Praise for Angela J

T0267487

"Set in small Troy, Alabama, *Untethered* tells a ... American story stretching far beyond city limits."

— ROY HOFFMAN, AUTHOR OF *THE PROMISE OF THE PELICAN* AND *ALABAMA AFTERNOON*

"There is no shortage of pain in this world, and certainly not for a Black woman trying to do good work against all odds. Katia Daniels, the protagonist of Angela Jackson-Brown's dynamic new novel, *Untethered*, spoke directly to my soul with her servant's heart, her hidden sorrows, and her resolve to be strong for everyone around her. This character gave me such a powerful mirror in which I could gaze and feel seen, and this novel showed me the ways that faith can waver but always win, love can delay but not be lost, and grief can sometimes give us pause so we can breathe into joy. Angela Jackson-Brown has once again proven that Black characters are fully human and that we, Black girls from Alabama who strive daily to make this world sing, are worthy of celebration and immortality in the pages of great literature. This is a remarkable book."

— ASHLEY M. JONES, POET LAUREATE OF ALABAMA

"This is a harrowing novel about the push and pull of fidelity, family, and faith under the crush of history. Angela Jackson-Brown has written a deeply emotional novel that feels timeless while also speaking to the particularly troubled times in which we live."

—WILEY CASH, *NEW YORK TIMES* BEST-SELLING AUTHOR OF *WHEN GHOSTS COME HOME*, FOR *HOMEWARD*

"[*The Light Always Breaks*] skillfully tackles romance, religion, and race relations in a tale that will appeal to readers who enjoyed *The Personal Librarian* (2021), *The Vanishing Half* (2020), and *Black Bottom Saints* (2020)."

—*BOOKLIST*

"Angela Jackson-Brown's reputation for digging deep and going wide at the same time continues to reward readers. Thoughtfully portrayed characters with deep minds and passionate hearts make *The Light Always Breaks* a memorable story that leaps off the page. You can see it, hear it, and feel it in your marrow. Hard and necessary truths are addressed, and as an avid reader of both historical fiction and historical romance, I found this novel struck a refreshing balance between the two. I highly recommend it."

—RHONDA MCKNIGHT, AWARD-WINNING
AUTHOR OF *THE THING ABOUT HOME*

"Jackson-Brown paints a vivid picture of family and community persevering in the pressure cooker of the Deep South. Readers will be drawn to Opal's intelligent and authentic voice, as the book confronts issues of racism, injustice, and white privilege head-on. This is a powerful Own Voices contribution to the historical fiction genre, joining titles such as Alka Joshi's *The Henna Artist* and Kim Michele Richardson's *The Book Woman of Troublesome Creek* in their unflinching look at the past."

—*LIBRARY JOURNAL*, STARRED REVIEW,
FOR *WHEN STARS RAIN DOWN*

"*When Stars Rain Down* is a book with religious themes, but if that's not your preference, don't let that stop you. The writing is beautiful, the story compelling, the characters vividly drawn, and religion is a backdrop, not the main story. Opal's voice is pitch-perfect, and the plot has enough surprises to keep you turning pages late into the night. I give this book a whole-hearted thumbs up."

—HISTORICAL NOVEL SOCIETY

"*When Stars Rain Down* is so powerful, timely, and compelling that sometimes I found myself holding my breath while reading it. Rarely have I been so attached to characters and felt so transported to a time and place. This is an important and beautifully written must-read of a novel. Opal is a character I will never forget."

—SILAS HOUSE, AUTHOR OF *SOUTHERNMOST*

Untethered

Untethered

A NOVEL

ANGELA
JACKSON-BROWN

HARPER MUSE

Untethered

Copyright © 2024 Angela Jackson-Brown

Published by Harper Muse, an imprint of HarperCollins Focus LLC.

Scripture quotations are taken from the King James Version. Public domain.

This book is a work of fiction. The characters, incidents, and dialogue are drawn from the author's imagination and are not to be construed as real. Any resemblance to actual events or persons, living or dead, is entirely coincidental.

Any internet addresses (websites, blogs, etc.) in this book are offered as a resource. They are not intended in any way to be or imply an endorsement by HarperCollins Focus LLC, nor does HarperCollins Focus LLC vouch for the content of these sites for the life of this book.

Library of Congress Cataloging-in-Publication Data
Names: Jackson-Brown, Angela, 1968- author.
Title: Untethered : a novel / Angela Jackson-Brown.
Description: Nashville, Tennessee : Harper Muse, 2024. | Summary: "Sometimes family is found in the most unlikely of places . . ."—Provided by publisher.
Identifiers: LCCN 2024030528 (print) | LCCN 2024030529 (ebook) | ISBN 9781400241132 (paperback) | ISBN 9781400241149 (epub) | ISBN 9781400241156 (ebook)
Subjects: LCGFT: Novels.
Classification: LCC PS3610.A355526 U58 2024 (print) | LCC PS3610.A355526 (ebook) | DDC 813/.6—dc23/eng/20240708
LC record available at https://lccn.loc.gov/2024030528
LC ebook record available at https://lccn.loc.gov/2024030529

Printed in the United States of America
24 25 26 27 28 LBC 5 4 3 2 1

This book is dedicated to all of the brave soldiers who served in Vietnam, especially Paw Paw Joel Hall and Uncle M.J. McCall.

1

I SHOULD HAVE STAYED IN BED, I thought to myself. But bed meant nightmares, from my reoccurring dream about leeches crawling all over me to the even worse dream I'd started having about my twin brothers, Aaron and Marcus, being chased down by the Viet Cong. Most nights sleep was not a place of peace. Most nights all I wanted to do was run from the images playing in my mind like something from a really bad movie. Mama said I've had nightmares all my life. I would think, at the age of forty, I would be over such nonsense, but the dreams just kept coming and evolving.

Rather than allow my overactive brain to torture me any more, I woke up with the intention of getting to work early. But instead of flying down the road toward my office, there I sat, pumping the gas pedal of my eighteen-year-old Chevy pickup in a valiant attempt to get it to crank. It was a cold November day, and my truck was not in the mood to make my morning easy. The truck used to belong to my daddy. He left it to me right before he died, and all these years later, I still held on to that truck like it carried the spirit of Daddy in it.

I whispered a prayer under my breath: "Please let this old clunker start up, and please, let there be no surprises, no grief, and no turmoil for me or the boys at the group home." I usually prayed some semblance of this prayer every morning, but this morning felt different. It felt weightier. I added the words my mother would always pray: "Dear Creator, today I need mercy."

I was the executive director at the Pike County Group Home for Negro Boys, and the last few years had been difficult, mainly because of the board of directors. At this point, I had no clue how much longer I would be able to do what had been my absolute dream job, stress and all.

After yesterday's board meeting, I wasn't sure if I'd be in that role much longer—whether that meant a firing or a quitting, I didn't know. Either way, things were not looking good. Samuel P. Arrington IV, the new board president of the group home, had become the proverbial thorn in my side. The group home was situated inside a stately old house that once belonged to Samuel IV's great-grandfather, Colonel Samuel P. Arrington, a Confederate soldier. Years ago, shortly before I became director, the Arrington family turned the house into a group home for Negro boys who weren't good candidates for adoption or who needed a place to stay before returning to their family or the foster care system.

Unlike his father, Big Sam, who'd recently stepped down as board president, Sam IV seemed determined to undermine my efforts. I'd been executive director for ten years, making great strides to change the paradigm for these boys, and in the span of a few months, Sam IV had tried to render null and void everything my staff and I had accomplished. I'd tried reaching out to Big Sam for help, but he said his son was in charge and he didn't want to have to choose sides.

No matter what I tried to do, from the mentoring program to my fundraising efforts to provide college scholarships for as many boys as possible, Sam IV insisted I was wasting time and resources on boys who didn't need or deserve that type of attention. He never worded it quite that way, yet the message was always clear.

"These boys need to learn a trade," Sam IV said at yesterday's meeting while a huge puff of cigar smoke encircled his head like a lopsided halo. He'd then looked around the room with an expectant expression. Clearly he assumed the other board members—six white men, six Negro men, and one Negro woman—would all chime in their agreement. But no one said anything, so he continued talking. *"These boys need to be taught useful skills like carpentry or plumbing or welding. The last thing they need is a whole lot of unnecessary book learning."*

Even though the six white men in the room didn't speak up, they all nodded. And even though the six Negro men didn't say a word, I knew they weren't far from agreeing too. On more than one occasion, they'd individually and collectively come to me and said that maybe I should lower the bar a bit, insisting that I was setting the boys up for disappointment with my "lofty goals." The idea that these Negro men who had overcome the odds to be successful businessmen, clergy, doctors, and lawyers would dare cheat my boys out of any opportunities to thrive kept me gritting my teeth anytime I had to deal with them. They all liked having "board member of a group home" on their résumés, but none of them really believed in what we were trying to do at the group home, which was to radically change these boys' lives.

The sole woman on the board, Mrs. Adelaide Hendricks, was my only staunch ally, and I knew that most of the time, it was her support alone that kept the Negro men from siding with Sam and his cronies. But she was slated to step down from the board this year, and I worried that everything would come crashing down after she left.

I took a deep breath and looked down at my watch. So much for leaving early this morning. If I didn't get on the road soon, I would miss saying goodbye to the boys before they left for school. I closed my eyes and said, "It's going to be okay," and then I turned the key one more time. Although the truck sputtered and coughed, mercifully it cranked. "Thank you," I muttered as I eased the truck out of the yard. I hoped all of the noise didn't awaken Mama. Like me, she sometimes found sleep elusive, especially with the boys being in Vietnam, so far away from us.

I turned the radio dial until it picked up a station that wasn't staticky, and almost as if on cue, I heard Big Mama Thornton singing "Hound Dog." Thornton was the original singer of the song, and I always got excited when I heard her infamous growl on the radio.

As was always the case, I joined in. Daddy, who'd died of cancer shortly after I graduated from college nearly twenty years ago, loved the blues, and Big Mama was from the same little town where Daddy was born—Ariton, Alabama. She and I were only a year apart in age, and I'd only recently started hearing her music on the radio. I didn't know if Daddy had known her or her people, but every time I heard her on the radio, Daddy felt a bit closer—even when she was singing about a good-for-nothing man, the absolute antithesis of Daddy.

Most days, Daddy's death didn't haunt my thoughts, but other days it felt like January 17, 1948, all over again—a day that, similar to what President Franklin D. Roosevelt said about the attack on Pearl Harbor, "will live in infamy" for me and my family. The twins were only little boys when Daddy died, and now they were twenty-five-year-old men trying to survive in the Marines. I well remember that cold day when we buried Daddy. Aaron and Marcus had clung so tightly to me and Mama, asking us why Daddy wouldn't wake up. Just thinking about it made my eyes water.

I wiped away the tears and allowed Big Mama to sing me through the back streets of Troy, past Troy State University, until I reached the group home on the corner of South Three Notch and Montgomery Streets.

"Let my boys have peace today," I said, echoing my prayer from before. I eased the Chevy into the spot marked Executive Director, then reached for my briefcase and threw my oversize shawl across my shoulders as I exited the truck. Before I closed the truck door, I heard loud yelling from inside the group home. It was shortly after six in the morning—too early for this much commotion.

I dropped my shawl and briefcase and sprinted—bad hip and

all—like I was still on the high school track team. I was used to some noise in the early mornings because the residence housed fifteen rambunctious boys ranging from ages eight to sixteen, but what I'd heard was not normal. When I reached the front door, nine-year-old Pee Wee, one of the boys, met me in tears. Pee Wee talked with a stutter that worsened when he was angry or excited. This morning, he was both.

"Miss Katia, c-c-come quick," he cried. "Chad g-g-got his caseworker and Mr. J-J-Jason cornered u-u-up in the family room. Chad s-s-say he gone k-k-kill . . ."

Kill was all I needed to hear. "Get my shawl and briefcase and bring them inside. Tell the other boys to go to their rooms," I instructed as I ran toward the ruckus.

"I ain't going back to that dopehead," Chad yelled. "You better step away from me. I'll kill everybody up in here 'fore I go back to live with her!"

"Put down the chair, Chad," Jason, the assistant director, said in a booming voice. Jason was a senior studying counseling at Troy State, one of very few Negro students admitted. He'd been raised by his grandparents while his mother and father drifted in and out of jail. Due to his childhood, he had a passion for working with boys like Chad. I'd hired him as a weekend counselor last year, and he soon became my second-in-command. Last month, I promoted him to assistant in anticipation of his graduation this December.

"I'm warning you, Chad—if you don't put down the chair, I am going to come over there and take it from you," I heard Jason say as I approached the room.

"You just try, you stupid mother—"

I burst into the room and saw Chad standing in the corner with a chair hoisted over his head.

Jason stood a few feet away, shielding the young white caseworker, Mrs. Gates, from Chad and his wrath.

"What's going on in here? Chad, put down that chair," I said as I walked to stand in front of Mrs. Gates and Jason.

"Miss Daniels, step back," Jason cautioned. "He—"

"Take Mrs. Gates to my office, Jason. *Now*," I interrupted, never taking my eyes off Chad. It wouldn't take much for him to send that chair flying, injuring one of us accidentally or, in the case of Mrs. Gates, intentionally.

"Chad, put down the chair and calm yourself," I said as I inched closer to him. Although I'd be considered a tall and big woman, at five foot ten and weighing 190 pounds, fourteen-year-old Chad was an astounding six foot one and weighed about 220 the last time I'd checked his chart. I looked at him as a little boy, but I knew the world didn't or wouldn't. They'd only see a dangerous Black man trying to attack a poor, defenseless white woman.

Chad had been in the system off and on since he was a baby. His mother, Lena, was strung out on heroin when she gave birth to him, and a few days later, his now deceased grandmother brought him to the Negro hospital in Tuskegee, Alabama, because he was having seizures from heroin withdrawal. After that, the state took Chad from Lena. Throughout the years, Lena would get clean, and Chad would return to live with her until something catastrophic happened, like the time when Lena's boyfriend, Cobra, and two other men got high and attacked Chad, leaving him with two cracked ribs, face lacerations, and a broken arm. One of the men also sexually assaulted Chad. He refused to say who. The detail about the sexual assault came out during a group therapy session. It had taken hours to calm Chad down, as well as the other boys. That night, one thing he did say and has continued to say is that he'd never go back to live with his mother.

Mrs. Gates knew his story, and it infuriated me that she'd chosen to overlook my cardinal rule: caseworkers must *always* speak to me before they speak to my boys, for reasons like the current situation. She should have known Chad wouldn't react kindly to the notion that he'd be sent back to his mother. And why in the world was Mrs. Gates visiting the group home this early in the morning? I felt as if she had been trying to spirit Chad away before I arrived. This felt calculated, but more than that, it was way out of order.

"That bitch over there talking 'bout me going back to live with Lena. I ain't going back to live with her no more!" Chad yelled, shaking the metal chair over his head like it weighed nothing. Normally I'd "check" a resident for using profanity, but my priority was getting Chad to put down the chair and calm himself.

"It's okay, Chad. I will handle this situation. Just put down the chair," I said.

"Miss Daniels, I must insist that—" the caseworker started.

I whipped around and faced her, my face hot with anger. "I said to leave the room, Mrs. Gates. You too, Jason."

As the words were leaving my mouth, Chad hurled the chair across the room. Jason pushed the caseworker out of the way as the chair crashed against the thin wall next to them, creating a gaping hole.

"Do you need me to call the police?" Jason rushed Mrs. Gates toward the door.

"No. I've got this." The last thing I wanted was a bunch of white police officers reporting to a disturbance between a six-foot-one Black boy and a tiny, blonde white woman.

I turned toward Chad, watching him as he stood panting, his hands tightly fisted.

"Enough, Chad. Enough." I walked to him and put my hands on his arms. He was trembling violently. I took deep, cleansing breaths until he slowed his breathing to match mine, a technique I often used with my boys when they spiraled out of control.

When I thought we were both calm enough to have a conversation, I touched the side of his face, which was wet with tears. "Are you okay?" I asked him.

He nodded. At no time had I feared for myself. My rapport with the boys made me feel safe around them, even when their tempers got the best of them.

"Are you in a safe enough space that I can remove my hands?" I asked, keeping my gaze locked with his. His eyes weren't as erratic as before. I nearly breathed a sigh of relief, but I knew it wasn't over yet.

He nodded again. I allowed my hands to fall to my sides.

"Good. However, I do not want you to mistake my calmness as acceptance of the display I just witnessed. That behavior is not and will not be tolerated at this group home. Do you understand me, Chad?"

"Yeah, but—"

I held up my hand to stop him. "No, sir. I will not listen to 'yeah, buts.' You just messed up royally, and you need to acknowledge that fact without throwing in some 'yeah, buts.' Do you understand what I just said to you?"

Chad swallowed hard, as if agreeing with me was too much, but finally he mumbled the words I was waiting to hear. "Yes, ma'am."

I motioned for Chad to follow me to the couch on the other side of the room. Once we both sat down, I looked at him with all of the steely reserve I could muster. I'd learned a long time ago that if the boys thought I was vulnerable to their tears and tantrums, they'd try to railroad me with their sob stories. God knows that every one of these boys had reasons to be angry. None of them had "good" stories. Almost every boy came from a home filled with drugs and abuse, and while I always wanted to honor their truths, I didn't want those truths to become crutches. I was determined for these boys to leave the group home stronger and better than they were when they arrived. That didn't always happen, yet I worked my butt off to make sure it happened for as many boys as possible. I wished to God that the board of directors could understand that, but I stopped myself from thinking about them. Chad needed me to focus on him and him alone.

"I want you to tell me what you did wrong, Chad. Starting with your reaction before I even arrived here this morning."

"Miss Katia, that woman said—"

I held up my hand again. "This conversation is about you. Not her."

Chad took a deep breath and started over. "I got angry when I heard I was gone have to go back to live with Lena again. Instead of getting angry, I shoulda been quiet and let Mr. Jason talk with the caseworker. Or I shoulda asked them if we coulda waited and talked when you got here. I shouldna thrown that chair and broke up the walls 'cause I ain't got no money to fix them. I shouldna been cursing and swearing. I shoulda been calm, 'cause when we are calm, we can make change happen," he said, concluding with one of the many mantras I constantly quoted to the boys and the staff.

I took Chad's hands in mine. "Yes, Chad. You are exactly right. Thank you."

I released his hand before I stood up and looked down at this young man who was still struggling to calm himself. "I want you to go upstairs and get cleaned up for school. Before you go into the dining room for breakfast, you are to come to my office and apologize to Mrs. Gates."

"But—"

I shook my head. "No buts. You were wrong. And when we are wrong, we apologize. It doesn't matter what the other person said or did. We acknowledge our own deeds. You also need to apologize to Mr. Jason and Miss Leslie."

Chad stood up, his face filled with every emotion he'd been feeling—from rage to fear. He nodded and said, "Yes, ma'am."

"Thank you, Chad," I said.

He started to leave the room but then stopped and turned around. "Miss Katia, please don't let them send me back to my mama. Fix it so I ain't got to go back. I'll kill myself before I'll go back to Lena."

I went to Chad and wrapped my arm around his shoulders. "No one is killing anybody or themselves. Do you understand?"

"Yes, ma'am, but—"

"No buts. I will do my very best to make sure you are never in harm's way again, Chad, but you must work as hard as you can to not make my job any more difficult than it has to be." I couldn't make too many promises. The courts were unpredictable. All I could do was fight for Chad like I did for all my boys.

Chad seemed satisfied with my reply and took off for the stairs, running up them two at a time.

On my way to my office, I paused in front of my new secretary's desk. Leslie had only been working at the group home for a few weeks, but that didn't stop me from being angry with both her and Jason. I didn't tolerate inconsistencies with the protocols I had set up with my employees. The main one was that no one could have access to my boys without my prior approval. My staff knew better than to allow anyone to have a conversation with my boys when I wasn't there. I didn't care if it was a parent, a caseworker, or President Lyndon B. Johnson himself. All dialogue concerning my boys started and stopped with me. I was quick to say that I ran a benevolent dictatorship—heavy on the dictatorship with rules that directly affected the boys.

"Is she still in my office?" I asked Leslie, referring to Chad's caseworker.

"Yes, Miss Daniels. Miss Daniels, I'm so, so—"

"We will all talk about this incident later," I said, my voice a little angrier than I intended. But I *was* angry, and I wanted Leslie to understand that protocol was everything in this line of work. One "small" goof could mess up a young person's life forever. I'd seen it happen too many times. Before I began my stint here at the group home, I was a caseworker myself. Seldom a month went by when I didn't witness an innocent mistake causing major headaches. I wouldn't allow my boys to suffer because of anyone's negligence, whether mine or any of my staff.

"Make sure Chad comes by my office before he leaves for school," I said. "He needs to apologize to you, Jason, and his caseworker. He can apologize to the other boys at breakfast."

"Yes, ma'am, Miss Daniels." Leslie looked like she might start crying at any moment.

I lightly placed my hand on her shoulder. The last thing I wanted to do was destroy the young woman's self-confidence. "I know that what happened this morning was all a misunderstanding, Leslie. We'll all discuss this during the morning staff meeting and put a mechanism into place so that nothing like this ever happens again."

I patted Leslie's shoulder before crossing to the other corner of the reception area and stopping in front of my office door. I lifted my hands to my head, gently massaging my temples to ward off the headache I could already feel coming. Then I quickly refluffed my Afro, a style I'd recently started wearing, much to my mother's chagrin. She said women of my stature did not need to be walking around with a nappy head. I didn't argue with her, but I didn't change my hairstyle either.

"So much for peace today, huh, God?" I said under my breath as I grasped the knob, pulling the door open wide and entering my office.

2

"THIS SITUATION IS COMPLETELY UNACCEPTABLE, MISS Daniels," Mrs. Gates said, speaking in a loud voice as she paced in front of my desk. I was used to her antics, so I forced myself to sit quietly until she wound herself down. She reminded me of that little yapping Chihuahua Mama used to have—saying a lot and nothing at the same time. After what seemed like hours but was actually only a minute or two, she stopped pacing *and* yapping, and looked at me.

"Are you going to say anything?" she snapped, glaring at me. Clearly even after all the visits and interactions, this white lady still didn't understand that trying me wasn't in her best interest.

I leaned back in my chair, crossing my arms. "I was simply giving you time to finish. Are you done?"

"This is no joke, Miss Daniels. I should—"

"First, no one is laughing, Mrs. Gates," I interrupted. I was tired of her and her attitude, and on top of that, I hadn't yet had one cup of coffee that morning. She was lucky I wasn't swinging chairs like Chad. "Second, you are out of line and out of place. If you had something to say concerning one of my boys, you should have contacted me first. Period. End of sentence."

"As Chad's caseworker, it is my right and duty to make sure he and his mother, when appropriate, are reunited," she said with a tone so snide that I felt a curse word rise up in my spirit—one of those words I'd need to immediately fall on my knees and pray about. Instead of losing my religion this early in the morning, I did what I taught my boys to do. I breathed. Deep breaths. Then I smiled, although I'm sure it looked more like a snarl to her. She backed away as if venom were spewing from my mouth.

"Coming to the group home at the crack of dawn—when you knew I wouldn't be here—was absolutely out of order, and you know it. I run a group home filled with high-risk boys from unstable environments. These boys had never known a day's peace until they came here. I will not allow you or anyone else to disrupt their routine or their peace of mind." I enunciated every word carefully and precisely. "I understand that you have a job to do, but neither your needs nor the needs of the foster care system will ever supersede the needs of my boys. Do I make myself clear?"

"I am here to take Chad Montgomery back to his mother." She placed her hands on my desk and leaned forward with a glare. "She has successfully completed a rehab program, she has been clean for three months, and she attends weekly AA meetings."

"Three whole months and AA," I said, clapping my hands slowly. "Well, she's ready for the 'Mother of the Year' award. Will you give her a trophy, or should I?"

"Your sarcasm is not benefiting either one of us or Chad. Lena Montgomery wants her child back, and there is no reason to stop her from getting custody of him again," Mrs. Gates said in a stern voice. The caseworker knew all of her Department of Human Services handbooks by heart and could recite protocol better than the originators of the rules could. I respected rules, and as often as I could, I honored them. But it would be a cold day in hades before I'd give Chad up to the system so they could return him to his mother—not without some assurances that she was ready to be a mother to her son again.

"This is not the first time Lena has 'turned things around,' according to your office," I said. "Time and time again she does all of the 'right things,' and in less than a few weeks or a month, Chad is right back in the system again. Aren't y'all tired of putting that young man through that torture?"

"The law states that—"

"You will need to submit the paperwork . . ." I started, but Mrs. Gates was ready. She reached into her briefcase and handed me a stack of papers. Of course the paperwork was in order. Some judge likely signed off on it during his lunch break, barely giving it a cursory look.

"This time we will need to go to court and stand in front of a judge. I am not surrendering Chad without a thorough investigation and the recommendations of a judge who actually knows something about the case." I resisted touching my pounding temples. I wouldn't give in to it. Not in front of her.

"There is no need for all of that, Miss Daniels. We can—"

"This is going to a judge, and we are all going to be in the room with the judge so he can hear Chad's case properly." I didn't care about her glaring at me. They always wanted to hurry up and wash their hands of Negro boys like Chad. If Chad were white, we wouldn't even be having this conversation. Mrs. Gates never would have tried to bypass me, and she absolutely would want to ensure that Chad was returning to a safe environment. As overworked as she was, I knew she'd make the extra effort to try to protect a white child. I'd seen it time and time again.

They knew Chad wouldn't be safe with Lena, but they saw him as collateral damage. I'd first read about the term in an article by Thomas Schelling, an economist who wrote about the concept in the early 1960s. He was referencing civilian casualties during war, but it was a perfect term to describe young Negro boys in the system. Everyone who worked in this field had unrealistic caseloads, so when it came down to who got sacrificed, they would rather it be the Negro children.

"This could take weeks or months to resolve if we do it your way," she said angrily. "Judge Smith signed off on Chad returning to his mother. There is nothing left to do but surrender him to me so that he can be returned to her."

"No," I said, looking at her unblinkingly. I was not surrendering Chad to her. Not like this. Not without everyone doing their due diligence to determine his mother's fitness. "I understand you are given much latitude when it comes to deciding when a boy can be returned to his parents, but with this particular case, you should be in agreement with me that we must do everything possible to make sure Chad is protected and Lena is ready to be a mother to him again."

"There is no way anyone can be absolutely sure that something bad won't happen again. But the law is clear: children belong with their parents, and it is my job and your job to return them to their parents without giving any resistance," she said.

"Children belong in safe spaces," I said firmly. "And my job is to protect Chad Montgomery—whether that be from his mother or a system that couldn't give two flying figs about his safety. I thank you for the paperwork. Now, as I have already said, get me and Chad in front of a judge."

"You do realize I could call the police and have Chad arrested for his violent behavior? Or I could just take him with me—I have legal documents saying I have the right to do so." Her eyes were fiery with emotion. Now she was the one who looked like she wished she had a chair to hurl.

I pointed toward the wall near the door. "Do you see those photos over there, Mrs. Gates?"

She glanced at the wall. "Yes, of course I see them. Yet I don't see how any of this relates to Chad Montgomery."

I stood up and walked over to my "wall of honor," as I called it. "This young man," I said, pointing at the photo at the top of the corkboard, "is entering his second year of law school. This young man below him is an assistant defensive football coach at Tuskegee Institute. This young man at the bottom right is a high school English teacher, and the young man beside him graduated magna cum laude from Howard University in May of this year. Do you want to know what all of these young men have in common?"

She sighed long and hard, but I had a point to make, and her snotty attitude wouldn't stop me.

"These young men were once residents of this group home," I said, returning to my desk where I gingerly lowered myself into my chair. My sciatica was messing with me again. Stress.

"The system said they weren't going to amount to anything, but they came here, and we helped them prove the system wrong. Don't make me call your supervisor, Mrs. Gates." I wasn't entirely sure that calling would make a difference, but I knew Mrs. Gates well enough to know she would hate being "reported."

"Fine," she said with a huge sigh. "I'll file the necessary paperwork for a judge to intervene with a hearing, but you know as well as I do that the judge is going to see it my way. You are just delaying the inevitable."

"Be that as it may, I will be awaiting the formal paperwork from the courts," I said. It could be weeks, even months before the case went in front of a judge—at the very least, after Thanksgiving, maybe not even until Christmas or New Year's. The court system was so bogged down that we both knew nothing would be done about changing Chad's living conditions anytime soon.

I just needed to buy some time. If Chad's mother followed her usual trajectory of drug addiction, before a judge could review the case, she'd once again be strung out on heroin.

Mrs. Gates seemed poised to say something else, but then we heard a light knock on my door.

"Come in," I called out.

Chad entered the room. He was cleaned up and dressed for school in a pair of freshly pressed blue jeans and a white button-down shirt. His expression could be perceived as sullen by those who didn't know him, but I knew he was scared—terrified that in spite of all my efforts, I wouldn't be able to protect him. I wanted nothing more than to embrace him, but he needed to own up to his behavior more than he needed hugs.

"Chad, do you have something to say?" I prodded.

"Yes, ma'am." His tone was wooden. "I'm sorry for cussing at you and throwing that chair, Mrs. Gates. I just . . . I . . . I won't do it again."

I was proud of him for not trying to deflect responsibility. I nodded, then looked at Mrs. Gates.

She sighed and then crossed her arms. "Thank you for your apology, Chad. Unfortunately, I will have to document your behavior in your file. I understand that you have reservations about returning home to your mother, but trust me when I say it is for the best."

Chad looked at me with panicked eyes. I had to say something fast or all the good he'd done with his apology might be wiped away by another impulsive outburst.

"You aren't going anywhere today but to school and back here, Chad." I smiled at him. "I promise."

I watched as he began to do the deep breathing we'd taught him and angrily swiped away a tear. "You're dismissed, Chad. Go and eat something before you have to leave for school."

"Yes, ma'am," he said and rushed out of the room.

"You are not doing these boys any favors by coddling them so," Mrs. Gates said.

If I had to hear one more white person tell me what was right for my boys, I might scream.

"What do you know about these boys besides what's in your files?" I snapped. "How many Black boys have you raised? How many Black boys are members of your family? You don't know anything about these boys other than what the DHS handbook tells you. Next time you want to come to my group home, Mrs. Gates, you call first. Otherwise, we are going to have issues with each other. Good day."

"You will hear from me soon, Miss Daniels," she said and huffily marched out the door.

I had some choice names to call her, but I released all of that and went to the dining room to check on the boys. All of them were sitting together at the family-style table. The room was usually filled with lots of noisy chatter and laughter. Today everyone was silent, barely eating their food. Pee Wee was trying to coax Chad into talking to him. I was pleased that Chad didn't snap at Pee Wee—he just shook his head.

Pee Wee had come to the group home a week after Chad did, and before long the unlikely pair became like brothers. Chad took up for Pee Wee if any of the other boys tried to pick on him for his stuttering or short stature, and when Chad's temper flared, Pee Wee was usually able to make Chad smile and forget his bad mood.

All eyes turned to me when I walked into the room. I went and sat at the head of the table. As often as I could, I tried to take my meals with the boys.

"I know you are all confused by what happened this morning," I said, looking from one boy's face to the next. "A lot of emotions were on display, and I am sorry you all had to witness it. But I hope you won't let it mess up your day. Your job is to go to school and learn new things, and my job is to take care of everything else. Am I understood?"

"Yes, ma'am," they said in unison.

"Chad, do you have something to say to the group?" I asked. The boys knew the routine. They put down their knives and forks and looked at Chad.

Chad stood up and made eye contact with each boy as I had taught all of them to do. "I'm sorry for messing up everybody's morning. I let myself get mad and I shouldna. Forgive me?"

"Yes, Chad," everyone said, Pee Wee loudest of all. "We forgive you."

"Thank you, Chad. Thank you, everyone," I said. "Someone explain why we accepted Chad's apology just now." Everything was a learning opportunity at the group home, and I wanted the boys to see merit in what we asked them to do, from taking out the trash to mowing the yard or saying "I'm sorry" when they did wrong.

Pee Wee raised his hand, waving it frantically.

I couldn't help but smile. He was such a lovable child. Always wanting to make sure he was on my good side.

"Yes, Pee Wee."

"We forgive Ch-Ch-Chad because we want to b-b-be forgiven when we m-m-make mistakes," he said, smiling broadly.

"That's right, Pee Wee," I said. "Good answer."

Jason entered the room and looked from the boys to me. I nodded, signaling to him that I was done talking.

"Y'all go wash up one more time and meet me out at the van," he said. "It's time for school." The boys got up and carried their plates to the kitchen. Instead of racing to the various bathrooms, they moved slowly and quietly, especially Chad. It was clear that they all were still a bit rattled. During their time together, they bonded like brothers, and whenever they saw one of their brothers in distress, they took it hard. Managing the emotions of fifteen rambunctious boys was no easy task. I was grateful for my staff. We worked well together, and even though I was displeased with this morning's outcome, overall they'd done the best they could.

I watched as Chad hesitantly walked up to Jason with his head down. Jason didn't move. He simply waited.

"I'm sorry, Mr. Jason," Chad finally said, raising his head and looking Jason in the eyes. "I didn't mean to disrespect you that way. You been nice to me, and I was awful to you. I won't do it again."

Jason considered Chad for a moment and then offered him a hand so they could do one of the elaborate handshakes Jason had taught the boys. "You and I are good, man. Just watch that temper of yours. Don't let nobody get inside your head like that. Every situation can be figured out. Breaking up walls ain't the answer. Now, go finish cleaning up for school."

Chad smiled for the first time that morning. "Yes, sir. Thank you." He hurried out of the room. I could see a lightness in his steps that almost caused me to tear up. We could offer them crumbs, and it would often be better than what they'd ever been offered before.

Jason came to the table and sat beside me, appearing almost as gloomy as the boys had looked. He was an earnest young man who took his work here seriously. He reminded me of my brothers in a number of ways. Studious. Hardworking. And anxious to gain my approval.

"I apologize, Miss Daniels," he said. His voice was solemn, and his eyes were shining, but he held back the tears. "I take full responsibility for everything that happened this morning. I should have been more proactive with shutting things down until you arrived, especially once I knew why she was here. I just didn't expect Chad to have that kind of reaction. With her having all the paperwork, and her insisting on seeing Chad, well . . . I just . . . I didn't think."

I nodded my head in agreement. I didn't believe in letting people off the hook when they messed up, even when it was unintentional. This work we did was important and none of us could risk falling down on the job.

"Thank you for your apology, Jason. You're right. Balls were dropped today. None of you followed protocol, and as a result things got out of hand. Thankfully, we all survived. When you get back from taking the boys to school, we'll have our staff meeting. The other houseparents plus the on-site counselors will be here as well, so we can all go over this incident together. No one is guilt-free, but as a team we will fix what is broken and move forward."

"Yes, ma'am," he said, getting up. "I'd better get the boys to school. Don't want them to be late."

"That sounds good," I said, getting up too. "I'll see you in a bit."

I made my way into the kitchen, where Mrs. Dorothy

Kennedy and Miss Theresa Grant were washing dishes and talking animatedly to each other. I was in desperate need of some coffee, and the heady scent of freshly brewed java was wafting throughout the house. I didn't have an appetite, but the coffee was calling my name.

Both Mrs. Kennedy and Miss Grant had worked as part of the kitchen staff since the group home opened. Every meal they cooked was like Sunday dinner, Thanksgiving, and Christmas all wrapped up into one. Both women were amazing cooks and made sure we ate well. The boys called them Mama K and Mama G, and it was typical to find one or more of the boys seeking them out for hugs, advice, or a freshly baked cookie from the cookie jar they kept on top of the refrigerator. Mama K and Mama G never overstepped their boundaries, but they were always ready to share a scripture or say a prayer with anyone who needed it, resident or staff.

When I entered the room, they both stopped talking and looked up, smiles on their faces as usual. It was a relief to see both women. I often sought their counsel as much as the boys.

"Good morning, Miss Daniels," Mrs. Kennedy said, walking over to the coffeepot. "I already know what you want." She poured me a cup of coffee, splashing it lightly with cream. She handed it to me, and I took a sip without even blowing on it. I coughed but continued to drink the fiery liquid that was burning my throat. I needed that caffeine in the worst kind of way. As I drank, I could feel the coffee-induced calm begin to wash over me. I felt the urge to do what my boys did and seek solace from these older, nurturing women, but I just smiled.

"Do you want some breakfast, Miss Daniels?" Miss Grant asked. "You've had a long day and it ain't even started good. You need some fuel in your gas tank. There's some eggs, toast, and bacon over here with your name on them."

"No, thank you. Thank you, ladies, for the coffee." I hurried out of the kitchen and down the hallway. Leslie wasn't at her desk, so I was able to make it into my office unnoticed. I wanted to take a couple of aspirins, but before I could reach inside my desk for the bottle, the phone rang.

I stared at it like it was a two-headed snake. Something wasn't right. I just knew it. I had a sixth sense that dated back to my childhood. On the night Daddy's mama died, when I was only five or six, I felt her spirit hover above my bed, reach down, and give me a ghostly kiss, and then evaporate like a cloud. No one believed my story, but ever since then, I'd had premonitions and ghostly visitations. Whoever was on the other side of the phone did not have good news for me.

"Hello," I said into the receiver.

"Baby," Mama said. That one word made me sink into my chair, bracing myself for what I'd hear next. "It's your brothers. They lost. The government letter say they lost."

I shook my head without saying a word. Not this. Not this of all things. Not my brothers. I squeezed my eyes tight, trying to get a feeling about their whereabouts and their condition. I didn't sense them being dead, but I didn't sense them being alive either. I didn't know which was more frightening.

"Baby, are you there?" Mama asked, her voice cracking.

"I'm coming home now, Mama," I said and hung up the phone.

I jumped up and grabbed my things. Even as fragile as Mama was, I needed her to wrap her arms around me and reassure me that my brothers would be found and be alright. Right before I ran out of my office, I stopped myself and took several deep breaths. In and out. In and out.

"Please," I said, the only word that would come out of my mouth at that moment. I prayed God could interpret everything that was encompassed in that one word. I prayed that God was, as Mama always said, on the throne and in control.

3

LESLIE HAD RETURNED TO HER DESK, so on my way out I explained what was going on and told her to let the staff know I wouldn't be long. I hoped I wouldn't be long. But I didn't know what Mama was going to tell me or the frame of mind we'd be in once the telling was done. Leslie reassured me that she'd relay the message and if I needed to postpone the staff meeting, to call and let her know.

I mumbled something but my main goal was to get home as fast as I could. By the time I turned onto Hubbard Street and neared the little white house with the white picket fence that I shared with Mama, I was nearly frantic.

I just kept repeating Mama's words. *They lost.* What did that even mean? Were they lost together? Did they somehow get lost separately? I didn't know, and as usual, my imagination was beating me up worse than the shaking and shimmying of Daddy's truck. I was grateful that my group home boys were at school, because I needed to be with my mother.

My mind drifted to the twisted dream I'd had about the twins the night before. Had God sent me a sign? Was that awful nightmare of them running in the jungle God's way of warning me that my brothers were in danger?

Once I reached our yard, I jerked the truck into Park and raced into the house. Seemed like running was all I'd been doing for such a long time.

Mama was in her favorite rocking chair by the front window, holding the letters from the government in her lap, still and unmoving. Her hair was uncombed, white curls splayed around her head. I had short, coarse hair like my daddy. Mama and the twins had what some deemed "good hair," curly and fine in texture.

She looked so fragile. Almost like one of my old discarded baby dolls I'd neglect for a good book back in the day.

"Mama," I called out.

"Both telegrams came today," she said as I walked closer to her. "I got one for Aaron and one for Marcus. They coulda just sent me one. They twins. One can't move without the other. One telegram woulda sufficed." She held them out for me, as if she needed to pass the burden off to someone else, and like always, I was that someone. My whole life had been about seeing after other people. My daddy. My mama. My brothers. The boys at the group home. All I'd ever known was giving to others and figuring out how to fix their problems. Right then, I needed her to hold me and tell me things would be alright. Yet she needed such reassurances from me more, so I had to set aside my grief and my fears to assuage Mama's.

I took the telegrams from her, my hands shaking as I wondered how in the heck I was going to be able to fix this. I began to read the first telegram out loud:

"'I regret to inform you that your son, Private First Class Aaron Lamont Daniels, has been reported missing in action since 2 October 1967.'"

"Why you think they just now contacting us?" Mama mumbled. "My boys been lost for over a month and the gov'ment just now seeing fit to let me know something. I coulda been praying different had I known they was missing. Just ain't right. Just ain't right."

"I know, Mama," I said. I kept reading.

> If further details or other information are received, you will be promptly notified. You have my sincere sympathy during this time of anxiety and uncertainty.

I glanced at the other telegram. Just like Mama said, it was identical. The only difference was that it had my other twin brother's name, Marcus Harold Daniels III. He was the oldest of the twins by seventeen minutes. Even though the telegram didn't say it, I could imagine that Marcus had gotten captured while trying to protect his younger twin brother, as he had done their entire lives. It was because of Aaron that Marcus was in the military. Aaron, who'd always had a fascination with the military, secretly joined the Marines. Once we discovered what he'd done, Marcus immediately joined the Marines too. *"We both got a better chance of surviving together,"* he'd told Mama and me.

Although it nearly cracked my heart open to know they were

both missing in action, I felt some semblance of gratitude that they had each other—at least I hoped they did.

"What we gone do?" Mama asked, shaking her head, tears streaming down her face. "I can't lose my boys."

Daddy's death had nearly destroyed Mama. For weeks after he died, I couldn't even grieve. I had to tend to her and the boys. I cooked. I cleaned. I read the boys bedtime stories. I went to the funeral home and took Daddy's good suit for him to wear one last time. I even selected his casket and arranged the program. I tried not to let my imagination wander to having to do the same for one or both of my brothers. I didn't think Mama could survive losing them. I didn't know if I could either.

I put the telegrams on the side table and knelt beside her chair, taking her hands in mine. "I will figure this out, Mama. I will get on the phone and see who knows what." I summoned every ounce of conviction I could find, saying the words for her and for me.

"You think they alive?" she asked, looking at me hopefully, like a little girl needing her mother's assurance.

I didn't know if they'd be found alive. From what I'd read in the newspapers about prisoners of war or soldiers missing in action, I didn't hold a lot of hope, but I couldn't say that out loud. The best I could do was kiss Mama's forehead. She sighed, a heavy sound emerging from the very depths of her soul.

"You'll find them for your mama." She said this as a statement, not a question. I prayed she was right. She leaned back in her chair, closed her eyes, and reached for the telegrams. She pressed them to her chest as she started singing one of her favorite hymns, "Farther Along."

As she continued to sing softly, a smile now affixed on her face, I got up from the floor, my hip crying out in pain. I grunted but was able to stand.

"Be right back, Mama," I said and hurried down the hallway to the bathroom, my strong emotions nearly crushing me. Once in the bathroom, I closed the door behind me. I turned on the water in the sink and the tub, as loud sobs wracked my body. I didn't want her to hear me cry, but I had to let it out. I knelt, hoping prayers would come, but none did. All that came was grief—unquenchable grief.

When I arrived back at the group home, everyone was waiting for me, gathered in the same room I had met with the board the previous day. I could still smell the stench of Sam IV's cigar in the air. It nearly made me puke. Even though it was cool outside, I walked over to the window and cracked it a bit to let in some fresh air.

"Are you okay, Miss Katia?" Jason asked as I walked back to the long table and sat down at the head. Jason was to my left, and to my right, Leslie was preparing to take notes. Two of the houseparents, Mr. and Mrs. Grambling, an elderly Negro couple who had worked with the group home since it opened in 1953, had been here the longest, along with Mrs. Kennedy and Miss

Grant. Whenever anyone had questions about protocol, on the rare occasion that they couldn't locate me, or if they couldn't find Jason, they'd reach out to the Gramblings. They ate, breathed, and slept this group home and I appreciated their dedication.

David Snell, another recently hired houseparent, was slightly older than Jason, and along with being a houseparent, he was the youth minister at one of the white Baptist churches in Troy. When he applied for the job, I was worried about hiring a young white man to help mentor and support Black boys. But it didn't take long for me and the other staff to see that David's passion to serve was sincere. He always treated the boys with the greatest love and affection, but he was also stern when necessary.

Cairo Fieldings was an ex-con who'd come to me shortly after I started working at the group home. He'd been arrested numerous times since he was a teenager, but he promised me he was done with that life. At first he begged for food and clothing. Over time, I started giving him jobs to do around the group home, like mowing the grass or deep cleaning the house and preparing rooms for new arrivals. Eventually he expressed an interest in becoming a houseparent. I was unsure about it, but Mr. Grambling spoke up for him and said the boys needed to see someone like them who had turned his life around. I checked with the board and the Department of Human Services, and they weren't concerned about Cairo's past, so I gave him a chance and he'd been with the group home ever since.

Finally, there were Mr. and Mrs. James, another Negro couple who had only been with us for a few weeks. They started around the same time as Leslie.

Such a dedicated group of individuals. They were like family. If the truth be told, I spent about as much time with them as I did my own family. Seeing their sympathetic faces almost did me in, yet I couldn't give in to my sadness. Right now, there was work to do.

"I'm okay, everyone," I said, forcing a smile upon my face. "We have much to talk about today." I tried to summon normalcy. I needed to put aside my personal feelings and emotions and focus on why we were here: the boys. "We need to unpack what happened this morning with Chad Montgomery and make sure nothing like that happens again. We also need to discuss the other boys and their progress. The holidays are coming soon. Most of the boys, God willing, will be returning to their families. I need you all to help set up the initial visits with their families before we relinquish the boys to them. Jason, please debrief the staff on what happened this morning."

I tried to pay attention to everything people said, but my mind kept drifting back to my missing brothers. On more than one occasion, Jason reached over and lightly touched my arm. Usually I could figure out what I'd missed and rejoin the conversation. We came up with some clear rules about caseworkers and the hours they were allowed to visit the group home. We also discussed specific punishment for Chad's behavior. We'd limit his television watching and ensure he and his therapist spent additional time talking about ways he could better manage his anger.

"Chad is a good kid," Jason said. "And he wants to do the right thing, but he gets afraid when he senses things aren't going to go the way he wants them to."

"Fight or flight," I said. "That's his way of coping, but we have to teach him—teach *all* of the boys—that there are other ways to cope. He'll get it. It will just take time. But until then, let's avoid doing anything that pushes Chad into believing fight or flight are his only options." The discussion went on a few more minutes, and then we transitioned to talking about the other boys.

Jason brought up each boy, and one by one we discussed their progress or any issues that needed addressing.

"Miss Katia," Jason said softly. I looked at him absently, realizing I had blanked out again. Thoughts of the jungles of Vietnam were crowding my mind. I sighed. There was no way for me to finesse this particular mind lapse. I had no clue what they were talking about.

"I'm sorry," I said, trying not to be embarrassed. "Would you repeat your question?"

"Larry Holten, the new boy, is still stealing food from the kitchen and hiding it underneath his bed in a shoebox," Mr. Grambling said. "I told that boy the food ain't going nowhere, but he still does it. Ants and roaches is gonna be all over the place. I just need some guidance on what y'all think we should do."

"From what I gather, it's something he's always done," David Snell said. "I asked him about it yesterday and he said when he was in foster care, sometimes there wasn't enough food, so he would hide food for himself and his little brother. He apologized, but I don't even think he's conscious of doing it. It is as much a part of who he is as walking or breathing."

"When his therapist comes tomorrow, let her know what's

going on," I said. "In the meantime, maybe offer him an apple or an orange that he can keep on his dresser. Just so he can feel safe for the time being."

"Feels like that's giving in to bad behavior. If we let him have food outside of mealtimes, the other boys will think they should be able to do the same," Mr. Grambling said in a gruff voice.

I looked over at him and smiled. He sometimes struggled with my methods. Before I started working at the group home, the houseparents were allowed to spank the boys or severely punish them by taking away their meals. I stopped all of that immediately. I had grown up in a household where my parents didn't use corporal punishment; instead, they would talk to me and my brothers. They emphasized love and respect over everything else. They always said, *"We can't teach you to be the kind of person who doesn't hit if we are constantly hitting you."* I wanted that same environment for the boys. It took a while to get everyone on board, but things had gotten better because the boys knew that no matter what they did wrong, there would be consequences, but no physical violence of any kind was tolerated—from the adults or the children.

Once we had discussed every boy in detail, I adjourned the meeting and told everyone to go to lunch. I was exhausted. My tank was empty, so for the rest of the afternoon, I sequestered myself in my office and threw myself into processing the stack of paperwork on my desk. I went back and forth between dealing with the paperwork for the group home and making calls about my brothers. The hours went by in a hurry, and by the end of the day my head was spinning from all of the unsatisfactory calls I had made to various people in the military who I thought might have some information for me and Mama. Every single person I spoke to, all the way up to a harried Department of Defense secretary, said the same thing: they were sorry for my family's "anxiety and uncertainty," but they had no new information.

By the time I called the last person on my list, it was four thirty, and the sounds of the boys' laughter and talking filled the hallways, a sound that usually brought me the greatest pleasure.

School was out and they were clearly happy to return to the place that felt most like home to many of them. Any other time, I'd be waiting for them at the door, greeting each boy, asking him about his day. But today I needed the sanctity of my office. I needed the neutrality of the paperwork that demanded my attention but required nothing of me besides my thoroughness and my accuracy.

Not long after the boys entered the house, I heard a light knocking on my door. I felt like hiding under my desk. I wasn't ready to see anyone. I needed another few hours to regroup, but I didn't have that kind of time. I was needed—here and at home. There was nowhere for me to hide.

"Come in." I took off my reading glasses and placed them on my desk as Chad opened the door and walked into the room, an uncertain look on his face.

"You still mad at me?" he asked, stopping in front of my desk. He shifted from one foot to the other, his eyes squarely on the floor.

"Look at me, Chad," I said. He didn't move. "Chad. Look at me."

He looked up, apprehension in his eyes. He was such a big

little boy. So afraid that his number one ally—me—was going to abandon him like everybody else in his life had.

"I'm not mad," I said, observing him closely. "You apologized and I forgave you. That's the end of that."

He observed me just as closely, as if he were trying to figure out my mood. "You look sad 'bout the eyes. You okay, Miss Katia?"

His astuteness stunned me. I cleared my throat. "I'm okay, Chad. It's been a long day. How was school?" I wanted to shift the focus off me.

"Okay." He paused for a moment and then said what I knew must have been on his mind all day. "Miss Katia, is that white lady gone send me back to live with Lena? I don't want to go back to live with her."

"Mrs. Gates," I corrected. "You know her name. We use names around here."

"Is Mrs. Gates gone send me back to live with Lena?" Chad had a fearful look on his face, as if he were bracing himself for my answer.

I sighed and got up from my chair, making my way around the desk to where Chad stood.

"Let's go sit. You're too tall for me to talk to you while you're standing and I'm not."

He went over to the couch, and I followed him. After we both sat down, I gathered my thoughts before responding to his question.

"Chad, what is the one thing I always tell you boys?" No matter how tired or overwhelmed I felt, I wanted to make sure

Chad wasn't confused about anything pertaining to his case. Some things I couldn't resolve, but the things I did have power over, I wanted him to know about, from my mouth to his ears.

"You say you won't ever lie to us. You say no matter how tough the truth might be, you'll always tell it to us."

I reached over and took his hands, big bear paws within mine. "I will fight with everything in me to keep you safe. But I'm just one person. I don't know what a judge will say."

Chad jerked away his hands, balling them into fists, his face instantly growing dark with anger. "I could just run away. I don't need nobody to look after me."

"Okay," I said slowly, as if I were considering his suggestion. "If you think you're prepared to live on your own, who am I to stop you?"

He looked at me quizzically. My words did not match up with what he'd expected me to say. "You would just let me leave? You would just let me go without a fight?"

He appeared hurt by my nonchalance, but I wanted him to see for himself how ridiculous and dangerous his impulsive idea was.

"Well, I would tell you that you need money to live on your own, and as far as I know, you don't have any money, or at least not enough money to take care of yourself, which means you would have to get a job, and because of your age, legal jobs would be impossible," I said. "So, how do you think you would be able to support yourself?"

"I know people," he mumbled. "Somebody would help me out."

"No one on the streets helps folks out without a price, Chad,"

I said. "You know that. I don't want you to make a hasty decision because you're afraid. Give me a chance to figure this situation out. Don't do something that will make things worse. Will you do that for me? Will you just hold on and believe that I am fighting for you day and night?"

Chad was quiet. Normally he was the kid with the slick mouth—no matter the question or point being made, he had a quippy response. I was surprised that he just sat and watched me intently. At last, he spoke.

"Your eyes are puffy," he said. "You been crying?"

I thought about lying to him, but I tried my best to always be honest with the boys. "I got some bad news about my brothers."

"Them," he said, pointing at a picture on my desk of the twins wearing their Marine uniforms.

Chad was such an observant child. He saw things most children his age didn't even notice. It worried me some. He looked like a grown man, and sometimes he sounded like one. I prayed no one ever took advantage of my gentle giant.

"Yes," I said.

"They dead?" he asked, looking at me intently. "They get shot up by them Viet Cong? I heard tell on the news that they some badasses."

"Watch your mouth, Chad. Say it different."

"I'm sorry. I should have said, 'Them Viet Cong is some bad men.' Is that better?" He looked at me for approval and I smiled, even though this conversation was breaking my heart. I didn't want to entertain the idea that either of my brothers might be dead instead of missing. Missing was bad enough, but at least they

might be captured somewhere, maybe by people who could see the
tragedy of this war and might practice a hint of compassion toward
my little brothers. I couldn't make myself believe that every person
over there wanted this war any more than many of us over here. I
had to believe that there was goodness everywhere on God's green
earth, including in the place where my brothers and others like
them were fighting for their lives.

"I pray they aren't dead, Chad, but unfortunately, I don't know
for sure. All we know is that they're missing in action."

Chad nodded. "My Uncle Lennie died over there. He wasn't
my real uncle, but he looked out for me when he could. He was
a junkie too, but he wasn't as bad as Lena."

"I'm sorry to hear that, Chad. This war is brutal. A lot of good
men and women are dying over there. My sincere prayer is that
it will end soon."

Chad stood up. "I should go do my homework."

I smiled. When Chad had first moved into the group home,
getting him to do his homework was almost impossible, but now,
six months later, he seemed to like to get his homework done, and
he even went out of his way to help Pee Wee with his. Every Friday
after school, if the boys had done their work and tried their best,
Jason took them to Dairy Queen for ice cream, and so far Chad
hadn't missed a trip. At the morning staff meeting, we'd discussed
whether he should forgo Dairy Queen due to his behavior, but I
argued in his favor. Rightly or wrongly, I blamed his caseworker
for his behavior more than I did him.

"Let Mr. Jason know if you need help with your math," I said.

"I don't need any help," he said with a wide grin. "My teacher say I'm good with numbers, and if I keep on, I could work for NASA someday."

"Oh. So you want to work for NASA?"

He nodded, and his face radiated with pride. When Chad acted the way he was supposed to, he was the sweetest boy. It was hard to believe he was the same young man who had smashed a wall with a chair earlier in the day. Thank goodness the damage was minimal. Cairo Fieldings had already patched up the wall and repainted it. Even if you stood close to it, you couldn't tell that anything had happened.

"Yes, ma'am. I want to be just like Scotty on *Star Trek*. I want to 'boldly go where no man has gone before,'" he said, proudly quoting the line from his and the other boys' favorite show. We didn't let them watch much television, and I wasn't exactly pleased with the skimpy outfits of the women on *Star Trek*, but I did like Uhura—and I did like that half the boys were into science and math, hoping that someday they, too, might fly around the universe like Captain Kirk and the crew of the USS *Enterprise*. Almost all of their playtime was spent pretending they were the *Star Trek* crew. They even allowed Pee Wee to join in. He always wanted to be Mr. Spock, but inevitably they'd offer him the role of Chekov or Sulu. It was always interesting watching them play, a sweet reminder that as tough as they could act sometimes, they were simply boys.

"Alright, Mr. Scotty," I said. "You go get that homework done. I'll check in on you before I leave."

"Yes, ma'am," he said and started walking toward the door, but before he left the room, he stopped and turned to face me. "Miss Katia . . ." His voice trailed.

"Yes. What is it?" I watched as he struggled, almost like he didn't want to say whatever it was that was on his mind. "Just say it, Chad. Whatever it is."

"I . . . I wish you were my mama," he said and then hurried out the door.

I was stunned. Not so much that he wished I was his mother. Other boys had said similar things to me over the decade that I'd worked at the group home. I usually let it flow over me, but his words hit differently.

My thoughts rushed back to last year when I'd had an emergency hysterectomy. I'd always had difficult periods, but they got so bad last year that I'd double over in pain while walking from the house to my truck. One day while I was getting ready for work, the pain became so intense, I passed out. The next thing I knew, I was waking up inside the Negro hospital in Tuskegee. I remembered looking around wildly, relaxing only when I saw Mama sitting by my bed. A doctor stood next to Mama, his skin dark like mine. There was something reassuring about having a Negro doctor— that is, until he shared his news.

"Miss Daniels, my name is Dr. Shaw, and I am going to be honest with you," he said, gazing down at me with the utmost compassion. "There is an unusually large mass inside your uterus, and although I won't know for sure until we get inside, I don't think I will be able to save it."

"A hysterectomy," I said as Mama squeezed my hand. "But I don't have any children. I'm not married. This isn't right."

He went on to explain everything to me, but all I could think about was the family I thought I still had time to have. With this news, I could no longer see that in my future. Unlike most women, I hadn't spent a lot of time thinking about getting married and having children. I was busy taking care of Mama, my brothers, and the boys at the group home, yet the thought of not being able to give birth was devastating.

Just like the doctor had warned, there was no saving my uterus. When I awakened after the surgery and saw the look on Mama's face, I instantly knew.

I cried in her arms, and then, in true Katia fashion, I tucked my pain away and focused my attention on everyone else. Right around that time was when I first dreamed about the leeches crawling all over me.

Mama said it was God telling me I needed to put myself first. I didn't know about that. I just knew that I had to figure out how to move forward with a future that held no babies and, as far as I could see, no husband. And now, Chad saying he wished I was his mother opened up every bit of heartache I thought I had packed away, and I didn't know how to cram those emotions back into the suitcase again.

4

"DANG IT," I SAID, HITTING THE steering wheel with frustration upon seeing the truck of my on-again, off-again boyfriend, Leon, in the driveway. I wasn't in the mood to make nice with him today. I just wanted to go to my bedroom and listen to Nina Simone's newest album on my record player. It had arrived in the mail the other day, and I'd been saving it for a day like this. One where I needed to relax and get carried away by the music. Instead, I'd have to entertain Leon. He wasn't a demanding boyfriend at all, but he required some attention—attention I wasn't in the right frame of mind to give. My mind was still filled with thoughts of my brothers, the boys at the group home, especially Chad, and my inability to bear children.

Leon was fifty-five years old, and we knew each other from church. "Boyfriend" wasn't the most accurate title for Leon—perhaps "gentleman caller" would be a better moniker for him. I'd started quasi-dating Leon a few months after the hysterectomy. He wasn't my type necessarily, but he was safe. He was the father of three children and the grandfather of seven. He wasn't seeking a wife to start a family with; he was seeking companionship. One Sunday after church, he asked me if I'd go have ice cream with him. From there, it became our routine. We'd shared a few awkward kisses, but mainly I filled a void left by his deceased wife, and he made me feel a little less alone. Sometimes.

I knew that Mama had called him. As a truck driver, Leon was on the road Monday through Friday, which worked fine for me since the group home consumed my weekdays and at times my weekends, depending on what crisis we were dealing with or trying to avoid. I wondered what he was doing in town on a Tuesday. Mama met me at the door with a huge grin on her face.

"Brother Leon is here," she said as if I wouldn't recognize his truck. I suppose I should have been happy she was smiling after the news we got today.

When I'd first told her Leon had asked me to be his girlfriend, she had nearly shouted with excitement because I was getting serious about someone. I was grateful that she liked Leon and that they got along so well. Probably because he would sit and watch endless hours of mindless television with her. It was nothing for us all to be in the living room sitting on the couch, with Leon between me and Mama. I'd be reading a book while she and Leon would cackle over *The Jackie Gleason Show* or *The Smothers Brothers Comedy Hour*. Sometimes it felt like "Brother Leon" was more Mama's boyfriend than he was mine.

"Just Leon," I muttered. "His name is Leon. You didn't have to call him."

Mama shook her head disapprovingly. "If a woman has a man,

she needs to lean on him during the hard times. It lets a man know he's important. Lean on your man, Katia."

I sighed heavily. I wasn't about to pick a fight with her. Definitely not on a day like this. "Okay, Mama."

Mama looked me up and down. From that look alone, I knew where this conversation was going. Where it always went with Mama when she took a good look at me: my appearance.

"If you hurry to the kitchen," she said in a loud whisper, looking around as if there was someone close by to overhear our conversation. There wasn't. She reached up and touched my hair. "I can take out the straightening comb and touch up those naps. I just don't know why you want to let your hair look like this. You weren't raised to have a nappy head. I straightened your hair every Saturday when you were growing up. This bird's nest on your head is an insult to me and to your daddy's memory. God only knows how you got the attention of a man like Brother Leon looking like this!"

I felt something bubble up inside me. At first I thought it was anger, but I'd heard this particular diatribe before. No, what I was feeling was good old-fashioned hurt. I knew Mama loved me and only wanted the best for me, but right now I needed her to stop nagging me about my appearance and focus on the fact that I was her one and only daughter, and through thick and thin, I had always stood by her without complaint. That was what I needed from her, but for me to say those words out loud would have crushed her spirit, so I said nothing.

"Katia girl," Mama said. "You heard what I said?"

"Yes, Mama. I heard you," I said, squaring my shoulders as

defiantly as I could. "And like it or not, I did. Get his attention, that is. Nappy hair and all. This hairstyle speaks to me. If it is all the same to you, I think I will leave it just the way it is."

I'd started wearing my hair in an Afro when I saw a picture of Nina Simone in a magazine a couple of years ago. It was like looking at myself, from her eyes to her nose, from her thick, luscious lips to her dark brown skin. That picture made me feel seen more than any picture I'd encountered of Diahann Carroll or Lena Horne. They were beautiful Negro women, but they made me feel more invisible because I knew that no matter how many times I straightened my hair or tried to diet and lose weight, I'd never look like them. Nina Simone wasn't a big woman like me, but she was beautiful and talented and, from the sound of her music, free. Free in ways I only hoped to be someday.

When I had gone to the barbershop my daddy used to go to and sat in the chair with the cutout from the magazine in my hands, shaking with excitement, I felt exhilarated as long pieces of hair fell to my shoulders. Mama was scandalized, but my brothers called me a Nubian queen. It saddened me that Mama looked at me and saw something to be ashamed of, in spite of all my accomplishments.

Mama shook her head and grumbled. "Too many good-looking women out here in these streets who would love a man like Brother Leon. You ought to try harder, Katia. You're no spring chicken. If you play this thing right with Brother Leon, he might just ask you to marry him. I might never see my boys get married, but you . . ." Her voice quivered as she stopped speaking and wiped away tears.

I had a mouthful of things to say, but I didn't. Mama needed to get her mind off the boys, and talking about my nappy hair and my last-ditch effort to gain a husband was the perfect distraction. So I smiled, gave her a quick hug, kissed her cheek, and walked past her into the house. She sighed as I passed by.

When I got inside, Leon was standing there waiting for me. He was a nice-looking man for his age. Not a gray hair on his head, and his skin was as dark and smooth as a teenager's. The only thing that belied his age was his thick, Coca-Cola bottle glasses. I was shocked he could drive big trucks with his poor vision, but as far as I knew, he'd never even received a parking ticket, let alone had an accident. Knock on wood.

As always, he was impeccably dressed in a pair of black polyester slacks, a white button-down shirt, a tie, and a red-and-black tweed jacket. He was so persnickety he wouldn't even remove his jacket or loosen his tie when he came over to visit. I always told him he was overdressed, but he said a man needed to look his best when he came courting. I could appreciate that, but I never worried about such things. If I was home, I'd be dressed in a pair of pants and a turtleneck sweater or a large muumuu, much to Mama's chagrin. That didn't seem to bother Leon. Of course nothing seemed to bother Leon. His emotional gauge was forever set at a comfortable seventy-five degrees.

He approached me and kissed my cheek.

"Are you okay?" he asked in his low-and-slow southern drawl.

Before I could stop myself, I burst into tears. I was overwhelmed at his innocent question.

"Now, now," he said, pulling me into an awkward embrace

while patting my back. It was the kind of embrace a well-meaning stranger gives to another person—not the way a boyfriend hugs his girlfriend. "Don't get yourself sick. Now, now."

I pulled away, brushing the tears away angrily. I hated getting emotional. "I'm fine, Leon. Just tired. Maybe you could come back tomorrow?"

"I guess I could," he said slowly, "but your mama made meat loaf and tonight's *I Dream of Jeannie* and *The Jerry Lewis Show*. I never get to watch them when I'm on the road, and your mama . . ."

"Never mind," I said quickly. "You stay. I'm going to go take a bubble bath and change."

He perked up. "Do you want us to wait on dinner?"

I didn't have time to answer before Mama walked back inside. "Everything's ready and if we don't eat now, we'll miss Cronkite at five thirty. He tells the news the best."

"Don't worry about me," I said, moving around Leon. "I'm not hungry anyway. Y'all enjoy your food and your television."

"Are you sure?" Leon called out to me, but all I did was wave and continue toward my bedroom. I went inside and gathered up the silk pajamas and matching robe I'd gifted myself on my last birthday. Mama could entertain Leon. I had no intention of returning to that living room tonight.

I picked up my newest book from my nightstand, *Valley of the Dolls*, by Jacqueline Susann. I'd been waiting to read it for a while. I knew Mama and "Brother Leon" would be appalled by my reading such things, but I made no apologies to anyone for my looks or my reading tastes. Reading had always been my escape, and when I first discovered *Lady Chatterley's Lover* by D. H. Lawrence during college, I became hooked on sexy romance novels. I'd long ago resigned myself to being confidant and best buddy to cute guys, never their girlfriend. I had female friends who'd leave me in the company of their boyfriends and whisper, *"Keep an eye on him for me. Make sure no other ladies get fresh."* Never once did they think I might be one of those *other ladies* getting fresh with their man. So I poured my attention into my books, and from them, I lived vicariously through the heroines' lives.

I made my way to the bathroom, put *Nina Simone Sings the Blues* on the record player I kept beside the tub, and started my bath, pouring in a liberal amount of Badedas bubble bath, a gift from the twins our last Christmas together. I turned up Nina just loud enough for me to hear the mournful wail of the harmonica, the guitar, and her sultry voice. Once the tub was nearly overflowing with bubbles, I undressed and slid into the water as I softly sang along with the album's first song, "Do I Move You?" The lyrics were so risqué. I tried to imagine listening to the album with Leon and almost laughed out loud. He was definitely a prude when it came to such things. One time, while we were sitting in the living room, I put Aretha Franklin on the record player, and he insisted I turn it off. Said she was blaspheming God and her daddy, the Reverend C. L. Franklin, with her "nasty woman" music. After that, I kept my music and my reading preferences to myself.

I sank deeper into the water, allowing my head to become completely immersed, something I couldn't do back in my press-and-curl days. When I came back up for air, I was more relaxed than I had felt in days. It was like baptism, going underneath that water—everything from the last few hours washed away.

I reached for my bath cloth and began to wash every part of my body. I tried not to judge the rolls of fat or the stretch marks from my constant gaining and losing and regaining of weight. My favorite cousin and dear friend, Alicia, fussed at me for talking badly about my weight and figure. She was a big woman too, but she carried her weight with far more confidence than I did. I also tried not to pay attention to the huge scar on my belly, where they'd cut and removed all possibility of motherhood in the traditional sense. I grabbed the towel on the rack next to the tub and dried my hands. Then I reached for my novel and started reading: *"The temperature hit ninety degrees the day she arrived."*

"Girl, is you drowned in there?" Mama's voice called out from the other side of the door, causing me to jump. The water was now cold, and my book was completely submerged. I jerked it out of the water but it was ruined. I chucked it into the garbage can. I'd have to get another copy. Thankfully, it wasn't a library book.

I looked at the clock on the wall. It said 8:05 p.m. I had read and then slept straight through Cronkite and *I Dream of Jeannie*.

"I'm fine, Mama," I called back to her. "I just fell asleep. Be out in a second." I stepped out of the tub and dried off. My skin was wrinkled from too much soaking. I slathered myself with Vaseline and then Jergens lotion, hoping the two products working together would revive my skin. I rubbed some Tussy deodorant on my armpits and then put on my pajamas, robe, and house slippers. When I walked out of the bathroom, Mama was still standing by the door, causing me to jump again.

"Lord, you scared me, Mama. I said I was fine."

"Brother Leon left," she said in an accusatory voice. "He watched the news and *I Dream of Jeannie* with me, but when you didn't bother to come back out, he said it was best he head on home. You ought to be ashamed, Katia."

Even though I'd evidently had a nice, long nap, I was still tired, and I didn't feel up to arguing with Mama. I was sorry that Leon probably left with his feelings hurt, but he would understand. One apology from me would clear everything up. It always did. But I wasn't going to call him tonight. I almost said, "I didn't invite him over," but I knew that would lead to more words, so I kept that comeback to myself.

"I'm going to bed." I inched around her and walked toward my bedroom, but she was on my heels, yammering away about "Brother Leon."

"I just don't know why you treat that man so disrespectful," she said as we entered my bedroom. "He ain't showed you nothing but the greatest care and love, and all you do is push him away. Do you want to be alone the rest of your life?"

I took a deep breath and forced myself to smile. "I'll never be alone, Mama. I've got you, and if you count the boys at the group home, well, my cup truly does runneth over, with no shortage of people in my life." I didn't mention my brothers. I didn't want to upset Mama, but my words still seemed to cause her grief.

Mama wiped tears from her eyes. "I'm not gone live forever, girl. And we don't know about your bro . . . your bro . . ."

I reached out and pulled Mama close. I couldn't stand to see her distraught. As much as she wounded my soul with some of her careless words, when it came to her, my protective nature would rival any mama bear. Before Daddy died, he made me promise to take care of Mama and the boys, and that was what I tried to do.

I gently stepped back so I could see her fully. Then I wiped her tears with a handkerchief I had in my robe pocket.

"What was *I Dream of Jeannie* about tonight?" If I could get her talking about her shows, I could get her to dry her tears. "Come get in the bed with me and tell me all about it."

We both climbed into my bed, something we used to do after Daddy died. Many a night, Mama would cry herself to sleep, her thin body pressed against my larger, thicker frame. I'd always been a big girl, but when Daddy took sick, I ate everything in sight, trying to fill the empty spaces his dying was leaving exposed.

"Lord, that Major Nelson is always doing something to vex poor Jeannie," Mama started, sniffling loudly. "He went and tricked her so he could go out with an old girlfriend. If I was her, I would just stay in that bottle and forget about Major Nelson. He don't mean her no good. You can tell by his eyes he ain't no good man. That's what Brother Leon said. He said you can always tell by a man's eyes if he 'bout something, and that Major Nelson ain't about nothing."

"Do tell," I said. "Then what?" Suddenly I was wide-awake again. My stack of books was calling my name. I figured that Mama would either grow tired of talking and fall asleep or go back to the living room and finish watching *The Jerry Lewis Show*. But she did neither. Instead, she rolled onto her elbow and looked at me.

"I'm not going to be here forever, baby," she said, repeating her earlier sentiment. "I don't want you living your whole life without knowing the love of a man. You deserve that and more, Katia. Every woman deserves it, but especially you."

"What about you then, since every woman deserves love? Don't you want the love of a man again?" I asked. Mama was only sixty, but as far as I knew, she'd never talked romantically to another man since Daddy. More than I wanted a man for myself, I wished she could find someone. Just like she said I deserved someone to love me, I felt the same way about her.

A smile crossed her face. "I don't need no other man. Your daddy was enough. I want you to experience that kind of love, Katia. I don't even care if it's not with Brother Leon. If he doesn't make you feel warm all over like those nasty books you like to read do, then find a man who does."

I opened and then closed my mouth. I had no clue Mama knew about the subject matter of the books I read, but more than that, I never thought Mama would ever say I should consider seeing someone else other than "Brother Leon." The way she'd been telling it, I should have married him several yesterdays ago.

"Mama, I don't know what to say."

She reached over and stroked the side of my face. "You deserve happiness, Katia. Large helpings of happiness. I need at least one of my children to get their hands on some happiness. Will you try?"

"Yes, ma'am," I said. What else could I say? Hearing her speak so sweetly and tenderly about her desire for me to experience love like she and Daddy had was more than I could ever have hoped to hear her say. This was the mama I needed. I knew the criticisms were all born out of love, but sometimes I just needed her to love on me.

Silently, I reached over and pulled her close, and that was how we lay until we both dozed off to sleep.

5

THE NEXT MORNING, I WOKE UP feeling refreshed in a way I hadn't felt in a while. I looked toward the other side of the bed. Mama was gone. I didn't know when she'd gotten up. I glanced over at my clock; it was five in the morning. I had to get up even though my bed was like a comfortable cocoon—a refuge from the turmoil in my life, a place where I didn't feel the pain of loss or the fear of more bad news. But duty called, and it seemed to summon me in loud yells rather than soft whispers. Plus, I wanted to call my cousin Alicia before leaving for work.

Alicia was an early riser too. Her husband, Curtis, was a garbageman and he woke up at the crack of dawn to start his work. Alicia got up before him and made him a hot breakfast and packed his lunch. I used to tease her about spoiling him, but when she said he was all she had to spoil in their house, I stopped with the teasing. Just like me, Alicia had no children. She and Curtis had been trying since they'd married three years ago, but unfortunately, she had miscarried every single pregnancy.

I padded quietly down the hallway, stopping to peek into Mama's room. She was asleep. I made sure, as I went to the kitchen on the other end of the house, not to be loud. I didn't want to wake her up. I picked up the phone and dialed Alicia's number. As usual, she picked up after the first couple of rings.

"Hey, cousin," she said. "What's new with you?"

I filled her in on my brothers being missing in action. We both shed some tears. Although Alicia was closer to me than to the twins, they were like little brothers to her too. We all grew up together. Alicia and I were only a few months apart in age. For a time, family members called us the Bobbsey Twins after the characters in the books.

Once I got her caught up on everything, we both expressed excitement about seeing each other for Thanksgiving. She'd visit for the holidays, along with as many of our Mobile, Alabama, family members who could come. Half of the family would stay with Great-Aunt Hess, my grandmother's only surviving sibling, and the other half would stay with Mama and me. Thanksgiving dinner rotated from house to house. This year it was our year to host.

"I want you to make sure you take some time to relax," Alicia said. "I know that group home has become your life, but you deserve happiness outside of those walls."

I didn't respond. Focusing on the group home kept me from being lonely. Those boys needed me, and that gave my life purpose. I'd be lying if I said my relationship with Leon was fulfilling in any way. Almost as if Alicia could read my mind, she brought up Leon.

"Listen, honey," she continued. "Leon is a good man. Don't get me wrong. But he is not the man for you. I want you to have someone who curls your toes, girl. Someone who makes you feel like those women in your paperbacks."

I touched my face as it grew hot. It seemed everybody knew about my vice of reading steamy paperbacks. It was funny. I could read all day about other women in romantic relationships, and I could even listen to Alicia talk about her love for Curtis and his love for her. Yet anytime I tried to imagine myself with a man who loved me like the men in my books loved their women or like Curtis loved Alicia, I started blushing and feeling awkward.

The only person I'd ever had a legitimate crush on was a boy I used to tutor in high school named Seth Taylor. He was a football player. The handsomest boy ever, who had no time for me. He was nice enough, but he barely glanced my way. I was good for helping his GPA but nothing more. I was a big girl with huge glasses and frumpy clothes, not much different than I was now. Definitely, I wasn't the kind of girl who attracted boys like Seth.

As tradition would dictate, he fell in love with the cheerleader captain, Denise, and the two, as far as I knew, continued to live happily ever after. The last I'd heard they were living in Atlanta. I dated a few guys here and there over the years, but I didn't vibe with any of them, and after a while I threw myself into my work, figuring I wasn't the dating or marrying kind. Then Leon came along and filled the void as best he could. I'd resigned myself to the fact that he was enough for me. He was kind to me and Mama. What more could I ask for?

"I can't wait to see you," I said, shifting the conversation.

Alicia laughed, but she didn't bring up my romantic life, or lack thereof, anymore. We continued to chat, promising to talk later today. Then I went to the bathroom and took a quick shower. No soaking in the tub this morning. No Nina Simone to lull me into a sexy mood. Just the quiet. I needed to get dressed and leave for work, so I didn't even listen to any music. I just mentally reviewed my day's schedule.

I had to get all of the paperwork in order for the boys who'd be returning to their families for the holidays. This meant all fifteen of them, minus Chad and Pee Wee. Some of them would be returning for good, hopefully. The others would be gone for a few days. The houseparents and I always scheduled appointments for the families to come in and review the visitation and/or reintegration plan. We did a lot of counseling and planning to make sure the environment was conducive to the child successfully reuniting with his family. Some of our boys had only been away from their families for a few weeks. Others had been away for months. Rejoining the family after living in such a structured environment as the group home can be hard, and we wanted to do everything we could to ensure success.

I was thinking about these things as I walked down the hallway, but I was nearly stopped in my tracks by the delicious aromas wafting throughout the house. For a minute, I thought I was dreaming. I entered the kitchen, and Mama had a full breakfast on the table— bacon, eggs, grits, toast, and orange juice. Normally Mama slept in. I'd hear from her about midmorning, but unless it was a special occasion—Thanksgiving, Christmas, or the twins' or my birthday— Mama never made breakfast. She'd throw down for the other meals, but for breakfast we were on our own.

"Mama? What's all this for?" I went over to the sink where she was washing dishes and hugged her. She was still wearing her dressing gown and robe, and her hair was in rollers, but she looked at me with loving eyes—no smile, but the love was there. It always was, even when she was scolding me about something or another.

"Thought I'd surprise you with a good hot breakfast before you headed out," she said. "Go sit down and eat before the food gets cold. I don't want you being late."

"Yes, ma'am." I wasn't really hungry yet, but I wasn't going to insult Mama by not eating. Anyway, the food sure was smelling good. I put some of everything on my plate and said a blessing, specifically mentioning my brothers by name. I wanted God Himself to know they had people who loved them, and we weren't ready to surrender them to the bosom of Abraham. Mama sat down but didn't fix herself a plate. She just looked at me.

"Do you think they'll find the boys?" she asked, dabbing the tears from her eyes with a napkin. I should have known that this brave face she'd put on was a ruse. "Last night I kept hearing one of the twins calling out to me in my dreams. But just one. Not the both of them, and I couldn't tell which one of them it was saying, 'Mama. Mama.'"

"Don't go getting wound up, Mama." I set down my fork and reached for her hand. "Yesterday I called everyone I could think of who might have some answers, but I am not giving up. I'll call them over and over until we find out something. Okay?"

Mama nodded and rose from the table. "I'm gone go lay back down. You finish your breakfast."

I watched as she walked out of the room. What little bit of an appetite I'd been able to muster was gone. I got up and straightened the kitchen, then made my way out to my truck, all the while praying that Mama's intuition was wrong. It wasn't as cold today as it was yesterday, but I felt like I might never be warm again after the conversation I just had with Mama.

I hoped that maybe the war would end soon and both boys would come home, but every newspaper headline seemed to indicate the opposite. Just yesterday I'd hidden the paper from Mama, something I'd been doing on and off the last few months as things seemed to escalate over there. The headline yesterday said "Communists Shell 25th Infantry, Kill Five, Wounding 27 Soldiers." My brothers weren't part of the Twenty-Fifth Infantry Division, but the panic I felt was as severe as if they were, and I knew Mama couldn't handle any more painful news like that. I didn't even like her watching Cronkite in the evenings anymore, but his soothing voice—even as he shared tragic news—seemed to calm her.

Mama had always been in tune with the boys in ways I didn't understand. I was Daddy's twin. He'd understood me in ways Mama never did. The boys were her heartbeats, and she could feel when something was going right with them or when something was going wrong. When they were seniors in high school, they'd plotted to wait until Mama and I went to bed and then sneak out and meet up with some girls. Unbeknownst to them, Mama had one of her "feelings" and got back up. When they finally tried to sneak out, she was sitting in the living room with a belt in her lap. She had never whipped them, but the threat was always there. She said they pretended like they were sleep-walking and hurried their butts back to bed. The next day, when it was just the two of us, Mama and I laughed so hard I thought we'd lose our breath.

"They snored like they sound asleep," she had said, laughing and snorting, holding her arms out to mimic them playacting like they were sleepwalking.

I wiped a tear from my eye as I started up my truck. What I wouldn't give right now to have them back home, roughhousing with each other or begging me for some spending money so they could go to the movies. My brothers were everything to me and Mama. Losing them would be unimaginable.

The ride to the group home was uneventful. It was so early, the roads were almost empty. When I exited my truck, I held my breath for a second and listened. All was quiet.

"Thank you," I whispered to God under my breath as I pulled my coat closer around my body.

I walked toward the door, continuing to thank God and all of the guardian angels that I wasn't hearing any commotion this morning. When you're in charge of a house full of rowdy boys, the best sound you will ever hear is silence.

Chad met me at the door with a huge grin on his face—a far cry from the previous day.

"Good morning, Miss Katia." He reached for my bags. "I'll take your stuff."

"Thank you." I handed over my bags and my coat. "What's got you in such a good mood this morning?"

"Last night after you left, I played Mr. Jason in chess and I won," he said.

"Hold up," Jason said, coming toward us, an equally large grin on his face. "If you're going to tell this story, tell it true."

"Okay, I didn't actually beat him, but we reached a . . . a . . . What you call it, Mr. Jason?"

"A draw. It means neither one of us could beat the other. It was a tie." Jason wrapped his arm around Chad's shoulders. "But I will admit, I have taught you all of my best moves. Miss Katia, when he opened with the King's Gambit, I knew I was in trouble."

We all laughed.

"I love the sound of this, Chad." I gave him a quick hug. "Anyone can play checkers, but it takes a brilliant mind to play chess. It takes an even more brilliant mind to beat Jason."

"I didn't beat him. This time." Chad grinned. "But next time? Just wait. I'm gone figure out how to beat' em. Miss Katia, you reckon I could get some books on playing chess? Nothing new. Like a library book or something?"

Even though the public library was integrated, just like the schools were, I was still hesitant about taking my boys there. I didn't want to risk something bad happening, and I saw how some people treated them after finding out they were residents at the group home.

One time we were at the grocery store, and though the boys never left the sight of the houseparents they were with, a store manager insisted he saw one of my boys pocket a candy bar. The accused boy emptied his pockets, proving he hadn't stolen anything, but the experience had left a bad taste in all of our mouths. I tried to make sure the boys went to places they were welcome, like the Black barbershop or church. Integration didn't equal fair treatment, and my boys had been hurt enough in their short lives. For now, I wasn't willing to put them into any situations where their emotions might get the best of them.

"I've got a couple of books at home I can loan you, Chad," Jason said quickly. I smiled at him, and he nodded as if he understood my hesitation. Knowing Jason, he probably did. Out of all the assistants I'd had over the last few years— and there had been many because this was a high-stress job that most people couldn't handle—Jason was the one I most trusted.

"I'll run by the house and get them before I pick you boys up from school this afternoon. You hurry up and take Miss Katia's things to her office, and then finish getting dressed so you can eat. The van will be leaving soon," Jason told Chad.

"Yes, sir," Chad said and rushed toward my office so he could deposit my things.

"Thank you, Jason." I put my hand on his shoulder. "I know we have to get used to a world where we can go wherever we like, but . . ."

"But this is still Troy, Alabama, at the end of the day," he said, nearly finishing my sentence. "We've come a long way, but we still have a long way to go."

"I'm glad you get it." I started to walk away, but then I stopped and turned back toward him. "Jason, when you get back from your classes today, I want to talk with you about the holidays."

"Yes, ma'am," he said. "Is anything wrong?"

I hated that the default for those of us in this line of work tended to be fear that the other shoe was dropping or had already dropped. I guessed, for those of us who worked with vulnerable populations, it sort of went with the territory.

"Nothing's wrong," I reassured him. "I've been talking to the caseworkers for all of the boys, and it looks like everyone except Pee Wee and Chad have a place to go for Thanksgiving, maybe even Christmas and beyond. Obviously, Chad cannot go and spend the holidays with Lena, and Pee Wee's grandmother has pretty much washed her hands of him. The poor woman has three teenagers of her own and at least three grandchildren living in her three-bedroom apartment. I'm going to call her this morning, but I doubt she's going to want him to come stay for any of the holidays. Of all of her grandchildren, she bonded with him the least, I think. It's sad. He's such a good little boy. I want to talk to you about some options for those two so we can shut down the group home during the holiday season and employees can have a break and be with their families."

I'd been toying with taking Pee Wee and Chad home with me for Thanksgiving. In the past, if there were only a few boys lacking stable homes to go to for the holidays, I'd sometimes give my staff the holidays off and stay at the group home with the boys, or if there was only a boy or two, I'd clear it with their caseworkers and take them home with me.

I didn't want to be away from Mama, especially this year, so I needed to see what Jason thought about me taking the boys to my house. I still needed to get things approved by their caseworkers. I didn't foresee having any issues with Pee Wee's caseworker, but I was clearly not one of Mrs. Gates's favorite people right now. If I had to stay at the group home with them, I would, but I hoped they could experience Thanksgiving at my house.

My mind briefly drifted to Chad's words from the previous day. *"I wish you were my mama,"* he'd said. I had pushed his pronouncement out of my mind, but his words had touched me. I knew the cardinal rule for running a group home: *stay engaged, but stay detached.* With Pee Wee and Chad, I knew I wasn't operating from a safe distance. I cared about both of them, especially Chad, and the idea of either of them going back to their old homes scared me. Fortunately, Pee Wee's caseworker agreed that Pee Wee wasn't safe with his mother and the grandmother wasn't a viable option for him right now, if ever. I prayed Mrs. Gates would figure out the same when it came to Chad.

"I'll come by as soon as I'm done with class. I only have one today," Jason said. I was so deep in thought, I nearly jumped.

"Great," I said quickly. Too many times over the last twenty-four hours or so, I had been unfocused. I hated that feeling and I was determined to pull myself together. "I'll see you then." As I approached my office, Leslie was hanging up her coat.

"Good morning, Leslie," I greeted her.

"Good morning, Miss Daniels," she said with a smile. I was happy to see she was back to her old self. I didn't want the Chad incident to get to her. This career was easy to burn out from because there was often more bad news than good. That's why I celebrated those young men whose pictures were on my wall. They were a constant reminder to me that our work was important and change was possible for the boys. Every night I had the houseparents ask the boys to repeat the following: *I am not my circumstances. Even when it feels like all hope is lost, I am still a winner.*

"Around nine or so, I need you to get Mrs. Gates on the phone," I said. "If she asks what it's about, just tell her Chad. I'll tell her the rest."

"Yes, ma'am," she said, writing down my every word. I stifled a smile. I didn't want to be the Big Bad Wolf with my staff, but I'd rather they fear my wrath than make a mistake that could lose a boy his freedom, or worse, his life. "Is there anything else you need me to do?"

"I've got a list of things a mile long. After you call Chad's caseworker, I need you to get Pee Wee's grandmother on the line. After that, I'll need you to call Pee Wee's caseworker." I figured I'd tackle the most difficult calls first. "Let me go get settled, get a cup of coffee inside my belly, and then we can get down to business," I said.

"Yes, ma'am," she said. "Your coffee is already percolating. I made it as soon as I walked in."

"Thank you, Leslie. Much appreciated." I went into my office and eased the door shut. I headed straight for the coffeepot, poured myself a full cup, and took a sip. It tasted delicious. I saw that Chad had neatly hung up my coat and placed my briefcase on my desk. I sat down and started on the paperwork. I hadn't been working long when someone knocked on my door.

"Come in," I said. Pee Wee and Chad burst into the room, their faces aglow. "To what do I owe the pleasure of this visit, young sirs? Don't you boys have things to do? Mr. Jason will be taking you to school soon."

"Yes, ma'am. You see, Pee Wee and me—"

"Pee Wee and I," I corrected, smiling because their enthusiasm was contagious.

"Yes, ma'am," he said hurriedly. "Pee Wee and I—"

"L-l-let me t-t-t-tell it, Ch-Ch-Chad," Pee Wee begged, hopping on one foot, something he did when he was excited. Some of the other boys used to tease him about it and call him Hop-along until Chad warned them to stop. Because Chad wasn't threatening about it, I allowed him to be Pee Wee's guardian angel. It helped the boys when they could see that others needed support, just like them.

"Okay, Pee Wee," Chad said with a huge sigh. "Slow down and say your words right. We ain't got all morning."

Pee Wee's face fell. I could tell he was hurt by his friend's words. "Y-y-you t-t-tell h-h-h . . ." He hung his head.

I looked at Chad expectantly. I tried to give the boys time to do the right thing before I chimed in. I knew Chad knew better than to make Pee Wee feel less-than because he stuttered.

Chad reached out and placed his hand on Pee Wee's shoulder. "Naw, buddy. You tell her. It was your idea. I'm sorry. I just got excited. That's all."

Pee Wee gazed up at Chad with the eyes of a true worshiper. Chad and I both watched as Pee Wee took a deep breath. Pee Wee saw a speech therapist at his school each week, and it was helping, but whenever he got anxious or excited, his ability to speak got worse. One thing we were all trying to do, staff and residents, was encourage Pee Wee to talk more, even when it made him uncomfortable.

"Last night, M-M-Mr. Jason told us about chess t-t-t . . ." He looked up at Chad helplessly.

"You doing good," Chad said, nodding and smiling. "Just take your time. Like you said, 'Last night, Mr. Jason told us about chess . . .' Finish it. You got it, buddy."

Pee Wee bit his bottom lip, but then he started talking again. "Tournaments. He said they have ch-ch-chess tournaments, b-b-but you have to have a cl-cl-club. W-w-we wondered if w-w-we could start one."

Chad looked over at Pee Wee, as if waiting for permission to speak. Pee Wee nodded with a grin. "T-t-tell her the r-r-rest."

So Chad shared elaborate details about starting a chess club at the group home and competing in competitions.

"Mr. Jason could coach us," Chad said excitedly. "It'll be awesome."

I smiled. That the two of them came up with such a thoughtful plan made me warm all over, in spite of the chilliness of my office. I wanted to say yes. God knows I did, but the group home wasn't set up to support an activity like that. It would require traveling money and tournament fees, not to mention permission from the state to transport the boys to and from tournaments. And because our doors were constantly revolving with boys coming in and leaving, I didn't see how this would work. However, I didn't want to shut down their enthusiasm.

"Let me talk to Mr. Jason during staffing today, and we'll take your well-thought-out proposal into consideration." I wasn't sure what we would come up with, but I wanted to at least try to figure out something. It wasn't often that the boys got passionate about a game like chess. Usually, they all wanted to play Monopoly or checkers. Somehow I just knew we could figure out something.

Chad and Pee Wee high-fived each other. "Yes, ma'am," they said in unison.

"Good. Now you boys hurry on so you aren't late for school. I'll see you this afternoon."

"Yes, ma'am!" they yelled and ran out of the room, chatting away about their brilliant plan.

I returned to my paperwork, a smile on my face as well. Moments like these were definitely ones to cherish. Leslie came in and we mapped out the 101 things I felt like we needed to accomplish today, knowing that we'd be doing well to finish even half of what was on my list. By the time we wrapped up, it was fifteen minutes before nine.

"Well, might as well get it over with," I said. "Go see if you can get Mrs. Gates on the line."

"Yes, ma'am," Leslie said and left the room. A few minutes later, she buzzed. "Mrs. Gates is on the line, Miss Katia."

"Thank you, Leslie," I said and waited until her phone clicked. "Good morning, Mrs. Gates."

"Good morning, Miss Daniels," she said, her dry tone reverberating over the line. "Your secretary said you needed to speak to me about Chad. Is everything okay?"

"Yes, it is. In fact, I wanted to talk to you about taking Chad to my home for Thanksgiving." I explained to her that the other boys would be leaving or spending time with family. Once I stopped talking, I held my breath. After what felt like several minutes, she spoke.

"That sounds alright with me," she said. "Barring a court order demanding Chad be returned to *his mother* between now and then, I see no reason why he can't spend the holiday with you and your family. Perhaps it will do Chad good."

"Thank you, Mrs. Gates," I said. "I do appreciate you being so gracious."

"I know you don't think much of me and how I conduct business, but I am merely trying to follow the guidelines," she said stiffly. "I truly do have Chad's best interests in mind. It would be nice if you could return my kindness with kindness of your own sometimes."

"Thank you," I repeated. I wasn't about to quibble and was okay with her getting the final word on the matter. "Take care, Mrs. Gates."

"You too," she said. "Make sure you get the necessary paperwork to me this week. I would hate for Chad to miss out on this excursion due to time constraints."

"I'll get the paperwork to you today, Mrs. Gates. And again, thank you." I eased the phone back into its cradle.

My next call was to Pee Wee's grandmother. The phone rang several times before she picked up.

"Yeah," she answered.

"Hello, Miss Staples. This is Katia Daniels, the executive director at the Pike County—"

"I know who you are. What you want?"

Anyone else might be offended by her abrasiveness, but I wasn't. I knew she was overextended with all of those mouths to feed and personalities to deal with in her tiny apartment.

"Miss Staples, I'm calling you about Pee Wee. The holidays are coming up and I wondered if you might want to see him. Even if for a few hours," I said.

"I ain't got time, money, or energy to deal with nobody else. I told his caseworker the same thang," she said harshly. "Y'all need to start talking to each other so you can stop calling me. I wish the boy well, but call his mama's people. I told Nathan to leave that trashy white gal alone, but he didn't want to listen, so now, because of her, he doing time in prison for selling drugs and shooting that white man. In the meantime, I'm raising my three teens, two of Nathan's other children, three grandchildren by my oldest two daughters, plus two nieces and one nephew that got dumped on me last week. Ain't no room in the inn."

Before I could say anything else, she hung up the phone. I couldn't be angry with the poor woman. A three-bedroom apartment with twelve people in it was unimaginable. I didn't bother looking up the number for Pee Wee's white family. They had disowned their daughter as soon as they heard she was sleeping with a Black man, and when she went to jail for selling drugs and being an accomplice to a murder, they'd sent a letter to DHS saying never to contact them again about Pee Wee or their daughter. Unfortunately, Pee Wee's story wasn't much better than Chad's. I understood more and more why the two of them had bonded. Pain recognized pain.

I called Pee Wee's caseworker, and she was thrilled that I was willing to take him home for the holidays.

"Maybe it will take his mind off what he doesn't have in his life," she said. "He's such a sweet boy. I spoke to his mother last week and she said, without any prompting from me, that she would like to relinquish custody of him so he can perhaps get adopted. We reached out to his father, but we haven't heard from him yet. I feel like we might have a shot at getting Pee Wee a family—a permanent family. He's so lovable."

"All of our boys are lovable," I snapped, then quickly caught myself. "I'm sorry, Mrs. Gonzalez. I know you mean well. Your words struck a nerve. If any of the boys get adopted, Pee Wee would be top on the list because he *is* lovable and easy to deal with, for the most part. I just wish that all of our boys could get the love and safety they deserve too."

I'd been in this business long enough to know the rules of how adoption often worked: the babies went first. Then the toddlers, and finally, children like Pee Wee, who were cute and cuddly. Boys like Chad were often ignored because they didn't look the part or their history was so fraught with bad behavior that no one wanted to take a chance on them.

After I said my goodbyes to Mrs. Gonzalez, I tried to shake my current mood. I reminded myself that the good part in all of this was that I'd be able to show Chad and Pee Wee what it was like to spend the holidays with a loving family, and really, wasn't that what it was all about?

6

NOT LONG AFTER I GOT OFF the phone with Pee Wee's caseworker, Chad's mother, Lena, called. Our group home was different than many. We encouraged parents to stay in touch, even if they were incarcerated. We strove to keep our boys' families intact while they were with us, through visits and phone calls when possible. Unfortunately, trying to maintain a relationship with Lena hadn't been easy. Half the time she wouldn't call or answer my calls, or when she did call, Chad would refuse to come to the phone, even when Jason or I offered to listen in. Visits were out of the question. Parents weren't allowed access to their children if they were using or selling drugs. Most of the time, Lena was doing both. This recent news that she'd gone through rehab surprised me. The last time I'd interacted with Lena, she had shown up to the group home drunk and high. Fortunately, Chad had been at school so he didn't get exposed to her vitriol.

"Hello, Lena," I said, trying to sound as pleasant as possible. "How are you—"

"Caseworker say you won't let my boy go. What the hell you doing keeping him hostage up there at that home? I want my boy released today," she said, her voice slightly slurred. Was she tired or sick? Or was she high or drunk?

"Lena, I understand that you're frustrated, but we don't want to send Chad back home until you're in a good place," I said. "Maybe once we—"

"This situation is fu—"

"Stop with the language, Lena," I warned, cutting her off. "I will not have this kind of conversation with you." I didn't do it with the boys, and I didn't intend to do it with her.

"Fine," she said, the slurring even worse. "I just need to know what the hell is going on. They cut off my money. No stamps. No housing. Nothing till I get Chad back with me. I ain't trying to be homeless up in here over a misunderstanding."

"I am not willing to have this conversation with you any longer, Lena," I said. "In a few weeks, you will have the chance to speak your piece to a judge. I suggest you prepare for that."

"God—"

I hung up the phone. I wasn't interested in hearing any more profanity-laden tirades from Lena. I couldn't say for sure if she was drunk or high, but she gave the impression of someone who was. Immediately, I began typing up my notes documenting the call. When, or if, Chad's case went in front of a judge, I wanted to have everything in writing. I planned to send copies of the notes to Mrs. Gates so she could see why I had serious concerns about Chad's mother.

I glanced at the clock. No time to sit and worry about Lena. I had a staff meeting. I went to the conference room and everyone was present. I smiled at my married couples, Mr. and Mrs. Grambling and Mr. and Mrs. James, who were all sitting together, laughing about something. I loved having married couples supervise the children at night because for many of them, it was their only opportunity to see a happily married couple up close. Most of the boys came from homes that didn't have two parents. Some of them barely had one, or if they did, it was often a dysfunctional situation.

We talked about the last twenty-four hours, including the recent phone call with Lena. Everyone was happy to learn that Chad and Pee Wee would spend the holidays with me and my family, and not just because that meant they'd get additional time off. My staff worked long hours, and the emotional time they put in went far beyond when they clocked out. Like me, even when they weren't around, their minds were still here, playing out the details of the day—thinking about everything they could have done better or differently.

After the staff meeting, we ate lunch in the dining room. Mrs. Kennedy and Miss Grant had prepared chicken salad sandwiches, homemade potato chips, and a large pitcher of peach-flavored iced tea. For dessert, they baked sweet potato pies. One thing was for certain: no one ever went hungry around here.

"Them sweet taters in that pie came straight outta our garden," Mrs. Kennedy announced, her grin spreading clean across her face. "Them boys picked them before they went to school this morning. Y'all enjoy."

Mrs. Kennedy believed in growing as much of our food as possible, and it was a good teaching opportunity for the boys. They loved working in the garden with her and listening to her explain the process of getting fruits and vegetables from the garden to the table. I looked at the smiling faces around the table. We were a family. Yes, we were coworkers, but at the heart of it, those boys were like children, grandchildren, and nephews to us. I loved every person around this table, and I knew they felt the same way about me.

Once lunch ended, I went back to my office to work on the release papers for some of the boys. As much as I missed them when they left, I was happy to see them reunite with their families, provided I knew they'd be safe. I looked at my clock. The day had scurried by, and it was almost time for the contractor Jason had recommended to stop by and discuss repairs we needed on the roof and, depending on the cost, some remodeling of the upstairs bathroom. Our benefactors, the Arrington family, were generous with their money, but I tried to be the best steward of their funds and our budget.

My phone buzzed, and I quickly picked it up. "Yes, Leslie?"

"Mr. Taylor from Big T Construction is here," she said.

"Very nice, Leslie. Send him in," I said absently. A few weeks ago, I'd asked the board for permission to get some work done on the roof and the bathroom, and they had approved my request. I then asked Jason to find someone to do the work and he recommended Big T Construction. I hadn't questioned him about it at all. I had only told him to set up a meeting with me and the owner as soon as possible.

"Hello, Mr. Taylor," I said without looking up. I was trying to balance the budget for the previous month, and as always, I was struggling. Math was not my forte. I could write reports all day long, but a simple math problem could leave me scratching my head for hours.

I heard the door close. "Have a seat. I will be with you in just a moment," I said.

"Take your time, Katia," he said, his voice deep and husky.

I looked up. A tall, dark-skinned Black man stood before me, showing all of his pretty white teeth. He was definitely a looker, but also there was something familiar about him.

"You don't recognize me, Kat?" he said, moving closer to my desk. He removed his Atlanta Braves baseball cap, revealing a head full of salt-and-pepper curls. Suddenly I knew who he was. *Seth Taylor.* I almost couldn't breathe. I'd been thinking about him the other day, and now here he was in the flesh. I couldn't believe it.

I could have kicked myself for not inquiring more about this Big T Construction company that Jason had recommended. So much had been going on, I'd only half listened to him tell me about this company, owned by a veteran named Mr. Taylor. It never dawned on me that it was Seth Taylor. Taylor was such a common name. Why would I make the connection? Plus, Seth had been away from Troy for decades. There was no reason for me to think they were one and the same.

But here I was, face-to-face with my high school crush.

I decided not to let on that I recognized him. I didn't want him to think I'd spent the last twenty-plus years fantasizing over some high school jock.

"I'm afraid I don't recognize you, Seth," I said, groaning internally because of my ridiculous slip. To his credit, he merely tilted his head slightly and grinned.

"Well, you got my name right," he said. "Good guess. You and I went to high school together. I wouldn't have made it through Mrs. Parks's senior English class without you. How are you doing?"

I stood, completely embarrassed but grateful that he didn't make a big deal about my faux pas. Feeling about as socially awkward as I used to in high school, I silently reminded myself that I was the boss around here and he was a potential contractor. Nothing more. I took a deep breath and forced a smile.

"I'm doing just fine, Seth," I said. "Good seeing you again. How is Denise?"

"Denise and I parted ways not too long ago," he said quietly. "Not all things were meant to be, I suppose. I went over to 'Nam and got discharged back in '65 after I lost my leg. I wear this thing now." He lifted his pant leg a bit, revealing a prosthetic.

"I'm so sorry, Seth," I said, walking around the desk, trying not to be self-conscious of my size. It's not like I'd been a stick in high school. In fact, I was probably only one dress size larger now than when Seth had seen me last, but old insecurities die hard.

When I motioned for him to come sit with me at my conference table, I noticed his slight limp. I wondered if he was as insecure about that as I was of my weight.

"So, you're doing construction?" I said as I sat down. I felt foolish as soon as the words left my mouth. I was usually the most confident person in the room, and here I was, making one verbal mistake after another. I waited for him to laugh, but he continued talking as if my question were perfectly normal.

"Yes," he said with a nod as he sat at the table. "I've always been good with my hands. After I got back to the States and things fell apart with me and Denise, I decided to come home. My parents were amazing with their support, and Dad helped me start this business. I do as much as I can, and my crew does the rest. It's honest work and it keeps me out of my head—most days."

I could feel my cheeks grow warm, which was silly since we were just having a simple conversation. I resisted the urge to reach up and touch my cheeks.

"It sounds like you have a busy life. That's good."

"Well, I could say the same for you, Miss Executive Director. That's a pretty fancy title. I bet your husband is proud," he said.

"Thank you. But I'm not married—although some would say I am married to this job." I placed my hands palms down on the table, mainly to keep them from shaking.

"I'm shocked that you haven't been snapped up," he said, looking at me with an intensity no man had shown me, ever. I was embarrassed. I wasn't like most women, who seemed to have a guidebook for how to flirt with a man. I'd never had that skill set. And anyway, I imagined that Seth was being nice. I was sure he still had to deflect women's attention left and right, just like back in high school. I was determined not to take his kind words seriously.

"How about I show you around so you can see the roof and the upstairs bathroom?" I stood and pushed my chair out of the way. "I know you're probably as busy as I am, so let's do the grand tour."

He looked at me with a strange expression on his face, but then he smiled. "Absolutely. You lead the way."

Finally, I was back to a topic I felt in control of. I led Seth to the upstairs rooms that had leaks, and he wrote extensive notes. Then I led him outside, and while I stood near the part of the house where things seemed to be the worse, he went to his truck and took out a ladder. I watched in surprise as he placed the ladder against the house and began to remove his prosthetic leg. He must have noticed the look on my face because he grinned.

"Don't worry," he said. "I do this all the time. I can't get up there with the leg on, but I can hop with the best of them with my one good leg. I promise I won't come tumbling down."

I stood in amazement as he climbed the ladder and then stepped onto the roof. I confess that I held my breath until he safely descended back to the ground. Just as deftly as he'd removed his leg, he put it back on. Then he turned to me.

"I see where the problems are, and I can get a couple of guys up here in a day or two to repair the roof. The question is, do you want something to tide you over for a year or two, or do you want something that will last you another twenty-five to thirty years, give or take?"

"I depend on the kindness of strangers around here," I said, smiling.

"*A Streetcar Named Desire*. Although I think the quote was, 'I have always depended on the kindness of strangers,'" he said and then laughed. He'd obviously seen the look on my face.

"I paid attention to you senior year when you tutored me in that English course. Yes, we read Shakespeare, but after graduation, I developed a liking for Tennessee Williams. I even got to see *Cat on a Hot Tin Roof* when it opened in New York in 1955. A friend of a friend got me tickets. Denise didn't care for it, but ever since, I've made a concerted effort to read his plays. My favorite to date is *The Glass Menagerie*."

"Well, Mr. Taylor. I don't know what to say about that, and it takes a lot to leave me speechless." I smiled. "Would you like to see the rest of the house?"

"You lead the way, Miss Daniels," he said, returning my smile with one of his own.

Seth and I went back inside so he could see the rest of the job. I was hoping to turn the single-person bathroom upstairs into a multiuser one with three or four shower spaces. When he finished looking around at the current setup, writing tons of notes, we went back to my office. After a bit more scribbling in his notebook, he quoted me a price, and I was pleasantly surprised. Although it would stretch the budget, with some tightening of our belts here and there, we could get the new roof *and* the renovated bathroom.

"You're not lowballing are you?" I asked. I wasn't going to argue with his quote, but I couldn't resist teasing him.

"No, Big T Construction Company is just very efficient. I promise," he said, smiling. "My company will make money from this project. Cross my heart."

"Well, I need to run this by the board once more, but I can't imagine them saying anything other than a resounding yes. I should be able to call you in—" Before I could finish, my office phone buzzed. "Excuse me one moment," I said and picked up the phone. "Yes, Leslie?" She told me it was Lieutenant Rogers. He was one of the many men I'd spoken to yesterday. I gripped my desk. "Put him through."

"Would you like me to leave the room?" Seth asked.

I shook my head. I was happy not to be alone. I put the phone on speaker and glanced toward Seth. His calm demeanor helped me to calm myself.

"Hello, Miss Daniels," the lieutenant said. "I won't beat around the bush. Your brother, Private First Class Marcus Harold Daniels III was found alive this morning. Unfortunately, your other brother, Private First Class Aaron Lamont Daniels, remains missing in action. He was last seen by his twin brother. The details are still getting sorted out. As soon as more is known, you and your family will be informed. I know this is not exactly the news you were hoping for. I know you wanted to hear that both young men are safe, but please know that the Marines are doing everything we can to find your other brother."

"Thank you, Lieutenant Rogers," I said after taking a large gulp of air. "Is Marcus hurt? Where was he found?"

I was trying hard to focus on the fact that Marcus was alive and Aaron wasn't dead—or at least he wasn't reported dead. There was still hope. I had to believe that because that was the message I'd have to sell to Mama.

"He was out in the jungle for weeks trying to find your other brother. From what I was told, he has lost a considerable amount of weight, but other than that he seems to be okay. As soon as he gets checked out more fully and they are sure he is good to travel, he will be sent home."

"When will that be?" I pushed. All I wanted to do at that moment was board a plane to Vietnam so I could pull Marcus into my arms and search high and low for Aaron.

"You should be getting a call tomorrow with better intel, Miss Daniels. I apologize that I can't tell you more today," he said.

"Thank you. I appreciate everything you did to find out what you could about my brothers. My mother and I are grateful."

"Yes, ma'am. Is there anything else I can do for you?" he asked.

"No, sir. Have a good day," I said and hung up the phone. I closed my eyes and took deep breaths, trying to regain my composure.

"What can I do?" a voice said, and I jumped. I'd forgotten Seth was in the room. I shook my head as tears began to fall down my face. I felt a strong hand on my shoulder. I looked up at him and tried to smile through my tears but I couldn't, so I continued to take breaths. After a few minutes, Seth sat back down in the chair beside my desk.

"Katia, this is a hard situation, but there is every reason for you and your mother to keep the faith, and from what I heard, your brother Marcus is going to need all of the strength you can come up with."

"Thank you," I said. "I appreciate that."

"Kat, listen," Seth said, looking at me seriously. "I run a program that supports vets. It's nothing formal and there aren't any doctors or head shrinkers involved—just a bunch of ex-military guys who get together on Friday nights to try to support each other. Once Marcus gets back home, let him know there are guys out there who understand what he is going through and he is welcome to join us."

I nodded. "Thank you."

"You're welcome." He stood up. "Why don't I head out of here and give you some space? We can deal with the construction stuff when things are a bit more settled with you and your family. No rush on my part. And Kat, if you need me, just call. They tell me I'm a pretty good listener."

I nodded again. It seemed like all I could do was nod. "Thank you. I appreciate your kindness."

"I would say I owe you. I'm a few decades late, but better late than never, I suppose." He headed toward the door. "I was for real when I said call me. And because I know you're probably not the type of person to ask for help, I'll check in with you a few days from now. As a friend. Is that okay?"

"Yes," I said. "I appreciate that, Seth."

He gave me a final wave and headed out the door. I started gathering my things. Now I had the hard task of going home and explaining all of this to Mama.

7

"MARCUS," I CALLED OUT TO MY brother, knocking softly
on his door. There was no answer. It was hard to believe that it had
been less than a week since I'd gotten the call that they'd found
Marcus, and now he was home. We'd met him at the bus station
two days ago, and even though he seemed happy to see us, he
hadn't said much on the drive home or since. Mostly he stayed in
the room he shared with Aaron, who was still missing in action.

Neither Mama nor I had asked him about Aaron. Marcus's
state of mind seemed so fragile that we didn't want to upset him.
I knew Mama had many questions, and I did too, but we agreed
that we'd give him more time. Marcus seemed barely able to
handle the most basic questions. Whenever I asked him how he
was doing, he'd look at me blankly, and then if I repeated the
question, he'd say in a monotone voice, "I'm okay."

Yesterday when I'd called Seth about starting the remodeling
job at the group home, I mentioned that Marcus was unusually
quiet.

"Give him time, Kat. Coming out of those jungles back to civilian life is difficult even under the best of circumstances. I can't imagine what your brother is going through after all he has seen, knowing his twin is still there. Time will be the best healer," Seth said.

I thanked him, and after I hung up the phone, I felt a bit better. I was determined to give Marcus the time he needed.

Meanwhile, Mama was determined to feed him back into good health. Thanksgiving was two days away, yet Mama had been cooking for Marcus almost relentlessly. Marcus's first night home she made fried chicken, collard greens, potato salad, baked yams, and coconut cream pie. Marcus didn't eat one morsel. Instead, he sat at the table, tears rolling down his face as Mama held a forkful of food in front of his mouth like she used to when he was a toddler. We had tons of leftovers, but the next day Mama fried fish and made coleslaw, macaroni and cheese, and sweet potato pie. This time Marcus took a few bites, but he still ended the meal crying—loud, wracking sobs that shook his frail body. Mama and I both held him tightly, but it was like a faucet of emotions had been turned on and he didn't know how to turn them off. But now Mama had a mission. Though her attempts at conversation with Marcus were failing, she seemed to think food was the key. So she kept cooking.

Marcus's favorite food had always been Mama's chitlins, and even though their smell makes me gag, I'd gladly helped her clean them yesterday when I got home from work, praying his appetite would be triggered. But when she placed them in front of him for supper tonight, he pushed them around on his plate and eventually excused himself. I wondered if the chitlins made him think about Aaron, who also loved the stinky delicacy.

Marcus's body was back in the safety of our home, but his mind and soul were clearly still in Vietnam, roaming the jungles in search of his twin, whose whereabouts remained unknown.

I had talked to Lieutenant Rogers this morning, and he didn't sound encouraging about Aaron being found. He didn't say it was impossible, but he also didn't say anything that made me think I'd ever again see my little brother's face. He mentioned that over six hundred men were reported missing in action. I'd seen the same number in the newspaper. For that reason alone, I had to fight for Marcus and his sanity. The jungles of Vietnam had swallowed up one of my twin brothers—I wouldn't allow them to take the remaining one. The idea of losing one brother was overwhelming enough. The thought of losing them both was enough to make me almost lose *my* sanity.

"Marcus, it's sissy," I said, knocking again. "Please answer me." I didn't want to barge in on him. But I was afraid for him to be alone. I had dealt with suicidal boys at the group home before. The thought of Marcus doing something to end his life nearly had me in a choke hold.

Mama was in her room, reading her Bible. I was glad the Word still brought her comfort. I couldn't manage dealing with them both melting down at the same time.

"Yes," I finally heard Marcus reply. His voice sounded soft and weak, like a baby bird crying out from its nest.

"Thank you, Jesus," I whispered and opened the door. The room was dark, and I could barely make out his shape on his bed. I went over and sat down, stroking his head the way I used to do when he was a boy. I heard him mumbling, but I couldn't understand it. "What did you say, Bubby?" I used my old nickname for him. He just kept mumbling. I lay down in the bed and wrapped my arms around him. He was sweating in spite of the room's cool temperature. I leaned in closer and then heard what he was singing:

> *If I die in a combat zone,*
> *Box me up and ship me home.*
> *Pin my medals upon my chest.*
> *Tell my mama I did my best.*
> *Mama, Mama don't you cry,*
> *Marine Corps motto is "do or die."*

"Oh, baby," I said, the tears streaming down my face. I pulled my brother closer, trying to ward away the crazy attacking his mind. "Sissy isn't going to let you go. Do you hear me? So, I need you to fight. I need you to fight harder than you have ever fought before."

But he didn't hear me. He kept singing that cadence over and over. I didn't know what to do. If we didn't figure out something soon, even if Aaron came back, there'd be nothing left of his twin when he arrived home. Then I remembered Seth. He had said to call him if I needed to talk. Well, I needed more than a talk—I needed a miracle.

I got up from the bed, leaving my brother, who continued singing underneath his breath, curled into a fetal ball. It was close to nine at night. I hated bothering Seth so late in the evening, but we were running out of options. Before I changed my mind, I walked to the living room, sat down on the couch, and dialed Seth's number. After a couple of rings, he picked up.

"Hello?" he said. I almost sobbed with relief just hearing his voice.

"Hello. It's Katia." I rubbed my hand on the leather couch, trying to calm myself.

"Kat? Is everything alright?" I could hear the concern in his voice. How, after all these years of not speaking to each other, could he have such concern for me?

I shook my head and took a huge breath. "No. Everything isn't alright." I then began explaining Marcus's behavior. "And now, he's in there repeating that cadence he learned at boot camp. I don't even know if my brother is still in there. Seth, I'm scared."

"Your brother is in shock," he said. "What do you know about your other brother and how he went missing? What did Marcus witness?"

"I don't know," I confessed. "He won't say. He barely eats and when we try to talk to him, he just cries."

"Do you mind if I come by tomorrow after work?" Seth asked. "Maybe Marcus will talk to me."

"You would do that?" I really felt like crying now.

"Of course I will do that, Kat," he said. "If you wanted me to come now, I would."

"No," I said. I could only imagine Mama's reaction if a strange man showed up at our house after nine in the evening. I was an adult, but over the years Mama's rules hadn't changed much as they pertained to gentlemen callers. "Tomorrow is good. Thank you, Seth."

"You're welcome," he said. "I wish I could say that everything is going to be alright, but I can't. But I can promise you that I'll do everything I can to encourage your brother and let him know he isn't alone."

"Thank you," I said. I gave Seth our address and told him I'd be home early tomorrow.

"I have one job to finish tomorrow, so I should be able to drop by around four," he said. "Does that work for you?"

"I should have no problem getting here by then," I said. The last of the boys would be leaving in the morning to spend the rest of the week and the weekend with their families. Once they left, the staff and I would straighten up and Chad, Pee Wee, and I would come home. I'd told Pee Wee and Chad yesterday about coming to my house for the holidays. I hadn't planned on telling them until the last minute, just in case something changed, but they'd both been so sad watching the other boys pack their things to leave with moms, dads, grandparents, aunties, and uncles for the week. I wanted to give them something to look forward to as well. I almost second-guessed bringing them home with Marcus being the way he was, but when I shared my concerns with Mama, she insisted they still come.

"*Having youngins around might help,*" she had said. She didn't say it might help Marcus, but I knew that was what she meant, so I pushed my reservations away and didn't change the plans.

After Seth and I hung up, I found myself praying that Marcus could hang in there until Seth came over. I wasn't sure if Seth could do anything, but I hoped that maybe a fellow veteran could reach him in ways Mama and I couldn't. At the group home, we sometimes allowed the residents to have free time with just each other or we'd be there but stay silent while they talked through their issues minus our voices. We found that they'd sometimes heed each other better than they would us. With this knowledge at the forefront of my mind, I checked on Marcus and Mama one more time, and then I was able to go to my room, say my prayers, and drift off to sleep.

"Are we st-st-still going to y-y-your h-h-house, Miss K-K-Katia?" Pee Wee asked me for what seemed like the one hundredth time today. Jason and I were in my office, finalizing paperwork for the last of the residents going home with relatives. School was out, so we weren't on our usual morning schedule. The boys who were still here, including Chad, were sleeping when I'd arrived, but Pee Wee was sitting on the front steps, and he hadn't left my side once. I knew he was fearful that I might change my mind. Pee Wee was used to the adults in his life disappointing him. Because of that, I tried not to get aggravated with his constant questioning.

"Yes, Pee Wee," I said. "You and Chad are still coming to my house for Thanksgiving. Nothing has changed. Now run upstairs and make sure you have everything you need inside your suitcase."

"I forgot a-a-about my su-su-suitcase!" he yelled and took off running. Jason and I looked at each other and laughed.

The joy on Pee Wee's face told me I'd made the right decision.

"So glad Mrs. Hendricks bought suitcases for all of the boys," Jason said as he filed a folder into one of the cabinets. "I've always hated having to send the boys away with their things in hand-me-down bags from the thrift store or worse."

Once in a while, a boy would come to the group home with a suitcase, but usually the boys were ripped away from their homes with nothing but the clothes on their backs. They'd often show up with a plastic bag filled with a couple changes of clothes and some toiletries provided to them by the police or social services—if they were lucky. When Pee Wee moved in a few months ago, he didn't even come with a toothbrush.

"I agree," I said. A few weeks ago, Mrs. Hendricks, one of the board members, had called and asked me what the boys needed that she could gift them since she was leaving the board soon. I told her they could use suitcases, and last week she'd dropped off fifteen brand-new suitcases, one for each boy. She also left me with a word of caution.

"Katia, they are coming for you," she said after we were alone in my office. Mrs. Hendricks was a beautiful, stately woman, a few years shy of eighty but still spry and one of the smartest women I knew. She wore her nearly all-white hair in a tight chignon and she dressed in all black with a single strand of pearls around her neck—a look she'd adopted after the recent passing of her husband, Mr. Gordon Hendricks. His death was the main reason she was stepping away from the board. She wanted to move to Florida to be near her sister, her last surviving sibling. She didn't have any children. She'd told me they'd been too busy making money to slow down enough to make babies. They owned fifteen supermarkets, five funeral homes, and a chain of diners across Alabama. Her sister's son was taking over the day-to-day operations of Hendricks Enterprises while she got to enjoy her "last chapter," as she referred to it.

I offered her a seat and a cup of tea. She delicately sipped the beverage while looking at me pointedly. "I've kept these menfolk off your back as long as I could, but my time is coming to a close, Katia. You need to be on the lookout for an ally or two who can replace me."

I didn't have to ask her what she meant. The last board meeting was proof enough.

We talked a little while longer, and right before she left my office, she said, "Arrington has it out for you, and he wants to replace you with a man. Any man at this point, but he's leaning toward somebody white. The only thing keeping him from making a move is that those other knuckleheads at least agree that this group home needs a Negro at the head. Up until now, I have convinced them that you are the someone this group home needs. Get you some people on that board you can trust, Katia, before it's too late."

With all that had been going on with my brothers, I hadn't had much time to think about new people for the board. To be perfectly honest, I wasn't even sure if I wanted to fight anymore. I felt overwhelmed by it all. And now I had Marcus to contend with, and Chad and Pee Wee. I figured I'd worry about all of that after the holidays. If Sam Arrington IV decided to replace me before the new year, then I just wasn't sure if I wanted to put up a fight.

I hadn't told anyone about the conversation I had with Mrs. Hendricks. I didn't want them panicking. So, as Jason and I finished the paperwork, I kept the conversation light. He asked how Marcus was doing, and I quickly said, "Okay," using Marcus's own go-to response. I wasn't up for any heavy discussions, and talking about Marcus and his state of mind was more than I could manage.

A few minutes later, Pee Wee was back at the door.

"I'm r-r-ready, Miss K-K-Katia," he said, gripping his suitcase in both hands.

"We have one more resident waiting to be picked up, Pee Wee," I said. "Once Larry's father gets here and I send him off safely, we'll head out soon after. Let's plan to leave here at noon. Put your suitcase by the front door, and then go see if Mrs. Kennedy needs any help making sandwiches for Chad, Mr. Jason, you, and me. Okay?"

"Okay," he said in a glum voice, walking ever so slowly out of my office.

"How much you want to bet he takes that suitcase with him to the kitchen?" Jason chuckled as he continued to file papers.

"That would be a bet I'd surely lose. Hopefully Larry's father comes by for him soon. Otherwise, Pee Wee might leave without me or Chad." We both laughed. I was sorting through the paperwork and Jason was filing it. Every boy who left, whether it was permanently or temporarily, had a mountain of paperwork associated with his departure. Between the caseworkers' documents and the group home's documents, it was nothing for my entire desk, floor, and conference table to be covered in mounds and mounds of papers.

Fortunately, Larry got picked up before long. Larry Holten was one of the boys who wasn't coming back. His father had landed a good job working as a janitor at the school, so he was now in a financial position to take care of Larry. Larry's mother had lost custody of him a year ago after a run-in with the police over selling narcotics. It had taken Larry Sr. this long to get his own life straightened out to take over raising Larry Jr.

"I'm going to miss you, Larry Jr.," I said to the eleven-year-old who, for the first time since I'd known him, was smiling ear to ear. When Larry Jr. had first arrived at the group home, a few weeks before Chad, he would rarely talk to anyone, and if he did, it would be one or two sentences at most. Many nights, he cried himself to sleep. It was only in the last few weeks, when he learned he'd be going to live with his father, that he started perking up and talking more.

"I'm going to miss you too, Miss Katia," he said. "And thank you for helping my daddy get me back." He gave me a brief hug.

I wiped away a tear. His words and affection meant the world to me because of how difficult it was for him to express both. This was why I did what I did—for experiences like this. And no matter how many times I said goodbye to one of our boys, whether he had been here for days, weeks, months, or years, it wasn't easy. I missed them all and fretted over them until I could check in and make sure they were thriving away from the group home.

"Take care of Larry Jr.," I said, looking at his daddy. "He's a good boy."

"I appreciate everything you did for me and this boy," Larry Sr. said, tears streaming down his face too. "I never would have got this boy back without you. May I give you a hug?"

I nodded, and then we embraced. "You are not alone. If you ever need anything, you call me," I whispered for his ears only. He stepped back and smiled.

"You ain't gone get rid of us this easy," he said, his voice thick with emotion. "I'll check in and let you know how we doing. You ready, boy?"

The two of them walked out the door arm in arm. This was what success looked like and it felt pretty good, especially after the last few weeks.

After Larry and his father left, Jason and I went upstairs, removed all of the bedding from the beds, and began washing it in the industrial-size washing machine. Then we got Chad to help us sweep and mop the floors. Mrs. Kennedy's husband usually came over to help with the cleanup, but he was down with back troubles, so Jason, Chad, and I tidied up before leaving.

"I'll make sure Pee Wee don't get on your brother's nerves, Miss Katia," Chad said, sounding far older than his years. "I don't want nothing messing up this weekend."

Yesterday afternoon I sat down Chad and Pee Wee and explained to them that my brother was, for the most part, physically well, but he was struggling emotionally.

"He m-m-miss his br-br-brother," Pee Wee had said with a nod of his head, as if he were speaking from experience. Pee Wee had siblings, but based on what he'd told me and what his files said, he'd only met them once or twice. They had different mothers, and Pee Wee's father and paternal grandmother hadn't made an effort to keep the siblings in touch with each other. Pee Wee didn't even know their names or ages. I wondered if he was thinking about them now.

"That's right. He misses Aaron, so he might not be very talkative," I said. "I just didn't want either of you to take his behavior personally."

Today I saw that Chad had been worrying about the weekend but for different reasons. Once again I tried to reassure him.

"You don't have to worry about Pee Wee getting on anyone's nerves," I said. "He'll be fine. In fact, my mother said the two of you might very well be exactly what my brother needs."

"Yes, ma'am," Chad said, but I could tell he wasn't convinced.

"Chad, no matter what, this weekend is going to be good. Do you know why?" I put my hand on his shoulder. "Because we are going to make it good."

"Good things don't just happen. We make things good by being intentional," Chad said slowly, enunciating his words like Mr. Jason had been teaching him. Sometimes Chad would slip into dialect, but we were working on it. I didn't mind if he was a bit more relaxed with his speech as long as he wasn't using profanity.

If nothing else, Chad's ability to recite my many mantras showed me that he was listening, even when he didn't follow through the way I'd like him to.

Once we were done cleaning and straightening the upstairs, we went to the kitchen, where Pee Wee was helping Mrs. Kennedy dry the breakfast dishes. He was wearing an apron that hung down to the floor and talking a mile a minute. Interestingly, he was barely stuttering.

"And Miss K-K-Katia's mama is gone stuff a turkey. And I'm gone help her l-l-like I help you. Miss Katia say I'm gone b-b-be a . . ." He turned around and smiled broadly when he saw us enter the kitchen. "What did you say I w-w-would be, Miss Katia?"

"A sous chef. That means you will be the assistant to my mama," I said.

"I know Miss Heloise is looking forward to having you be her helper. Cooking a Thanksgiving dinner is not easy," Mrs. Kennedy said.

"It's not a helper, Mama K-K-K. It's a . . . Say it a-a-again, Miss Katia."

"Sous chef. S-o-u-s c-h-e-f." I repeated the words and letters slowly.

"It's a sous chef, Mama K-K-K." He beamed at all of us.

"Well, y'all better go on and have your lunch so you can be on your way." Mrs. Kennedy looked at me and winked.

"Absolutely. We have a lot to do to get ready for Thanksgiving tomorrow," I said, guiding the boys over to the table, where Mrs. Kennedy had laid out a platter of ham-and-cheese sandwiches, a bowl of leftover macaroni salad, and more of her delicious peach iced tea. Jason said grace and we all dug in. The boys had a lot of questions about Thanksgiving at my house and what it would be like.

"As we speak, Miss Heloise, my mama, is busy baking cakes and pies." I put another ham sandwich on my plate. For whatever reason, I was starving. Then I remembered that I'd skipped breakfast. "Once we get there, Mama will have us washing collard greens and peeling potatoes—both sweet and Irish—and I imagine she'll have me outside washing chitlins."

"Wh-wh-what's chitlins?" Pee Wee asked.

Everybody but Pee Wee laughed. He looked around the table and Chad finally answered him.

"They the nastiest, smelliest part of the pig. I tried 'em once, and they taste pretty good," Chad said with a grin. "You just have to remember to put some hot sauce on 'em."

"Gross," Pee Wee said, squinching up his nose.

"I hear you, Pee Wee," I said, taking the last bite of my sandwich. "I had them once in my lifetime, and that was enough for me. Pee Wee, you and I can stick with the baked ham. I promise you, between all of the aunts, uncles, and cousins, plenty of people will be eating the chitlins." I stood up, and immediately Pee Wee stood up too.

"Time to g-g-go?" he asked, hopping from one foot to the other.

"Yes," I said. "Time to go."

Pee Wee started clapping and while Chad was trying to act all cool, he came over and hugged me.

"Thank you," he whispered in my ear.

I hugged him back. "You're welcome. And thank you. I'm excited about having you boys over as well."

We all wished Jason and Mrs. Kennedy a happy Thanksgiving. Mrs. Kennedy promised to lock up the house before she left. The boys and I made our way outside to my truck.

I looked over at them. "Ready?"

"Ready," they said.

"Next stop, home." They both cheered as we took off down the road.

Even though I didn't know how the rest of the week would turn out, I was thankful that right now things were looking pretty good. After all that these boys and my family had endured, that was definitely a blessing.

8

"GRAN, I FINISHED PEELIN' THE SWEET potatoes. What you want me to do next?" Chad asked, using the name Mama had insisted the boys use. She said she might never get to hear someone call her by that name, so as long as the boys were here, they could call her Gran—the same as the grandkids called her mother.

It hurt a bit to hear her say she might never be a grandmother. Not just because I couldn't have biological children but because she worried that Marcus might never be well enough to be a father. That probably hurt the most. I tried to block all of that out and focus on the preparation before us.

The house was filled with pre–Thanksgiving Day smells, and Mama had everyone working on something. Except Marcus, who was in his room with the door closed and window shades lowered. The boys and I went to say hello, but he'd barely raised his head off the pillow to speak. They didn't take his stand-offishness personally. I had warned them earlier that Marcus might not behave in the friendliest of ways, and they understood. Chad had said that he hadn't felt very much like visiting with people when he first came to the group home. Pee Wee had chimed in that he also had struggled with talking to folks right away. I was so grateful that these boys had so much empathy in their hearts for other people.

I looked around the kitchen, and the boys and Mama were smiling. Even with the uncertainty surrounding Aaron and Marcus, we were all trying to find ways to celebrate moments of happiness.

"Chad, you want me to show you how to clean some chitlins?" Mama asked, glancing over at me with a sly grin. "My daughter acts like she's dying from the smell whenever I ask her to help."

I shook my head as I washed collard greens and turnips in the sink. I was very happy to turn that job over to Chad if he wanted it. Mama and I cleaned the chitlins outside on the back porch, where she cooked them in the same cast-iron pot her mama used to cook chitlins in. I had already helped her prepare a small batch of chitlins the other day. I wasn't looking forward to a repeat performance. Anytime I finished helping her clean them, I'd make a cocktail of different bubble baths in the tub and soak and scrub and scrub and soak until the odor was removed from my body. Every year I prayed that Mama and the boys would lose their taste for the high-blood-pressure-inducing delicacy. Sadly, their appetite for them only seemed to grow. At least they only ate them on Thanksgiving or Christmas.

"I'll help," Chad said. "I ate 'em once before and they don't smell all that bad to me."

I laughed. He was trying hard to fit in and be agreeable to anything and everything Mama suggested. She could have asked him to fly with her to the moon and he would have been tracking down a space suit to wear. "Chad, one thing we do in this house is tell the truth, and you know chitlins are some foul-smelling thangs. Don't let Mama twist your arm."

Chad laughed. "Yes, ma'am. But I still don't mind helping Gran with 'em."

Mama went over to Chad and hugged him. "Pee Wee," Mama called out. "You want to help us clean these chitlins?"

"N-n-no, m-m-ma'am," he said as quickly as his stutter would allow, his eyes on me. I knew he wanted to make sure I was on his side.

"Pee Wee, you are a wise young man," I said. "Come on over here and help me wash these greens. You don't have to be part of the chitlin brigade."

He got up from the table where he'd been "assisting" Chad with the potatoes and hurried to my side.

"Alright, baby," Mama said to Pee Wee. "But you're gone have to at least try a bite of chitlins. Don't let my daughter turn you 'gainst them before you even give 'em a try. Okay?"

"Yes, m-m-ma'am," he said. After Chad and Mama walked out of the house, he stopped washing the collard leaf I'd handed him and looked at me with a helpless expression. "I d-d-don't have to eat the ch-ch-chitlins, do I?"

I shook my head. "Not if you don't want to. But let me warn you: Gran will be sad if you don't at least give them a try. Before we say no to a food, we should at least try it. They aren't terrible. Just an acquired taste."

His face clearly showed that he was torn. I was about to relate my first experience with chitlins, when I was around his age, but then the phone rang.

"Excuse me," I said, wiping my hands on a towel before I went to the other side of the room to pick up the phone. "Hello?"

"Hello, Kat," the deep voice said. "This is Seth."

My heart began to race. I couldn't believe that at age forty I was having high school reactions to men. I took a breath before replying.

"Hello, Seth," I said, impressed with myself for sounding so calm while my emotions were swirling. I felt bad for being giddy over someone who wasn't Leon. Granted, Leon and I had never been demonstrative with our affection, but the way I was feeling about someone I hadn't seen in over twenty years wasn't a good sign for my relationship with Leon.

"I wanted to see if this is a good time for me to come by," he said.

Earlier, I'd talked to Marcus about Seth coming over, and my brother had shrugged. Thankfully, he wasn't singing that awful cadence, but he definitely wasn't my good-natured little brother. He was broken, and short of his twin coming home, I wasn't sure if anyone could get him back. But I was sure willing to try.

"Come by anytime," I said. "We're cooking for tomorrow, so if you don't mind the usual Thanksgiving scents wafting throughout the house, you're welcome to drop by. I told Marcus you might come to see him."

"All of my folks went to Birmingham to visit family for the holidays. I have too much work, so I stayed behind. I welcome those good scents," he said. "And I'll keep our talk as light as Marcus wants it to be. One thing I've learned is that every man heals at his own speed. My old commander used to love to quote Ecclesiastes 9:11. When we'd begin to grow weary, he'd say, 'The race is not to the swift, nor the battle to the strong.' Then he'd follow up on his pep talk with some expletives telling us to get our butts in gear."

We both laughed. Then, before I could stop myself, I invited him to Thanksgiving dinner. After I said the words, I wished I could take them back. Leon would be here tomorrow too. How would I keep myself from being moony-eyed over Seth in Leon's presence? This was a bad idea.

"Thank you, Kat. I appreciate your hospitality," he said before I could pull back the invitation. "I was going to make do with some Vienna sausages and some Ritz crackers. Mama promised to bring back some food, but I'm afraid that right now the cupboards are pretty bare at my house."

"Well, that would never do," I said, trying to sound decisive. "We always have way too much food. You're welcome. To come over, I mean . . ." I wasn't used to feeling awkward and uncertain, and I was both at the moment. This man had me in a dither.

"Excellent," he said, then paused. I wondered if he was feeling as uncomfortable as I was. I was suddenly forty going on fourteen. Finally, he spoke again. "I'll see you soon?"

"Absolutely," I said. As soon as I hung up, I glanced down at my water-splotched clothes. I looked over at Pee Wee, who was still washing that same piece of collard green. "Pee Wee, I'm going to run and change. Will you be okay in here by yourself for a few minutes?"

"Yes, m-m-ma'am," he said. "You w-w-want me to w-w-wash another c-c-collard green?"

"Yes, please," I said. "You keep washing and I'll be right back. If you need anything, Gran and Chad are right outside the door."

"Yes, ma'am," he said, but his attention had already returned to washing the greens. I'd given him a step stool and he was concentrating on each leaf. I'd told him we had to look for bugs, and he was turning the leaves over multiple times. No bug would get past his watchful eye.

I went to my bedroom and started searching through my closet. Lord, I needed to go shopping. I was never a fashion girl. I always focused on neat and comfortable clothes, not clothes to catch a man's attention. Then I groaned at that thought.

"Girl, you have a man," I said, trying to sound convincing to my own ears, even though saying those words in connection to Leon didn't fit. He was more of a "male friend" than "my man." Seth was "a dream," as my cousin Alicia would say, but I knew he wasn't the dream for me. He'd want children and I couldn't have any. Me having designs for him would be unfair to both of us. "Just put on something clean, Katia, and stop making a fool of yourself. That man ain't thinkin' about you. He's just being nice. That. Is. All."

But I still decided to clean up and wear something nice. It

couldn't hurt. I settled on a brown, long-sleeved cotton dress with a V-neck and a gold tie belt in the front. I put on leaf-shaped gold earrings and a matching necklace. Then I freshened up my hair, sprayed it with oil sheen, and picked it out so it stood up in all its natural glory. I tried my best to channel the sass of Miss Nina Simone. I wasn't bold enough to believe that, like Nina, I could put a spell on anybody, but I at least wanted her onstage confidence. I wanted to believe I was beautiful and desirable as much as I believed I was talented and smart. I wanted desperately to believe that even though I couldn't bear any children, someone was out there who could, like my cousin Alicia said, "curl my toes."

After I was done dressing, I went to Mama's room and borrowed some of her Elusive Red lipstick by Avon, and then I spritzed myself with her Here's My Heart cologne mist, also by Avon. I went to the bathroom mirror and stared at my reflection. I looked okay, but the lipstick was probably a reach.

"You look desperate and ridiculous," I muttered, wiping off the lipstick with a tissue and tossing it into the garbage can. I still had the lipstick in my hand when Mama came up behind me.

"You don't look desperate or ridiculous," Mama said. She grabbed the lipstick and began to reapply it. "You look beautiful. I wish you dressed up like this more often. Is your friend coming over now?" Mama looked at me knowingly. I blushed and turned away.

"Yes, ma'am," I said. "He's coming over to see if Marcus would like to talk." I wanted to make sure she knew I wasn't inviting Seth over for me. "And, Mama, I invited him to

Thanksgiving tomorrow. He's going to be all alone. I didn't even think about it—I just invited him. I can uninvite him when he gets here."

"No. Let the invitation stand. Ain't no harm inviting some-one to break bread on Thanksgiving," she said with a smile. "Just make sure you don't disrespect Brother Leon. If he's not the one for you, let him know that. Don't lead him on."

"Yes, ma'am," I said. Breaking things off with Leon was complicated. He wasn't just my "gentleman caller." He was also a good friend of Mama's. I didn't want to take her TV buddy away from her.

The doorbell rang and my heart jumped again. I closed my eyes to steady myself.

"You better go to the door," Mama said.

I looked at her staring at me and again I felt embarrassed, but I took a deep breath and walked as calmly as I could out of the bathroom. As I went to the front door, I heard the boys laughing in the kitchen. When I opened the door, once again I had to mentally settle my nerves. Seth was wearing his Marine uniform and had never appeared more handsome. He stood with a confidence that belied a man with a prosthetic leg who was dealing with demons from the war. I forced a smile.

"Hello, Seth," I said. "Come on in." He removed his cap. I turned and saw Mama standing right behind me. I pulled her close. "This is my mama, Mrs. Heloise Daniels. Mama, this is Seth Taylor. He owns Big T Construction. He and his crew are going to be doing some work at the group home and he's here to talk with Marcus. That is, if Marcus is up to it and . . ." I realized

I was babbling, so I stopped talking midsentence. I felt sweat beading above my lip.

"Afternoon, Mr. Taylor," Mama said, extending her hand. He shook it gently.

"Good afternoon, Mrs. Daniels. It's a pleasure to meet you," he said.

"Come on in," she invited, stepping aside. "I'll go see if I can get Marcus to join us in the living room. Katia, you offer Mr. Taylor something to eat or drink. God knows there's plenty to eat in that kitchen. Mr. Taylor, I was happy to hear you'll be joining us tomorrow."

"Yes, ma'am," he said, stepping into the house, which seemed very small with his large frame filling up much of the entryway. The space was so cramped, his arm and mine touched. I tried not to shrink away.

"The living room is this way," I said, thankful that my voice didn't break. I led him to the living room and then asked him if he'd like something to drink or eat.

"No thank you, Kat," he said, taking a seat on the couch. I sat in the recliner opposite him. "I had a big lunch, and in the truck I have a gallon jug of water I've been drinking on all day."

"Miss K-K-Katia," Pee Wee called from the door, causing me to jump.

I turned. "Yes, Pee Wee? But before you tell me what you need, say hello to Mr. Taylor."

"Hello, Mr. T-T-Taylor," he said and then went over to shake hands like I had taught him.

"Nice to meet you, Pee Wee," Seth said as they shook hands.

Once the pleasantries ended, Pee Wee turned back to me. "Th-th-the greens are w-w-washed. Ch-Ch-Chad helped. We didn't s-s-see any b-b-bugs. Come check, p-p-please?"

"Okay," I said. "Excuse me, Seth."

When I got to the kitchen, Chad was cleaning up the mess. I smiled at them both.

"Thank you, boys. You have done such a good job helping Mama and me with the preparation for tomorrow. Why don't you take a break?" I said. "In the storage room out back, there are some footballs and basketballs that used to belong to my brothers. The key to the room is hanging by the door. You can go outside and play until dinner. Chad, make sure you bring the key back and hang it up for me."

"Is that your man?" Chad asked abruptly.

I looked at him curiously, my cheeks growing warm. "No. He's a friend. He's here to see my brother. Hopefully he can help him feel better."

"Then he's a doctor?" Chad's question startled me—not the words but the tone, but then it dawned on me what was happening. Because I was one of the few people in Chad's life who was a stable presence, he worried I might somehow stop being that person on a whim or, in this case, because of a man. Right then I needed to establish clearer boundaries with him. I had allowed us to become too close. That was my fault. But I had to be the one to make sure Chad and I didn't cross a line. Chad was not my son, and we couldn't pretend like he was, even for these next few days.

"Those are personal questions, Chad," I said in a firm voice.

"Don't overstep. You and Pee Wee should go outside and play. I will check on you shortly."

"Yes, ma'am," he muttered. "Come on, Pee Wee."

I watched as the two of them left out of the kitchen door. So many broken men and boys underneath this roof today. All I wanted to do was heal them and take away their pain. But all I could do was what I *was* doing, and it felt hopeless at times. I'd had that dream again last night. Leeches. Everywhere I turned. I woke up just in time to stifle a scream. Maybe I needed some therapy myself, but who had time for it? My life was filled with one thing after another. Looking after myself wasn't at the top of my priority list.

When I went back to the living room, Marcus and Mama were entering from the other direction. I scanned my brother's face. He looked absent from this world. He seemed to be barely hanging on. He wore a pair of camouflage pants and a white T-shirt. Both hung on him like he was a scarecrow.

I watched as Seth stood. He, too, gave Marcus a once-over. I wondered what he was thinking. Was Marcus typical for the men Seth saw at the group sessions he ran, or was my brother so far out into the deep waters that no lifeboat could save him? If I could plunge my body into those waters and swim out to where my brother was, I'd do it in a heartbeat. But I didn't know the first thing about reaching him. It pained me that I could help so many boys at the group home yet couldn't do the same for my own brother.

When Daddy died, Marcus and Aaron had allowed me to be their anchor. Maybe because they were so young and I, their big sister, was a giant slayer in their eyes. Now all Marcus knew of the world was that it could rip away the other part of his soul—his twin and best friend—and no one could do anything about it.

Seth walked over to Marcus, the limp more noticeable now than when he'd entered the house. Seth stood at attention and saluted Marcus. Marcus pulled himself up into a stiff position and saluted Seth back.

"At ease, my friend," Seth said. "At ease."

Marcus's body seemed to crumble, as if that salute took everything out of him. He wasn't quite stooped over, but Mama leaned into him to support him. She guided him into the recliner, where he sank like a stone.

"Mama," I said. "Let's give Seth and Marcus some privacy."

Mama looked at Marcus like she used to when he was a child. I knew she didn't want to leave him alone with a stranger, but I trusted Seth. I didn't think he'd do anything to hurt Marcus. In fact, I had planted all of my seeds in that garden of hope, trusting that Seth might be able to pull my brother back from the abyss.

"It's okay, Mrs. Daniels." Seth smiled at her reassuringly. "We're just going to visit. That's all. I lost my leg in the Battle of Ia Drang on November 16, 1965. But I lost a lot more. Sometimes we war veterans just need to bear witness to each other's stories. That's all I'm here to do, if that's what Marcus wants. Otherwise, we'll chat about whatever—maybe the Alabama–Auburn game coming up in December. Or maybe the sharp rise in the price of lumber and plywood. Or maybe the fact that Nina Simone released three studio albums in one year."

My head jerked up at the mention of Nina Simone, but I was more interested in my brother's reaction.

He looked up sideways at Mama. "I'm okay, Mama." His voice was barely above a whisper, but I heard something—something that sounded a bit like my brother. And for that, I was willing to entrust him to Seth.

"Okay," Mama said. "But if you need me, I'll be in the kitchen."

Mama and I walked out of the room arm in arm. She looked up at me and I smiled at her with as much assurance as I could muster.

"Seth is a good man," I said, and somehow I knew that to be true. I had no hard evidence to prove that claim, but I believed it with everything in me. Maybe because I had to. We needed to get Marcus back on his feet, and my fervent prayer was that Seth could help with that. "They're just going to talk. Let's you and me go and get started on those sweet potato pies. Okay?"

A tear trickled down her face. "I can't lose him too."

"I know." I hugged her tight, hoping to pour some of my hopefulness into her empty cup. I wanted her to believe that Marcus would be alright, for both of our sakes.

9

THE LIVING ROOM HAD BEEN QUIET for more than an hour. A couple of times, Mama walked to the doorway to see if she could hear anything, but she always came back saying she didn't hear a peep. We both wondered if Marcus was talking to Seth at all. We could barely get a coherent sentence out of him, so it wouldn't be surprising to us if Marcus clammed up. If Seth was able to coax my brother into talking, it would be a miracle.

Rather than sit and wring our hands, Mama and I got busy in the kitchen. I had started working on the sweet potato pies and Mama had turned her attention to making the dressing when we heard Marcus wailing. We immediately stopped what we were doing and ran to the living room. Mercifully, the boys were still outside playing. I didn't want them to witness this. They'd had enough trauma in their lives. Witnessing my brother's meltdown wasn't what I wanted them to experience during this time away from the group home. Once again I questioned if I'd made the right decision to bring them home with me.

When we entered the living room, both Marcus and Seth were sitting in their same seats. Seth wasn't speaking. He was just watching as Marcus rocked and cried, loud sobs filling the space.

"What happened?" I demanded, rushing over to Marcus, who was inconsolable. I tried to embrace him, but he fought me. Mama tried to do the same, but Marcus wasn't having any of it. It was as if the grief was so great, he couldn't bear to be held.

"Baby, do you want to go to your room? Or maybe a walk? You and I could take a walk if you like." Mama looked at Seth angrily as Marcus continued to rock and say no, over and over again. "What did you do to him? You promised you wouldn't cause him any pain."

"No, ma'am, Mrs. Daniels." Seth moved forward in his seat, his eyes trained on Marcus. "I did not promise that. But as it stands, it's not me causing Marcus pain. It's Marcus's memories. Tell them, Marcus. Tell them what you told me."

Marcus shook his head, still sobbing loudly. Seth stood up and faced my brother with a stern look on his face.

"Marine, stand at attention," Seth barked.

Before Mama or I could protest, Marcus stood. It was like he was in a trance. Once again his body was stiff and rigid, yet other than a few sniffles, he'd stopped crying. In this moment, years of training overshadowed his grief.

Marcus saluted. "Yes, sir."

"Tell your mother and sister what you told me." Seth folded his arms across his chest. With that move alone, he reminded me of the military men at Fort Lejeune, where the twins had completed basic training. Mama and I had visited them there before they'd shipped off to Vietnam. Those soldiers had seemed like they were devoid of emotions—their backs never bent and their faces steely. Just like Seth right now.

"He doesn't have to tell us anything he doesn't want to," Mama insisted. Her Christian upbringing was the only thing preventing her from throwing Seth out of the house. I could see it all over her face.

"Let Marcus tell us what he needs to tell us, Mama," I said. "It's going to be okay." And somehow I knew that to be true. Mainly because this was often the case with the boys at the group home. So many of them would arrive burdened with untold stories—stories that ate at them worse than any cancer could. I didn't want my brother to carry this load alone anymore, no matter how upsetting it might be to me or Mama to hear his truth.

"It's okay if he isn't ready to talk," Mama said, resting her hand on Marcus's shoulder. He continued to stand stiff and un-moving. I think his Marine training was holding him together. As difficult as it was to witness, I understood what Seth was trying to do. I prayed Mama would go along with it.

"Let him talk, Mrs. Daniels," Seth said. "He needs to tell his story to you and his sister. That is how we heal. Silence is what kills us slowly. Trust me. I know firsthand." Seth walked over to Marcus, too, but he stood behind him and leaned in, close to Marcus's ear. "We're waiting, Marine."

"We're the shadow warriors. Death in the dark," Marcus muttered as a tear rolled down his left cheek. I wanted to wipe it away. I wanted to wipe away all of his tears, but this was one thing I couldn't fix.

"Speak in civilian language, Marine. They don't understand that kind of talk. Speak plain." Seth didn't raise his voice, but his tone was ominous. I knew Seth had been an officer in the Marines. Up until now, I couldn't imagine him as anyone but the soft-spoken man I'd just recently been reunited with, but this man . . . this man was all military—fire and steel. "Tell your mother and sister what happened, Marine," Seth pushed, his voice deep and cold.

Marcus wiped the tear from his eye and stood even straighter. "We were responsible for clearing the Ho Bo Woods. Viet Cong were everywhere, or at least that's what they told us. No matter where I was, I could hear them Viet Cong breathing down my neck. Still see them now in my dreams—hear them, smell them. We got there in the middle of the night. Ain't never seen dark like that before. Air so thick it was hard to breathe. So hot I couldn't imagine hell being any hotter."

Marcus's face was devoid of emotion. I almost held my breath as he continued to talk. I didn't want to break the spell he seemed to be under.

"Two artillery battalions got stuck in the mud. It took two days to get them unstuck. In the meantime, we built a log road for them to cross over on. Aaron got antsy. He wandered off. I should have been watching. I should have been paying closer attention." Marcus began to shake, and his eyes started to blink erratically. I feared we were losing him again.

"Marine. Focus," Seth warned. The tone of Seth's voice brought Marcus back. He started talking, still in a monotone, but at last, he was telling his story.

"I was busy putting down them logs. When I noticed he was gone, I looked everywhere. I asked around, and somebody said he saw Aaron walk toward the woods. I took off in the woods after him. I couldn't find him nowhere. Everywhere I looked, he wasn't there. I didn't even see no Viet Cong to see if they had stole my brother. Mama, I looked. I didn't stop looking till they come and drug me outta them woods. 'Fore we left for 'Nam, you said, 'Look after your brother, Marcus. He ain't strong as you, Marcus. You the oldest, Marcus.' I failed. I failed, Mama."

Then he dissolved into tears. I sensed a release—or at least I prayed that he was experiencing one. Mama gathered him into her arms. She pulled him in so tight, it was a wonder he could breathe.

"You didn't do nothing wrong, son. I'm so proud of you for looking for your brother. You did more than most would do in that scary, awful place y'all was in. I ain't angry. I'm grateful that you are here. Do you hear me?"

Marcus continued to cry, but the sounds he was making were different than before. This one moment of breakthrough wasn't a sign that he was healed, but Lord, I hoped it meant he was heading in that direction. I whispered thanks to God. At church, the preacher always said a testimony will free you. I prayed this experience freed Marcus from some of the guilt he was carrying.

I motioned for Seth to follow me. From what I could tell, Marcus had said everything he needed to say for now. I wanted to give him and Mama some privacy. Seth followed me into the kitchen, and before I could speak my own tears began to fall.

"Thank you so much, Seth." I dabbed at my eyes. These last

couple of weeks had turned me into a crier. Since Daddy died, I'd held my emotions inside. I didn't have time to release them. I had too many people who were leaning on me. But now I couldn't help myself. I was exhausted and all I could do was weep. "I don't know what you said or did, but it helped. I can already tell."

Seth reached out and put his hand on my shoulder. "You don't have to thank me, Kat. Marcus has a long way to go, but he can heal. I've seen soldiers worse off than him make it back from the brink of destruction. I don't know if you'll ever get your other brother back, but if Marcus is willing to do the work, I'm happy to continue talking with him. If he wants to come to the group meetings, we get together every Friday night. I warn you: the things we talk about and the way we talk about them isn't fit for a civilian's ears. You can drop him off, but you can't be part of our meetings."

"I understand," I said, nodding as more tears fell. "If Marcus wants to attend the meetings, I'll make sure he gets to them."

"Excellent. I should go. I have a crew working on a house. I want to check it out before we get into the holiday weekend. I hope I'm still invited for tomorrow." He glanced at me sideways with a smile that told me he absolutely knew he was still invited but wanted to tease me.

"Of course you're still invited. And, Seth—thank you again."

He smiled. "Anytime. See you tomorrow, Kat."

I walked him to the door and watched as he made his way to his truck.

"Get your head out of the clouds, Katia Daniels," I muttered. I went back to the living room and peeked in on Mama and

Marcus. They were sitting together on the couch, talking softly to each other. I backed away and went outside, where the boys were still playing football. I sat down on the porch and listened to them banter back and forth with each other. If there were any two boys closer than Pee Wee and Chad, I had not met them. Their brotherhood was so strong, and I worried about how they would take it when someday they would be forced to be separated from each other.

"I'm number nineteen, Johnny Unitas, quarterback for the Baltimore Colts!" Chad yelled, spinning around, posing with the football in the throwing position. "I'm the best quarterback in the U.S. of A. Can't nobody tackle me, boy!"

"I'm D-D-Deacon Jones," Pee Wee declared, jumping up and down with excitement. "I pl-pl-play for th-th-the . . . Who d-d-do I pl-pl-play for again?"

"The Los Angeles Rams. You're part of the Fearsome Foursome. You, Merlin Olsen, Lamar Lundy, and Rosey Grier are the best defensive linemen in the entire NFL," Chad declared as he ran toward Pee Wee, sidestepping him with an over-exaggerated move. "But you ain't better than me."

I laughed as he raced across the yard, Pee Wee at his heels. Football was another television treat we granted the boys, mainly because the houseparents enjoyed watching it too. By default, the boys knew everything about the sport, from the top players to their stats.

"Hey, boys," I called out to them. "Are y'all ready to come inside and eat? We still have some leftovers we need to use up before we jump into all of that good Thanksgiving food tomorrow."

Upon seeing me, they both ran over to where I sat.

"Miss Katia, I know you don't like us watching a lot of television, but could we watch *Lost in Space* tonight?" Chad looked at me with a hopeful expression. "Please. We was good helpers today, and we ain't fussed at each other once. Have we, Pee Wee?"

"No, ma'am. W-w-we been g-g-good. Please." Pee Wee leaned against my knee and gazed up at me with those big green eyes of his. I knew he couldn't care less about *Lost in Space*, but if Chad was for it, he'd never be against it.

I sighed. How could I resist them both? On Wednesday nights, we usually took the boys to Bible study at my church, but since we had so much cooking to do and what with Seth coming over, I told the boys we'd stay at home.

"How do you even know about *Lost in Space*?" I asked, but I knew. Chad had asthma, and on a few occasions he'd stayed behind with one of the houseparents while the rest of us went to church. I was sure that he had sneaked and watched the show. If space travel was involved, Chad was all for watching it. He just grinned at me.

"This one time," I said. "And afterward, I expect you both to head to bed. Don't go talking to me about no *Beverly Hillbillies* or *Green Acres*, because the answer to that will be a resounding no. Understood?"

"Yes, ma'am," they said.

I could already hear Mama begging on behalf of the boys to let them stay up and watch *Beverly Hillbillies* and *Green Acres* with her. Mama didn't enjoy TV watching until she had a TV buddy or two to watch her shows with her. I was never interested, so having the boys around would definitely cause her to lobby on their behalf.

"Y'all go get washed up and I'll start heating up the leftovers," I said. Mama had taken a lot of the leftovers over to Great-Aunt Hess's house, but there was still some fried chicken and potato salad in the refrigerator.

I got up from the steps and went to the kitchen. The boys raced by me to go wash up in the bathroom. Mama was already heating up the chicken, and I could smell the sweet potato pies for tomorrow baking in the oven.

"Where's Marcus?" I asked as I kissed her cheek.

"He wanted to rest before we ate supper."

"How's he doing?" I went to the refrigerator and took out the potato salad. I noticed there were also enough baked yams for each of us to have one, so I pulled them out and placed them in the oven next to the pies.

"Better," she said, turning around to face me. "He ain't never gone get over this, but I pray God protects his mind, 'specially if we get the news that . . . 'specially . . ."

"I know, Mama." I didn't want her to get upset. I was praying we could get through the holidays with some semblance of peace. Aaron would be sorely missed tomorrow, and tears would be shed, but I hoped we'd find ways to honor him as we prayed for his safe return.

The phone rang and Mama answered it. After a moment, she held the receiver out toward me. "It's that young man from your work, Jason."

I hurried over and took the receiver from Mama. "Hello."

"Hello, Miss Katia. I'm sorry to bother you at home," Jason said, then paused. That pause had me nervous. Jason was never at a loss for words, so his seeming need to gather his thoughts had me extra concerned.

Sometimes a boy would go home and things wouldn't work out. Each family was given my number, as well as Jason's and the houseparents' numbers, in case something went wrong. I wanted to prompt Jason to tell me what was the matter, but I waited, trying to exercise the patience I expected from my employees and the boys. Finally, he continued.

"I left one of my schoolbooks at the office, so I went back over and there was a letter in the mail from family court."

"Did you open it?" Of course he had. I'd given Jason permission to open mail related to the boys. I trusted him more than any assistant I'd ever had.

"Yes, ma'am. It's about Chad. They've set a date for the hearing. December eleventh."

"Oh no. So soon?" I said. I didn't think it would happen this quickly. I figured that we'd have until after the holidays, and at that point we'd reassess where Chad's mother was in relation to her ability to parent Chad. I didn't wish evil on her, but I needed enough time to pass for her to either stay on the straight and narrow or fall off the wagon like she normally did. Judging from that phone conversation I'd had with her, she wasn't far from falling.

I looked around to make sure the boys weren't within earshot. "He's going to be heartbroken. I know the courts want to clear their books so they can enjoy the holidays with their families and perhaps reunite some other families, but this is too fast. However, there's nothing we can do until after Thanksgiving. Thanks for calling, Jason."

"I'm so sorry about this, Miss Katia. I almost didn't call, but I figured you would want to know," he said.

"You did the right thing, Jason. It's just . . . Well, you know. We'll figure it out. We always do. You have a good Thanksgiving tomorrow. Give my best to your family." After I hung up the phone, I stood staring into space. What was I supposed to say to Chad? How was I supposed to make this sit well with him? I knew this would set him back when he'd been making so many great strides forward. For a time, I forgot where I was, until I heard Mama calling out to me.

"Katia. Katia baby, what's wrong?"

As I turned to tell her what Jason had told me, the boys bounded into the room.

"Hello, fellas," I said. "Go and set the table for dinner. Chad, the plates are in the cabinet. Pee Wee, the silverware is in the drawer to the left of the cabinet."

I went over to Mama and whispered in her ear, "I'll fill you in later."

She nodded.

"Hi, Mr. Marcus," Chad said, causing me and Mama to look up. Marcus entered the kitchen and much to my surprise—and from the look on Mama's face, to her surprise too—he had showered, changed clothes, and shaved.

"Hi, Chad. Hi, Pee Wee," he said. I was amazed that he remembered their names. He'd been so out of it these last few days.

I hadn't been sure what computed and what didn't. I didn't want to make a big deal out of it, but I couldn't help but rush over and hug him.

"It's good to see you, little brother," I said down low. I hoped he knew what I meant by my words.

"Good to be seen," he said, using the words Daddy used to say. I wasn't sure if he knew he was repeating what our daddy had spoken or if it was just a phrase he'd picked up, but either way, it took me over the moon to hear the words come out of his mouth. He still looked and sounded exhausted. We had a long road ahead of us, but I prayed that today's breakthrough meant we'd turned a corner, even slightly. As upset as I was about the Chad situation, I had to celebrate this win, no matter how small.

"Okay, y'all. Everything is heated up and ready," Mama said, her hands on her hips as she smiled broadly at me and Marcus. She was as thankful as I was for this moment.

I linked my arm with Marcus's and we walked together to the dining room.

I wasn't sure what the next several weeks would bring, but I was grateful that tonight my little brother was here—with us. And for now, that was enough.

10

OUR HOUSE WAS SMALL. WHEN MAMA, the twins, and I were alone in the house, it felt cramped. Yet somehow, on family holidays like this, it was as if the house expanded to include all of our loved ones. Every room would be occupied, whether someone was eating, taking a nap, or playing a game of bid whist or dominoes, but the house never felt overcrowded. Most of the children were outside playing football, basketball, and tag, or sitting on the front porch talking and catching up with each other. I was enjoying the quiet kitchen, where I was finishing up with the cleaning.

"Hey, girl," my cousin Alicia called out as she reentered the kitchen, carrying another armful of dirty dishes. "Your mama needs to let go of the rule that we have to eat Thanksgiving dinner on the good china. Chile, it's like these plates is out here having babies."

I laughed. "Just put them in the sink. Surely this is the last of them."

"Until they all get ready for dessert or seconds or thirds. I promise you, one more person comes in here asking about a clean plate, I'm going to go all the way off."

Alicia was always the cousin I had sought out, from childhood until now. We were alike in so many ways, but in other ways, like her sense of humor, we were exact opposites. Alicia was always good for a laugh and the first to crack a joke, usually at the most inappropriate times. Like me, she had recently started wearing her hair short. We both had dark skin and a mole, though they were on opposite sides of our faces—exactly like mirror twins. Since Daddy died, she frequently checked in on Mama and me, and seldom did a morning go by that we didn't call each other, at least to say good morning. Alicia was close to being the sister I never had.

Mama had three sisters and one brother, and all of them took the Scripture "Be fruitful and multiply" to heart. In total I had twenty first cousins, forty-five second cousins, and God knew how many others. Not all of them made the trip this year. Most of them lived in Prichard, Alabama, near Mobile where Mama grew up. But for Thanksgiving everyone who could made the trek to Troy. At first it was because Grandma lived here with us, but after Grandma passed away, they still made the trip here because Mama was the oldest sibling and Great-Aunt Hess was Grandma's last surviving sister. Mama guilted everyone into continuing to come here, and they did. Plus, she said she didn't have the energy to take her cooking on the road for the holidays. No one seemed to mind. Everyone would pack up and come to town, bunking wherever they could.

Uncle Rob, Aunt Marion, Alicia, and her husband, Curtis,

came last night. I gave my room to Uncle Rob and Aunt Marion, next to Mama's room, because it was the nicest. Marcus tried to offer up his room, but I knew he needed the familiarity of his bedroom. The boys gave up the room they were sleeping in to Alicia and Curtis. I provided sleeping bags and they camped out in the living room. To tell the truth, I think they enjoyed sleeping on the floor in the living room more than they did in the twin beds in the guest room. Plus, it was only for a few days. As always, we'd make it work.

"Marcus seems to be doing a little bit better," Alicia said as she scraped the food off the plates before handing them to me to wash.

"I think so. One day at a time." I remained cautiously optimistic. I'd been watching him all day, making sure all of the people didn't overwhelm him. Yes, they're family, but for the last few days, the house had been pretty low-key. I didn't want all of the loving wishes and endless questions to cause him to be overcome with too many raw emotions—emotions he was just coming to grips with. "I just pray we get some word about Aaron. It's torture not knowing if he is alive or dead."

"I know, honey. One day at a time, like you said."

"Sorry to interrupt you," a voice called out.

Alicia and I both turned to see Seth standing in the doorway. Other than greeting each other when he'd first arrived, he and I hadn't had much of an opportunity to talk. He'd arrived right when we were gathering in the dining room for Great-Aunt Hess to say the family blessing. The oldest relative was always tasked with blessing the family for the upcoming year and giving thanks for all who were still able to congregate. All of our names were written in the family Bible that the oldest family member kept, and on Thanksgiving, she called each name, and if any new births or deaths had happened, they got documented in the Bible.

When Seth walked into the dining room, looking good in a blue button-down shirt and blue jeans, all eyes went to him and then to me. My cheeks started burning. I looked at Leon, but he was busy chatting with Mama. I introduced Seth to everyone, including Leon, who shook Seth's hand and turned back to Mama. They were discussing some TV show. I was glad no one seemed to think it odd for Seth to be here. I didn't want to set tongues awaggin'.

Now, as he stood at the door with dirty plates in his hands, I was thankful Alicia was here. I relied on her to carry the conversation. It was easy talking to Seth about the group home or Marcus, but everyday small talk I wasn't very adept at.

"Oh, you've got more dishes," Alicia groaned. "Those dang plate babies. Well, bring them on in. Seth? That's your name, right?"

"Yes," he said with smile. "And you're . . . Cousin Alicia?"

She smiled back. "That's right. Good memory. There are tens of thousands of us running around here today, all with the same daggum faces. The Collins genes are strong, I tell you. I commend you for getting my name right. So, how do you and my cousin know each other?"

Seth and I looked at each other, yet neither of us spoke right away.

"Uh, cat got y'all's tongues?" Alicia asked, peering over her glasses at me. "Let me ask my question a different way. Where did you two meet?"

"School," we said in unison, and then we all laughed.

"Seth and I were in high school together. I tutored him in English. He was the quarterback." I couldn't stop myself from blushing. Thank God my skin was dark enough to hide it.

Alicia grinned. I knew there'd be a million questions later.

"Well," he said slowly. "I'll head back. I'm supposed to be partners with your uncle Travis in a game of bid whist."

"Careful," Alicia warned. "Uncle Travis don't play when it comes to whist. You better not make no mistakes, or you'll never hear the end of it. I tried being his partner once, and that was enough for me. Who y'all playing?"

"I think the guy's name is Leon. His partner is Kat's mama."

Alicia looked at me and laughed. "Uh-oh. Well, have fun."

Seth shook his head, waved slightly, and walked out. I turned back to the dishes, hoping Alicia would ignore the awkwardness that had just transpired. Of course, she wouldn't be Alicia if she didn't tease me.

"Kat, huh?" she said, coming over beside me, bumping her hip to mine. I flicked some suds at her as her face split into a grin. "Now explain to me why you ain't said a doggone thing about that fine specimen of a man. How long has Seth been in the picture? You introduced him like he was nobody special. Clearly he's special."

"He's not in the picture," I said gruffly. "I'm seeing someone. Remember?"

"Old Deacon Leon?" She snorted. "Chile, please. You need to

give that crotchety old thang to your mama and get yourself some Seth. Why are we even debating this?"

"I'm not having this conversation with you, girl," I said, laughing in spite of myself. "Finish cleaning those dishes off so I can wash them and we can get out of this kitchen."

"Katia, all jokes aside, you can't be putting all your chips on Leon—or Brother Leon, as your mama calls him. That man got to be at least sixty-five or seventy."

"He's fifty-five," I said defensively as I continued to wash the last of the dishes Seth had brought into the kitchen. "And age doesn't matter to me. He's a good man. A really good man, and I won't do anything to hurt him. At least not intentionally."

"Katia," Alicia said, taking my hands out of the dishwater and holding them in hers. "This isn't about whether he's a good man or not. I'm sure he is, but your entire life you have been settling. Stop settling. And I'm not talking about age differences. I'm talking, does he make the hairs on your arms stand up? Does he make your breath quicken? Does he get you all hot and bothered?"

I let my hands slip from hers and dropped them to my sides. I was really blushing now. "Stop, Alicia. Stop with all of that."

"Baby girl, it's clear that there isn't a lick of chemistry between you and Leon. Anybody with eyes or insight can see it."

I looked down at the floor, but she lifted my chin, and the look on her face was so tender and loving, I felt tears start to stream down my face.

"I get it, Katia," she whispered, drying my tears with a napkin from the counter. "Until I met Curtis, I thought no one would want me. I was almost forty, a big girl, with the kind of sense of humor that a lot of folks don't get, so before Curtis, I settled for whoever would laugh at my jokes and tell me I was 'pretty in the face.' It wasn't until I met Curtis that I realized I never should have accepted crumbs when I deserved the entire cake. Sis, you deserve the cake. You deserve a man who looks at you the way that fine brother looked at you when he came into the kitchen."

I clicked my teeth and turned back to the dishes. "You're just making stuff up. He didn't look at me no kinda way. He's just nice. That's all."

"Ain't that much nice in the world, cousin," she said with a laugh. "That man looked at you the way a man should look at a woman. You think he brought them dishes in here just to be nice? Honey, has it been that long?"

I wiped away another tear. "No man has ever looked at me the way you're describing. Leon is nice to me, and he's good to Mama. And the boys. That's enough."

"No, ma'am," Alicia said, shaking her head firmly. "That's not nearly enough. I don't know what's wrong with these men in Troy, Alabama, but if I have to drag your butt all the way down to Prichard where menfolk love a girl with some meat on her bones, then that is what I will do. But like I said, I saw how Seth looked at you, girl."

"I can't have babies," I said softly. "A man like him wants a woman who can give him babies. I'm not that woman."

Alicia reached for my hand, tears streaming down her face. "Don't think that way, Katia. I saw goodness in that man's eyes. At least give him a chance."

I pulled away. I couldn't allow my mind to go where Alicia was trying to take it. "I'm going outside to check on the boys."

She sighed. "Okay, Sister-Cousin. I'm not going to argue with you anymore about this. Plus, I'm tired. I think I'll go lay down."

I looked at her with concern. Alicia was never tired. "Are you okay?" I couldn't handle more bad news about someone I loved.

She smiled. "I'm fine, cuz."

Now I was really worried. Her words said one thing, but her tone said another. "No. Something is wrong. Please, tell me. Alicia, if you don't . . ."

"I'm pregnant," she burst out. "Four months yesterday."

I knew my eyes must have looked like they were going to pop out of their sockets. "A baby? A baby, Lish?" I said, using my old nickname for her.

"Shhh." She giggled, putting her hand over my mouth, but then her face got serious. "We ain't told nobody yet. What with the other babies . . ."

I pulled her into a hug. I knew about the miscarriages she had suffered. I also knew how much she wanted children. "I'm so happy for you and Curtis. Let's just pray that this pregnancy is the one."

"From your lips to God's ears," she said as we parted and the tears rolled down her cheeks. "The doctor says everything is looking good. I'm just too scared to actually believe him."

"Like I said, we will pray, without ceasing, for this pregnancy." I put my arm around her waist and kissed her cheek. "Now go rest. You shouldn't have been on your feet this long anyway."

"I'm alright. But I'm going to head to the room for a while. I love you, girl."

"I love you too." I watched as she walked out of the room. I tried to focus on the joy of the moment, but sadly I only felt one emotion: jealousy. It enveloped me like a winter coat.

"When do I get my 'happily ever after'?" I whispered, trying hard not to cry. I didn't want to cry anything but happy tears over Alicia's news.

I felt awful for giving in to jealousy for even a second, but I had to acknowledge it so I could then release it. That's what I'd tell the boys, especially on days when a boy went back to his family or to a new home and others had to stay behind. We'd sometimes spend hours talking to them about their feelings. I knew what I was feeling was similar. It hurt to know that for the first time in a lot of years, my sister-cousin was about to embark on a fantastic journey that I'd never experience. That hurt. Bad. But I had to push forward and bring myself back to the joy of the situation. Otherwise, Alicia would pick up on it and it would make her feel bad. I couldn't bear for that to happen. So I breathed . . . and released. Breathed . . . and released.

Once I felt more like myself, I put down the dish towel and walked outside where the kids were playing. I wanted to make sure Chad and Pee Wee were still getting along with the other kids. The last thing I wanted was any drama with the boys, especially since Chad's hearing was coming up soon.

Just like before, they were all ripping and running. They didn't even notice me coming outside. I sat on the porch for a few minutes, and then I went back inside. Leon was in the kitchen, fixing himself a plate of dessert. He looked at me and smiled.

"Got a little hungry," he said, rubbing his belly with a laugh.

"With this gut though, I reckon I could just leave this sweet potato pie where I found it. Did you make this?"

I nodded. "Are you done playing cards?"

"Yeah," he grumbled. "Travis and that young buck beat me and your mama like we stole something."

I hid a smile. "Well, that happens. I guess I'll go see what everyone's doing."

"Wait a minute," he said, placing his plate of pie on the counter. "Would you walk out a piece with me?"

I looked at him curiously. "Sure. Let me put my shoes on."

I went to my room and put on my sneakers. When I got back to the kitchen, Leon had finished off the piece of sweet potato pie. "Ready?" he asked.

"Yes." I followed him out the door, and we wandered down the road. We reached a big rock that the twins used to jump from when they were younger, and Leon motioned for me to sit. But then he didn't say anything.

"What is it, Leon?"

"I don't really know how to say this, or even if I should say this today." He fidgeted a bit and then took my hand. I nearly panicked because I feared he might be proposing, and that was the last thing I wanted.

"Maybe we should just do this another day," I said as I pulled my hand away, but he took it back into his grasp.

"I need to say this now," he said. "And I apologize for the timing. I know you are stressed, but if I don't say what I need to say, it's just going to make things worse."

I was really confused. I didn't have a clue what he was talking about, so I waited. Finally, he took a deep breath and said something I never imagined he'd say.

"Katia, I'm in love with your mama. And before you say anything, I know how wrong that is. I have been fighting this feeling for the longest time, but I don't know what to do about it no more. You are the sweetest, kindest woman there is, and you deserve better treatment than this, but I can't pretend no more."

I was stunned. Then I became overcome with laughter. Alicia was wanting me to give Leon to Mama, and lo and behold, Mama already had his heart. My laughter started off as low chuckles, but soon I was laughing so hard tears rolled down my face.

"Oh, Lord. You done got the hysterics," he said, and that made me laugh even harder. The sheer irony of that word nearly took me over the top. No babies. No man. No nothing. I shook my head, wondering how I managed to get here in this moment. "Oh, honey, don't cry." He patted me on my shoulder as awkwardly as always. I should have known a long time ago that I wasn't the object of his affection. But Mama? Not in a million years did I think she'd take my man.

"I'm not crying," I managed to say, even though my face was covered with tears. "I can't believe you are dumping me for my mother. I think that is one for the books."

"I'm not dumping you for nobody, Katia. I would never be so disrespectful as to try and date your mother after dating you. That's not godlike," he said firmly. "But I can't keep seeing you and being around her. It's just too much."

I wiped my tears with the handkerchief he handed me. "Who says it's not godlike, Leon? Not me. If you fancy my mama that way, then go for it. Life is too short, and death is too long for people to not be with the one they love. Go talk to her, and tell her you both have my blessing."

He looked at me with an expression like he didn't believe me. "Are you sure you not going through some kind of shock?"

I nodded. "I'm sure. And if it makes you feel better, I was thinking about doing the same thing—tell you that this thing between us wasn't working out. You are a good, good, godly man, Leon. The kind of man any woman would love to have. I'm not that woman, but maybe Mama is. I know she cares for you deeply. So go, Leon. Tell Mama that you like her. I'll let her know I'm all good with it, if you think that will help."

"You are an incredible woman, Katia," he said. "I don't think I'll do that with everybody around, but maybe next Saturday when I get off the road. As long as you're sure."

"I'm sure," I said in a firm voice, and I was. I'd feel far less guilty if he and Mama did get together. I didn't want to hurt anyone by breaking up with Leon, so this was a solid compromise. Oh, I knew folks' tongues would wag, but like I said, life was too short. I hoped against hope that Mama would say yes to Leon. They were already the best of friends. They might as well take it to the next level.

"Well, I think I'll be moseying on home." He leaned over and gave me a quick peck on the cheek.

I watched as he walked away. A few minutes later, I heard his truck crank up and then drive off, dust flying everywhere. That was when my tears began to fall—not from laughter but from true sadness.

"You couldn't even keep Brother Leon," I said with a harsh laugh. I had to confess that it stung a little. Okay, a lot. It was one thing to break up with someone yourself. It was something altogether different when that someone broke up with you. Leon and I didn't have a romantic relationship, but it was consistent and familiar. Now I was alone again. I put my hand to my mouth to keep from wailing loudly, like someone out of their mind.

"Are you okay?" I heard someone ask.

I turned toward the direction of the voice. It was Seth. I furiously swiped at the tears. The last thing I wanted was for anyone, let alone him, to find me outside crying. But then I decided to tell him the truth—about Leon at least.

"I think I just got dumped." I laughed, turning my head away from him. He came and sat beside me on the rock.

"I didn't know you were dating anyone, Kat. I'm sorry." He lightly touched my arm.

I shook my head, feeling silly for being so emotional. "Well, the fact that you didn't notice who I was dating in this crowd is a sure indication that nothing was that deep. It was Leon. The guy who partnered with my mama in bid whist." When I told him what Leon had shared about his feelings for Mama, Seth whistled low.

"Damn, Kat," he said. "I'm sorry. That's messed up."

I shook my head. "It's fine, and it was obvious now that I think about it. Neither one of them did anything wrong. At this point, Mama doesn't know about Leon's feelings, and I'm not

crying over him. If he and Mama got together, I'd be their big-
gest cheerleader. I'm crying because I'm alone again. I'm forty
years old, I have no man and I have no children except for the
boys at the group home, and I don't really have them either. At
the drop of a hat, the state can take them away, whether it be to
a good home or a bad one. So, I'm just having myself a good ol'
pity party—minus the fancy hats and the sparklers."

"Any man would be lucky to have you, Kat." His voice was so
soft I almost missed it.

"What did you say?" I didn't want to come across as someone
fishing for compliments, but I wanted to make sure I'd heard
him correctly.

"I said, any man would be lucky to have you."

"We shouldn't be having this conversation," I said and moved
to leave, but he gently pulled me back down beside him on the
rock.

"I know this is all of a sudden. I apologize. But I like you, Kat.
A lot. I'm still working on healing from this war, and I don't
know when that will happen. I mean, I'm not as bad off as a lot
of the men who came back from 'Nam, but I'm not whole either.
I have nightmares, both when I'm asleep and when I'm awake.
I haven't had a drink of liquor in ten months, but I have to be
vigilant so I don't give in to the darkness. I'm taking everything
one day at a time, and I know it is a lot to ask anyone to deal with
me and my demons. Denise couldn't. But having said all of that,
I want to give us a chance."

I felt awful that I sat there and allowed Seth to bear his soul
while I held on tightly to my insecurities and secrets. But I just

couldn't tell my truths. I felt too vulnerable. I didn't want to see the pity or the disgust in his eyes. I stood up.

"I'll bring Marcus by your group and I'll see you at the home next week. Have a good rest of your week." As I started walking back toward the house, I felt tears forming again. But I refused to let them fall.

11

I COULDN'T SLEEP. I WAS IN Mama's room with her, and normally I slept my best when I was nestled up against her, but this night was different. My mind wouldn't let me have a moment's peace, so after tossing and turning all night, I got up at five. I thought I'd be alone for the next few hours, but when I got to the kitchen, Alicia was sitting at the table.

"You okay, Lish?" I walked over to her. She was sipping from a mug and leaning back in her chair with her eyes closed. When I spoke, she opened her eyes and smiled. Relief washed over me.

"I'm fine. This baby just likes to give me fits every morning. I woke up with heartburn. It probably didn't help that I ate two or three plates of food and desserts yesterday. I warmed up some milk to drink. It's helping, and moving around some helps too. I just got back from a walk." She cupped her belly with her hands. Because we both carried our weight in our stomach and hips, I hadn't noticed anything different about her until she'd told me she was pregnant. Seeing her cradle her belly, it was so obvious.

I couldn't believe I missed it. What did it feel like to touch your belly and know that life was living inside your womb? I forced away my envy and instead focused on my cousin, who deserved this happiness.

"I'm sorry you aren't feeling well," I said as I went over and started a pot of coffee. "I couldn't sleep either."

"What kept you up?" She set her mug on the table and looked at me expectantly.

I told her about my conversations with Leon and Seth.

"Oh, girl. I'm sorry." She came over to where I stood and wrapped her arms around my waist, leaning her head against my back. "What did Grandma always used to say? 'God's got a bigger blessing waiting for you.' Don't let them menfolk run you crazy, girl. It's all gonna be okay."

I swiped at the random tear that fell down my cheek. It frustrated me that I was so emotional these days. It made me feel weak, and I didn't like that. I was the strong one. Always. This new me, with the tears and the over-the-top emotions, was foreign and uncomfortable. But I had more on my mind than babies and boyfriends. I was also worried about Chad.

"I also got a call about Chad," I said, turning around and facing her. "Family court set a date for his hearing. I don't know how to tell him. He's been so happy and has been trying so hard to be good. I just don't want him to experience a setback."

Suddenly I heard footsteps. I went to the kitchen door and saw Pee Wee creeping down the hallway.

"Pee Wee," I called softly. I didn't want to wake up anyone else. "Pee Wee, come here."

He turned around and walked back toward me.

"M-m-ma'am?" He wouldn't meet my eyes, which let me know that he'd heard what I said.

"Let's go sit in the kitchen and talk for a minute. Okay?"

"Yes, m-m-ma'am." He reluctantly followed me back to the kitchen. I often scolded the boys about eavesdropping. They came from families where eavesdropping had sometimes saved their lives, but I wanted them to learn the importance of respecting others' privacy. Yet I understood that old habits were hard to break.

During a one-on-one session, Pee Wee had shared with me that he'd overheard his mother saying she was going to "loan him out" to a dude who was going to give her some drugs. He had said he didn't know what "loaning him out" meant, but he knew it didn't sound good. He'd run away and hidden in the woods behind his school for over a week, until the principal found him scavenging for food in the trash can. On more than one occasion, Pee Wee had ended up on the streets, knowing it was safer out there than at his home.

"I'm gonna go see if I can get a little more sleep," Alicia said as she gave me an encouraging smile and then left the kitchen.

"Come sit with me, Pee Wee," I said, pulling my robe tight. I fixed my cup of coffee, then joined him at the table. "You heard what I said to Miss Alicia, didn't you?"

He nodded as tears rolled down his face. "I don't w-w-want Ch-Ch-Chad to go back to that b-b-bad place."

I reached for his hand. "I know. I know you and Chad have become like brothers. But Pee Wee, I promise that I'm going to fight as hard as I can to make sure Chad is in a safe place." I wish I could have said, "stays with us at the group home," but I knew the courts well enough to acknowledge that if Chad's mother showed even a glimmer of improvement, they'd return him to her. No further questions asked.

"Me and Ch-Ch-Chad talked and we w-w-wondered could we st-st-stay here with y-y-you?" Pee Wee said, the pleading in his voice almost causing me to weep along with him. "We pr-pr-promise not to get in no tr-tr-trouble, and we can help o-o-out around here. Gran said we're g-g-good helpers."

Once he finished his request, he began to cry in earnest, and I couldn't stop my own tears from flowing. I pulled him into a tight embrace. I wished I had the power to hug away all of his fears and sorrows. No little boy his age should have to beg for the bare bones when it came to love and attention.

There was so much I wanted to say to him, but I had to remain the "executive director," not the fortysomething, childless woman who'd give anything to be the mother of Pee Wee and Chad. When I first had the hysterectomy, I wallowed in the pity of never being able to conceive a child. I didn't wallow long because I had boys who needed me—yet they weren't my boys. I only had them temporarily, and then they went on their way. But hearing Pee Wee beg me to somehow create a situation where I could parent him and Chad broke my heart wide open. I wanted it, but this was a dream that had no chance of coming true.

I eased Pee Wee out of my arms so he could see me as I spoke. "Pee Wee, you and Chad are two amazing little boys. I would love nothing more than to have you around all of the time, but unfortunately, I'm not allowed to do that. The court system wants to reunite families when the parents are in a better place to take care of their children."

"But can't y-y-you stop them fr-fr-from sending Ch-Ch-Chad back to his m-m-mama?" Pee Wee implored.

"I ain't going back to live with Lena." Pee Wee and I both turned and saw Chad standing at the door. I didn't know how long he'd been standing there, but it was long enough for his face to have the appearance of a storm cloud. His body was rigid, ready to turn his anger on anyone in his path. This wasn't how I'd wanted either one of them to hear this news.

"Pee Wee, let me talk to Chad." I watched as Pee Wee walked slowly out of the kitchen, not looking at his friend as he passed by. Pee Wee, more than anyone, knew how volatile Chad's temper could get. Chad never put his hands on Pee Wee, but he'd sometimes yell, causing Pee Wee to run and hide in the closet of the room they shared. He'd stay there until Chad came and apologized.

Once Pee Wee was out of the room, I turned my attention back to Chad.

"Will you come sit with me?" I prayed I could calm him before we awakened the entire house.

"Don't want to sit," he grunted. His eyes looked cold and distant. His anger wasn't directed at me, but if he lost control, whoever ended up in his path could feel the full strength of his rage.

"I know you aren't in the mood to sit, Chad, but our conversation will go much smoother if you do. Will you join me?" I motioned for him to come, and after a moment he complied, slumping in his chair with a face looking like a hurricane ready to break loose. "Thank you, Chad. I'm so sorry you had to hear that. I wanted to give you this weekend to relax before we had to deal with it. Please accept my apology?"

"I ain't going back to live with Lena," he said, folding his arms across his chest. "Ain't no judge gone make me. Lena the devil. She ain't gone stop till I have to do something awful just to survive."

His feelings were valid. I couldn't, in good conscience, disagree with what he was feeling. I agreed that him living with Lena wouldn't be good, but my job was to uphold the law. I'd stalled as long as I could, but now that a court date was set, all I could do was comply.

I also was troubled by his lightly veiled threat. What did he mean, "do something awful"? I didn't know if I should ignore his words or specifically address them. For now, I tried to divert his attention to the things we could control.

"We will have our day in court, Chad. We will have the chance to tell the judge all of your concerns," I said, reaching for his hand, but he snatched it away.

"Courts ain't thinking 'bout me, Miss Katia," he snapped. "They don't care shit about me. They gone send me back to her, and this time somebody gone die."

My breath caught at those words. "What do you mean, 'somebody gone die,' Chad?"

He looked at me with unblinking eyes—eyes that were like empty shells, void of all emotion, void of all hope. "I ain't taking no more beatings and I ain't taking no more nasty touching from them awful men she brings around either. Ain't nobody else gone put they hands on me again. I'll do what I have to do to survive, but I'm done getting treated any kind of way by Lena and them menfolk of hers."

I felt an awful chill roll over me. Chad was speaking from an honest place. Without a doubt, he'd do whatever he had to do, which meant his future was bleak. I'd supported the child services system my entire career, but what they'd done to Chad and Pee Wee—not to mention the infinite other boys and girl like them—was unconscionable. If you caged a lion long enough and you kept poking it with a stick, eventually it would roar and fight with all its might to survive. Chad had been a caged-up lion cub for way too long, and now he was ready to fight back. I feared that the courts would not realize it when they made their decision soon.

"What about what Pee Wee say?" He looked at me wildly as he pleaded even harder with his eyes than Pee Wee had. He wasn't shedding any tears, but the desperation on his face was hard to witness. "Can't we stay with you? Pee Wee ain't got it much better than me. They'll be trying to send him back to his mama soon. Can't you take us in? I'll get a job somewhere. Maybe the supermarket. Or construction with that dude who came by earlier. I'm big for my age. They'll hire me and I can help pay for whatever me and Pee Wee might need. Please, Miss Katia. We won't be no trouble. I promise."

His words were causing my chest to hurt. He was proposing something I'd love to do, but I didn't see a way toward the future he and Pee Wee were trying to paint. I was a single woman and they were clients at the group home where I worked. The courts wouldn't give me even one of them, let alone both. And what about the ethics of it? If I took in two boys from the group home, the others would begin to wonder why I didn't choose them. This was an impossible situation, and I had no clue how to fix any of it.

"Chad, what you and Pee Wee are proposing is the sweetest thing anybody has ever said to me," I told him, hoping he could tell I meant what I was saying. Having these two boys tell me they wanted me to be their mother was a dream I never thought to dream for myself.

"But you don't want us," Chad said, his shoulders dropping in defeat.

"That's not what I said. The laws are strict about such things, Chad. The court wouldn't agree to it."

"Then I hope the court burns in hell," he said, jumping up and rushing out of the door. I was about to follow him, but Marcus walked into the kitchen. He was already dressed and still looked tired, but he appeared more like himself. I was grateful for small victories.

"Let me go see about him, sis," Marcus said. "Sometimes one broken person just needs to hear from another broken person. I'll make sure he's alright."

I simply nodded. It seemed the entire house was eavesdropping this morning, but I was thankful that Marcus was willing to step outside of his own grief and go see about Chad. He walked out the door, and when I went to the window, I saw him join Chad on the swing set in the far corner of the backyard. The swing set was a destination the twins used to head toward when one or both of them got into trouble or felt bad. I had bought it for them the first Christmas after Daddy died. They'd go out there and swing for hours, talking in their secretive twin language that only they understood.

"Fix this," I prayed. It was close to six thirty. Everyone would be waking up soon, so I started making breakfast. Most relatives would be driving back to Prichard this morning, and I wanted to send them on their way with full stomachs. It was only a two-and-a-half-hour drive, but I wanted them to leave feeling good mentally, physically, and spiritually. That's what Grandma used to say when family visited and got ready to head home. She wanted to feed the entire person.

I was surprised Mama wasn't awake yet, especially since I'd made the coffee. She'd done so much cooking in preparation for Thanksgiving yesterday, she was probably tuckered out. I started making my grandmother's Butter Swim Biscuits. They were a favorite and pretty easy to make, and like the name implied, they were swimming in butter. Once I placed three pans of biscuits in the oven, I started working on a pot of grits. The cooking took my mind off everything going on.

Before long Mama wandered into the kitchen, yawning and stretching, wearing the new purple gown with matching robe and slippers that I'd bought for her. My tradition with Mama was to buy her new sleepwear when company was coming to visit. It made her feel special, and I'd spent the better part of my life trying to put a smile on Mama's face.

"Girl, you shoulda come for me to help," she said. "I heard you when you got up, and I planned on getting up too, but Lawd, that bed started calling my name."

I smiled at her as I began whisking the eggs. Mama always made the eggs according to everyone's preference, from poached to fried. I, on the other hand, knew one way to make eggs: scrambled. "You were resting so well. I didn't want to disturb you."

"I looked in on Marcus, but he wasn't in his room. Is everything alright?" she asked.

"He's fine," I said and then told her about the situation with Chad.

"Just ain't right," she said, going to the toaster and loading it with bread. "They need to be thinking 'bout what these children need 'stead of trying to hurry up and get 'em off their plates. It's a scandal and a shame."

I brushed away a tear as I stirred the grits. "I agree, Mama."

She looked at me hard, her hands on her hips. "You okay, Katia? I know you care about all them boys that come through the group home, but I ain't never seen you take on like this. Is something else going on?"

I wasn't going to tell her about Leon or my conversation with Seth. Leon deserved the right to tell Mama about his feelings, and as far as Seth went, there was nothing to tell. I wasn't going to guilt him into choosing a woman incapable of ever making him a daddy. It wouldn't be fair.

"I've allowed myself to care too deeply for these boys. I normally keep a healthy distance. It's just different this time," I said. Mama came over and hugged me.

"Your hormones are talkin' to you. Women your age usually want children. Not all, but a good many of them. You done spent most of your life taking care of everybody else's children, but I know you want your own. I'm so sorry your body wouldn't let you carry a baby," she said. "But if you and Leon would just go on and get married, you could adopt you some babies. I know he's a daddy already with grandbabies, but he'd consider children if you said that was what you wanted. You want me to talk to him about it for you?"

I turned back to the grits. "No, Mama—I don't want you to talk to Leon about us adopting children. None of that is in the cards for us."

"Well, I don't know why," she said in a huffy voice. "You and Leon ought to be at a place where y'all is at least discussing marriage and children. You can't tell me that conversation ain't come up at least once or twice."

"I'd better check on the biscuits," I said, opening the oven door. The smell of buttery biscuits filled the room. "They smell just like Gran's biscuits, don't they?"

As I'd hoped, Mama got distracted. "They sure do. Every time you make them, I think about my mama. Here, let me put some bacon in the oven while it's hot."

Soon after the grits were done and the biscuits were out of the oven, Marcus and Chad walked back into the house.

"Come here, Chad," Mama said. Chad walked over to her, and she pulled him into an embrace. Marcus and I watched as our petite mother imparted every bit of love and concern she had into that hug. After a moment or two, she stepped back and looked at Chad. "I'm praying for you, son."

To Chad's credit, he nodded and said, "Yes ma'am." Then he left the room, probably to find Pee Wee. He looked at me but didn't say anything. I understood that he wasn't happy with me. I was okay with that for the time being. I only needed him to eventually accept that I was doing everything in my power to protect him.

Shortly thereafter, the rest of the family began to stir. My uncle Rob and Curtis started lugging suitcases out to the car. Aunt Marion and Alicia started setting the table. That gave me an opportunity to question Marcus.

"How did y'all's conversation go?" I whispered after cornering him by the window. He was staring outside, looking like he was far, far away. I imagined he was somewhere in the jungles of Vietnam, still searching for Aaron. He looked at me sadly.

"He's in a bad place. Understandably." He raised his hand as I was about to interject. "I know you fight for those boys at the group home every single day of your life, but these two have become more than your clients. I can see it in your eyes when you look at them," Marcus said. "Do what you can for them."

"I don't know what to do, Marcus," I said, frustrated and overwhelmed. "I can't make the laws operate differently just because I want them to."

Marcus kissed my cheek. "I know you will do whatever it takes, sis."

He and I watched as the boys came back into the kitchen, fully dressed. They went over to Mama, who gave them platters of food to carry into the dining room, where we'd eat breakfast.

The room was solemn. The laughter and jovialness of the

previous day was gone. Alicia had probably filled everyone in on what was going on with the boys. She wouldn't have mentioned Leon or Seth, but the situation with Chad and Pee Wee was overwhelming enough on its own.

"Let's all join hands," Uncle Rob said, and as he prayed, I silently asked the Creator to please send me wisdom and knowledge to handle this situation. I beseeched God to send a miracle our way. To bring Aaron home and to protect these boys, and all of the other boys in the group home, from the danger they had to face when they weren't in my care.

12

SAYING GOODBYE TO OUR FAMILY WAS always hard, but especially today. I needed them close by, yet one by one they were loading up their cars to go home. It felt like they were driving to the end of the earth.

Seeing Alicia prepare to leave was even sadder for me than usual. I wanted my cousin to be closer than a phone call. The way we clung to each other told me that she felt the same way, but as was the case with us, she was being the strong one. With everyone else I had to be the Rock of Gibraltar, but with Lish I could be the one needing someone to lean on.

"I'm just a couple of hours away, Katia. All you have to do is call, and I'll jump on the first thing smoking back to Troy, Alabama," she whispered in my ear.

"You can't do that. You've got to take care of yourself and this baby," I said, wiping away the tears. "Nothing should come before that."

She laughed softly. "This baby better learn sooner than later that you are my sister-cousin and my best friend. When you need me, I'm here. No matter what."

I nodded, hugging her even tighter. I touched her belly and said a prayer, silently pleading with God to let this baby stay put for the five months needed for it to be full-term. We hugged once more, and I stood at the door, crying and waving. After everyone else had left, I went looking for Chad and Pee Wee. I found them sitting on the floor in the bedroom Alicia and Curtis had occupied. As much as I knew it would hurt my hip, I lowered myself to the floor. My knees made an obnoxious cracking sound. Normally the boys would laugh at the sound of my old, noisy bones, and I'd laugh with them, but neither they nor I were in a laughing mood. One look at their faces told me they were still discussing Chad's upcoming hearing.

"You boys okay?"

"Ch-Ch-Chad and me tr-tr-trying to make a pl-pl-plan," Pee Wee blurted.

"Shut up, Pee Wee," Chad ordered. "You ain't got to have such a big mouth. Some things is just between you and me."

"Tell me what you're talking about. Maybe I can help." I kept my voice calm. I had learned that the less I reacted to the things the boys said to me, the more likely they were to trust me and tell me the truth. Sometimes the truth was hard to hear. These boys I took care of had complicated and heartbreaking lives. The things they thought about and dealt with were adult-level situations. Who was I kidding? The average adult hadn't experienced half of what my boys had experienced. But somehow they kept getting up after life punched them down. That's why I took their truths to the chin without allowing myself to become overwhelmed in front of them. I felt as if I owed them that.

After a brief silence, I spoke again. "It's okay. Just tell me."

"N-n-nothing," Pee Wee muttered, looking down at the floor. He hated displeasing Chad more than he hated lying to me. I knew he wouldn't reveal any more intel, so I turned my attention to Chad.

"Chad? I'd love to hear more about this plan you guys are cooking up. Maybe I can help," I said again, waiting and watching as their eyes met, and they had a silent dialogue with each other. They reminded me of the twins when they were younger. Aaron and Marcus could have entire conversations without uttering a single word.

Finally, Chad rolled his eyes at Pee Wee, and then he spoke. "We trying to figure out what to do when we get separated. Ain't neither one of our mothers got an inside phone like you, so we figured we'd come up with a plan for staying in touch or getting help when we need it. I know y'all don't like us kids to do stuff like that, but this's 'bout survival, Miss Katia."

I didn't know what was sadder—that they'd made a plan or that they were resigned to the fact that they'd be separated from each other soon, in addition to likely being in danger. I knew better than to argue with them concerning the impending separation. The two of them had spent enough time in the system to know the reality of their fate. I knew it too. It would take an act of God to keep Chad from going back to live with Lena. The court system nearly always erred in favor of the mother, regardless of how terrible she was. The thought of them being out of my protective care was painful. I had allowed myself to get too close to these boys, and now, when the day came when we all had to say goodbye, I already knew that they and I would be inconsolable.

"I can understand why you boys would want a strategy in place." I resisted the urge to reach for both of their hands. Neither they nor I needed the sentimentality at the moment. Right now, we all needed a concrete plan. "Let's see if I can contribute to what you have already put into place."

The three of us discussed things like memorizing my phone number at the group home and here at the house. We talked about safe spaces they could go to, like churches or fire departments, if things became too dangerous at home. It broke my heart that we had to have such conversations, but the more we planned, the calmer the boys seemed to become.

"I know h-h-how to find m-m-my old sch-sch-school. I'll h-h-hide there if I-I-I need t-t-to. Just like be-be-before," Pee Wee said with a smile, belying the seriousness of his words. It was clear he was proud of his problem-solving skills. I was too, but at the same time, hearing him speak that way pained me. "Is that a g-g-good idea, Miss K-K-Katia?"

I had to will away the sob trying to form deep inside my throat. That I had to sit on the floor with these boys and come up with ways for them to escape from harm was almost too much. Before I could answer him, Chad chimed in excitedly.

"Yeah, man. That's smart," Chad said, patting Pee Wee on his back. "And then you can go to that lady's house you said was across from the school and tell her . . . I mean, ask her if you can use her phone. Tell Miss Katia her name so she can write it down in your file. Then, if Miss Katia needs to get in touch with you, she can call that lady."

"Yeah," Pee Wee said. "Her name M-M-Miss Cordell. She lives on S-S-South Union Street. S-S-Same as m-m-my school. Wh-wh-what about you? What's your p-p-plan?"

"I'm gone try to tell that judge to send me to foster care or juvie. Either one of them be better than going back to Lena," Chad said.

"Wh-wh-what if j-j-judge say no?" Pee Wee questioned. "What you g-g-gone do th-th-then?"

"I'll just stay outta her way and her boyfriend's way." He shook his head up and down, as if he'd just come to that conclusion. "Don't worry about me though. I'm gone be fine. I'm gone try to get a part-time job if they do make me go back to her. Save up some money and then come back here to Troy and go to school where Mr. Jason goes. I know some folks who might can help me if I need help before then."

"Chad," I said in a warning voice.

He grinned. "No criminals. Good people. Like you and Mr. Jason. If I end up here in Troy, I can leave word at that barbershop Mr. Jason takes us to, but I doubt they'll let me stay here. If I'm down in Ozark, I can run over to that AME church or to the gas station down the road from it. I promise I won't break no laws, Miss Katia, and if I can't get a legal job, I'll make sure I don't get on Lena's nerves. How old I got to be before I'm a legal adult?"

"Twenty-one in the state of Alabama," I said softly.

"Twenty-one?" Chad said, raising his voice. "How is it I can fight in a war at eighteen but I ain't no adult till I'm twenty-one? How the hell I'm supposed to stay safe and out of trouble if I've got to take care of myself for another seven years? Don't make no damn sense."

His point was valid, and considering the situation, I did not scold him for using foul language. I understood where his feelings were coming from, and if anyone had a right to be angry, he did. I didn't have any good answers for his questions, so I did what adults often do: I tried my best to divert their attention from the worst parts of their stories. I got them back on track fine-tuning their "plans," which took most of the afternoon.

I was exhausted when we finished, so I let them go watch television. The local news was on, but they were looking forward to watching *The Wild Wild West* and then *Star Trek*. Mama promised them they could watch *The Guns of Will Sonnett* with her when *Star Trek* ended. She planned to enjoy her television buddies, and I wasn't about to try to take away their fun, especially since she didn't know Leon and I had broken up. I had no clue how she'd respond to Leon's advances, but I had an inkling I'd be returning to television-buddy status soon. After the boys and Mama were happily preparing to settle in for a night of TV viewing, Marcus and I got ready to go to his first session with Seth's veterans' group. Marcus was dressed in his Marine uniform. Mama came up to him and wrapped her arm around his waist.

"You sure, baby?" she asked. She didn't elaborate, but it was clear what she was talking about.

"I'm sure, Mama," he said, bending down and kissing Mama

on top of her head. "If things get too rough, I'll walk outside and get some air."

"We should go," I said softly. I didn't want him to change his mind about going and I didn't want to give Mama any more time to potentially sway him to stay.

We gave Mama hugs and left. My truck decided to be co-operative tonight, and I was grateful for that. Marcus didn't talk much on the drive, and I decided not to prod him. In some ways, I welcomed the silence. My mind was overrun with so many thoughts that I, too, needed some time to process everything. When we arrived at the church, he sat in the passenger seat, neither speaking nor moving.

"Are you sure you want to go to this meeting?" I asked, repeating Mama's sentiments. The parking lot of First Missionary Baptist Church had about five or six cars in it, and I recognized Seth's truck even though it was nearly dark outside. I reached over and touched his hand. "It's okay if you don't want to go, Bubby. There's always next week."

He shook his head, wiping away a tear. "If I don't go today, I won't go. I need to get my head right. Talking to these guys . . . who know a little something about what I'm going through . . . might help. At least I hope it will help."

"Then you go inside, and I'll be right here waiting. Okay?" He looked at me and nodded. I kissed his cheek and held him for a few seconds before releasing him with a gentle pat on his cheek. He exited the truck and I watched as he slowly made his way toward the door.

This moment reminded me of when he and Aaron went back

to school after Daddy died. They were afraid and lost, even though they had each other. For their first week in class, I sat outside of their classroom window so that if they got scared they could look outside and see me.

I wasn't sure where the meeting would be inside the church, but I wanted Marcus to know I'd be right here, just like always. Waiting for him. I was glad he was being so brave in tackling his depression, but more so for tackling his sadness and fear concerning Aaron. Even though we hadn't talked about it much the last few days, we understood that with each passing day, the likelihood of Aaron being found alive grew smaller. I was terrified that when and if we received that call, I'd lose Marcus too.

I leaned back in the seat of my truck and closed my eyes. It was cool outside, but with a light jacket on I was fairly warm inside the truck. I kept an old blanket in the back for really cold days. Before long, I started feeling drowsy. I fought sleep at first, but then I gave into it, grateful for peace and no nightmares. What felt like only a few seconds later, a knock on my window startled me awake. I was unaware of how long I'd been asleep or how long the person had been knocking. I put on my glasses and realized it was Seth. I rolled down my window.

"What's wrong? What happened? Where's Bubby—I mean Marcus?" I demanded, ready to hop out of the truck the second he told me what was wrong.

"Nothing is wrong, Kat," he said quickly. "I just wanted to come tell you that Marcus was still talking with a couple of the guys he knew from basic training. I didn't want you to worry."

"When it comes to my family, worry is my first, middle, and last name." I almost cried from sheer relief that there was no immediate need for me to panic, but I was determined not to shed more tears anytime soon. I was tired of being a water fountain.

"Do you mind if I sit with you for a minute?" Seth's voice was quiet. I truly wanted to say no but found myself inviting him into the truck anyway. My heart needed protecting right now, and I was the only one who could do it.

I watched as he rounded to the passenger side. As soon as he opened the door, I caught a whiff of his cologne. I steeled myself against the attraction I felt for him. I didn't say anything, but he began to talk.

"When I came back from 'Nam, Denise told me she couldn't handle being with a crippled man," he said. "Turns out, before I even made it back to the States from the hospital in Saigon, she'd packed up all of her things and moved back home with her parents. Mama and Daddy moved me back here with them. I wanted to die. I even tried once. I took a handful of sleeping pills, but I threw them back up before they could do any damage."

I gasped. How could anyone be so cruel to another person, particularly someone they had stood before God and promised to love "in sickness and in health"? I only vaguely remembered Denise from school. She didn't hang around people like me. The nerds. The awkward girls. She was pretty and popular, but I didn't remember any stories of her being hateful. I reached over and touched Seth's hand. "I'm so sorry, Seth. That is deplorable. You deserved better treatment than that."

"She didn't want me to enlist. She said I was stupid for signing up for a white man's war." He took a deep breath. "The draft is escalating, Kat. It's just a matter of time before every eligible man is sent over there. I figured if I enlisted, what with me having a medical degree in psychology, maybe I wouldn't get sent off to the front lines like so many of my buddies in the military already were, but soon as I was done with training, they sent me to the worst of the fighting. Maybe she was right. Maybe I was stupid."

"No, you are not stupid, and she was not right, Seth." I turned to face him. Even though it was dark outside and the parking lot lights barely illuminated the inside of the truck, I hoped he could sense my sincerity. "What you and all of these young men have done is the height of bravery. You all went over there to fight for freedom. That's never stupid."

"I don't know, Kat. I was thinking back to what Muhammad Ali said. He said he wasn't going ten thousand miles from home to kill other poor folks—poor brown folks. Maybe he was right. Maybe I signed up for a fool's errand. I just don't know."

I took his hand in mine. "Seth, being a Black person in this country ain't easy. We love America a whole lot more than it loves us, but this is the only country we've got. I'm not disagreeing with Muhammad Ali that something feels off about us fighting against other poor brown folks, but those same people shot off your leg and kidnapped my brother. They're not innocent in all of this either. There is enough blame to go around for everybody. So, you doing what you thought was right is all you, my brothers, or any other man or woman can do in this lifetime. Daddy used to say that when the Judgment comes, we all might be surprised at who got it right and who got it wrong and who just made some good guesses. That's all I know."

Before he could respond, Marcus and some of the other men walked out the front doors of the church. They weren't jovial, but they didn't look beaten down. I said a quick silent prayer for each one of them, that their steps would become lighter and their minds freer.

"I should go," Seth said and patted my hand. "Thank you, Kat. I appreciate you listening."

"We're friends," I said. "And if you want to know how amazing you are, look at those men coming out of that church. You set aside your grief and your pain and your sadness to help them. That's not a stupid man. That is a man with integrity."

He ducked his head with what I assumed was embarrassment. "Thank you. I do it for myself as much as for them."

"Why are you doing construction instead of working with men like my brother and the others full-time?" Construction work was noble, but helping others seemed to be Seth's calling. I wondered why he had left it behind.

"I don't think I could handle the weight of this work full-time," he said. "Volunteering to meet with the guys once a week is about all I can manage. At least for now."

I instantly understood what he meant. Sometimes running the group home was more than I could bear. Days like today made me question if I could continue, especially when it didn't feel like it was truly making a difference.

"I'll see you next week. Take care, Kat." He exited the truck as Marcus walked up to it. They shook hands, and then Seth limped away. I looked over at my brother as he sat down in the truck, closing the door sharply.

"How was the meeting?" Because of the darkness of the night, I couldn't make out his features to read his emotions, so I waited for him to speak. I listened as he sighed deeply.

"It was definitely overwhelming at times, but helpful, I think." He leaned back wearily against the seat. "All the guys were welcoming and encouraging."

"Seth said you met some people from your basic training?"

"Yeah. Both of them got injured over there. Not as bad as Seth, but enough for them to get sent home. One of the guys is trying to see if the Marines will send him back," Marcus said.

I was surprised to hear that. I couldn't imagine anyone wanting to go back to that awful place. I said the same to Marcus, and his words shocked me.

"I'd go back tomorrow." He hugged himself tightly. "All they would have to do is say the word."

"Because of Aaron?" I questioned, trying to understand where he was coming from.

"Partly, but also because I'm a Marine, Katia," he said. "A Marine only wants to come home for one of two reasons. Because we destroyed our enemies or because we're inside a body bag. There's no honorable discharge for a Marine."

He didn't sound like my little brother who used to cry over a baby bird falling out of its nest or a squirrel lying dead on the road. It was scary to know this was how he thought these days. While I was still processing his words, he reached for my hand.

"I just want my brother back. I want to hear him call out my name, and I want to see him running toward me, ready to give me a big bear hug. I don't know if I can do this life without him, sis." I touched his face, which was wet with tears. My heart was breaking for him, and for the first time ever, I didn't know how to ease his pain.

I pulled him to me, holding him as tightly as I could. "Don't say that. Don't say that, Bubby."

But I knew he was just being honest. He and Aaron had never been apart before, and it was wearing Marcus down. I imagined, if Aaron was still alive, the separation was doing the same to him. Once again I prayed that God would give us a miracle, more so for Marcus than for me and Mama. I knew that somehow Mama and I would survive even if the worst happened, but Marcus . . . I truly couldn't imagine him living without Aaron, just like he said. When they were babies, Mama tried putting them in separate cribs, but they'd cry and cry until she put them together again. They'd snuggle up next to each other and sleep for the remainder of the night. I prayed that Aaron wasn't suffering out in the jungle, wanting nothing but the warmth of his big brother beside him.

"Let's go home, Bubby," I said.

Suddenly I was more tired than I'd ever remembered feeling before. I wanted to go home and escape all of the bad feelings and thoughts. Maybe I'd play Nina Simone's album *High Priestess of Soul* when I got home. A nice long bubble bath and Nina singing in the background seemed perfect. Already I could hear her singing the words to that familiar song that was always sung during baptisms at my church, "Take Me to the Water." When I first discovered it on her album, I was intrigued. I'd always thought of that song in the context of church. Hearing her sing it with both a churchy and bluesy growl added another level of meaning for me, one I'm sure my mother wouldn't appreciate. But I did believe that just as there was healing in the act of baptism, there was healing and redemption in the voice of my favorite singer. And tonight I desperately needed Nina to calm my mind.

13

IT WAS MIDDAY ON SATURDAY WHEN Leon arrived back in town. I was sitting on the porch swing watching Chad and Pee Wee play basketball. Marcus had played with them for a little while, but he soon grew tired and retreated to his room. It was nice seeing him out and about.

Leon parked his truck near mine and slowly approached me. I could tell he wasn't exactly excited about sharing with Mama what he had shared with me the other day. He normally walked with purpose. Now he was dragging. He was dressed up as usual. I hoped Mama would be receptive to what he had to say.

As he stepped onto the porch, I impulsively stood and hugged him, then whispered in his ear, "It's gonna be okay, Leon. Just speak from your heart."

When I pulled away, he had tears in his eyes. "You were always too good for me with your book smarts and your ability to lead. I'm just an old country boy who can drive a big rig better than most. Your mama's too good for me too."

"Not true. We're all looking for love and acceptance. Nobody is better than anybody else," I said and patted his back with a smile. "Go get her, tiger." A good night's sleep and an early morning conversation with Lish helped me put things back into perspective. She had told me I needed to stop acting like I was pining for Brother Leon.

"You are sad about being alone," she had said wisely. "That's normal. But don't get that confused with loving that man, because you didn't. Not the way a woman loves a man. There was zero passion between you and him, and you, girl, need the passion. Period."

She was right. As many romantic novels as I'd read, I knew exactly what I was looking for. Not textbook love. Not storybook love. But definitely not the love I felt for Leon. He was more like a brother or an older cousin to me. As much as I liked Leon, he wasn't the man I wanted to wake up next to for the rest of my life. Yet now I couldn't imagine finding love. Most men my age were still thinking about starting families of their own, and that wasn't my future, unfortunately. I mean, maybe there was a man out there who wouldn't mind adopting a child with me, but from my experience, most men seemed to want biological children. I didn't know for sure if that was how Seth felt, but I was too scared to find out.

"Go on and talk to her, Leon," I said, pushing him slightly, trying to put my feelings aside. "Tell Mama the truth. Tell her about our conversation, and then, after that, it's out of your hands."

He nodded. I knew this was out of his comfort zone. Leon

didn't like displaying his feelings, but I hoped he'd move past that, and I equally hoped Mama would be receptive. They were perfect for each other. I wish I had seen that sooner.

"Boys," I called out. "Let's go to town and get ourselves a burger and fries at Mr. Miller's restaurant." Both of them immediately stopped what they were doing and ran to the porch. Mr. Miller was a member of Bethel Missionary Baptist Church, where my family had attended since Mama and Daddy moved to Troy. Mr. Miller and his family had one of the few Black-owned restaurants in Troy. Integration would lead you to believe that Black folks could go and eat anywhere we pleased, but the truth of the matter was that the cold reception we often received at a white-owned establishment wasn't worth the effort. So, as much as possible, my family and I went to places where we knew we'd be welcomed.

"Th-th-that place we a-a-ate at before?" Pee Wee asked, his face radiating with excitement. He never cared where we went, as long as we went somewhere. I looked at Chad. His excitement was more tempered, but I knew they were ready for a change of scenery. Besides, I wanted to give Mama and Leon some privacy.

"That's the one," I said. "I'm going to run inside and get my purse, and we'll be on our way. Y'all keep Mr. Leon company until I get back."

I hurried inside, where Mama was heating up leftovers. I noticed she'd changed out of the housedress she'd been wearing. Clearly she'd heard Leon's arrival, and her words confirmed my suspicions.

"I see Leon is outside," she said, sliding the dressing into the oven. "I know he's probably hungry. Bless his heart. You can finish heating this up for him."

I kissed Mama's cheek. "Nope. I'm about to take the boys out for a hamburger. You can entertain Leon all by yourself."

Mama shook her head. "You need to stop being so careless with the attention you give that man. Brother Leon ain't gone keep coming around here if you don't make him feel like his time and energy matters to you, Katia."

I kissed her cheek again. "Brother Leon is just fine, Mama. In fact, he wants to talk to you about something. Something important."

Her face split into a grin and she clapped her hands with glee. "Hallelujah and thank you, Jesus. He wants to ask for your hand in marriage. It's about time."

Rather than contradict her, I squeezed her shoulders and rushed to my room in search of my purse. It was underneath a pile of clothes I'd washed this morning but hadn't put up. On my way out, I peeked inside Marcus's room. He was sound asleep. When I got back to the kitchen, Leon was coming inside the door.

"Okay, y'all. See you later," I said and left before either one of them could say anything to me. This was definitely not a conversation I wanted to be privy to. "Dear Lord, open her heart and mind to what she is about to hear," I muttered under my breath.

The boys were already standing next to my truck. "Y'all ready for some big, fat, juicy burgers and some salty, salty french fries?"

"Yes, ma'am," they said in unison.

"Well, get in the truck." I laughed as they battled to see who'd sit in the middle and who'd sit by the window. The twins used to do the same thing, so I knew exactly how to handle the scuffle. "Pee Wee gets the window going and, Chad, you get the window on the way back. Deal?"

They looked at each other and then grinned. "Deal," they agreed. Chad slid in from the passenger side first; then Pee Wee slid in after him.

"Can I r-r-roll down the w-w-window?" Pee Wee asked, bouncing up and down in his seat.

"It's a bit too cool for the windows to be down," I said, but after seeing his disappointed face, I gave in and told him he could roll it down until we got to the end of the street. Compromise was always key with my boys.

When he first came to the group home, Pee Wee had told me that he'd never ridden in a car or truck before. He said he and his mama walked everywhere they needed to go. He then told me that he'd ridden inside an ambulance when his mother had knocked him unconscious, but of course he didn't remember that ride. Riding in my truck was as exciting to him as being on the Ferris wheel at the county fair.

The ride to town didn't take long. The boys chatted animatedly about our current adventure, which allowed me to ponder the conversation going on back at the house. I couldn't imagine what Mama's response might be. Well, actually . . . I knew exactly what her response would be. She'd ask him if he'd lost his ever-loving mind. I imagined she'd ask me the same question when the boys and I returned. My hope was that at some point, she'd realize she felt the same way about Leon as he did about her.

"Miss Katia, can we stop at the store over there? I want to get your mama a thank-you present from me and Pee Wee," Chad said, pointing toward The Mercantile. He must have caught my look because he grinned broadly. "It's okay, Miss Katia. I got money. Not a lot but enough for maybe something small."

I nodded. "Okay. But I don't want you spending your money." I didn't want to say that, with the uncertainty of his situation, he might need that money soon. "Let me buy the gift for you. It can still be from you and Pee Wee. Nobody ever has to know." I eased the truck into a parking spot across the street from The Mercantile. Crowds of people were out shopping, no doubt already thinking about Christmas.

"But that's not the same," Chad insisted. "If you buy it, it's not from us."

I could tell it meant a lot to him to buy the gift himself. I decided to acquiesce for now. If I had to slip the money back into his pocket at a later date, I would. But for now he needed to buy this gift on his own.

"Okay." I smiled. "I won't have anything to do with it. It will be all you and Pee Wee. I know Mama will be so excited."

Both boys grinned, giving each other high fives. Their unselfishness knew no bounds. Most boys their age would be clamoring to buy things for themselves at the store, and here they were, thinking about my mama.

"Can we go into the store by ourselves?" Chad asked, glancing at me sideways. "We want what we get to be a surprise to you too."

"No," I said in a firm voice. "That's pushing it and you know it. I can't let you boys out of my sight."

"Okay, okay," he said, holding up his hand. It was clear he was about to negotiate the terms. I hid a smile. I loved it when the boys asserted their independence. I wanted them to be able to vocalize their thoughts and wishes, even if that meant I had to do some tap dancing of my own to keep up with them.

"Miss Katia, what if," Chad said, slipping his arm through the crook of mine, "you stayed near the front door of The Mercantile and me and Pee Wee went shopping? You would still be right there, but we'd have some privacy. What you think about that?"

I shook my head, unable to stifle a laugh. "You boys are something else."

"I-I-Is that a y-y-yes?" Pee Wee looked at me eagerly.

"That's a yes. But don't make me regret my decision." I looked at them sternly. Both Pee Wee and Chad had stolen before. Mostly food, and not since they'd been at the group home. The last thing I wanted was for them to impulsively snag something that caught their eye. "Make sure you only pick up what you have money to buy, and do not spend all of your money, Chad. Is that clear?"

"Yes, ma'am," he said. "We won't touch it unless we plan to buy it."

"No sticky f-f-fingers," Pee Wee said in a serious voice.

I reached over and ruffled his hair. "That's right, silly boy. No sticky fingers. Let's get out of this truck so y'all can go shopping. That money is about to burn a hole in Chad's pocket."

We got out of the truck and stood for a minute as the traffic drove by. Then I took Pee Wee by the hand, Chad took his other hand, and we crossed the street.

Before we walked inside The Mercantile, I faced them. "Repeat the rules, Chad. You're the oldest, so you're in charge."

He nodded solemnly. "We're supposed to find what we're looking for and not touch anything unless we plan on buying it. And I am not to spend every dime in my pocket."

"Good." I turned to Pee Wee. "Anything you want to add?"

"No st-st-sticky fingers," he said with a nod.

"Exactly." I made sure not to crack a smile. "I will stay over there by the front of the store, but if you need me, come there and find me. Also, do not put your hands in your pockets for any reason. Why is that?"

"'Cause white folks all the time thinkin' we stealing something," Chad said.

"I wasn't specifically referring to white people, but yes, we don't want to raise anyone's alarm when we enter into their stores. Speak to people. Look them in their eyes. And keep it moving. Okay?"

"Yes, ma'am," they said.

"Alright then. Let's go." Pee Wee rushed to open the door for me, holding it as Chad and I walked inside. I was happy to see a familiar face at the register. It was Mrs. Gayle Cherry, the white lady who lived about a mile from our house.

"Hello, Katia," she said, greeting me with a smile. "Happy Saturday after Thanksgiving. Who are these boys with you?"

I knew the boys were self-conscious about being from the group home, so I fudged my answer a bit. "Friends of the family. The taller one is Chad and the other young man is—"

"Mason. M-m-my name is M-M-Mason," he said. "Pleased to m-m-meet you, m-m-ma'am."

Chad and I smiled at each other. I, of course, knew Pee Wee's real name, but he'd always insisted on being called Pee Wee. I wasn't even sure if Chad knew his real name. Pee Wee had told me that Pee Wee was the nickname his daddy had given him. It was interesting to hear him use his birth name in this instance. I guess he wanted to come across as a big boy, and maybe, in his mind, Pee Wee sounded childish.

"Pleased to meet you, Mason, and you too, Chad. What are y'all here for?" Mrs. Cherry asked.

"Presents," Pee Wee said. Chad gave him a look, and then I knew. They weren't here solely to get something for Mama. They were here to get something for me as well. I pretended like I didn't hear the *s* at the end of "present."

"These young men want to get my mama a present."

"Well, that is the sweetest thing ever," she said. "Y'all should go over to aisle three. There's some toilet water over there that Mrs. Daniels might like."

"No, ma'am," Chad said quickly. "I don't think she'd be wanting no toilet water. We want to get her something nice."

Mrs. Cherry, to her credit, didn't crack a smile or laugh at Chad's misunderstanding. "Oh, Chad. I apologize. I should have been clearer. That's another name for perfume. Don't ask me why someone came up with toilet water. Seems downright silly, doesn't it?"

Chad grinned. "Yes, ma'am. But now that we know what it is, we'll go check it out. Is it okay if we smell it? We'll be careful, and we won't drop any of it. Promise."

"Absolutely," she said. "You smell as much as you want. And if you need my assistance, you just call out for my help."

Chad and Pee Wee thanked her and slowly walked away. I was proud of them for taking their time and not rushing through the store.

"They are some well-mannered young boys, Katia," she said. "Whoever is raising them is raising them right."

"Thank you," I said. I turned back toward the direction they'd gone, fighting the urge to go hover over them. They soon returned and Chad asked me to turn around. I heard Mrs. Cherry ask if they wanted her to wrap the presents. I could hear Chad whispering, and I pretended to be engrossed in a display of Tide laundry detergent near the front of the store.

"I'll put your purchases in this bag, Chad," Mrs. Cherry said.

I felt arms around my waist. It was Pee Wee. "Gran is g-g-going to l-l-like her present."

I gave him a firm hug. "Of course she is. As long as it's from you boys, she will absolutely love it."

I turned just in time to see Chad walk toward us with a bag. His smile was bigger than any I'd ever seen on his face.

"You didn't spend all of your money, did you?" I looked at him intently. He grinned wider.

"No, ma'am." He patted his pocket. "I still got some money. I could buy us our burgers and fries if you wanted me to."

I shook my head. "You've spent enough. Let's go so we can get our food and head on back home."

We said goodbye to Mrs. Cherry and headed out the door. None of us noticed the man standing outside. As soon as we exited the store, he roughly grabbed Chad's arm.

"Come to Papa, you son of a—"

"Take your hands off of him!" I yelled, reaching for Chad, but the man pulled him out of my reach while simultaneously pushing me away. I almost fell, but I didn't care about myself. I only wanted to get Chad away from this man. "Let him go!"

"Let me go," Chad whimpered. "Let me go, Cobra."

"It's okay, baby," a woman's voice said, getting out of the beat-up Chrysler parked in front of the store. "Cobra ain't gone hurt you. I told him that was you. We was right over there at the thrift store. Mama gone take you home."

"St-st-stop!" Pee Wee screamed.

"Go back inside, Pee Wee," I yelled. "Now!"

He immediately ran back inside the store. I was grateful for his obedience. I needed all of my attention on Chad.

Lena's thin body was dressed like a woman of the night, in all red—go-go boots, short skirt, and halter top—with a matted wig on her head. I didn't understand how she wasn't shivering, but she didn't seem aware of the cold. Her eyes were bloodshot, and her skin appeared ashen. It was clear that she was high on something. I prayed she wasn't so far gone that she wouldn't listen to reason.

"Lena," I said softly. "This isn't the way. A judge has to—"

"Shut up," she snapped. "Don't say nothing to me about no judge. This 'tween me and my boy. Get in the car, Chad."

"Let me go, Cobra," Chad grunted, pulling and twisting, but the big man had him in a tight grip.

"Please let him go," I ordered. "You have no right to hold him like that. Let him go."

Vaguely, I remembered that name. *Cobra.* But where? Then suddenly, it all came to me. This was one of the men who'd hurt Chad. In that moment, my fear increased exponentially.

"I said let me go, Cobra!" Chad yelled, continuing to try to break free, but the man only held him tighter, laughing like a hyena.

"That's Mr. Cobra to you, punk," he said, and I noticed he had a knife pushed against Chad's right side.

I began to sweat in spite of the cool temperature. Cobra had light skin and an awful scar on his face, and his teeth were nearly all rotten. He grinned at me wildly. He was high on something too. "Chad, my boy, you, me, and Lena is about to go for a ride."

By this time a sea of white faces stood at a distance, staring. I scanned the crowd, hoping to see even one familiar brown face, but there was none. In that instant, I knew we were the entertainment for the afternoon.

"Mr. Cobra," I said, trying to sound calm. "Let him go. Let him go and I won't say anything to anyone. Tell him to let Chad go, Lena."

As if in response, he waved the knife toward me, and people shrieked, yet no one came to our aid. "Lady, you don't make the rules. This son of a dog owes me a dance. Don't you, Chad? Lena don't like to dance with me no more, so I reckon you'll have to do the two-step with ole Cobra tonight."

"Noooooo," Chad wailed and tried to pull away, but Cobra was at least a good fifty or sixty pounds heavier. Cobra repositioned himself and held the knife to Chad's throat.

Lena let out a nervous laugh, tugging at a halter strap that had slipped down her shoulder. "Stop all that, Cobra. You ain't gone do nothing." She reached out and put her hand on Chad's arm. "He ain't gone do nothing. Just come on. We need to get gone 'fore the ofays call the law. Come on now."

I heard someone holler for the police, but if any cops were around, they didn't respond. I didn't have time to worry about them. I was a pro at defusing tough situations with my boys. I prayed God would give me strength to talk this madman down.

"It's okay, Chad." I tried to make my voice as soothing as possible. "Mr. Cobra, you seem like a reasonable man. The police will be here any second. Just let Chad go and you two be on your way."

"You ain't the boss of me!" he yelled. "I aim to take this boy, and maybe you, too, if you keep running your mouth."

"Ain't nobody taking her nowhere," Lena snapped. "You always—"

"Let the boy go," I heard a familiar voice order.

I turned from Lena in time to see Seth grab Cobra from behind and wrestle the knife from the man's hand. I quickly reached out for Chad and pulled him close, his body trembling.

"Cobra," Lena called out as she hopped back into the passenger seat of the car. "Come on. We'll get Chad later. Come on."

Cobra pushed Seth away and ran for the driver's side. He and Lena raced off just as the police drove up.

"Bring him inside," I heard Mrs. Cherry say from the door of The Mercantile. "Y'all move and let her and the boy in."

She stood with her arm around Pee Wee, who was crying in loud gulps. As I led Chad to the door, Pee Wee hurled himself into my arms, nearly knocking Chad and me to the ground. Once we were inside, people were coming toward us, but Mrs. Cherry shooed them away.

"Lord, have mercy," Mrs. Cherry said, escorting us to some chairs she'd pulled out. "What was that all about? Who was that monster trying to get at this boy?"

Chad slumped into a chair. I noticed he was still clutching the bag with the gifts he and Pee Wee had bought. I sat down beside Chad and pulled a crying Pee Wee into my arms. I just shook my head at Mrs. Cherry as I held the boys as close to me as I could.

"It's okay," she said. "Y'all just get yourselves together."

I saw Seth talking to a policeman. I knew they'd want to speak to Chad, but he wasn't up for talking. Since Seth had wrestled the knife away from Cobra, Chad hadn't uttered a word.

"Chad," I whispered. "Chad, honey. Are you alright?" I knew it was a ridiculous question as soon as the words came tumbling out of my mouth, but at that moment I didn't know what else to say.

"Don't. Let. Him. Get. At. Me." Chad said each word as if uttering it hurt.

"No one is going to get at you," I said. "No one."

He nodded, tears streaming down his face. Seth and the

policeman walked into the store together. Seth hung back, but his eyes stared straight at me. I mouthed, *Thank you*, to him.

As the officer came toward us, Chad began shaking his head back and forth. I was afraid he might jump up and start running.

"It's going to be okay," I said over and over, trying to calm him as well as myself and Pee Wee, who was holding on to me for dear life.

When the officer neared us, I stood, extracting myself from Pee Wee's death grip. I glanced at the man's badge and saw that Perryman was his name.

"Officer Perryman," I said, reaching out to shake his hand. He paused, then accepted my hand for a quick handshake. I didn't care if he didn't want to shake hands or be cordial to me. I just wanted to buy as much time as possible for Chad. "My name is Katia Daniels, and I am the executive director at the Pike County Group Home for Negro Boys. Sir, these two boys are in my care. Chad here is traumatized. Is it possible for us to make a statement once I get him back to my house, where they both have been staying for the holidays? You can follow us there," I said.

He looked at me for a moment, and then his eyes shifted from Chad to Pee Wee. Before he said anything, Mrs. Cherry inserted herself between us.

"Hello there, Officer Perryman. Good to see you. How's your mama?" She had a huge smile on her face.

He smiled back at her. "Just fine, ma'am. Mama was grateful for the casserole you sent over the other week. She's feeling much better."

"Good," she said, placing her hand on his arm. "You do right by my friends here. They've been through a lot today. You hear?"

"Yes, ma'am, Mrs. Cherry." He then looked back at me. "I will follow you to your home, ma'am."

I didn't want to take a chance that he might change his mind. "Let's go, boys." I hugged and thanked Mrs. Cherry.

Chad got up slowly and took my hand. I squeezed it. I then reached my other hand for Pee Wee's. When we got close to Seth, Chad barreled into his arms. Seth held Chad close, patting him on his back. I reached for Chad's arm. We needed to go. I didn't want the policeman to change his mind.

"I'll follow y'all back home. I'll be right behind you," Seth said reassuringly.

I was grateful he was going back to the house with us. I felt as if my strength was waning, so knowing he'd be there reassured me.

"Let's go, boys," I said as we all made our way out of The Mercantile. I prayed that Chad would be able to tell the police what they needed to know. And then I prayed he'd be able to somehow put this awful ordeal behind him.

14

AS SOON AS I STOPPED THE truck, Chad jumped out and ran toward the house. Leon's truck was gone. I didn't have time to wonder about that. I could tell Pee Wee was about to sprint after Chad, so I reached out and stopped him.

"Let him have a moment, Pee Wee. Or would you rather be called Mason?" Pee Wee ducked his head. I rubbed his shoulder. "It's okay if you want to be called by your given name now. I think Mason is a wonderful name."

He looked up and smiled, although the sadness and fear remained in his eyes. "P-P-Pee Wee is g-g-good. I j-j-just didn't want that wh-wh-white lady to think I didn't have a r-r-real name, like y-y-you and Ch-Ch-Chad."

Once again his stuttering was pronounced. He obviously was stressed. I looked up at the porch where Mama was now standing. From a distance, I could tell she wasn't in a great mood. I turned my attention back to Pee Wee.

"Well, I think it's pretty cool that you have two names. You wear both of those names well, Mason 'Pee Wee' Jones."

Pee Wee didn't say anything. I watched him closely. He always packed his emotions away. It was a coping mechanism, but I wanted him to know he didn't have to do that with me. "I was scared, too, Pee Wee."

Wordlessly, he scooted over and laid his head against me. I put my arms around him just as Seth and Officer Perryman drove into the yard, parking their vehicles next to mine. Pee Wee glanced up, a look of terror on his face.

"Is he g-g-gone t-t-take Chad to j-j-jail?" Pee Wee's voice was barely above a whisper, like he was afraid the policeman could hear our conversation.

"No, Pee Wee. He's not here to do anything to Chad. Chad did nothing wrong. We should get out of the truck now and go talk to the officer." I gave him one more hug and opened my door as Mama ran toward us.

"What's going on, Katia? What is this policeman doing in our yard and what's wrong with Chad? He ran clean past me with nary a word." Mama's face was beyond distraught. She was wringing her hands. "And you and I need to talk about other things, and you know what," she hissed.

Before I could answer, the officer walked over to where we were standing.

"Hello again, Miss Daniels. Is the boy available for me to ask him a few questions?" he asked.

Mama was uncomfortable being around the police. Images of white police officers bashing in heads on the Edmund Pettus

Bridge in Selma, Alabama, were still fresh in our minds, even though that was two years ago. Troy was a small community, and we all knew John Lewis's family, so when Mama saw how they'd done John, bloodying and battering him nearly unconscious, she was inconsolable for days. Because of the nature of my work, I was more relaxed around the police, but not by much. I reached over and touched Mama's arm. She jumped and looked at me with fear in her eyes.

"Mama, this is Officer Perryman. He's here because of an incident that happened when we were downtown. Chad's mother and her boyfriend tried to get him to go with them. Officer Perryman just needs to ask Chad some questions. Would you mind going to get him?" I wanted to offer her a way out of being present for this questioning, but Mama looked at me like I was crazy.

"I ain't going nowhere," she said in a firm voice.

I turned to Pee Wee. "Pee Wee, go tell Chad I said to come outside, please."

Pee Wee nodded and ran for the house. Seth made his way over to us.

"Hello, Mrs. Daniels," he said to Mama. He came and stood by me, giving me a quick hug, which I so appreciated.

"Hey, Seth," she said, looking from me to him. "You know about this?"

"Yes, ma'am," he said, removing his baseball cap and running his fingers through his hair. "I was there when it happened—or rather, I came up at the end of it."

"When what happened, exactly?" she asked, looking back at me.

I filled her in on the details, and as I talked, Officer Perryman occasionally stopped me with his own questions. Mama was beside herself.

"They could have killed y'all," she exclaimed several times.

"It's okay, Mama," I said, reaching over and grabbing her hand. "Seth was there, and he defused the situation." I tried to smile at Seth. Recounting what had happened and realizing the danger overwhelmed me. I glanced toward the door, wondering where the boys were.

Finally, Chad and Pee Wee came outside. Chad dragged his feet, looking like it would take nothing for him to run off. Pee Wee, who must have sensed what Chad was feeling, took his hand and guided him toward us. In that moment, Pee Wee seemed more like the older of the two.

"Hello, Chad," Officer Perryman said, looking at Chad with a serious expression. "I have some questions for you."

I prayed that Officer Perryman would be sensitive to the fact that while Chad might have the stature of a grown man, he was a young boy. Mama must have been thinking something similar, because she reached for Chad and pulled him close. Chad didn't say anything. He just looked at the officer, seemingly prepared for the worst.

"How do you know the two people involved in this incident?" Officer Perryman had his notebook out and his voice was clipped and businesslike. I tried to make eye contact with Chad, but his gaze stayed directed at the ground.

"Chad," I called out softly. "Answer Officer Perryman."

"I don't know nothing," he mumbled, still not looking up.

Seth moved toward him and patted his back. Seth and Mama looked like two ushers at church, standing with a fallen sinner between them at the altar.

"Speak up, boy, so I can hear you," Officer Perryman snapped. He was clearly getting impatient with the entire process. I imagined he'd never taken this much time with a case involving a Black person. "Who were the two people trying to get you to go with them? How do you know them? Don't waste my time, boy."

Chad whimpered and shifted closer to Mama. She tightened her arm around him and glared at Officer Perryman. Seth looked like he was about to say something, so I jumped in.

"He's afraid," I said quickly. "Chad, look at me." I didn't want to raise my voice, but I needed him to snap out of his reverie enough to get through these questions. "Chad, I said look at me—now." His head popped up faster than a jack-in-the-box. "Officer Perryman needs you to say out loud who the two people were. It's okay. Just tell him."

"The woman was my mama, Lena," he said gruffly. "The other one was her man, Cobra."

"Where are your mama and Cobra now?"

Chad looked at me with a helpless expression.

"We don't know," I interjected. "As I explained, Chad lives at the Pike County Group Home for Negro Boys. I can reach out to his social worker on Monday and try to find out exactly where Lena and Cobra are staying."

"What did your mother and this man—Cobra, as you call him—want with you?" Officer Perryman asked, turning back to face Chad. The policeman was tapping his foot, appearing frustrated with all of us. I prayed that everyone, but especially Chad, kept his cool. Pee Wee eased between Chad and Seth, taking Chad's hand in his again.

"He wanted to . . . to . . . to dance," Chad muttered, as the tears began to lap underneath his chin.

"You're okay, baby," Mama said, squeezing Chad around the waist. "We got you. You're doing good."

"Dance?" Officer Perryman snapped. "What you mean 'dance'?"

"Officer Perryman, would you walk over there with me for a second?" I was trying to hold my temper, but this white man was about to really anger me. The tone he was using was not the tone an officer of the law should use with a child—especially a child who was nearly kidnapped by two drug addicts and was still extremely upset and frightened.

He looked at me coldly, grunted, and then followed me across the yard near the swing set.

"'Dance' is Cobra's code word for sex," I said, striving to appeal to whatever better angels were hopefully guiding Officer Perryman's steps. "I don't know if he has ever abused Chad in that way before, but he threatened him with that today."

The officer stared at me for a moment before nodding his head. "I see. Well, I need the boy to tell me these things. No offense, but I can't take your word for it. I'm just following protocol."

"Officer Perryman, I know you are a reasonable man. A God-fearing man, I'm sure," I said as calmly as I could, resisting the urge to cry. "Chad is like a wounded baby bird right now. Please don't ask him to regale you with all the sordid details of his past life with that man. I have folders filled with accounts from him of the physical abuse he experienced at the hands of Cobra and others, and if you check with the Troy police and the Pike County Sheriff's Office, you'll find numerous police reports about the abuse Chad has experienced. I am begging you not to put him through any more today. Please."

Officer Perryman seemed like he might want to argue with me, but instead, he responded in a weary voice. "I just need him to explain what happened today. Then I'll get the rest of the information from you, our records, and the sheriff department's records."

"Thank you," I said, letting out a deep breath. "I appreciate your kindness."

He gave me a curt nod, and then we walked back to where everyone was standing. This time Officer Perryman asked Chad only a few questions, to confirm what me, Seth, and some of the onlookers had already told the policeman. Once he was satisfied with the answers, he thanked us and left. After he drove off, none of us said anything. I think we were all shell-shocked—I knew I was. This afternoon had worn me out, and I knew it had done the same to Chad.

"Miss Katia, can I go lay down?" Chad asked. Mama, Seth, and Pee Wee were protectively clustered close to him. I went and stood in front of him, putting my hands lightly on his cheeks, which were still wet with tears.

"I am so sorry this happened to you today. If I could take away what you are feeling right now, I would." I wished I could cram his pain inside me and carry it so he wouldn't have to. I hated that we'd run into Lena and that awful monster of a man.

Chad nodded but didn't speak. The tears started to roll down his face again, and I could tell that he was emotionally spent.

"You go on in the house and rest a bit," I said, hugging him. "I'll come check on you in a little while." If I thought talking would help him, I'd push the issue, but he needed to go somewhere and sleep this off or at least rest his mind.

"You w-w-want me to g-g-go with y-y-you?" Pee Wee looked up at Chad hopefully, but the older boy shook his head.

"Not right now. Just . . . just give me a minute," he said, and without another word he ran into the house.

Instantly, Pee Wee started crying. The way I was feeling, I could have joined him. I was almost out of energy to deal with even one more meltdown, including my own. Seth must have sensed it because he squeezed my shoulder and then plastered a smile on his face.

"Hey, Pee Wee," Seth said, putting a hand on Pee Wee's shoulder. "How about you and me take a little walk? I saw a deer dart across the street a few minutes ago. Maybe we can get a glimpse of it up close."

Pee Wee looked up at me, hiccuping slightly as he tried to stop crying. I nodded to let him know he had my permission. For the second time today, I mouthed, *Thank you*, to Seth. He patted my shoulder again as he and Pee Wee slowly wandered toward the wooded area across the street.

"Katia," Mama said, using a tone I hadn't heard since I was much younger. A tone that told me I had more drama to deal with before I could go inside. I wanted to collapse into the recliner in the living room, not deal with Mama's fury. I wanted the sounds of Nina Simone singing to envelop me like a warm blanket on a cold winter's night. I didn't want to listen to more angry words, but as I raised my eyes to look at my mother, I knew that was exactly what I was about to do: receive an earful of vitriol.

I sighed and answered her the way I always did. "Ma'am?"

"I know you have a lot on your mind, Katia, but we need to discuss the situation with Leon," she said in a stern, no-nonsense voice. "I am not pleased. At all."

"Mama, can't we talk about this another time? I need to write out a report of what all happened today with Chad," I said. I did need to fill out a report, but it could wait. No one would see it until Monday anyway. And I could tell by one look at Mama's face that she wasn't picking up what I was putting down.

"No, ma'am. I want to deal with this now. How in the world could you have encouraged that man to come say what he said to me?" she demanded, her voice full of righteous indignation. "How could siccing that man on me make any kind of sense to you, Katia? How?"

"Mama, I did not sic anybody on you," I said wearily. "Leon confessed to me on Thanksgiving that he had feelings for you, not for me. All I said to him was it wouldn't hurt my feelings if the two of you did decide to date."

"How you gone pass a man around like he's a collection plate at Sunday service?" she said. "And you actually thought I would want a man my daughter had dated? You think I'm just some no-account woman like that?"

"Oh, Mama," I said and tried to pull her into an embrace. She was reluctant, but she didn't pull away. "I think you are the most amazing woman there is, and I would never do anything to disrespect you. If you don't think Leon is a good man for you, then I honor that opinion."

"Nobody said he wasn't a good man," she mumbled. "I just don't like how any of this looks. Can you imagine what people would say? First, he was with the daughter and now he's with the mother? Just scandalous. Just plain scandalous, Katia."

"Mama, if you and Leon went forward with a relationship, it would look like a good, godly woman was saying yes to a good, godly man," I said. "Who cares what other people think? Life is too short. If you're remotely interested in Leon, you have my blessing—not that you need it. And if anyone says anything about it, they can come and talk to me." Mama shook her head. I kissed her forehead. "Just think about it. No rush. You know Leon. He has the patience of Job, so however long you need to think about this, take that time. He's not going anywhere. How did y'all end the conversation?"

She lifted her chin defiantly. "I told him this was highly inappropriate and unless he wanted to sit and watch *The Lone Ranger* with me, I didn't have anything else to say."

I stifled the laughter bubbling up inside me, threatening to escape, because Mama surely would have given my butt a good pop. "What did he say?"

"He said he didn't think it would be appropriate for him to stay and watch television with me, and he left," she said. Part of her obviously was miffed by his departure whether she admitted it to herself or not.

"Everything will work out the way it should," I said. "Isn't that what you always tell me and the boys?"

"I don't have time for this, Katia," she said, tears shining in her eyes. "I have a son missing in action and another one who is fighting to maintain his sanity. This is not what I need on top of all of that."

"Oh, Mama," I said, hugging her tightly. "Maybe having a man who can love on you and tell you everything is going to turn out fine is just what you need. You ever thought about that?"

Just then, we both turned at the sound of Pee Wee and Seth coming back into the yard. Pee Wee's voice was excited, so Seth had been able to get the boy's mind off everything that was going on.

"Miss K-K-Katia! Gr-Gr-Gran!" he yelled.

"Slow down, Pee Wee," I called back. "Take your time."

"We saw a d-d-deer and we s-s-saw a sq-sq-squirrel. I want to g-g-go get Ch-Ch-Chad and show him," he said, hopping from one foot to the other. "Is th-th-that okay?"

"Absolutely," I said. "But if he's inside the bedroom with the door closed, make sure you knock first."

"Yes, m-m-ma'am," he said as he took off running, but he stopped before entering the house. "Mr. S-S-Seth. Don't l-l-leave. Okay?"

"I won't. I'll stay right here until you get back," Seth said with a grin.

The three of us laughed as Pee Wee ran into the house, breaking Mama's cardinal rule of slamming the door. But considering the afternoon we'd all had, one slammed door didn't seem to be that big of a deal right now.

"Seth, I don't know how to thank you for everything you did today," I said, swallowing hard so I wouldn't get choked up. "If that awful man would have . . . had he been able to . . ." I couldn't continue.

Seth rested his hand on my arm. "It's okay, Kat. I know those boys mean a lot to you. I'm grateful that I was there to intervene."

Pee Wee ran back out of the house, waving a piece of paper in his hand, letting the door slam behind him once more.

"Pee Wee, I let you get away with one slam of my door, but now you need to slow down," Mama scolded. "Where's—"

Pee Wee didn't wait for her to finish. He interrupted, something he seldom did, which immediately caused me to be alarmed. "M-M-Miss K-K-Katia. Ch-Ch-Ch . . ."

"Take your time, Pee Wee," I said, placing my hands on his shoulders. "What's wrong?"

"R-r-read," he managed to spit out.

I took the piece of paper from his hand, recognizing Chad's slanty handwriting.

> Dear Miss ~~Kacia~~, I mean, Katia,
>
> I'm sorry, but I can't stay. I ~~ain't~~ am not gone let them send me back to Lena. I ~~ain't~~ am not letting Cobra get at me no more. No more dancing. I'll call you when I find a safe place to stay. Tell Pee Wee he my brother for life and when I figure out how to take care of myself, I'll come looking for him so I can take care of him too. Brothers

have to stick together. Don't be sad, Miss Katia. You did the best you could. Tell Mr. Jason I preshate all he did for me. Tell Gran her present from me and Pee Wee is on her bed. Tell her it ~~ain't~~ is not real toilet water. Your present is on your bed too.

Love,

Chad

"Dear God," I moaned.

"Let's go," Seth said quickly. "He can't be far. Let's go in my truck. We'll find him."

"Mama, stay by the phone and don't let Pee Wee out of your sight!" I yelled as I turned to leave, but then I paused and looked at Pee Wee. "Don't you worry, Pee Wee."

I ran toward Seth's truck, where he was getting into the driver's seat. My hip hurt from all the physical emotion I had been exerting today, but I paid it no mind. I just wanted Chad back with us before something terrible happened, and my intuition was telling me that he was heading headlong toward something awful. I opened the passenger-side door and got in beside Seth. For a brief second, I closed my eyes and silently prayed. *Please, protect him. Don't allow any more pain to come his way.*

15

FINDING CHAD FELT MORE AND MORE unlikely as the day progressed. As the minutes and hours slipped by, it seemed that Chad had done everything in his power not to be found. Every passing second caused my panic to rise. Seth wisely didn't try to converse as we drove around. He just asked for suggestions on where to look next. Other than that, we rode in silence.

Seth and I had driven up and down every backcountry road near my house, and then we drove up and down the streets of Troy, stopping anywhere we thought someone might have seen him, from the barbershop where Jason took the boys for haircuts to the local high school where various boys were hanging out playing basketball on the playground. No one had seen him. We even stopped at The Mercantile to see if Mrs. Cherry had by chance seen him walk by. She said she hadn't seen Chad but she'd keep her eyes open. When we left the store, I told Seth we should probably head home. As soon as we drove into the yard, the back door swung open and Pee Wee ran outside. He probably had been standing watch for a while. It was crushing to see the expression on Pee Wee's face when he saw we didn't have Chad with us. His expression also told me that Chad hadn't returned.

"Wh-wh-where is h-h-he?" Pee Wee said as he opened the passenger door for me. He was angry and frustrated, but his manners were still intact. Yet another small victory to celebrate. We taught the boys to always put being kind at the top of their list of things to do, even when they didn't particularly feel like being kind.

"I don't know." I put my hand on his shoulder as we all walked back inside the house. Mama looked up at me expectantly, and I shook my head. Her shoulders slumped. I hated having to be the bearer of more bad news. "Listen, y'all, I am going to do everything I possibly can to bring him back. Just don't give up hope. Okay?"

Both Mama and Pee Wee nodded. Pee Wee knew Chad was smart, and if the older boy didn't want to be found, he knew how to stay hidden. Troy, Alabama, wasn't a big town by any stretch, but if a person really wanted to hide and not be seen here, it was absolutely possible to do. And for someone like Chad, who was used to being on the streets, I feared that our efforts wouldn't have a good outcome.

Marcus, who walked into the room shortly after we returned, was kind enough to offer to take Pee Wee to the living room while I made some phone calls. He kissed my cheek before they left the kitchen.

"You're doing the best you can. But you can't save everybody," he said in my ear before leading Pee Wee toward the living room. I wondered if he was referring to Chad or also to himself. I prayed not. I'm greedy. I wanted to save them all. I didn't want to lose Chad or any of my group home boys, and I didn't want to lose my brothers.

I sat down by the stand where Mama kept the house phone. I slowly dialed the first number from memory. That call was to Jason. He and I stayed in constant communication, so his number came to me almost as easily as my own. When he answered, I filled him in on what was happening and asked him to reach out to the other houseparents. I needed all hands on deck, combing the streets for Chad. I also called Chad's social worker and her supervisor at their home numbers, but no one answered. Which I'd expected, since both women said they'd be out of town for the holidays. Probably the soonest I'd be able to speak to either of them would be Monday, and by then I hoped to have Chad back with me. Next I called the police and reported him missing. They assured me they'd send someone out to look for him. They also suggested I stay at home in case he returned, but I wasn't ready to give up on the search. Plus, I'd go stir-crazy sitting around twiddling my thumbs. I needed to feel like I was doing something. Finally, I called Sam Arrington IV, the board president.

"What you mean he's missing?" Sam said angrily.

I explained once more what had happened, from the incident at The Mercantile to Chad running off after we returned home.

"You should have called me the second the police got involved," he said, his voice rising with anger. "This situation is out of hand, Katia. You've made a mess of things. Find that boy, and y'all get yourselves back to the group home. I expect regular updates."

"Yes, Mr. Arrington," I said. I took deep breaths after I hung up the phone. He was right—I had made a mess of things. Nothing my staff had done the day Chad had his outburst measured up to this, and I had no one to blame but myself.

I felt a hand on my shoulder. It was Seth.

"Where to next?" he asked. I was grateful he didn't ask me about the phone call. It would hurt too much if I saw that he agreed with Sam. However, even though I appreciated his commitment to sticking with me on this search for Chad, I didn't feel right asking him to continue to ride around, especially since my heart told me it was a lost cause. I could have kicked myself for not picking up on the signs. Chad wasn't in a good place after the morning's incident, and I should have stayed with him and forced him to talk through his emotions. The only good thing about this situation— and calling it "good" was a stretch—was that Pee Wee didn't run off with him.

"Seth, you have done enough today," I said as I went to the hallway coat closet, Seth following close behind me. The temperature outside was continuing to drop, and if I'd be driving for a while tonight looking for Chad, I needed a warm jacket. Instantly, my hand went to Daddy's coat. Sometimes when I was feeling particularly lonely or sad, I put on Daddy's coat and my spirits lifted.

I even kept his favorite brand of pipe tobacco, by John Middleton, in the coat's breast pocket. The walnut scent transported me back to cold evenings on the front porch, sitting on Daddy's lap as he filled the air with the sweet, woodsy smell from his pipe.

Seth helped me into it, and when I turned around, he put a hand on each of my shoulders.

"I'm not going to let you do this alone, Kat. We're in this together." He had a firm look on his face. Such a kind man, always wanting to help others.

"I just don't know where to go next, Seth," I said, trying not to feel defeated. "We've gone to all of the places that I know to look. He's probably hunkered down in the woods or hiding in some old abandoned building. There are dozens of places he could be, not to mention that, by now, he may have hitchhiked to God knows where with God knows whom."

Seth draped his arm around me. I warmed to his touch but reminded myself it was nothing more than a friend consoling a friend. "Then we'll start all over again and revisit the same spots, just in case. With so many people looking for him, we're bound to find a clue. We have to be patient and not give up hope. Like you said to Pee Wee."

I nodded. I went and told Mama that Seth and I were leaving. She was back in the kitchen, sitting by the phone. I knew she was hoping, just like me, that someone would call and say they found Chad. Even in this short period of time, I knew she'd grown fond of both boys. I tried not to feel guilty for being part of the cause of her grief. Loving people is simply what Mama did. I wouldn't have been able to stop her from worrying, even if she didn't know Chad and had only heard about him in passing. Yet another reason why I loved her so much and wished that she could find happiness with someone other than Daddy.

"Y'all be careful out there," she said, standing up from her chair. "Them redneck boys take to the streets after dark. I don't want to see something happen to y'all too."

"We'll be careful," I said, kissing her cheek. "I won't be late. We're going to revisit a few more places, and then we'll call it a night."

Mama looked up at Seth. "Thank you for going with my daughter. I'd be scared to death if she tried to go searching for that boy on her own."

"I wouldn't have it any other way, ma'am," he said with a smile.

"Be back soon, Mama," I said and walked toward the door. I turned around. "You should call your friend."

"What friend are you . . . ?" She stopped, her face turning into a grimace. "Girl, hush. I don't have time for all of that. Leave sleeping dogs where they are."

I laughed a little and then went out the door. It was a bit of a stress relief to tease Mama. I needed all the laughs I could get at the moment.

Seth followed me out of the door. I noticed that his limp was a bit more pronounced.

"Do you want me to drive?" I asked. "You seem tired."

"I can drive a truck," he snapped and then reached out and placed his hand on mine. "I'm sorry. That was uncalled for. You were just being nice. I am still learning the difference between kindness and pity. Forgive me."

"Nothing to forgive," I said. "We're both tired. Let's just go. You drive."

We got back on the road, starting the process all over again. Like before, we didn't talk much. Just as I feared, we continued to run into the same dead ends. No lone Black boys were walking along the roads, and I supposed that in and of itself was a blessing. The idea of some "redneck boys," as Mama called them, stopping and harassing Chad was more than I could manage to think about. That wouldn't bode well for Chad. But the other alternatives were equally grim.

Our one glimmer of hope occurred when we stopped at the school. A couple of young Black boys were milling around the playground—one taller and one shorter, reminding me of Chad and Pee Wee. The streetlights illuminated the spot, casting an eerie glow over the basketball court. I didn't recognize the boys, but that wasn't surprising. A lot of people were moving to Troy, and as much as I tried to integrate myself into the community and get to know folks, I hadn't had the pleasure of meeting many of the new Black families.

Seth and I introduced ourselves to the boys, but neither one of them seemed interested in revealing their names. When I explained who I was looking for, the one who appeared to be the oldest of the two looked at us suspiciously.

"Y'all cops?" he asked as he dribbled a ball between his legs, keeping an eye on us the entire time. The other boy glared at Seth and me as if he already knew something wasn't right about the two of us, but he was letting the older boy take the lead.

I shook my head. "No. We're just two people who care very much about Chad's safety. That's all." I didn't think it wise for me to bring up the group home. I understood that these boys mistrusted all types of authority and, often, rightly so. The system hadn't always been good to boys like Chad. I understood how I could be perceived as the enemy too.

The older boy gave us both a curt nod. "How much it worth to you for me to tell you what I know?" he asked, eyeing me slyly. I doubted this was this first time he'd made "deals" for information.

"It's worth everything to me," I said in a steady voice, trying my best to keep the panic from rising and bubbling over. Seth placed a hand on the small of my back. I glanced at him gratefully. Several times today he'd been the reason why I hadn't dissolved into hysterics, a feeling I wasn't accustomed to, mainly because most of my life had revolved around me being everyone else's rock. These last few months had forced me to acknowledge that I also needed to be vulnerable and taken care of sometimes, and needing those things didn't make me weak. It merely made me human.

I looked at the young man standing before us, trying to come up with words that would move him to share what he knew. "Young man, Chad—the boy we are looking for—is potentially in harm's way, and all I . . . we . . . want to do is save him from any more pain in his life. Can you understand that?" I reached inside my purse for my wallet and pulled out two ten-dollar bills and seven ones. "That's all I have. That's it. Is that enough? Will you please tell us what you know about Chad's whereabouts?"

"We ain't gone say no to no money," the youngest one said as he came and snatched the money out of my hands and handed it to the older boy. For a split second, I thought they might bolt, but they stayed put, the older one continuing to bounce his ball and the younger one glaring, in an attempt to appear tough. He reminded me of a tougher version of Pee Wee.

"About an hour after y'all left here the first time, he showed up," the older boy said in a flat voice, tucking the basketball underneath his arm. "He sat over there watching us play ball until finally a car pulled up, and the dude in the car motioned for y'all's boy to get in. A woman was in the car too. Your boy tried to run, but the dude ran after him and then made him get inside the car. Wasn't long before they rode off. That's all we know."

"Oh my word," I said. Cobra and Lena had found Chad.

"That's all the info I got for y'all," the older boy said.

"Thank you," I said. "I appreciate your help."

"I'm only telling you because I don't like seeing grown folks screw with young kids," he said. "I'm in the streets, but the streets ain't in me, if you get what I'm saying."

Seth patted him on the back. "I get it, young blood. Good looking out."

I thanked them again and followed Seth back to his truck. Once we were seated inside, Seth sighed.

"This situation is going to be more complicated than we previously thought, Kat," he said, putting his key into the ignition and starting the truck with a loud roar. "I think we need to go to the police."

"I understand what you're saying, Seth. I'm not ruling out involving the police," I said. "But we both know how quickly things like this can escalate when Black- and brown-skinned boys are involved. I have to try to find him and deescalate the situation, if possible. I don't have a current address for her. From what I can tell, she is either living on the streets or living with Cobra."

"I know a few places we could go and try to get some information," Seth said in a grim voice. "Reach down and pull out the box underneath your seat."

I looked at him curiously, but I did what he asked. I pulled out the heavy metal box and placed it on the seat between Seth and me. Even before he opened the box, my heart quickened, and when he pulled out a handgun, I gasped.

"What are you going to do with that, Seth?" I demanded.

"Nothing, I hope. This is insurance," he said. "I'm not putting us in harm's way without protection. If you want to be the hero tonight, we very likely will need backup. That gun is our backup."

"Seth, I don't want guns involved," I said softly. "I know this Cobra is a character, but bringing a gun will only escalate things."

"Kat, I don't want guns involved either," he said. "But I also don't want to get caught with my pants below my legs—excuse the metaphor. So, let's get this over with before it gets any later. I know some guys who might know where Cobra hangs out. Troy is a small town. Roughnecks know about other roughnecks."

Once again we rode in silence. I couldn't shake my fear over having a gun sitting between us, but more than that, I couldn't fathom not at least trying to rescue Chad from his mama and Cobra—especially Cobra. We rode around until Seth finally stopped at a local hole-in-the-wall juke joint known for violence, gambling, and prostitution. One might think the police would have shut it down, but from what I'd heard, some of them frequented the spot too. Judging from the cars parked outside, they had a full house tonight. If Mama knew I was at a place like this, she'd have a fit.

"I'm gonna go inside and see what I can find out," Seth said, reaching inside the metal box for the gun. I put my hand on top of his before he picked it up.

"Seth, please," I begged. "Maybe we should go contact the police like you said before. I don't want something to happen to . . . to anyone." I wanted to say, *You. I don't want anything to happen to you, Seth.* But I didn't.

He reached over and lightly touched my shoulder. "I'll be fine. Remember, even with this bum leg, I'm still a Marine at my core. These local thugs ain't got nothing on what I've seen. No one will even know I have the gun unless they force me to reveal it. I'm just going to ask a few questions. Slide over into the driver's seat. If anything pops off, I want you to hightail it out of here. Okay?"

"I'll get in the driver's seat, but I'm not leaving without you. Seth, please be careful."

He slid the gun inside his pocket. "I'll be right back."

I could barely make out his shadowy frame as he limped toward the run-down juke joint. I heard loud music playing inside. I prayed that the people were so engrossed in the music that no one would be interested in starting trouble.

I continued to pray silently, and a few minutes later Seth returned to the truck. I slid back to the passenger side with relief.

"We're in luck. I saw a dude I knew, and he said Cobra and some woman live out near Goshen in a trailer park. I know right where it is," Seth said. "Do you want to go check it out?"

Part of me knew we should probably leave well enough alone

and go to the police, but I knew firsthand that the police wouldn't do much. I looked at Seth. Even though it was too dark to see his face, I knew he'd do whatever I asked.

"Let's go get Chad," I said, praying I wouldn't regret my words.

Seth started the truck and drove out of the parking lot, the sounds of the juke joint filling the night air. I didn't know what we were about to encounter, but I sure hoped it involved bringing Chad back home.

16

WHEN WE GOT TO THE TRAILER park, my heart felt like it might leap outside of my chest it was beating so fast. Part of me wanted to tell Seth to turn around. Everything about this situation felt wrong, but I didn't say anything. At this point, I was too nervous to even try to formulate a prayer.

The more we drove around, the more I wondered why Cobra and Lena would pick this trailer park, of all places, to reside even temporarily. It was only a few steps above a garbage dump. If I didn't know better, I would think these were old abandoned trailers, but clearly people lived here. It was sad to think of anyone residing in places like this, let alone Chad.

There were only a few cars scattered about, and half of them were propped on cinder blocks. None of the vehicles we saw matched the car we'd seen Cobra and Lena in earlier. I'm not sure why, but I was surprised that the trailer park was filled with white folks—or at least that's who was sitting outside underneath a tree, with a fire burning inside a trash can. Seeing a sea of white faces in the moonlit evening was unnerving.

"We should get out of here," I said in a loud whisper, as if the white men outside could see or hear us inside the truck.

"We came all this way," Seth said. "Let me just pull up to those fellas by the tree over there and see what they say. I won't even get out."

I noticed that he'd slipped the gun out of his pocket and placed it between us. I don't know what terrified me most—the men by the open fire or Seth's gun.

When Seth stopped by the tree, one of the white men walked over to us. He was a tall, skinny man who appeared to have had some rough days in his life. Even in the dark, his posture had a defeated look about it. Again, I wondered why Cobra and Lena were lying low in a place like this. As Seth rolled down his window, the deep, earthy scent of reefer filled the air.

"Y'all looking for something or somebody?" the white man asked, his southern drawl so thick it made his words almost unrecognizable.

"We're looking for Cobra," Seth said. "He around?"

"Cobra comes and goes, but he ain't been around for a minute. Can I help you?" he asked. Even though his voice sounded friendly enough, I was beginning to feel nervous.

"I don't think so," Seth said. "I appreciate your offer of help."

"Ain't nothing Cobra can do for y'all that I can't," he said, shifting his weight, as he spat out a wad of tobacco, then took a long gulp from a beer can before crumpling it and throwing it to the ground. "Unless y'all is the law."

Suddenly his previous pleasantness was replaced by a surliness that made me glance at Seth, who seemed calm enough, so I tried to match his energy. I focused on controlling my breathing instead of letting out a cry of fear.

"I said no thank you, and no, we are not the law," Seth said and began rolling up his window. But the man stepped closer to the truck and reached inside, grabbing at Seth's left arm. I was surprised by the man's strength. Before I could say or do anything, Seth picked up his gun and aimed it toward the man's head. Seeing Seth with that gun, ready to shoot, forced me to suppress a scream that rose in my throat. "Get your hand off me, now. I said no thank you. Now move away from my truck so me and the lady can leave. Don't test me tonight."

The white man raised his hands in the air and backed away from the truck. The second he moved away, Seth peeled off. I was terrified that we might have gunfire at our backs, but neither the man nor his companions did anything. Once we were back on the road, Seth slowed down.

"Are you okay?" he asked.

"I'm okay," I said, even though my teeth were chattering. I gulped air until I was calmer. "I'm so sorry for getting us into this situation. I think we should call it a night." As much as I wanted to keep searching, I realized we were out of leads, and at this point, Chad could be anywhere.

"I'm sorry," Seth said. "I wasn't planning on any of this happening."

"I know," I said. "But this has become way too dangerous. You were right. We should have contacted the police and allowed them to handle things. I just worried that . . ."

"I worried about the same things," he said. "Involving the cops any more than they already are over the disappearance of a young Black boy could go any number of ways, few of them good. To be honest, I thought we might find him here, but we'll keep our eyes and ears open. What's next?"

"I go home and call the chair of the board, and then Monday I face the music with social services—more specifically, Chad's caseworker," I said in a voice that sounded weary even to my ears.

"If you want to go back out tomorrow, just give me a call. I'll be at church the first half of the day, but I should be home a little after one in the afternoon," Seth said.

"Thank you, Seth." I reached over and touched his arm. "I appreciate everything you have done today. I truly do."

"Anytime," he said. "There are a lot of good people looking for Chad, Kat. I'm hopeful that someone will see him. Keep the faith."

"I'm going to try my best," I said.

I stared out the window as Seth drove. The roads were empty. It was as if the entirety of Pike County had turned in for the night. I tried to hold back the tears. I put my hand over my mouth to stifle a sob, but it was too late. The floodgates burst wide open.

"Slide over," Seth said, his voice gruff. I didn't think about his words, I just scooted closer and allowed him to pull me close. As we turned onto my road, I took several deep breaths, determined to tame my emotions. I couldn't go into the house like this.

Seth drove into the yard and parked underneath the pecan tree my family and I liked to gather under for picnics. He rubbed my back in such a tender way, it almost set me off into another torrent of tears.

"You okay, Kat?"

"I'm okay," I managed. His arms felt good around me, but I was afraid to crave his affection even in a moment like this. Especially in a moment like this. Men like Seth never stuck around for women like me. I wasn't the pretty former cheerleader like his ex-wife, Denise. I was just Katia. The woman whom men wanted as their friend and nothing else. I slid toward the passenger door. "I'm just a bit overwhelmed. Oh, who am I kidding? I am *very* overwhelmed. I'm sorry for falling apart on you. This isn't like me at all."

"You have every right to feel overwhelmed, Kat," he said. "You and your family are going through a lot, and now this Chad situation is only adding fuel to a large fire. I can't imagine what you must be feeling right now. It's okay for you to not be strong sometimes."

The house was dark. I imagined everyone was in bed, although I knew without a doubt that Mama was still awake, waiting for the sound of Seth's truck to drive into the yard.

I squeezed his hand. "Thank you, Seth. I appreciate everything you've done today to help. I'll let you know how things go. And I'll see you at the group home on Monday." As much as I appreciated Seth's offer to help me look for Chad the next day, I felt as if I had to say no, because the more I allowed myself to rely on him, the worse it was going to hurt when eventually he gave up on this idea of liking me.

"Okay," he said in a quiet voice. "But if you should need me tomorrow, call me. I'll happily help any way I can."

"Thank you—drive careful," I said, getting out of the truck and closing the door without facing him again.

As I walked toward the house, all I could think about was going to bed. I wanted to block out the day and regroup in the morning. Most nights I fell asleep listening to Nina Simone or Billie Holiday, but tonight I wanted silence. I didn't even want to hear the night sounds of owls hooting or our neighbor's billy goats bleating under the moon.

I'm a problem solver, and for the last couple of weeks I hadn't been able to do much to fix things for the people in my life who depended on me. I hoped that a good night's sleep would get me to the other side of the self-doubt I'd been battling since Chad first went missing.

"You will figure this out," I said to myself as I heard the crunch of Seth's tires as he drove away. When I got to the door, Mama opened it as if she had been waiting there all night. Without a word, I went into her arms and allowed myself to be enveloped by her strong embrace. I was bigger than Mama, but right now she felt ten feet tall. I felt like I used to when kids at school would pick on me for being fat. Mama would grab me into a tight hug and say, *There is just more of you to love, baby girl.*

"Don't you worry none, baby," Mama said. "Everything is going to work out just the way it's supposed to. Leave it in God's hands."

"Thank you, Mama," I said, continuing to stay in her arms. Continuing to let her be the strong one.

Sunday passed in a blur. We woke up and went to church, and then, as soon as service was over, I went with Jason to look for Chad. My fingers wanted to dial Seth's number, but I fought the impulse. It was better for me to go with Jason, or at least that was what I told myself. He and I drove around for hours searching, and we didn't find even one clue to lead us toward Chad.

"What do you think Mrs. Gates is going to say?" Jason asked after I pulled back into his yard later that afternoon. It was still light outside, but night was rapidly approaching. I just looked at him. He got the picture. "It wasn't your fault."

I smiled sadly. I appreciated his loyalty, but I couldn't let that idea stand. "Chad was in my care. That makes me responsible. That makes it my fault. No one else's. You go on and try to enjoy the rest of your day off."

"Take care, Miss Katia," he said and then exited the truck. I knew he wouldn't find any joy in what remained of our Thanksgiving holiday. Like me, he'd spend the rest of the night trying to figure out where Chad might be.

I watched as Jason slowly walked across the yard toward his house. The defeat he felt showed in how he squared his shoulders. He loved these boys, and he gladly took on the role of older brother or uncle with every boy who came through our doors. That had been especially true with Chad.

The drive home was emotionally draining. I continued to keep my eyes peeled, but I didn't see Chad, Lena, or Cobra, or their car. Once I made it home, I was surprised to see Leon's truck parked in the yard. At first I wasn't sure what to do. Should I go in or stay out? Should I gather up Pee Wee and give Mama and Leon privacy? Did Mama even want privacy? Again, I was unsure of myself, and I hated how this felt. In high school I was voted "Most Likely to Succeed" and "Most Confident Senior." Right now, neither of those monikers felt appropriate.

"Get it together, Katia," I muttered, then stepped out of the truck into the refreshing cool air. I leaned my head back and allowed the late-afternoon chill to wash over me. Before I even reached the back door, Pee Wee bounded out.

"Hey, Miss K-K-Katia. Did you f-f-find Ch-Ch-Chad?" he asked, looking around as though he expected to see his friend trailing behind me.

"I'm afraid not, Pee Wee," I said, putting my arm around his thin shoulders. "I am so sorry. I'm not giving up and neither should you. Are Gran and Mr. Leon talking?" I asked, changing the subject.

"They w-w-watching *Lassie*," he said.

I nodded and smiled. Hopefully the two of them had decided at least to remain friends. For now, that was enough. "That sounds about right. Why don't you and I go inside and get your suitcase packed? Tomorrow we go back to the group home."

His face fell, but he didn't say anything. Sadly, disappointment was something my boys were used to.

"I know you aren't ready for the holiday to end," I said, rubbing his back. "I'm not either, but we do what we have to do. Right?"

"Yes, m-m-ma'am," he said.

Mama met us at the door. I noticed that she'd put her church dress back on and had even applied a bit of pink lipstick. Not her usual *Lassie*-watching clothes. Mama always made sure she looked decent when company was around, even when that company was Leon, but today she seemed to be paying a little extra attention to her appearance. I couldn't help but smile.

"I'll meet you in the bedroom, Pee Wee," I said.

He nodded and hugged Mama before running inside.

"No Chad?" she asked.

I shook my head. "No Chad. I don't know where he could be."

"God's gone work this out. All of it," Mama said.

I walked toward her and slid my arm around her waist. "Looks like God is working something out in the living room."

My mother blushed and shoved me away.

"We watching *Lassie*. That's all," she said.

"That's a start," I said and kissed her cheek as I made my way around her. "I'm going to help Pee Wee pack."

"Make sure you speak to Brother Leon," she said. "You know, if you tried just a little bit, the two of you could probably work things out."

"It's not me that he wants to work things out with, Mama, and that's just fine," I said. "I promise. But I will go speak to him."

I walked to the door of the living room and waved at Leon. He waved back.

"Hey, Katia," he said awkwardly. "I hope you don't mind I stopped by to . . . to . . . to watch *Lassie*."

I almost laughed at his discomfort, but I didn't want to embarrass him any more than he already was. Anyway, I was too tired to play games. This weekend had been long. I just wanted to go to bed—maybe listen to some music or read my latest book.

"No apologies needed," I said. "You and Mama enjoy your shows. I'm turning in. Good night."

On my way to help Pee Wee pack, I peeked in on Marcus. He was already asleep, and judging from his posture, he seemed to be resting okay. When I got to the bedroom the boys had shared, Pee Wee was underneath the covers, lightly snoring. I decided not to bother him. He and I could wake up early the next morning and gather his things.

I continued to walk slowly down the hallway to my bedroom. I didn't even bother to shower. I just slid into my gown, said a quick prayer, and got between the sheets. I hoped that sleep would find me in a hurry because I knew the next day or two were not going to be easy.

17

ONCE PEE WEE SAID HIS GOODBYES to Mama and Marcus, he and I hurried out to my truck and drove to his elementary school. It wasn't far from the house, and Pee Wee spent most of the time talking about Thanksgiving and all the fun he had. As he talked about everything but Chad, I knew he had a lot of sadness, and much of it was centered around Chad's absence, but boys like Pee Wee learned the hard way to find some good in any situation if they could. It was a survival tactic, and Pee Wee did it more than most.

I admit, I was only half listening to him. They say you never worry about the child in front of you—you worry about the child who's out of sight. I understood that quote more than most people, especially right now.

"Have a good day, Pee Wee," I said, reaching over and ruffling his curly hair. He looked at me with hopeful eyes.

"M-m-maybe he'll c-c-come b-b-back today or m-m-maybe he'll b-b-be at school," Pee Wee said. "M-m-maybe."

"I hope so. But you don't worry about that. You just focus on school, and Mr. Jason will pick you up this afternoon. Just like always." I wanted him to know his life still had some continuity and that all he needed to do, as best he could, was focus on being a little boy. I didn't want him carrying the burden of worrying about his friend.

After dropping him off, I went straight to the group home. No one else was there, and I was grateful I'd have privacy to deal with the drama related to Chad. As much as I didn't want to have to call Mrs. Gates, I preferred that she heard about Chad's disappearance from me rather than from a police report landing on her desk. After brewing myself a pot of coffee and pouring myself a large cup, I dialed Mrs. Gates's number. She answered the phone on the first ring.

"Good morning. This is Shirley Anne Gates. May I help you?" she said in that efficient-sounding voice of hers—a voice that sounded like someone who'd never had a child go missing on her watch. Suddenly I felt like a student being brought into the principal's office. I didn't think I could feel worse, but once we started talking, I did.

"Good morning, Mrs. Gates. This is Miss Daniels at the Pike County Group Home for Negro Boys," I said, and rather than draw out this uncomfortable conversation, I quickly filled her in. After I had told her the complete story, for a long while she said nothing.

"This is very disappointing, Miss Daniels," she said. "We trusted you to properly take care of Chad. I will have to write this up. I have no choice but to recommend to DHS that the group home be investigated for negligence. I recognize that these boys are not the cream of the crop, but one would think that you, of all people, would do a better job of keeping them safe, what with you being Negro like them. You've put me in a very precarious position, Miss Daniels."

"I understand," I said, swallowing hard. I wanted to come back with something harsh and biting, but she was within her rights to say what she said. "I would ask that you not penalize the group home. I take full responsibility for everything."

"As you should," she said in a firm voice. "But that changes nothing, Miss Daniels. You represent the group home, and whatever you do affects it. I will be in touch. If you learn anything about Chad's situation, please call me immediately."

I listened as she lightly hung up the phone.

I wanted to cry, but my crying time was over. I'd created this mess, and somehow, someway, I had to fix it.

Next I made another difficult call, to Sam Arrington IV. I phoned his office, not expecting him to be there so early in the morning, but his secretary picked up and immediately transferred the call to his office.

"What news do you have?" he said briskly.

"We still don't know where Chad is," I admitted. "And . . ." I took a deep breath. "Chad's caseworker says she will be recommending DHS investigate the group home for negligence."

Sam released a tirade of angry words laced with profanity. I winced. I wasn't used to being spoken to in that manner. A tear slid down my face, but I kept silent.

"I'm very sorry, Mr. Arrington," I said.   •

"The board will be meeting about this. Today, if possible," he snapped and hung up the phone.

Before I could process everything Mrs. Gates and Sam had told me, the phone rang. I picked it up and said hello.

"Good morning, Miss Daniels," the woman said. "This is Mrs. Gonzalez, Pee Wee's caseworker. I hate to call so early in the morning, but I wanted you to know right away. Late last night, Mason 'Pee Wee' Harrison's mother, Veronica Harrison, died from a heroin overdose. The police are still trying to figure out how she got it in prison, but . . ." She didn't have to continue. We both knew that when inmates wanted to partake in drugs, they'd find a way to do it.

"Have you been able to contact her parents?" I asked.

"The police said her mother and father hung up on them," she said. "The next step is to check about burying her, but if her parents aren't willing to talk, I'm afraid—"

"I'll make sure she's properly buried," I interrupted in a firm voice. There were many things going on that were out of my control, but this—this I could manage. If I had to pay for the funeral out of pocket, I'd make sure Pee Wee's mama got a final resting place. Plus, situations like this had happened before. If I called my church's pastor, he'd help ensure that Veronica Harrison was laid to rest with dignity. "Give me about an hour or two, and I'll call you back. Just make sure they don't . . . dispose of her remains."

"Nothing will happen before I hear from you," she said. "Would you like for me to go to the school and tell Pee Wee?"

"No. Let him finish out his day at school. I'll tell him when he returns to the group home this afternoon." I needed to be the one to tell Pee Wee. It would be hard no matter who shared the news, but I felt like maybe he would take it better if he heard it from me. He tried to act as if he didn't care about his mother, but like any other child, he truly did, regardless of their relationship.

"I'll await your call concerning Miss Harrison's burial. I appreciate your willingness to get involved. Tell Pee Wee I'll come by tomorrow and check on him," she said.

I thanked her, and as soon as I got off the phone I called Pastor Bennett. Just like I expected, he said he'd take care of the details. He even offered to have a small service the day after tomorrow. I was grateful that Pee Wee would get the opportunity to say goodbye. I knew Pastor Bennett would handle things diplomatically, and unlike some pastors in town, he wouldn't judge Pee Wee's mama harshly for the choices she'd made in her life. I remembered him once saying that funerals were for the living, not the deceased.

Normally I stopped at two cups of coffee, but today felt like a three-cup day for sure. I heard a noise out front—probably Seth and his team of workers—so I got up from my desk, poured my third cup of coffee, and walked to the front door just as it swung open. It indeed was Seth.

"Good morning," I said. "How are you doing?"

"Pretty good. This weather has my leg stiffening up a bit, but other than that, I feel fine," he said. "I wanted to check in with you before the fellows started working. I have another job site I need to go to, but I hoped they could begin before it gets too late in the morning."

"Thank you," I said as I smoothed the wrinkles on my suit

pants. Mama hated when I wore pants to work. She said, *"A lady always wears dresses, especially when she is the boss."* Yet another thing she and I didn't see eye to eye on, but she hadn't said anything this morning. I guess she figured I had bigger things to worry about than my attire.

"Is everything okay? Any news about Chad?" Seth asked, the concern clear on his face. It made me feel good that he cared. I told him about the conversations with Chad's caseworker and Sam Arrington IV. I also told him about the passing of Pee Wee's mother.

"Wow. That's terrible. I so feel for Pee Wee," he said. "I'll be saying a prayer for your strength today, Kat. None of this is easy. When I hear about stories like Chad's and Pee Wee's, it makes me feel awful for complaining and whining about my situation."

"Thank you, Seth. I have mountains of paperwork to complete before my new residents show up. If you need any assistance or if you have any questions, just let me know," I said, trying to make my voice as efficient and professional as possible.

He looked at me with an expression I couldn't quite identify.

"The guys are going to start on the roof," he repeated. "That should take them about two days or so. Then we'll get to work on the bathroom. As I mentioned before, the bathroom will take about three weeks, maybe a little longer, but not by much. I promise, my guys are efficient, and they don't waste time. All of them are military vets. They have dealt with their fair share of disappointment and shame, but they work hard, and they just want a chance."

"The work you provide for these men is invaluable, Seth. They are blessed to have you as their advocate and support." I hoped he knew that I meant every word of it. I knew how taxing it could be, trying to be a lifeline for others. This type of work we did, although different, was similar in a lot of ways.

"Thank you," he said. "Kat, I—"

"I'd better get back to that paperwork." I cut him off. I didn't want to get into any more deep conversations this morning.

"Sure," he said slowly. "I'll check in with you later."

The door closed, and I could hear him talking to the men outside. All I wanted to do was follow behind him, but I refocused and went in the opposite direction. When I got to my office, the phone was ringing. It was Mrs. Adelaide Hendricks.

"Katia," she said after we both said hello, "Sam is calling for an emergency meeting of the board. He's fit to be tied."

"When are you meeting?" I asked.

"He wanted to get together today, but I was able to buy you a bit more time. The meeting is scheduled for the end of this week. I'm going to call the other board members and try to reason with them, but I need you to prepare yourself for the possibility that I might not be able to talk them down from letting you go, honey."

I closed my eyes. Sam Arrington IV had been wanting me gone since he'd stepped into the role of board president. Nothing I did seemed to please him, and the issue with Chad became the springboard he needed to ensure my departure.

"I appreciate everything you're doing, Mrs. Hendricks. And I'm sorry you've been put in this position." I felt awful. She was such a nice woman and had always tried to support any initiative I put forward. I'd miss her once she left the board, assuming I remained the executive director until then. Of all the board members we'd had over the years, she was the only one I could honestly say was doing the work for the boys' benefit.

But I didn't have time to dwell on my phone conversation with Mrs. Hendricks. Jason knocked on my door to tell me the two new boys we were expecting had arrived. It turned out, the boys were cousins. The paperwork I'd received didn't mention they were cousins, but their caseworker filled me in on that detail, explaining that the boys' mothers were sisters. She also said both boys asked if they could share a room. I reassured them that we'd make sure that happened. I wanted them to be as comfortable as possible. The older boy, Darren, was fourteen years old, and the other boy, Charlie, was twelve.

The caseworker, Mrs. Crawley, had shared with me that both sets of their parents were arrested for selling drugs and prostituting girls under the age of seventeen. I knew without seeing the police report that none of them would see the light of day anytime soon.

"Welcome to the group home, boys," I said, sitting in the recliner facing the couch where they sat. "We are happy to have you here."

"We ain't staying long," Darren said in a gruff voice, looking down at the floor. "Soon as our granny finds out where we at, she gone come get us."

I looked at Charlie, but he stared at the floor too. When my eyes met the caseworker's, she shook her head. Clearly there was more to the story than the boys were aware of.

"However long you stay, you are welcome," I said and turned to Jason. "Why don't you take the boys upstairs and show them their room? Also, take them to the clothes closet and find them some clean clothes to wear."

"I ain't wearing nobody's raggedy-ass clothes," Darren said. "We ain't no charity case."

"Darren!" Mrs. Crawley said, raising her voice. "Do not speak that way. Say you're sorry. Immediately."

Darren looked away. I knew apologizing wasn't something he was interested in doing, but I had to establish early on that the boys didn't run this group home.

"Darren," I said. "We do not speak to each other that way. I know you're frustrated and angry with a lot of people in your life right now, but you don't get to take your emotions out on others. Do you understand?"

He looked at me. "Yes, ma'am," he grunted.

"Good," I said. For now, that was enough. I suspected that he and I would have many more conversations about attitude and behavior. "Darren, the clothes Mr. Jason will be showing you aren't hand-me-downs. Some very nice people have bought new clothes and donated them to our closet. We have almost any size you can imagine. I'm pretty sure we can find a few things you both can wear until later today when Mr. Jason takes you shopping for anything else you need. We don't want any boy to feel less-than while staying with us, whether that be long term or short term. You'll get to meet the other boys after school is done and they'll be able to share with you about their experiences here."

"Yes, ma'am," Darren said, the exhaustion suddenly showing on his face. He'd processed all that he could for now. His cousin, Charlie, was still silent. I hoped he might warm up to Jason once they were alone.

I looked at Jason and he read my mind, something that often happened between the two of us.

"Let's go, boys," he said, patting Charlie's back. "Time to get you settled in, and Charlie, I want to hear your voice. Right now, I'm wondering if your voice box got lost along the way."

Charlie gave Jason something akin to a smile. It wasn't much, but it was a start. Mrs. Crawley and I watched as they left. I then turned my attention to her.

"Is the boys' grandmother not an option?" I asked.

Mrs. Crawley shook her head. "The maternal grandmother, who's the only other relative in the boys' lives consistently, has expressed that she's too old to take on the burden of raising them. She has quite a few health problems and she has said that Darren and Charlie are too much for her to deal with full-time. Sadly, there are no other relatives who are interested in or capable of taking on raising them."

"Does the grandmother still want to be involved in their lives?" I asked. Sometimes, in cases like this, I was able to work with family members to at least take part in weekly, biweekly, or even monthly meetings. That often staved off a lot of problems, but Mrs. Crawley shook her head again.

"The grandmother says it would be too hard on her because she knows they will constantly beg her to take them with her," Mrs. Crawley said, sadness evident on her face. "I pleaded with her to at least stay in touch with them via phone, but she refused. I get it. Her daughters have put her through a lot. Between the two of them, they have three other children who were taken away. Those children are with their fathers and their families."

This was one of the most challenging parts of our job. It was one thing to have a parent or guardian die. It was another thing altogether for the boys to know they had family but that no one wanted them.

"Well, that's that. Maybe she'll change her mind, but for now we'll deal with the reality of the situation," I said before sighing and leaning back in my chair, trying to stave off a migraine.

Today was already proving to be a day filled with tears and heartbreak, and there was nothing I could do to fix any of it.

18

"D-D-DO I HAVE TO G-G-GO LOOK at h-h-her?" Pee Wee asked as he, Mama, and I drove toward Bethel Missionary Baptist Church, where Pee Wee's mother's funeral would be held. Somehow we had managed to pull this together in just a couple of days. I glanced over at Mama, who was dabbing at a tear. I'd told her that if this would be too much for her, she didn't have to go, but she said she was Pee Wee's gran and she had to be there for him.

Everyone on staff would meet us there. I canceled the Thursday morning staff meeting so that all who wanted to attend could attend. The other boys were in school, but I would not have brought them anyway. This day was all about Pee Wee. We wanted him to feel as if he truly had a family to support him since Veronica's family made it clear that they wouldn't be attending. Their callousness stunned me. I'd spoken to Veronica's mother— Pee Wee's grandmother—and the things she'd said horrified me.

"She laid down with that dirty Black dog and the fleas got her," she said without a hint of emotion in her voice. *"We ain't coming to no funeral to celebrate that life or to be around that mongrel she gave birth to."* Then she hung up,

In some ways, I was grateful they didn't want Pee Wee. He was just Negro enough for them to make his life miserable.

I looked over at him, his face troubled yet without tears. Even when I'd told him she had passed away, he hadn't shed a tear. I knew he'd be distraught with grief, but he merely nodded his head and asked me if he'd be able to stay at the group home. That question nearly broke my heart. This child had been through so much in his short life, and the only stability he'd known was the group home. I reassured him that nothing would change concerning that. He nodded again, but I could see the relief on his face. Then he asked to be excused. I allowed him to go to his room, but I asked Jason to keep an eye on him. I didn't want to have the same situation with Pee Wee that we currently had with Chad. And I couldn't bear the thought of losing another boy.

We still hadn't heard anything from Chad. The police, I was sure, had stopped looking—assuming they'd even bothered to look for him in the first place. Young missing Black boys weren't necessarily top priority on any missing person's list in the South. That was why Jason and some of the other staff continued to go out and talk to people. We couldn't find any sign of him, Lena, or Cobra.

"No," I finally said. "You don't have to go look at her." I remembered how traumatized I was seeing my own daddy in the casket, and I was in my twenties when he died. I made a mental note to enter the church before Pee Wee and make sure the casket was closed. This situation was hard enough. Pee Wee didn't deserve any more trauma related to his mother's untimely death.

When we pulled into the parking lot, the number of cars shocked me.

"Who are a-a-all these p-p-people?" Pee Wee asked.

I turned and looked at Mama. She smiled. "I let folks at church know about Pee Wee's mama passing. I guess a few of them decided to come and pay their respects."

I mouthed, *Thank you*. She nodded and continued smiling.

"Th-th-they came f-f-for M-M-Mama?" Pee Wee asked.

"And you," I said. "Everyone wants you to feel loved and protected today."

This was his breaking point. As he started to cry, I pulled him close, my own tears mixing with his.

"It's okay," I said. "It's okay, Pee Wee. You have every right to be sad—and angry, too, if that's what you are feeling."

"Sh-sh-she didn't e-e-even try. F-f-for me," he cried.

"Your mama struggled hard, Pee Wee," I said, rubbing his back. "If Veronica could have stayed for you and been the mama you needed, she would have. You are an incredible young man. I don't want you to believe for a moment that any of this has anything to do with you. Your mama was sick. Now she isn't suffering anymore. That doesn't take away the pain you're feeling, but at least we know that much."

"D-d-do you think sh-sh-she went to h-h-hell?" he asked, wiping away his tears with the back of his hand. This time Mama leaned forward.

"Absolutely not," Mama said, placing her hand on Pee Wee's cheek. "Your mama is in heaven, where she never has to worry about those awful drugs or awful people ever again. She's at peace, and when you're an old, old man, she'll be waiting at the pearly gates to welcome you home."

"You r-r-really th-th-think so, Gr-Gr-Gran?" he asked.

"I absolutely know so, Pee Wee," she said. "Your mama is resting in the bosom of Abraham, and that is a place of peace."

The worry on his face seemed to evaporate. Clearly this was something he'd been worrying about. I was grateful that my faithful mother had just the right words to reassure him. My faith was sometimes weak when it came to such things, especially after Daddy died. Thankfully, Mama's faith never wavered. Even when Daddy died, she refused to question God and she absolutely wouldn't allow me to voice my doubts. As soon as it seemed like I was headed down a dark path with my faith, she always had a good word to pull me back.

"Y'all let me go inside first. I won't be long," I said.

As I got out of the truck, Seth drove up in his truck, parking beside us. The other day, when I'd told him about the funeral, he'd asked if it was okay if he attended. Of course I said yes and thanked him. I also said Pee Wee would appreciate him being there.

I waited as he turned off his motor, then exited his truck wearing a dark blue suit. I was wearing a dark blue fit and flare dress with a white Peter Pan collar that gave the illusion that I had a small waist.

"Hello, Seth," I said. "Thank you for coming today."

Before he could respond, Pee Wee hopped out of the truck and ran into his arms. Seth hugged him tightly.

"H-h-hey M-M-Mr. Seth," Pee Wee said, stepping back and looking at him solemnly. "I d-d-didn't know y-y-you were coming. D-d-did you know m-m-my m-m-mom?"

"No, Pee Wee," he said, bending over so he was eye level with Pee Wee. "I didn't know her. But I know you, and I wanted you to know that you did not have to do this alone. Are you okay with me being here?"

Pee Wee nodded. "Yes, s-s-sir. Th-th-thank you."

"Y'all give me a minute while I go talk to Pastor Bennett," I said.

"We'll wait right here," Mama said as Seth helped her out of my truck.

I hurried toward the sanctuary, greeting various people and thanking them for coming. When I reached the door, Pastor Bennett was standing there, also greeting arrivals. I explained to him that Pee Wee was concerned about seeing his mother in the casket. He assured me that her casket was closed and that unless I told him otherwise, it would remain that way.

"I promise to keep this service short and sweet," Pastor Bennett said. "We want to make this event as pain-free as possible for young Pee Wee. The ladies of the church have prepared a lunch for afterward. By the time this is over with, Pee Wee will have a whole host of aunties and uncles. This is what we do here at Bethel Missionary Baptist, which you already know."

"I appreciate everything you and everyone else is doing to make Pee Wee feel supported in this moment," I said. The words almost caught in my throat, but I got them out.

Pastor Bennett hugged me. "The work you do with those boys is invaluable. The least we can do is show up when one of them is hurting. It means nothing to talk about God if we aren't living godly lives. I think back to when I lost my wife, Tillie. All of you stood with me for as long as I needed to be held up. Surely we can do the same for Pee Wee."

I could hardly speak, so I just nodded and smiled. He patted my back, and then I went back outside to get Pee Wee, Mama, and Seth. Pee Wee looked at me with concern.

"I d-d-don't have to l-l-look, do I?" he asked, his little face filled with fear.

"No, Pee Wee. You do not. I told you that we are going to take care of you. I meant that," I said, hugging him. "Let's go inside so the service can start," I said. I took one of his hands and Mama took the other one. Seth walked beside Mama. When we got to the door, Pastor Bennett gave Pee Wee a hug and explained what was going to happen. The night before, Pastor Bennett had come to the group home to ask Pee Wee if there was anything about his mama that he wanted mentioned during the service.

"Sh-sh-she made g-g-good spaghetti," Pee Wee had said. *"Wh-wh-when she didn't b-b-burn it."*

To his credit, Pastor Bennett didn't even crack a smile. He dutifully wrote down everything Pee Wee said. Pee Wee also said she had pretty hair and that she knew all the words to the Smokey Robinson and The Miracles song "The Tracks of My

Tears." Pastor Bennett promised that he'd work that into his sermon.

After we were seated, Pastor Bennett began the service. "I asked Pee Wee to share some memories with me of his mom, and without hesitation he gave me a list of things that I will share with you." Pastor Bennet then talked about the burning of the spaghetti, causing some people to smile and laugh. I put my arm around Pee Wee and he looked up at me and smiled.

Pastor Bennett continued sharing anecdotes Pee Wee had told him about Veronica, and he concluded by talking about the Smokey Robinson and The Miracles song. "Church, I understand that the song 'The Tracks of My Tears' is a secular song. But when you pay attention to the lyrics, you'll hear that Brother Smokey was preaching a word when he wrote that song. It talks about how we often walk around with smiles plastered on our faces, pretending to be okay when, in fact, we are dying inside, bit by bit, day by day. I never got to meet Pee Wee's mother on this side of life, but I think she gravitated to that song because she was in pain, struggling to be present physically and emotionally for Pee Wee. My sincere belief is that on the other side, where our Master resides, there are no more tears. There is no more sorrow, but most of all, there is no more pain. Today, saints, we are going to pray a fervent prayer that Veronica Harrison's soul is now at peace. We pray that Veronica is in a glorious place where pain and suffering can no longer find her. Rest, Veronica. Rest."

"Is i-i-it over?" Pee Wee whispered.

"Almost," I whispered back. "We're going out to the cemetery where your mama's grave will be."

"C-c-can I come v-v-visit sometime? Br-br-bring flowers?" he asked. The innocence of his voice nearly took me out. I gave him a huge squeeze.

"Absolutely. Mr. Jason or I will bring you anytime you want," I said, looking at Jason, who was sitting beside me.

"We're here for you, buddy," he said to Pee Wee.

Once the pallbearers were ready, we walked behind the casket toward the cemetery, which was right across the street. A light rain had started, and it was getting colder. I pulled my coat tighter around me and made sure Pee Wee was wrapped up in his coat and scarf. We gathered around the casket while Pastor Bennett said his final words.

"The Bible says in Matthew 11:28, 'Come unto me, all ye that labour and are heavy laden, and I will give you rest.' We stand united in the belief that Sister Veronica has found rest in the presence of our Lord. We therefore commit her body to the ground, earth to earth, ashes to ashes, dust to dust."

By this time, Pee Wee was sobbing. It had fully hit him that he'd never see his mother again.

"Let's go, baby," I said, taking his hand and leading him away from the graveside. I didn't want him to watch them lower his mother's casket into the ground. Unfortunately, I'd stayed to see them do that to my daddy, and it was an image I'd never be able to scrub from my mind. For a moment, I thought about my brother Aaron. Would we be doing this for him soon? We still hadn't received any updates. Mama called every day, and every day they told her the same thing: *We are diligently looking for*

Private First Class Aaron Lamont Daniels. We'll let you know as soon as we find out something new."

Marcus had wanted to attend the funeral and support Pee Wee, but he didn't think he could handle it. I understood. This was a lot.

When we got to the dining hall, the women of the church took over, enveloping Pee Wee in love. They plied him with food and hugs and prayers. It was good that we'd had the funeral here. These women had dedicated their lives to being rocks for others. They had been that for me and my family, and it did my soul good to see them do it for Pee Wee. I tried to bring the boys here to church as much as possible, so Pee Wee recognized many of the people. Yet this was the first time he'd experienced the full measure of agape love. After some time passed, he ran up to me at the table where I was sitting with Mama, Seth, and a few other people from the church. His excitement was evident as he wrapped his arms around my neck.

"I h-h-have more gr-gr-grannies," he said, looking up at me with a huge grin on his face. "Gran is th-th-the main one but m-m-maybe it's okay if I-I-I have more?" He looked over at Mama, who nodded and smiled.

"You deserve all the grannies and all the aunties there are," I said. "I'm so happy you get to feel the love the ladies at church have shown me my entire life."

"S-S-Sister Miller s-s-said I could come pl-pl-play with her gr-gr-great-grandson sometime," he said, hopping up and down. "Is th-th-that alright?"

I wanted to pretend like he was an ordinary boy and allow him to have every regular boy moment he could experience, but sadly he wasn't some ordinary boy. He was a ward of the state in the custody of the group home and in my care. We had protocols for such things, and I couldn't say yes without giving it some thought and coordination.

It was times like these when my heart broke for my boys. They just wanted to be ordinary kids, yet sadly, in spite of the normalcy my staff and I were able to provide for them, we couldn't make them the kind of boys where something as simple as going to play with a potential friend didn't require meetings involving multiple people and maybe even paperwork. Circumstances beyond their control and mine deemed them anything but ordinary.

"Let's talk about this later," I said. "Right now, we need to get back to the group home."

"Okay," he said, the happiness leaving his face. "M-m-may I go s-s-say goodbye to th-th-them?"

I nodded. "Yes, you may. And, Pee Wee, I promise that I'm not dismissing your request. I just have to make sure it's okay. Alright?"

"Yes, ma'am," he said and walked away dejectedly. It took all of my willpower not to pull him back and into an embrace. But hugs weren't what Pee Wee was wanting in this moment.

"Why couldn't you have said yes?" Mama whispered angrily. "On a day like today, you could have just said yes."

"I won't lie to my boys," I said in a firm voice. I understood where Mama was coming from, but she didn't grasp the full measure of my role and the weight I carried when it came to the boys at the group home. "I answer to social services, Mama.

There are a lot of decisions I'm confident making on my own, but taking them out of the group-home environment isn't a decision I feel comfortable making alone. Especially right now."

I didn't tell her that the group home was possibly under investigation and the board of directors was only one meeting away from deciding my fate as the executive director. I had to make sure everything I did was according to the rules, because the last thing I wanted was another incident I had to explain to the higher-ups.

Mama's face softened. "I'm sorry. Of course you know best. I just hate to see him disappointed."

"Me too, Mama. Me too," I said. We both watched Pee Wee hug all of the church ladies who'd come out today. When we got back to the group home, I planned to make sure he wrote thank-you notes to them and Pastor Bennett. That would make him feel a bit better. Pee Wee loved writing letters and notes and often gave thank-you notes to one of the houseparents, thanking them for soothing him after a nightmare, or to Mama K and Mama G, thanking them for not making green beans (which he hated). I figured that if I could get him focused on writing notes, he might forget about going over to Sister Miller's house.

"I'll be right back," I said and walked over to where Sister Miller was busy wiping down a table. I lightly placed my hand on the older woman's shoulder. She and my grandmother used to be good friends before Gran passed away. Sister Miller was eighty-five, the same age Gran would have been had she lived.

Sister Miller turned around and smiled. Such a dear, sweet woman. All of the ladies at the church were, but she held a special place in my heart because of Gran.

"Sister Miller, I just wanted to say thank—"

She held up one hand and put her other hand on her hip. "No, you don't. We don't say thank you for such things as this. That baby lost his mama, and we all did what the Good Book commanded us to do. No need to say thank you for that."

"Yes, ma'am," I said, wiping a tear from my eye. "Sister Miller, Pee Wee mentioned coming over to play with your great-grandson. I'm afraid the process for approving that involves background checks and all sorts of paperwork. I didn't want you to think I didn't appreciate your offer, but I can't ask you to do all of that."

"Tell me what I need to do so it can happen," she said. "My great-grandson lives with me most of the time. My granddaughter works out of town and the daddy is hit or miss. Bud would absolutely love spending time with Pee Wee. Whatever I need to fill out, I'll do it."

"Bless you," I whispered as I hugged her.

"I already am," she whispered back. "And, Katia, I been talking to the Lord about you, and He told me He's got somebody for you. You just got to be brave. I don't know what that means—I just heard it in my prayers."

I took a step back and looked at Sister Miller and then my eyes went toward Seth, who was talking to Pee Wee.

"That one ain't hard on the eyes," Sister Miller said. I looked back at her, and she was grinning, her eyes shining. "Let yourself be happy, Katia, and don't settle for less than what God has for you. Be brave. Just like He said."

"Yes, ma'am," I said. I gave her one last hug, and then I went to the restroom, the whole time thinking about Sister Miller's words. *Let myself be happy.* What an idea. I always thought I was happy, but I suddenly realized I hadn't been happy for years. Decades even. I buried my happy in the cemetery when Daddy died, and I hadn't made much effort to resurrect it since then.

By the time I came back, Seth was no longer at the table. I was both relieved and disappointed.

"Seth said he needed to head out and go check on his crew," Mama said.

I was embarrassed that she'd realized I was looking for him.

"We should go too," I said. We thanked people as we left the church. Once outside, I was surprised to see Seth in the parking lot. The rain had stopped, but the temperature had dropped. I braced myself against it—and against facing Seth. Mama touched my arm and then led Pee Wee to my truck. Once they were inside, I turned toward Seth.

"I didn't know you were still here," I said as I tried to make eye contact. I didn't want him to know how much he affected me.

"I couldn't leave without saying goodbye," he said, his hands clasped behind his back. "I also wanted to see if you'd be interested in going to dinner with me one night this week. Whenever you have time."

"I don't think that would be a good idea," I said. "Thank you for coming today."

"Kat, wait. I—"

"I'll see you later at the group home," I said. "Take care, Seth."

I turned and got into the truck. I was emotionally spent. Of course I couldn't let on that anything was wrong, so I flashed a smile at Mama and Pee Wee. "Let's get Gran home, and then you and I will head back to the group home. Everyone should be back from school soon."

"You okay?" Mama asked, looking at me knowingly. I smiled again.

"Yes. I am just fine," I said.

Mama nodded, then resumed her conversation with Pee Wee. I let the two of them chat all the way back to the house.

Once we made it home, Mama asked me what time I'd be getting back after work. I told her I planned to stay at the group home tonight. I didn't want to take any chances with the boys, especially Pee Wee, having a difficult night without me being there to support them. Of course the houseparents were more than capable of handling any emotional outbursts. But I was feeling the need to focus on someone or something other than myself. Other than Seth. My mind kept drifting back to him asking me out on a date. Me. On a date with an amazingly handsome man like Seth. Too good to fathom.

I'd decided to wait until after the funeral to tell Darren and Charlie that their grandmother wasn't going to take custody of them. I'd hoped that over the last few days she might have changed her mind, but Mrs. Crawley had said the grandmother was holding firm. I'd tell them tomorrow. If possible, I needed one peaceful night.

"You don't rest when you stay at the group home," Mama said after I told her my plans.

"I'll try my best," I said. She was right—I didn't rest well when I slept over at the group home. But my presence was needed. I looked at Pee Wee, whose eyes were already at half-mast. "Do you want to go inside with me while I pack?"

"I'll st-st-stay here. Is that al-al-right?" He looked exhausted.

"Absolutely," I said. "I'll be right back."

By the time I packed and returned to the truck, Pee Wee was sound asleep. I was grateful he could rest. I prayed that he'd have a good night. I prayed we'd all have a good night. I didn't know how much more any of us could take emotionally.

19

IT WAS TIME FOR DINNER WHEN Pee Wee and I returned to the group home. Mrs. Grambling, one of the houseparents, had made chili with jalapeño corn bread since both Mrs. Kennedy and Miss Grant had gone home after the funeral. It looked and smelled delicious, but I couldn't get my appetite going. We were all around the table, and Pee Wee was stirring his chili but not eating it. My soul was aggrieved, as Mama would say. Nothing seemed to soothe me, including food, which was unusual because most of my life, food had been my balm in Gilead. Finally, Pee Wee asked if he could go take a nap.

"I hate for you to be alone. Why don't you just stay here with us? You don't have to eat if you don't want to." I was afraid to let him out of my sight.

I glanced at Darren and Charlie, who were looking sympathetically at Pee Wee. These last few days had been difficult for them too. They were both sensitive boys, and they'd gone out of their way to be nice to Pee Wee, from giving him the last piece of chicken at dinner the night before to Charlie offering Pee Wee his dessert, insisting that he didn't like banana pudding. These boys in the group home didn't have much, but what they did have, they were willing to share with each other.

"I'm o-o-okay," Pee Wee insisted. "Just t-t-tired."

Jason leaned over and spoke to me in a low voice. "I'll sit with him until he dozes off and stay close until he wakes up."

"That might be good," I whispered back. I turned to Pee Wee. "Pee Wee, Mr. Jason will go with you. I need to get some work done in my office. If any of you boys need me, just come knock on my door."

I patted each boy's head, then went to my office. Almost as soon as I entered, the phone rang. I sighed and answered it.

"Hello," I said, hoping whoever was on the other end would get to the point quickly so we could hang up and I could catch my breath.

"Hey, Miss Katia." It was Chad. He spoke in a low voice, but I recognized it immediately.

"Chad," I said in a hurried voice. "Chad, where are you?"

"I shouldna called. I gotta go," he said. My panic set in. I couldn't let him hang up. This might be my last chance to convince him to tell me where he was so I could go get him.

"No," I said. "Don't hang up. Just talk to me. Tell me where you are. I can come get you. You don't have to stay there."

"You can't fix everybody's problems, Miss Katia," he said gruffly. "Some problems is bigger than what you or anybody on the right side of the law can handle."

"Chad, you're not safe there. You know that."

"How's Pee Wee?" He changed the subject, but I didn't give up. If I could continue talking to him, I could find out where he was.

"Pee Wee is as well as can be expected. He misses you, Chad," I said. I decided not to tell him that Pee Wee's mama died. I didn't want to add to his already huge burden. "Chad, are you hurt? Has anyone hurt you? Please, let me or Mr. Jason come get you."

"I can't come back there," Chad said. I heard the turmoil in his voice. "Tell Pee Wee I'll be checking in on him from time to time."

"Tell me where you are, Chad, please."

"I gotta go, Miss Katia."

"Please don't hang up," I begged. "Are you with your mother? Is Cobra there?"

"Naw. They had to run out for something. They told me to stay in the house. Cobra say he can tell if I use the phone, but I had to take a chance. Had to see how y'all was doing."

"Chad, if they aren't there, just run," I said, feeling my panic rise anew. "Just run or let me come get you, and—"

"He say he'd kill Lena if I left. Said if I even went outside this house without his permission he would kill her. I believe him, Miss Katia. I don't think I could live with that. I know she ain't been the best mama, but I can't let him kill her."

"What can I do to get you out of this situation, Chad? We need to get you away from Cobra and Lena."

"There's nothing you can do," he said in a resigned tone.

"Yes, there is. Tell me where you are—let me come get you," I begged again.

He paused for a long time. I didn't want to rush him, but I also worried that Cobra would return before I could get to Chad or get help to him.

Once more, he went quiet but then finally spoke in a near whimper. "Okay. I'm not far. I'm at—"

"Give me that phone," I heard a deep voice order that I immediately recognized as Cobra's even though I had only heard him speak a few times.

"Who this?" he snapped at me.

"Cobra, this is Miss Katia from the group home. Please let me come get Chad." I hated having to ask that awful man for anything, but I didn't have a choice.

"Chad ain't going nowhere and he gone pay for using this phone when I told him not to," he said in an angry voice. "Busybodies like you gone get this boy killed. If he calls you again, you best hang up. You dig?" He slammed down the receiver.

I wiped away a tear and called the police. They assured me that "someone would get on it"—code for *we'll do nothing*. I called Mrs. Gates and told her the same thing I told the police.

She sighed. "I am sad to hear this news. Sounds like Chad is lost to the system for now. Hopefully he'll turn up before things get any worse than they already are. Thank you for keeping me in the loop."

She hung up. Everyone was washing their hands of Chad. I always grieved the loss of a boy, whether it be to the system or to the streets. I wanted every one of them to be a picture of success on my wall. The idea that Chad might not end up on my wall, wearing his cap and gown, was almost more than I could handle. I dropped my head into my hands.

"Are you okay?" someone asked me.

I lifted my head and saw Seth standing at the door, a look of concern on his face. I hated having him see me, yet again, in tears.

"No, I can't say that I am okay," I admitted. "But I need to go check on the boys." I stood, but Seth entered the room and eased the door shut.

"Tell me what's wrong, Katia." He walked over to me and led me to the couch. We sat side by side, and as my eyes met his, I almost had to turn away because of the amazing amount of kindness shown in them. "What happened? Did the police call with some news about Chad?"

I shook my head and filled him in on my conversation with Chad, ending my update by sharing what Cobra said.

"That bastard," he said, his eyes filled with fire. "How could he do a young boy like this? Look, Chad said they aren't far from here. Let me ride around and see what I can see."

"No. Please don't. No one should go after Chad, because that would mean going after Cobra. I couldn't bear it if anyone else I care about gets hurt or worse. For now, we try and believe in the police."

Seth's face softened. "You care about me?"

My cheeks grew warm. I didn't think about what I'd said before I said it. I didn't want him to think I was having feelings for him—even though I was.

"I didn't . . . I mean . . . I . . ."

He moved closer to me and placed his hand on the side of my face. "I care about you, Kat, and I know this is very sudden, and I know we need to take things slowly, but maybe we could . . ."

He leaned in. I could almost feel his lips on mine when there was a discreet knock at the door. Thank God the door was closed. We jerked away from each other like guilty teenagers. I stood and went back to my desk.

"Come in," I called, and Jason entered the room.

"Hello, Mr. Taylor," he said. One of your men was asking for you."

"Thank you, Jason. And please—call me Seth. Mr. Taylor is my father," Seth said as he got up. "I'll see you later, Kat?"

I just nodded. He looked at me for a few extra seconds but then left my office. I cleared my throat and turned to Jason, who was looking at me quizzically.

"Everything okay, boss?" he asked.

I told him about the conversation with Chad. Like Seth, he offered to ride around and try to find Chad, but I told him the same thing I told Seth, which was we should give the police time to look.

"I don't know that they will have much luck, but let's at least give them the rest of the day. Cobra is dangerous and I don't want to do anything to make the situation worse," I said, releasing a loud sigh. "How's Pee Wee?"

"Knocked out," he said, going over and sitting on the couch. "He barely made it to the room before falling sleep, hard and fast. I'll keep an eye on him."

"Good," I said. "I haven't been sharing some of the things going on with the board, but I think it's time to bring you up to speed." As I told him about my conversations with Mr. Arrington and Mrs. Hendricks, his face contorted with anger.

"They can't get rid of you. You've turned this group home into a sanctuary for these boys."

"If they have the votes, they can get rid of me. So I need you and me to spend the rest of this week preparing you to take over. I can't guarantee that they'll offer you the executive director position, but I want you to be ready in case they do."

"I wouldn't take it. Not this way."

I reached out and placed my hand on his. "This is bigger than me or you. This is about the boys and this group home continuing to thrive. If they offer you the position, you'll take it because you've earned it and the boys need you. Period."

"Maybe it won't come to that," he said.

I smiled sadly. "We shall see. But for now, grab those files over there on the cabinet. You and I have work to do."

The idea of leaving the group home and trying something different had crossed my mind over the years. This work was sometimes thankless and heartbreaking, but most of the time it was the most rewarding job a person could ever do. I looked up at the wall of honor, filled with photos of young men who'd passed through these doors and exited them to become successful men who worked hard and had established families of their own. They were the reason I continued to show up every day. I truly prayed that I'd be able to continue the work I'd started, but if not, I vowed to make sure Jason was ready to take the helm.

20

"MISS KATIA," A VOICE CALLED OUT to me. "Miss Katia. Miss Katia."

I sat straight up in the bed, looking around frantically. For a moment, I forgot where I was, and then I realized I was at the group home. I'd slept in one of the unoccupied rooms. The bed was full-size but not as comfortable as my bed at home.

"Yes," I said as I clicked on the light. "Who is it?"

"It's Mrs. Grambling."

"Come in," I said, swinging my legs over the edge of the bed.

The door slowly opened. Mrs. Grambling, one of my longest-serving houseparents, walked inside. She was wearing a robe and a headscarf covering all of her pin curlers. I glanced at the clock. It was two in the morning. Regardless of the reason she was waking me this early, it couldn't be good.

"What's wrong, Mrs. Grambling?" I stood up.

"I'm sorry to bother you. We got a phone call." When I saw her wiping away tears, I braced myself. I was wide awake.

"What happened?"

"Chad's been shot," she blurted out.

"Who told you this? Who called?" I needed facts—now.

"Police called. He's at the hospital in Tuskegee. Miss Katia, they don't know if he's going to make it."

"What else did they tell you?" I ignored the part about him possibly not making it. I couldn't process that information, so I kept myself in executive director mode. I hurried to my suitcase and took out the clothes I'd packed for later that day.

"Not much," she said. Mrs. Grambling began making up my bed. I didn't stop her, because I knew she was nervous, and like me, she coped by keeping busy. "The policeman said Chad has several gunshot wounds, and a couple of them are life-threatening. He said Chad will need surgery."

"I'm going to Tuskegee," I said. I started taking off my pajamas. If this made Mrs. Grambling uncomfortable, she didn't let on. I didn't have time for modesty. I needed to get to Chad. I slipped on the gray skirt and matching sweater I'd packed. "For now, don't mention this to the other boys. Especially Pee Wee. Wait until I'm able to find out more."

"You don't need to go alone," she said, sounding exactly like Mama. "Let me get Mr. Grambling so he can go with you."

"I'll be fine," I said. "I need you and Mr. Grambling here, and the other staff will need to be on hand in case . . ."

"I'm so sorry, Miss Katia. That boy means a lot to all of us, but I know he was special to you."

I rubbed her arm. "Don't give up on him. I don't care what the police said. Chad is strong. We're not counting him out. I need you to pray like you have never prayed before."

"I ain't stopped praying since I heard the news, and I won't stop until we get that baby home," she said. "I'll leave out and let you finish dressing."

After Mrs. Grambling left the bedroom, I took several deep breaths. This wasn't the time for me to break down. I thought about Mama. She'd want to know what happened, but since I didn't really know myself, I decided I'd call her once she'd awakened to start her day later. Also, Mama would want to come or try to send Marcus with me. Neither one of them was emotionally well enough to sit in a hospital right now, especially with all of the uncertainty concerning Aaron. Mama would just have to fuss at me later about driving to Tuskegee by myself in the middle of the night.

Once I was ready, I threw some folders that needed my attention into my briefcase, as well as the book I was reading, *Invisible Man* by Ralph Ellison. I then put on my coat and hurried outside to my truck. I barely noticed the cold.

I believed that if I could get to the hospital and let Chad know he wasn't alone, everything would be alright. Tuskegee was only a little over an hour drive from Troy, but it felt like I was trying to reach the other side of the world.

The drive there was dark and ominous, on nothing but unwieldy backcountry roads. Between the curves and the potential for deer to dart into the road, I had to drive slower than normal. I tried to convince myself there was nothing to worry about, but when I finally arrived at John A. Andrew Memorial Hospital, I had to stifle the sobs threatening to overwhelm me. All I could hear over and over inside my head was: *"They don't know if he's going to make it. They don't know if he's going to make it. They don't know if he's going to make it."*

Then my thoughts drifted back to the conversation from a few days ago, when Chad and Pee Wee begged me to take them in. How I wish I could have done just that. Chad wouldn't be lying in a hospital, fighting for his life. I allowed the tears to flow but got out of the truck and hurried inside.

Even though it wasn't quite four in the morning, the hospital was already bustling with activity. There was something reassuring about seeing Negro nurses and doctors in their element. The white hospitals did accept Negro patients, but we all knew we were better off with our own kind, even if Negro hospitals didn't have the latest and greatest equipment. Because the staff saw in us their aunties, cousins, siblings, nieces, and nephews, they went above and beyond to provide us with a healing environment.

I rushed to the front desk and explained to the young-looking Negro woman who I was and who I was here to see.

"Yes, ma'am," she said with a gentle smile. "Chadwick Montgomery is in surgery right now. You are welcome to wait in the room over there to your left."

"Can you or someone explain to me what his injuries are?" I asked, trying to keep the panic out of my voice. I'd prayed that I'd arrive before they took him to surgery—so I could hug him and tell him, "I'm here, and I won't leave you alone." I needed answers. I needed to know what we were up against.

"I'm afraid I can't answer your questions, ma'am, but I'll get the nurse who was seeing after Chad to come and talk to you."

I thanked her and went to the waiting room. Four other people were waiting. One was an older couple. The woman was crying softly, and the man was rubbing her back. On the other side of the room sat a very pregnant woman with a toddler on her lap. Before long a nurse entered the room. Those waiting sat up expectantly and were clearly disappointed when she approached me. The nurse looked like a baby. Either I was feeling especially old right now, or all of these medical professionals looked like they were fresh out of high school. I motioned for her to follow me into the hallway. I didn't want anyone overhearing the conversation.

"Good morning, ma'am," she said in a soft but firm voice. "I was told you had questions about Chadwick."

"Yes," I said. "Thank you for coming to speak to me. Please, tell me what you know."

What she knew was grim. Chad had sustained a gunshot wound to his chest that narrowly missed his heart. But the worst news was that he was also shot in his neck and spinal cord. He was paralyzed from the waist down, and she didn't sound confident that the surgery would restore his movement.

"How long do they think he'll be in surgery?" I asked.

"This could take several hours," she said. "I'll be in contact with the doctor, so if I receive any news, I'll let you know."

I just nodded. I didn't know what else to say. I went back into the waiting room, sat down, and pulled my book out of my briefcase. I hadn't started it yet, but my eye was drawn to one of its lines: *"I am invisible, understand, simply because people refuse to see me."* I put my hand to my mouth to stifle the cry welling up inside me. That line perfectly described my boys at the group home and how the world treated them, but especially my wounded, big little boy, Chad. Beating up on myself wouldn't fix anything, but, my God, how I wish I could have done more.

"You okay, honey?" the older Negro woman asked, easing down in the seat beside me. She had a gentle look on her face. Somehow she had climbed outside of her own grief to come and see about me.

I almost lied and told her I was fine, but I couldn't tell an untruth to those knowing eyes, so I just shook my head as the tears continued to fall.

"It's okay, honey," she said, putting her arm around me. She was small in stature, but her embrace felt strong and protective. "This room is filled with suffering and heartache, but it's also filled with God and love. I'm going to pray for you and for that young woman over there with the baby on her lap. I'm going to ask God to protect our loved ones and protect us too."

"Thank you," was all I could say.

She patted my arm one more time; then she walked over to the pregnant woman and sat down beside her. She held her hands out for the toddler, who went to her without reservation. Soon she and the young mother were deep in conversation. Mama always said God sends you an angel when you're feeling most alone. I got the feeling that this older Negro woman was exactly who Mama was talking about.

I looked down at my watch. It was almost four thirty. Mama

wasn't a morning person, but when I wasn't at home, she slept with one eye open. I decided to go call her. I needed to hear my mother's voice. I needed her to tell me that Chad would live and walk again.

I'd noticed a pay phone near the front door of the hospital. I put on my coat and stuffed my book back into my briefcase. As I exited the hospital, the cold air caused me to catch my breath. I pulled my scarf around my neck. I entered the phone booth, which wasn't roomy at all. My hips were touching each side.

"They sure know how to make a girl feel ginormous," I muttered. I dialed the operator and told her I needed to make a person-to-person call from Katia Daniels to Mrs. Heloise Daniels. I waited while the operator dialed the number. Mama came on the line, sounding wide awake and panicked.

"Where are you, Katia?" Mama demanded, her voice trembling. I filled her in on the details.

"You shouldn't have driven all the way to Tuskegee by yourself in the middle of the night. Anything could have happened to you, Katia, and then what good would you be to anyone, but especially those boys you look after?" she fussed.

"I just . . . I . . ." My voice cracked. I heard Mama draw in her breath.

"It's alright, baby," she said. Mama's soothing voice felt so good to my ears. It was cold outside, but I focused on the warmth of her voice. "I'm so sorry, Katia. I know you're worried sick. Chad is a strong young boy and if anyone can beat this, he can. He and Pee Wee will be running and playing again before you know it."

Mama then began to pray, and I listened, my head bowed. At this moment, God seemed to be more of a taker than a giver. Since I couldn't find anything to say that I believed God would care to hear, I stayed silent and allowed my mother's fervent prayers to hopefully find their way to what felt like God's normally deaf ears. When she finished, I whispered, "Amen."

"I'd better go back inside, Mama," I said, clearing my throat. "I'll call you as soon as I know something."

When I reentered the waiting room, the elderly woman and man were gone. For a moment, I questioned whether they'd ever been there, suddenly wondering if an angel had visited me. But when I asked the young pregnant woman about them, she said their grandson came out of surgery and they went to see him.

"Are you okay?" I asked. "Do you need anything?"

"No, ma'am," she said. "I'm just waiting to find out some news about my son's daddy. He got mixed up in some mess tonight. The crazy lady he been cheating on me with shot him. Some would say serves him right, but I love him and this boy needs his daddy."

I didn't have time to respond because a very tired-looking doctor came into the room. From the look on his face, the news wasn't good. Instinctively, I reached for the young woman's hand. She couldn't be much older than twenty. I could easily be her mother and this toddler and unborn baby's grandmother. We looked at each other with fear in our eyes, not knowing who the doctor was there to see. He sat on the other side of the girl. She started to wail before he could open his mouth. I put my arm around her while patting the back of the toddler, who was now screaming at the top of his lungs. A nurse hurried into the room, took the baby, and sat on the other side of the doctor, bouncing the boy on her lap. Within seconds, he stopped crying and began cooing.

"Are you her mother?" he asked, looking at me sympathetically.

I shook my head. "Just another person waiting for news." I squeezed her shoulders. "Let the doctor talk to you."

She nodded, seeming grateful for my presence.

"I'm afraid the wounds were too extensive. He made it through the first hour of surgery, but he lost too much blood," the doctor said. "Is there anyone we can call to come and be with you?"

"He ain't got a lot of people in his life 'sides me and that boy over there, and this baby in my belly. His mama ain't got no car," the girl whispered hoarsely. "I can't believe this. Cobra dead?"

I got lightheaded when she said the name Cobra, but I strained to stay focused.

"Are you okay, ma'am?" the doctor asked as he eyed me with concern.

"I'm fine." I sat up straighter in the chair, continuing to hold the young woman's hand. Being other people's support was the one job in life I excelled at.

The doctor continued to look at me until I smiled and said, "I'm okay."

"Ma'am, I hate to have to ask such probing questions, but were you and Leonard Parker married?" he asked.

"Who that?" She looked confused. I figured she didn't know that Leonard Parker was Cobra's given name.

"He means Cobra," I said. She and the doctor looked at me.

"Do you know Cobra?" she asked suspiciously. "Why you

saying his name like you know him or something? Who is you, lady?"

"No, I didn't know him. You said his name, and—"

She snatched her hand away from mine. "I think I'd rather talk in private," she said, her voice now cold as ice. "I don't know this lady and I don't want her in my business."

"Very well," the doctor said.

"And give me my damn baby," she snapped at the nurse, who hopped up and handed the now sleeping toddler to his mother.

They all left, but before exiting the room, the young woman graced me with a backward glare. I stood up to stretch, but before I could work out the kinks in my neck and back, another doctor came in. I tried to read his face, but he gave nothing away. I quickly sat back down. In my mind I sought words to speak to God in the comfortable, trusting way Mama did, but no words came.

"Are you Miss Daniels with the Pike County Group Home for Negro Boys?" His voice was formal. He appeared to be in his late fifties or early sixties. He still wore his surgical cap, but white curls spilled out from underneath it.

"Yes, I'm Katia Daniels," I said, rubbing my hands on my skirt.

"My name is Dr. Lowe and I performed surgery on Chadwick Montgomery," he said, his voice softening. "But unfortunately—"

"Wait," I said, closing my eyes, gripping the edges of my seat. "Wait . . . Just wait." It felt as if the room was spinning.

"Miss Daniels, I'm so sorry, but Chad—"

"I should have done more," I whispered, and then, as if the

words couldn't be contained, I spoke them louder. "I should have done more."

"You didn't do this, Miss Daniels," he said firmly. "You didn't cause any of this. Chad sustained so much trauma from the bullets and then the surgery. His body wasn't strong enough to fight everything. You're not to blame for any of this."

"I need to see him," I said finally. "May I have some time alone with him?"

"Yes," Dr. Lowe said. "And I am so sorry that I wasn't able to save him."

This time I reached out and put my hand on his arm. "You did the very best you could. Thank you."

I fell back into the seat, all energy evaporated from my body. I needed to call the group home and Mama. I even thought about Seth, but I pushed that out of my mind. Right now, I needed to sit with this news. Chad was gone.

"I am so sorry that you never got the life you deserved, Chadwick Montgomery," I whispered, allowing the sobs to overtake me.

21

I WENT BACK OUTSIDE TO THE pay phone and called the group home, telling them what happened. Jason was nearly inconsolable. I was relieved the boys were at school, because he needed the time to gather himself. *We* needed the time to gather ourselves. I told him I'd drive straight there so we could tell Pee Wee together. After I finished talking to Jason, I called Mrs. Hendricks from the board. I didn't want to talk to Sam. She said how sorry she was and that she would let the rest of the board members know what happened. I knew I would have to speak to Sam eventually, but I just didn't have it in me now. After that call, I dialed the number to Chad's caseworker. As usual, she was efficient with her words. No sorrow. No pain. Just iciness. Maybe people like her were needed in jobs like this. Maybe they're the ones who are better suited to simply do the work and stay detached.

"I am very sorry to hear that Chad passed away," she said, but there was no true sorriness in her voice. I imagined that once the phone call ended, she'd have Chad's case closed out before her first morning coffee break. "I will be in touch if I need any additional information from you." Before I could respond, she hung up the phone.

I went back inside the hospital and asked to see Chad. One of the nurses said he was in a private room, where I could go be with him. She guided me down the hallway and was courteous enough to leave us alone. It was a nice space. I imagined other families had been in this room with their loved ones. It was dimly lit and peaceful. They had removed the wires and tubes and had washed him clean. He looked like he was taking a nap. I sat down beside him and took his hand and kissed it.

"You are going to love it on the other side, Chad." I stroked his hand as the tears rolled down my cheeks, falling onto the crisp, white sheet that covered him from his feet to his neck. "My daddy and gran are going to love you and spoil you like you will not believe. I'm so sorry that no one on this side of life could be what you needed us to be. I'll never forget the day you said you wished I was your mom. Just know that in my heart, you were mine. I love you. And I release you."

For the next two hours, I sat talking softly to Chad, sharing the good memories I had of him. Promising that I'd look after his best friend, Pee Wee. If Chad's spirit was lingering, I wanted him to know his existence mattered to me and that he was loved.

When it felt as if my heart might burst from grief, Mr. Clemmons from the funeral home that had handled Pee Wee's mother's body arrived. I gave Chad one final kiss on his now cool forehead and watched as Mr. Clemmons and an assistant moved him to a gurney and wheeled him out of the room. I tried not to think about the fact that the next time I'd see him he would be inside a casket, stiff and absent from his body.

After they left, I didn't know what to do with myself. Once again I needed to hear Mama's voice. One of the nurses insisted that I use the office of one of the RNs who was away today. I was grateful not to have to go back outside to the pay phone. I dialed home, and Mama picked up so fast I figured she'd been waiting by the phone.

"Oh, baby," she said with tenderness when I told her about Chad. Her words and tone caused me to start crying all over again. "Bless his sweet heart. He's with God. God's got him, baby."

I didn't expect to feel a rush of anger at her words, but I was almost consumed with rage. How dare God take yet another person I cared about? Losing Daddy had been hard and losing Gran had been expected but still difficult. But this death . . . This was too much. I wasn't sure where I was going to be able to store this grief and rage over losing Chad. I wanted to lash out at someone—maybe even Mama—yet I didn't. Her words came from a good place, and she was only trying to comfort me.

Mama asked me if I wanted someone to come and bring me home. I reassured her that I could make the drive back to Troy by myself. I needed that time alone in the truck, but more importantly, I didn't want to leave Daddy's truck behind here in Tuskegee.

"I'll be okay, Mama," I said. Before she hung up, Marcus got on the phone.

"Big sis, I'm so sorry," he said, his voice gruff with emotions. "Those boys have a way of connecting with your heart. Chad will be greatly missed. I love you."

Marcus was still battling his own demons as he worried continuously about Aaron, so his acknowledging my grief meant a lot to me.

"Thank you, Marcus," I said, wiping away tears. "I appreciate your love so much. I'll see you later."

I hung up the phone and went back into the hallway. Several of the nurses who had tended to Chad were waiting outside the office for me. One by one, each of them hugged me and whispered kind words.

"We are so sorry for your loss," the head nurse on duty said, taking my hands and squeezing them. I nodded and smiled at her, the tears streaming down both of our faces.

"Thank you," I said, the only words I could manage.

"You take care of yourself, Miss Daniels," she said, giving me a hug. For a moment, we stood in this embrace. I knew that, like me, she'd seen her fair share of Black boys and men dead at such young ages. Our boys and men seemed to be on a trajectory of leaving this earth well before their time.

Once we finished our goodbyes, I went outside to my truck. The finality of it all hit me hard.

I started the truck and turned the radio to my favorite station, WRMA. The disc jockey, Ellis Ford, was on the air, playing a favorite Nina Simone song of mine, "Willow Weep for Me." I cried and sang along with her as I drove out of the hospital parking lot. The words hit particularly hard today. I imagined the willow weeping extra hard for Chad, and like the song said, I wished I could be covered by it—covered by something, anything. I felt vulnerable and exposed, and as the song ended, I was crying so hard I had to pull the truck to the side of the road. My sobs were violent. I thought about Pee Wee and how much this would hurt him. I felt like an absolute failure, and even though a part of me understood this wasn't my fault, I didn't know how else to feel at this moment.

After a while, I collected myself and I got back on the road. It felt like every tune on the radio was a sad song that prompted me to shed more tears. It was like Ellis Ford knew my mood, and the playlist reflected that. From "The Tracks of My Tears" by Smokey Robinson and The Miracles to "Ev'ry Time We Say Goodbye" by Ella Fitzgerald, I felt like my emotions were playing out on the radio. I barely paid attention to the roads and was thankful I didn't pass many cars along the way. I didn't feel as if I was as present as a driver should be.

I made it back to the group home around two o'clock, which gave me just enough time to pull the houseparents, Jason, and the kitchen staff together in our meeting room so we could begin to process everything before Jason went to the school to pick up the boys.

I looked from one tearstained face to the next. I would have loved to say Chad didn't suffer, but I didn't know that to be true, and I would not lie to them. I wanted to throw my arms around each person, mixing my tears with theirs, but I had to show strength. We still had a group home to run, and I couldn't give in to my hurt and pain. There would be time later for more of my tears, but my staff needed me to be their fearless leader. "We all loved Chad, and we're all hurting something awful right now, but we have to be strong for the other boys, especially Pee Wee and the new boys. They've grown fond of Pee Wee and it will hurt them to see his pain."

Jason put his head in his hands and sobbed. Mrs. Kennedy, our resident grandmother from the kitchen staff, reached over and pulled him into her arms. Hurt filled the room, and I felt responsible for all of it.

"I'm going to go pick up the boys," I said. "You all take care of each other, and when I get back we'll bring them together and tell them about Chad."

It was still a bit early for me to pick up the boys from school, but I was overwhelmed and needed to escape the overpowering grief. I walked over to Jason and squeezed his shoulder. Before I burst into tears, I rushed out of the room and ran right into Seth. I tried to rush past him, but he pulled me into an embrace.

"I'm so sorry, Kat," he said in a voice full of emotion.

I struggled in his arms, but he continued to hold me. I allowed one sob to escape from my throat, but I stopped myself before it became a torrent of tears.

"I have to go get the boys," I said, trying to sound firm even though all I wanted to do was stay in his arms. He stepped back but kept his hands on my shoulders to steady me, which I was grateful for. I was exhausted and my knees felt as if they might buckle.

"Let me go with you," he said. "The guys are outside working. They'll be fine while I go with you. Please. It will make me feel better."

"Okay," I said.

He looked at me with surprise. "I didn't expect you to say yes."

"I don't have a lot left in my emotional gas tank, Seth," I said honestly. "So, I'm not going to argue."

"Do you mind if I drive you then?"

I shook my head, handing him the van keys. "I appreciate your kindness."

"I'm not just being kind, Kat," he said in a quiet voice as he led me out the door. "Let me go talk to the guys and I'll meet you at the van."

Somehow I had to find energy to deal with the boys' emotions, especially Pee Wee's. I squeezed Seth's hand and then went over to the van, which was parked near the front fence. Once I climbed inside, I leaned my head back and closed my eyes. I could feel a slight headache forming behind my eyes, but I was determined not to give in to the dull ache. I reached inside my purse and took out a BC Powder. I normally would take the BC with a Coke, but I didn't have anything to drink in the van. So I opened the package and took the BC dry. It tasted horrible, but within seconds the bitter powder began to work. I felt the tension in my head begin to melt away just as Seth joined me in the van.

"Are you going to be okay, Kat?" he asked as he put his hand on my shoulder.

"I don't have a choice but to be okay, Seth," I said, keeping my voice calm. "I'm the person in charge. I have to make sure everyone else is okay. Even if it means I'm not."

"You don't have to be okay with me," he said, so solemn and

earnest. "You can be as vulnerable as you need to be. I know this is a lot. You shouldn't have had to go through this alone."

"Thank you. I appreciate the kindness you have shown me."

"Again, it's not just kindness, Kat—I care about you."

"We should go. I don't want the boys to have to wait around for me to show up."

He looked at me one more time, then cranked up the van and eased onto the road. I closed my eyes and didn't even realize I'd dozed off until I felt a gentle touch on my arm. I sat up straight in my seat.

"We're at the school, Kat," he said. I glanced down at my watch. It would be another fifteen minutes before the boys rushed out to the van. I was glad for that time. I didn't want the boys to see me in tears. "Do you want to talk, or would you rather have some quiet time?"

"Quiet time," I said and closed my eyes again. The only thing I planned to give energy to today was the boys. Before long I heard the laughter of children. I opened my eyes just as Pee Wee and the other boys hurried toward the van. I got out and Pee Wee ran to my arms.

"H-h-hi, Miss K-K-Katia. I m-m-missed you." His thin arms around my waist felt good. He didn't know how much his innocent affection was soothing my broken heart.

"Hello, Pee Wee. Hello, Darren and Charlie. Did you boys have a good day?" I swallowed the lump trying to form in my throat and watched as Seth got out of the van and greeted the boys too. He instructed them to put their things in the back, which allowed me a moment to gather myself. Darren and Charlie hung back, so I turned my attention to them. "Did you boys have a good day? I know this is a new school for you."

"It was okay," Darren said gruffly. As usual, Charlie let his cousin do the talking.

"Well, let's get into the van and head back to the group home," I said as the three of them climbed in and Seth helped me into the passenger side.

Once we were all inside, Pee Wee leaned forward, resting his chin on my shoulder. "Where is M-M-Mr. Ja-Ja-Jason?"

I wasn't ready to reveal the news about Chad, so I danced around the question. "I wanted to pick you boys up since I didn't get to see you off this morning. Is that okay?" I turned to look at Pee Wee.

"D-d-do we get to g-g-go to Dairy Qu-Qu-Queen today? We were all g-g-good at school," Pee Wee said, hopefulness on his face.

"I like Dairy Queen," Charlie said. I looked at the excited expression on his face. They had earned their Friday afternoon ice cream.

"Absolutely," I said. "We will go get ice cream."

Pee Wee and Charlie smiled broadly. Darren didn't look very excited, but he didn't say no. I then looked at Seth. "Are you okay to stop for ice cream?"

Seth smiled. "Absolutely. Let's go to DQ."

Before we left the school parking lot, I walked to the pay phone and called the group home to tell them I was taking the boys for ice cream before bringing them back home. Mrs. Grambling answered the phone.

"That sounds good, Miss Katia," she said. "I'm glad they're getting a little bit of normalcy before we have to talk to them about Chad."

"Me too," I said. "How's Jason?"

"He's doing okay. Of course he's still sad—we all are—but he's gonna be alright. That news caught all of us off guard, but we're gonna support these boys and support you, Miss Katia."

I thanked her and told her we wouldn't be long.

The drive to Dairy Queen was noisy. The boys chattered on about their day at school and Seth joined them, allowing me to sit and listen. It was nice hearing their enthusiasm. Even Darren admitted that he liked his math teacher. When we got to Dairy Queen, Pee Wee hung back and took my hand.

"Miss K-K-Katia, do you th-th-think Ch-Ch-Chad might show u-u-up? He likes ice cr-cr-cream, and tonight is *St-St-Star Tr-Tr-Trek*. Maybe he'll go back h-h-home with u-u-us." I couldn't speak, and so I just pulled him into a hug. "Y-y-you okay, Miss K-K-Katia?"

"Yes," I managed to get out. "You hurry and catch up with the other boys. We don't want them to get all of the ice cream."

He didn't need further encouragement to run and catch up with the boys. They went inside and Seth waited and held the door open for me.

"You okay?" he asked.

I shook my head. He put his arm around my shoulders and gave me a gentle squeeze. I followed the boys to the counter, where they were already deciding what to order.

"I want a banana split with extra whipped cream," Charlie said.

"M-m-me too," Pee Wee said, then turned to look at me. "Can w-w-we order wh-wh-whatever we w-w-want?"

"Whatever you want," I said with a smile.

I listened as each boy placed his order. I didn't want any ice cream and evidently Seth didn't either. I asked for a cup of water instead. Thankfully, the boys didn't notice. They took their orders and sat at a table in the back of the restaurant. Seth and I sat a few tables away so we could keep an eye on them but still have a bit of separation.

"I'm so sorry that they'll have to deal with so much grief later on today," Seth said softly.

I took a sip of water. "Unfortunately, these boys are used to it. Their norm is pain and sadness. But I pray they don't become de-sensitized to the pain of loss. As much as I hate to see them have to suffer any more in their young lives, I pray that they continue to feel emotions, both good and bad."

Seth reached across the table and took my hand. I pulled it away.

"Seth, I can't do this with you right now. I'm sorry." I stood up and walked over to the boys' table.

"We need to head back to the group home," I said. "Make sure you clean up after yourselves."

They took their plastic bowls and spoons and tossed them in the garbage. Darren went to the front and asked them for a damp rag to wipe down the table. He cleaned the table, then took the rag back to the front. As we were preparing to leave, an elderly white woman approached me and lightly touched my arm. I turned and looked at her. She had a huge smile on her face.

"I just wanted to say that you and your husband have some wonderful sons. They are so well-mannered. You are a very lucky woman," she said.

"Thank you," was all I could say. Her words stung in the worst way because what she said was so impossible in my mind, but what I wouldn't give for her words to be true.

As we walked outside, Pee Wee was checking out the parking lot. I had no doubt he was hoping to see Chad. When we were all in the van again, I turned to the boys.

"Tell Mr. Seth thank you for picking you up from school and taking you out for ice cream," I said. Each one of them said thank you.

The drive to the group home was as lively as the drive to Dairy Queen had been. Before the boys could scatter, I told them to go to the meeting room for an early group session. None of them questioned me, and when we pulled up, they jumped out of the van and ran toward the house. I exited the van and slowly followed them, with Seth close behind me.

"Katia," Seth called to me. I turned and waited. "Katia, I never want to do anything to make you feel overwhelmed. I know you're going through a lot right now. Can I at least be a friend? Will you accept that from me? Friendship?"

I thought about it and realized that a person can never have too many friends. And Seth had done nothing but try his best to be that, especially today.

"Thank you, Seth," I said as I touched his arm. "I gladly accept your offer of friendship. With all that is going on in my life, I definitely need it." I turned around and looked toward the house.

I needed to go support my boys and staff as we negotiated our way through this new grief. "I'll talk to you soon."

"I'm just a phone call away if you need me," he said.

I thanked him, took the van keys from him, then slowly walked toward the house, girding myself for what I was about to face.

22

THE SOUNDS OF SOBS, INCLUDING MINE, filled the group home meeting room after I shared the news that Chad had been shot and hadn't recovered from his injuries. Normally this quasi–meeting/living room was filled with laughter while the boys played card games or watched *Star Trek* or *Lassie*.

I'd debated the best way to tell them the news, but eventually I handled it the way I always have: I opened my mouth and told them the truth. Although blurting it out might seem cold and uncaring, I'd found that when it came to telling the boys bad news, the best course of action was to spit it out. And there was no way to soften the blow of this particular news.

At first Pee Wee stared at me as if he didn't understand. When the full impact of my words hit him, he began to cry the most bitter tears I'd ever seen from him. He cried harder than he did when I'd told him about his mother's death. It was heartbreaking to see him this inconsolable.

I was shocked that the news of Chad's death even affected

the new boys who'd never met him. Charlie, who was being comforted by David Snell, the houseparent who also served as a youth pastor, was shedding tears, and his cousin, Darren, looked sad and stoic. Maybe it all hit too close to home. Maybe they were moved by the obvious pain the news caused their new friend Pee Wee. Whatever the case, from the houseparents to the boys to me, we were a group mourning the loss of someone we cared about, and the pain in the room was almost suffocating. At first I stayed quiet and let everyone handle their grief in their own way, but as time went on, I needed to step in and help everyone get a handle on how we were processing our thoughts and feelings. I didn't want the boys to become sick because they were so overwrought, and I could tell they were feeding off each other's emotions.

I cleared my throat, checking my own emotions as I held tightly to Pee Wee, who was still sobbing in my arms. Jason sat on the couch with us, his face drenched with tears and his hand on Pee Wee's back.

I asked David to say a prayer. After the suicide attempt by one of our residents last year, David had offered up such a cleansing and healing prayer that Mrs. Kennedy said, *"That boy prays like an old Negro deacon on the last night of a revival meeting."* I'd laughed at her words, and right now we needed David to summon up that same fervor. We stood in a circle and held hands.

"Heavenly Father, we are confused and hurt and a little bit lost right now," David prayed, his pale face also covered with tears. "But we are believing in Your infinite wisdom, that through this and all of life's heartaches and heartbreaks, You are in control, and You make no mistakes. We ask that You give each of us the peace of mind necessary to deal with the loss of our dear brother Chad. Please."

The sobbing and crying continued. We were all drowning in grief. Once David finished the prayer and everyone choked out an "Amen," I asked him and Mr. Grambling to take Darren and Charlie to their room and talk to them one-on-one. After everyone else left the room, only Jason, Pee Wee, and I remained. I took deep, cleansing breaths.

"Pee Wee," I said, lifting his chin to make eye contact with him. "I know you're hurting right now, and I wish you'd talk to Mr. Jason and me and let us know what emotions are the strongest so maybe we can unpack those feelings and help you to begin the very difficult process of healing." My words sounded like a textbook. But in that moment, that's what we needed.

At first Pee Wee shook his head back and forth, the sobs continuing to rack his body. Even though he was a hardy eater, he was still small, almost frail. With every shake and tremble, it felt as if he might shatter into even tinier pieces.

"I know this isn't easy, Pee Wee," I said, continuing to rub his back. "This isn't easy for any of us. But we have to be able to talk through our feelings. Please. Will you try for me and Mr. Jason?"

"Mad," he managed to rip out of his throat. "I'm m-m-mad. H-h-he said he w-w-would n-n-never leave me. He j-j-just l-l-like everybody else. E-e-everybody always l-l-leave me."

I looked at Jason and nodded at him. I wanted him to take charge of this moment. I'd dealt with the boys' grief at this group home for nearly ten years, and if you counted my years helping my brothers, for over twenty years. It felt like my entire life had been devoted to helping others overcome their sadness. I was used to it, but Jason wasn't, and as hard as it was for me to relinquish control, I knew Jason needed to step up. As my assistant, I wanted Jason to be able to manage his own sadness and devastation while also dealing with the boys' emotions. I knew he said he didn't want to take over as director if they let me go, but I knew, even if he didn't yet, that this job was meant for him, and I wanted him to be ready if the offer came.

Jason looked at me and nodded, showing me that he understood my unspoken request.

He took Pee Wee's hands in his. Without prompting, Pee Wee began taking several deep breaths along with Jason, both of them closing their eyes. I closed my eyes and breathed deeply along with them. I was certain that David and Mr. Grambling were doing the same with the boys in their care.

The boys in the group home knew that when any of the house-parents, Jason, or I held their hands, it meant that we wanted them to take a breath. To focus. To calm down. After a few minutes of deep breathing, Pee Wee stopped crying. He was still upset, but he was in control of his emotions enough to carry on a conversation. The same was true for Jason. He'd needed those cleansing breaths as much as Pee Wee did. Me, too, for that matter.

Finally, Jason spoke. There was a slight quiver in his voice, but he was in control, and that was what mattered.

"I understand that you're angry, Pee Wee. I'm angry too," he said.

Pee Wee looked at Jason with surprise. "Wh-wh-why are you m-m-mad, Mr. J-J-Jason?"

"I'm angry because we couldn't protect Chad. I'm angry someone would hurt Chad in such an awful way. I'm angry because none of this is fair," Jason said, tears flowing down his face. I appreciated that Jason wasn't afraid to show his emotions in front of the boys. They needed to know that even though they would someday be men, it was never wrong to show emotions. My goal was always to encourage them to feel their feelings but also to figure out how to harness those emotions into something that would ultimately serve them in a positive way.

"I'm m-m-mad because someone h-h-hurt Ch-Ch-Chad too." Pee Wee turned and looked at me. "A-a-are you m-m-mad, Miss K-K-Katia?"

I nodded and wiped away a tear. "Yes, Pee Wee. I'm terribly angry. I'm angry because Chad is no longer with us. Like Mr. Jason, I'm angry that someone hurt Chad. I'm angry with myself for not protecting Chad and keeping him safe."

"I don't w-w-want to go to another f-f-funeral," he whispered. "Are y-y-you m-m-mad at me?"

I placed my hands on the sides of his face so he could look into my eyes and know that I spoke the truth. "No, Pee Wee. I'm not angry with you."

"You don't have to," Jason said. "No one has to go."

"Does th-th-that make me a b-b-bad friend?" Pee Wee asked.

"Absolutely not. The friendship you and Chad shared is deeper than any funeral. You don't have to go, and you don't have to feel bad about not going," I said.

Relief softened his face. "Can w-w-we watch *St–St–Star Trek* t-t-tonight?"

I nodded and smiled. "I think Chad would like that. Let's go check on the other boys and see if dinner is ready."

We all stood, but before Pee Wee left the room, he turned back to me and hugged me. "You're b-b-better than a m-m-mama, Miss Katia."

I was thankful that he ran off without seeing my face. The pain from those words almost made me buckle. Jason grabbed me around my waist. I couldn't stop the flood of tears.

"They carry too much," I managed to gasp, my tears once again threatening to overpower me. "They carry too damn much, and I don't know how to fix it."

"I know," Jason muttered. We embraced, holding on like we were each other's lifeline, and in that moment, we were.

"Thank you for everything you do, Jason," I said. "You are an amazing assistant director. On days like this, I couldn't do this without you."

He smiled. "That means a lot, Miss Katia. Thank you."

I patted his arm. "I'll go and make sure supper is ready. You go check on the boys and the houseparents. Tell the house-parents that I'd love for them to stay for dinner tonight if they can. I think it will do the boys good to see us all here as a united front."

"Yes, ma'am," he said and hurried away to locate everyone.

Meanwhile, I made my way to the kitchen that, as always, smelled like a little piece of heaven. If my nose was telling me the truth, we were having Chad's favorite meal: spaghetti and fried catfish. Mrs. Kennedy and Miss Grant turned around when I entered.

"Chad would be very pleased with this meal," I said, smiling through the tears. I wondered when I'd get back to a place where I wasn't shedding tears every single day.

Mrs. Kennedy smiled back. "Theresa and I wanted to make sure we did our part to honor our boy. We got a chocolate cake over there on the counter, and I made a huge pitcher of peach iced tea. All of Chad's favorites."

"Thank you, ladies," I said. "I'll go and make sure the table is set."

When I got to the dining room, the boys were busy setting the table together. The houseparents were gathered around the room, watching. I went to each of them and squeezed their hands. I hoped they knew how much they meant to me. Then I walked to my office and called home. I told Mama that I'd most likely stay at the group home tonight. I just wanted to make sure the boys would be okay.

"I figured as much," she said. "You and them boys take care of yourself tonight. Me and Marcus already said we was gone watch *Star Trek* tonight in honor of Chad. We remembered how much he loved that show."

"Thank you, Mama," I said. Mama went silent for a moment, and I worried that something else had happened. "What's wrong, Mama?"

"Nothing," she said quickly. "Nothing is wrong. I just . . .

Well, Leon came by and I asked him if he wanted to stay for dinner and watch some television, but if . . ."

"I'm fine with it, Mama," I said. And I truly was. "I have no feelings about Leon. I don't want you or him to feel awkward about anything. If you and he have designs on each other, please, Mama, act on them."

Mama sighed. "I just want you to have a little happiness yourself, baby. And the last thing I ever want to do is cause you any more heartbreak in this life."

"What is it you used to tell me when I'd get sad when I was a little girl? Do you remember?"

Mama didn't hesitate. "I'd say, 'Your happy is right around the corner.'"

I smiled, though it wasn't a happy smile. "My happy is around the corner, Mama, but your happy can be right now. And your happy feeds my happy, so enjoy your dinner and your TV. I'll see you in the morning."

Mama said goodbye and I returned to the dining room, where everyone was still seated. When I walked in, all of the men and boys rose from their chairs. Even Darren and Charlie stood. I sat down while Charlie and Pee Wee went to the kitchen to help bring in the food. Pee Wee and Chad used to have Friday dinner duty. It was nice that Pee Wee and Charlie were working together tonight. I watched as everyone dug in. The boys' laughter was subdued, but they did laugh, and it sounded like a beautiful symphony. I still wasn't hungry and Pee Wee, who was sitting beside me, noticed.

"Just eat s-s-something, Miss K-K-Katia," he leaned over and whispered. "It will m-m-make you feel b-b-better."

I smiled at him. Those were my words coming out of his mouth. These boys didn't miss a beat. I picked up my fork. "You're right. And it would be rude of me not to enjoy this phenomenal meal prepared by Mrs. Kennedy and Miss Grant."

"And if you e-e-eat all of your f-f-food, you get d-d-dessert," he whispered with a twinkle in his eye.

"You're right," I said. "And I definitely want some of Mrs. Kennedy's chocolate cake."

I took a few bites and he smiled. Then he turned his attention back to Charlie. I listened as the two of them discussed tonight's upcoming episode of *Star Trek*.

"This e-e-episode is c-c-called 'Friday's Ch-Ch-Child,'" Pee Wee said.

"How you know that?" Charlie asked.

"*TV G-G-Guide*," Pee Wee said. "We always l-l-look up sh-sh-shows before th-th-they come on. Ch-Ch-Chad liked to . . ." He stopped. I looked over and saw his bottom lip quivering. I reached over and put my hand on his.

"It's okay," I said. I tried to smile. "Chad loved checking the listings in the *TV Guide* every week so he and Pee Wee could make a case for watching various shows. Isn't that right, Pee Wee?"

Pee Wee looked at me and nodded. "Yes, m-m-ma'am."

"One day we'll be able to talk about Chad and smile for real. I promise." Right now, that seemed unlikely, even to me. But I needed to give these boys something to hang on to. I needed them to believe that somehow we'd be able to have fond memories of Chad that didn't cause us to erupt into tears. That day wasn't today, but I hoped and prayed it would be sooner rather than later.

Once everyone was done eating, the boys worked together to clean up the dining room. They talked in hushed tones as the staff and I went into the meeting room.

"Thank you, everyone. I know this has been a difficult day for all of us," I said. "I'm going to stay over tonight so, other than Jason and David, you're free to go. You're welcome to stay and watch *Star Trek* if you want. We're going to keep the evening as lighthearted as possible."

The others lingered for a little while, but soon it was just Jason, David, the boys, and me. I decided to go to my office and call my cousin Alicia. I needed to talk to someone I could be vulnerable and open with and not feel guilty about it. Her husband, Curtis, said she hadn't been feeling well and was sleeping. I told him to tell her I'd call the next day.

I looked at the clock. It was almost time for *Star Trek*. By now, Seth was done with his meeting with the men at the church. I'd asked Marcus if he wanted to attend the meeting tonight and he'd said next time. I tried not to let myself worry about him too. Impossible. Before I had time to second-guess myself, I dialed Seth's home number. After a couple of rings, a woman answered.

"Hello. Taylor residence," she said. I assumed it was Seth's mother, although her voice sounded extremely youthful.

"Hello. Is this Mrs. Taylor?" I asked.

"It depends on which Mrs. Taylor you are trying to reach," she said pleasantly. "This is Denise Taylor. How might I help you?"

My mind wouldn't allow me to process what it meant for Denise to be at his house. I mumbled something, apologized, then hung up the phone.

For the longest time, I sat at my desk, mentally replaying the idea that Denise was back in town, and this could only mean one thing: she was back to reclaim what was hers. Eventually I went and sat on the couch in my office. I didn't feel like going to the room where everybody was watching the show, but I also didn't feel like going to bed, so I just sat. I didn't realize how much time had passed when I heard a light rapping on my door.

I cleared my throat. "Come in."

It was Pee Wee. He walked over to me, putting his arms around my neck. "*Star Trek* is o-o-over."

"Well, did Captain Kirk and the crew save the universe?" I listened patiently as he told me all about the episode. I tried hard to focus on what he was saying—not on my feelings concerning Denise being in town.

"Not the u-u-universe, but they s-s-saved a b-b-baby, and guess what the m-m-mama named him?" he asked.

"I wouldn't even be able to guess." I smiled, knowing he wanted to tell me anyway.

"Leonard J-J-James Ak-Ak-Akaar," he said with excitement. "He g-g-got his name from C-C-Captain Kirk and D-D-Dr. McCoy. His m-m-mama named h-h-him."

"They must have done something really nice for her to name her baby after them," I said as Pee Wee sat on the couch beside me.

"D-D-Dr. McCoy helped h-h-her. I think she w-w-wanted to be n-n-nice." Pee Wee laid his head on my shoulder. "You've been cr-cr-crying again. H-h-haven't you?"

"Some," I said. "What about you?"

"S-S-Some," he admitted. "I d-d-don't want anything t-t-to happen t-t-to you, Miss K-K-Katia."

"I know." I wasn't going to make promises about something I had no control over: life and death. Instead, I hugged him. "Why don't we focus on making sure we always tell the people we care about that we love them? That is the best and greatest gift we can give to each other."

"Yes, ma'am."

"It's time for you to go and get ready for bed."

"I'm sc-sc-scared," he whispered.

I hugged him even tighter. "I'm going to be here all night. Mr. Jason and Mr. David are going to be here too."

Pee Wee didn't say anything at first. But after a long pause, he said words that almost broke my heart. "I'm n-n-not worried about m-m-me."

I sighed. I didn't want him to be afraid that someone else he cared about might die, but I couldn't, in good conscience, promise him that his heart might not get broken again. At the end of the day, none of us could predict the day or the hour of our last breath here on earth. Gran used to say the challenge of growing older was saying goodbye to so many people she'd loved along the way.

"Pee Wee, I wish I could calm all of your fears, but I can't. But I will say this: no matter what, you are loved and cherished, and God willing, I'll be on this planet for a long, long time so I can remind you of that fact often. Okay?"

He nodded. "Yes, ma'am." He got up from the couch and turned to leave but then stopped.

"Would you like me to walk you upstairs?"

"Yes."

He offered me his hand, and I pulled myself up from the couch. "Let's go."

I prayed that this wouldn't be another long, sleepless night. I prayed we'd all find a way to sleep. I prayed my thoughts wouldn't drift back to the phone call I'd made to Seth's house. My already crowded brain didn't need any more turmoil.

23

"I'M SO SORRY, KATIA," MRS. HENDRICKS said over the phone, her voice cracking. "The vote was thirteen to one to let you go as executive director. I tried."

Mrs. Hendricks and I had spoken this morning before the board convened, so I knew the vote would more than likely go this way. It hurt that any of the board members would vote against me, but it particularly hurt that the Negro men on the board didn't have my back. When it came down to it, I'm not sure why I felt they'd be on my side. After all, Mrs. Hendricks was the only person who'd ever supported me unwaveringly.

I'd given everything I had in me to this group home and the young men we served. It was hard for me to grasp that everything I'd tried to do wasn't enough. My time at the job I'd loved more than any other was over.

I took a deep breath and then spoke. "Thank you for informing me, Mrs. Hendricks. I'm saddened that the board felt they needed to take such a drastic measure without even having a conversation with me about it. When is my last day?" I was surprised at how calm my voice was. Inwardly, I was screaming, *How dare you? I have given this group home my everything! How dare you throw me away like yesterday's newspaper? How dare you?*

"The end of day on Monday," she said. I sucked in air. So soon. I had a lot to wrap up, and they expected me to do it by Monday? I supposed it could have been worse. They could have said by the end of today or immediately, but acknowledging that didn't relieve the sting. "Sam will be in touch with you soon. I just wanted you to hear the news from me first. I wish I could have done more."

"Did they say who they might select to take my place?" I prayed they'd at least do the right thing and let Jason stay on as the interim director.

"I insisted that they keep the rest of the staff intact, so your assistant director will become the interim director if he wants the position," she said. I sighed with relief. "I can't promise you they'll vote to retain him as executive director, but hopefully . . ."

As Mrs. Hendricks continued to speak, my eyes wandered around my office. So many memories here. Over the years, I'd made this space my own, from decorative knickknacks on the bookshelves to the wall of honor filled with photos of the boys who'd "graduated" from living at the group home. Yet there were a lot of reminders that this office had once belonged to Colonel Samuel P. Arrington, a Confederate Army officer. I remembered my first day on the job and how overwhelming it was to walk into this expansive room that the family called "the Colonel's chambers," a name I'd continued to call it until a few years ago.

His portrait used to hang on the wall opposite my desk, but eventually I'd convinced the family that it was better suited out in the hallway where everyone could see it. Every day when I walked by his portrait, I wondered what he'd think, knowing a Negro woman who favored Nina Simone now occupied his office—an office where he probably met with other white, Southern men to discuss ways to keep my people enslaved. The irony of it all was never lost on me.

"Katia . . . Katia . . .," Mrs. Hendricks called to me. I'd almost forgotten she was on the phone.

"I'm sorry, Mrs. Hendricks. Thank you for all you have done."

"I'm sorry that things ended this way. You deserve much better." I could hear the tears in her voice. I had no tears left at this point.

We said our goodbyes, and shortly after we hung up Sam called. The call was short. I had nothing to say, so I listened while he relayed the details of my exit. Once he was done, we hung up.

I sat there for a moment, reliving the two vastly different conversations about my firing. When I looked at the clock, I saw it was a little after noon. On the weekends, the boys mostly raided the kitchen for leftovers or they ate sandwiches. I imagined they were either eating or playing basketball outside with Jason. Probably the latter, since it was a sunny day and Jason believed in keeping the boys moving.

There was a knock at my door. "Come in," I said.

Seth stepped inside. Memories of the phone call from the night before when his ex-wife answered the phone flooded my mind. I didn't want to talk to him, but I realized he might need to speak with me about the work his crew was doing on the group home. I tried to put on my most efficient face.

"Good morning. May I help you?" I asked, my voice sounding cold and distant. I wasn't trying to be rude. I was just overwhelmed.

"Good morning." Seth moved closer to the desk—the same mahogany desk Colonel Arrington once sat at. I imagined he was somewhere in the spirit world, cackling with delight at my firing. "Are you okay, Kat?"

"I'm fine," I said. "Do you need something?"

He looked at me with curiosity but quickly turned serious. "I have a few questions about the bathroom remodel. I have a couple of new guys working with me now. They can work on the bathroom while the other guys finish repairing the roof."

"Sounds good," I said. "Do we need to go upstairs to the bathroom?"

"That would be best. Kat, you sound so . . . I don't know. You just don't sound like yourself." He continued to stare at me, as if he were trying to figure out the pieces to a puzzle. If I'd had the energy to smile in order to stop the scrutiny, I would have. I wanted to go home and hide in my bedroom like I used to do in elementary school after the kids had picked on me at school. *You're not little Katia anymore*, I thought and tried to make myself believe those words.

"I'm just busy," I said and stood up. Evidently I moved too quickly, because the room was spinning. I plopped back down into my seat and Seth came over and placed his hand on my shoulder.

"Kat, what just happened? You almost fell."

I gripped my desk and closed my eyes. "I'm okay. Just a bit lightheaded. Give me a second and we can go see about the bathroom."

"I know Chad's death has to be weighing on you. Maybe you need to take a break. Go home and start fresh on Monday."

I couldn't stop the half sob that escaped my throat, and as much as I hadn't planned to say anything to him, the words spilled out. "I'll have plenty of time to take a break after Monday. The board fired me this morning."

"Oh, Kat," he said softly. "I'm so sorry. That's so unfair. Can you fight it?"

I shook my head. "Other than one board member, the vote was unanimous. They want me gone and I'm not going to beg any of them for my job."

"Kat, I'd bend down, but this leg won't let me. Will you sit with me on the couch?"

I shook my head. "We need to take care of the bathroom situation. I'll be fine." This time I rose more slowly and steadied myself. Seth was standing so close I couldn't move around him. He smelled amazing. Whatever his cologne was, it was meant for him. I looked up into his eyes. I truly could get lost inside them. But I reminded myself of two things: one, Denise was back, and she clearly didn't see herself as his ex, and two, nothing had changed about my circumstances. I couldn't have babies and it was too much to ask any man to give up on being a father. It was one thing to date Leon, a man who had children and grandchildren, but it was something altogether different to date a young, vibrant, childless man. While at first he might say it didn't matter, I knew that at some point it would.

"Are you ready to go upstairs?"

Seth reached out and put a hand on each of my shoulders. "We vowed to be friends. Let me be your friend. You've been hit with two terrible blows within just a few days, not to mention the stress of your brothers' situations. This is a lot. It's okay for you to lean on someone else sometimes."

It would be so easy to allow myself to be folded into his embrace. My body was sure craving it. If I closed my eyes, I could imagine the feel of him holding me, caressing me. But I refused to take his pity, and that was all it could possibly be. Pity.

I shook my head. "Show me what you need me to see."

Seth's hands fell away from my shoulders. I tried not to dwell on how much I wanted his hands to stay where they were.

"Okay," he said. He moved aside, I walked around him, and together we exited the office. There was no sign of the boys, so I knew they were outside playing with Jason. We went upstairs and everything was businesslike. I made what was probably the final decision I'd make for the group home: where to position the urinals. Any other time, I'd find that amusing, but I couldn't muster even a hint of a smile, let alone laughter. Once we finished our discussion, we went back downstairs and stood near the front door.

"Kat, I . . ."

This time I placed my hand on his arm, and I managed some semblance of a smile. "It's okay. I'll be fine, Seth. I appreciate your concern."

"Call me if you need to talk."

"Thank you for the offer, but I'm pretty sure your wife would not be pleased." I was about to walk away, but he reached for my arm.

"Wait, Kat. What are you talking about?"

I wished I'd held my peace and said nothing.

"Last night I called your house and Denise answered the phone—or should I say, Mrs. Taylor answered. That was how she referred to herself," I said, folding my arms across my chest for lack of a better place for them. "I understand you and I are just friends, but I don't want to complicate things with you and Denise and I don't want her thinking there's something between us when there isn't."

"Oh, Kat," he groaned. "I didn't know she was at the house until I got there, and I sure didn't know she was answering the phone, referring to herself as my wife. She's not my wife. She's my ex-wife and that's the lane she'll always occupy in my life."

"It didn't sound that way when she answered." I wanted to believe him, but Denise didn't sound like a woman who believed she was merely water underneath the bridge.

"Kat, I didn't invite her to the house," he said, stepping closer to me. "I didn't even know she was in town. She came over and spent the afternoon with my mother. Yesterday I left the group home and went straight to the church for the group session. When I got home, she was there, and I asked her to leave. I also told my mother that if she intends to continue being friends with my ex-wife, I wouldn't be able to stay in the house. My father agreed, and finally my mother did too. She even apologized to me."

"Oh," I said. That solved one part of my dilemma, but the issue of my not being able to have a baby was a fixed issue that wasn't going away.

"Kat, you could have just said something. I'm hopeful that at some point you'll give us a try. Just know I'd never do anything to jeopardize that possibility."

I took a step back. My closeness to him was too much. I didn't want to allow myself to weaken. I could tell he was about to say more, but mercifully the doorbell rang.

"I need to see who that is," I said, rushing to open the door. An elderly Negro woman stood there, clutching her purse in one hand and a Bible in the other. I wondered if she was a Jehovah's Witness. Sometimes they came by and offered to do Bible study with the boys.

"Good morning, ma'am," I said. "May I help you?"

"Uh, yes, ma'am," she said. "My name is Irma Staples. I'm Mason Jones's grandmother. On his daddy's side."

"Yes, ma'am," I said, smiling. "Come in."

"Good day, ladies," Seth said, nodding at both of us. "I'll check in with you later, Miss Daniels."

I appreciated the professional tone he used. I also appreciated the fact that we didn't have to continue our conversation. "Thank you, Mr. Taylor." Mrs. Staples and I watched as he walked out the door. Then I turned back to her. "Would you like to follow me to my office?"

Until Monday, it was my office, and I was treating it as such. Mrs. Staples clutched her purse and her Bible close. I guided her to the back of the house. I couldn't deny that I was surprised to see her. Judging from our last conversation, I didn't think we'd ever hear from her again. Once we entered my office, I offered her some coffee or tea.

"No, ma'am," she said. "Though I 'preciate the offer. I wanted to come by here and talk to you about Mason."

I motioned for her to sit in the chair in front of my desk. Once we were both seated, I asked her how I could be of service.

"I want to do right by that boy," she said, the tears streaming down her face. I slid the tissue box closer to her. I was used to sadness and crying in this room. Sometimes the sadness would be from the boys, but sometimes it was my own. I waited for her to calm down. After a few seconds, she took a deep breath and spoke. "My son Nathan called me from the jail. Seems somebody got word to him that the boy's mama died. I talked to God about my last conversation with you about Mason, and I got the feeling God was not pleased with me."

"Mrs. Staples, I know that you have a lot on your plate. I understand." I couldn't imagine how she was managing to raise so many children and grandchildren all by herself, not to mention three of her nieces and nephews. She had every right to feel overwhelmed.

"I was rude to you when we last spoke. I apologize for that. But I want to do right by Mason. I ain't got a lot, but what I have, I want to share with him. He's my grandboy too."

"I accept your apology," I said, leaning forward in my chair. "Are you saying what I think you're saying?"

"I want Mason to come live with me," she said. "That other

family of his ain't gone ever take him in. He should be with people who love him."

"Mrs. Staples, everyone at the group home loves Pee Wee—I mean, Mason," I said. "You could always let him stay here and you and the other children could be part of his life through visitation. It isn't perfect, but I've seen it work."

There had been occasions when the biological parent or parents were deemed unfit to raise their child, but through our efforts and their child's caseworker's efforts, we'd been able to create a family structure that worked for all involved. I'd be honored to do this for Mrs. Staples and Pee Wee. I'd rather this be my legacy than picking out bathroom fixtures.

"I appreciate what you're saying, ma'am, but he's my responsibility." She dabbed at her eyes again. "Mr. Staples died when my children were young, and I wasn't sure how I was gone make it, but every single time, God helped me to find a way. I gotta believe in the power of that same God now. One more mouth to feed ain't gone make that much difference. When can I take him?"

"Mason's caseworker will have to work out the details, but I'm sure . . ." I pulled out Pee Wee's file from the cabinet by my desk. I saw that both Vanessa, Pee Wee's mama, and Nathan, Mrs. Staples's son, had listed her as the next of kin. For that reason alone, her chances of getting custody of Pee Wee were very good. "I imagine that if everything checks out okay, you'll be able to take him home before Christmas." Christmas was a few weeks away. Ample time for the paperwork to be processed. On Monday I'd make it a priority to speak to Pee Wee's caseworker,

Mrs. Gonzalez, before I finished my last day at the group home. I needed to leave on a high. I needed to believe that even though I wasn't able to give Chad a happy ending to his story, maybe, just maybe, I could give one to Pee Wee.

"Would it be alright for me to see him? Just for a few minutes?" she asked, still wiping away tears. "I don't even know if Mason remembers me. It's been a couple of years since we last saw each other. He probably forgot he has a grandmama."

I stood up from my chair. "Don't worry, Mrs. Staples. Even if he doesn't remember you, this is a good time to get reacquainted. Pee Wee is a sweet soul and the only thing he wants out of life is to love and be loved. Until everything is worked out, it's best not to mention him going home with you."

She nodded, hugging her Bible to her chest.

"I'll be right back," I said. I went to the back porch of the house, and as I'd imagined, Pee Wee, Darren, Charlie, Jason, and David were playing basketball. When they saw me at the door, they stopped playing, and Pee Wee ran toward me.

"I sc-sc-scored four p-p-points, Miss Katia," Pee Wee said excitedly.

"Good for you," I said, lightly squeezing his shoulder. "Pee Wee, there's someone here to see you."

He looked at me with confusion. "S-s-see me? Th-th-there's someone t-t-to see m-m-me?"

"Yes," I said, smiling down at him. "Your father's mother— your grandmother—is here to see you." I didn't want to say more than that. Until the caseworker became involved, I wasn't going to give him any additional details to worry about. "Would you like to see her?"

Pee Wee nodded. "Yes, m-m-ma'am."

"Good. The rest of you can stay outside and continue playing basketball. Jason, would you mind going inside with us?"

"I don't mind at all," he said. "Ready to go see your grandma?"

"I s-s-sure am. Th-th-think she'll l-l-like me?"

"Absolutely," Jason said, putting his arm around Pee Wee's shoulder. Jason looked at me and mouthed, *Everything okay?*

I tried to smile. I needed to tell him what the board had decided, and then we needed to figure out our strategy over the next two days. But before then, we needed to make sure that Pee Wee's reunion with his grandmother went well.

"Let's go," I said, and the three of us went inside.

Jason and I walked Pee Wee to my office, and when we opened the door, his grandmother was standing, looking expectantly toward the door.

"Mason," she said, stretching open her arms. Pee Wee didn't move.

I bent over and whispered in his ear. "It's okay. Go to her."

Pee Wee looked up at me and I nodded as reassuringly as I could. He went over slowly to Mrs. Staples, stopping just out of her reach.

"Hey, Mason. I'm Grandma Staples," she said in a soft voice, as if she didn't want to scare him away. "Can I give you a hug?"

He walked into her embrace. "Th-th-they call me P-P-Pee Wee."

"Alright then, Pee Wee. They call me Grandma Staples."

I looked over at Jason. He had a huge grin on his face. It wasn't often that we got to experience moments like this with our residents. More often than not, their stories didn't end well, but I prayed that this story would.

I went over to Jason. "I need you to pull together the staff. Tell them I need all hands on deck."

His grin immediately disappeared. "Yes, ma'am," he said and left my office to make the calls. I appreciated that he didn't ask any questions. I only had it in me to tell everyone I'd been fired one time.

Pee Wee and his grandmother went over and sat on the couch. I decided to give them some privacy, so while they talked quietly, I eased out of the room and went to the staff meeting space, where once again I'd be the bearer of bad news.

24

AFTER I TOLD EVERYONE MY NEWS, the room went silent. Everyone was shocked. Just like I didn't mince my words with the boys, I didn't with my staff either.

Pee Wee's grandmother had left, promising to come back the following week for another visit. When the staff arrived, I sent the boys back outside to play with one of our volunteers. I'd called him to come by so the staff and I could meet. Jason was the first to speak.

"This is bull," he said, standing up and pacing. "This is some bull, Miss Katia. There's no way they should have fired you. No way at all. If they fired you, they should have fired all of us. We can all resign. If they see we're a united front, they'll have to back down."

Everyone murmured in agreement.

"Jason's right," Mrs. Grambling said. "Me and this old man love these boys, but if it wasn't for Miss Katia, we would have hung up our hats a long time ago. Ain't that right, Albert?"

Mr. Grambling nodded. "We ain't staying around here if Miss Katia is let go. It ain't right."

"Sure isn't," David Snell said, his face bright red. "Miss Katia, we've got your back on this one and so will half of Troy. All we have to do is get on the phone and call some people. They will stand by you, just like we will."

"Everyone," I said, motioning for their attention. "Settle down. Jason, come and sit." I waited while he sat down beside David. "I appreciate everything you all are saying and I'm sad to leave you and these boys, but there's something more important at stake: the continuation of the work we've been doing here at the group home. As much as I appreciate your support, I don't want to fight them."

"You *are* this group home, Miss Katia," Cairo Fieldings said. "This place wouldn't run if you weren't leading it."

I shook my head. "Not true, Cairo. This place wouldn't run if it didn't have a great team of dedicated workers, and it has that. All of you, along with me, made this group home a success. And sitting right among you is the best person on the planet to take over—Jason."

"I'm not ready. I graduate in a few days, but I'm not ready to take your place," Jason said.

I reached over and placed my hand on Jason's. "I don't want you to take my place. I want you to take *your* place as the new executive director of the group home. I saw how you handled yourself these last few weeks. You're ready." I turned to everyone else. "And he's going to need all of you to stay put and support him. Okay?" After further discussion, everyone agreed to stay and not to fight the board. I stood.

"We have two more things to do before I step down. One is to tell the boys the news about my departure, and two is to make sure Chad is represented by this family at his funeral next week." I'd spoken to the funeral home and the church, and it was decided that the funeral would be next Wednesday. I'd no longer be employed with the group home, so that would likely be our last time together as a team. I hated that it had to be for such a solemn event, but I was grateful everyone said they'd attend Chad's funeral. I was satisfied that this conversation had gone as well as it could have.

"Thank you to everyone who came back for this meeting. I'm sorry I had to pull you in for this. I'm going home for the night, but I'll be back tomorrow to tell the boys. I want to give them some time to process the information while I'm still here," I said. I turned toward Jason, who was scheduled to work over the weekend. "If you need me, I'll be at home."

"I know what you said, honey," said Mrs. Kennedy as she hugged me. "But this ain't right. It just ain't right. But I'm gone pray to the good Lord that He sees you and us through these hard times."

I hugged Mrs. Kennedy tightly. She and Miss Grant had been godsends during my time at the group home. I couldn't imagine life without them—without any of the staff. "From your mouth to God's ears. Thank you, Mrs. Kennedy."

"Me and Theresa gone make all your favorites on Monday. We gone send you off in style," she said, putting a brave smile on her face.

"Thank you," I said, a tear falling down my cheek. Mrs. Kennedy's kind words brought out the waterworks.

I hugged everyone else as they filed out, but Jason lingered. Once it was just the two of us, he turned and looked at me with fear in his eyes.

"I can't do this, Miss Katia," he said, sounding as terrified as one of the boys would be if I'd just told him he was in charge. "I'm not ready. I'm not prepared to take over. Not now. Not yet."

I sighed and motioned for Jason to join me on the couch. Once we were both seated, I took his hands and smiled at him. He nodded, closed his eyes, and breathed in deeply. I did the same, and for a short while, we held hands and breathed. Once a few minutes had gone by, I released his hands.

"You are ready," I said.

"Miss Katia, I . . ."

I shook my head and continued to smile. "You are ready. And if you weren't ready, I would tell you so. I have nothing left to teach you. You have been an amazing assistant director, and, Jason, you're going to be an even more amazing interim director. Do you hear me?"

He nodded. "Yes, ma'am."

"Tomorrow, after we tell the boys the news, you and I will hole up in *your* office, and I'll answer any lingering questions you might have, and we will discuss any remaining issues on my desk that you might not be aware of, although I don't think there is anything. Okay?"

"Yes, ma'am. Thank you for the trust you have in me. I will make you proud."

I lightly placed my hand on his shoulder. "I cannot imagine being any prouder of you than I already am. You're going to be a phenomenal interim director, and if they have any sense at all, they'll make you the permanent executive director. Now, escort me to my chariot."

"You mean your pickup truck," he said with a smile.

"Same thing," I said. After he stood, he extended his hand to help me get off the couch. "Let me go check in with the boys before I go."

Even though I'd put on a very good face, and even though I believed this was the right path for me to be on, I'd be lying if I didn't admit that leaving those boys behind was going to be difficult. I walked into the dining room, where Pee Wee, Darren, and Charlie were studying. All of them looked up as we entered the room. "Boys, I'm going to go home for a little bit. I probably won't be back until the morning, so I want you to be good and listen to your houseparents. I'll see you later. Okay?"

They said yes and returned to their schoolbooks. Part of me felt bad for going home, but I needed to sleep in my own bed. Jason walked me out to the truck. It started easily. It amazed me that over the last few weeks, my truck—Daddy's truck—hadn't given me a moment of trouble. It was if it knew I needed it to cooperate. I looked upward and whispered, "Thank you, Daddy."

I took my time driving home. I was tired and didn't want to get distracted or, worse, fall asleep at the wheel. I turned on the radio, and Dionne Warwick was singing a fairly new song of hers, "I Say a Little Prayer." I loved the sound of Dionne's upbeat, jazzy voice—not quite as much as I loved Nina Simone's, but close. By the time I drove into the yard at home, I was more relaxed. But then I remembered I still had to tell Mama that I'd been fired.

However, Leon's truck was parked near the back door, so maybe I could sneak in a nap before I had to tell her. If I remembered correctly, *American Bandstand* was on, and if I was lucky, some Negro would be on the show today so that Mama's and Leon's attention would be held.

I exited the truck and slowly walked toward the house. My entire body ached and the only thing I wanted to do was to go inside and fall into my bed. But Mama must have heard me drive up, because she met me in the kitchen. She was dressed in a gorgeous pink chiffon dress. In comparison, I felt dumpy in my polyester pantsuit.

"You didn't call me today," she said, wagging a finger at me, but then she stopped. She must have noticed the look on my face. "Is everything alright, baby?"

"I got fired, Mama," I said, my voice cracking. "The board voted this morning to let me go."

"Oh, Katia," she said, opening her arms wide. I stepped into her embrace and it felt good to be held by her. "I'm so sorry, baby. This week has been too much. Way too much."

My heart felt like it was ready to burst. Between losing Chad and now losing my job . . . I wasn't sure how much more I could handle.

"Why don't you come watch television with me and Leon?" she suggested. "Your brother went running. He said he wanted to clear his head."

I shook my head. The last thing I wanted to do was be a third wheel with Mama and Leon. "I'm going to call Lish and then I'm taking a nap. Thank you though."

Mama hugged me again. "You don't have to be alone in all of this." She then leaned in and whispered, "There's a handsome young man who seems like he'd be interested in being a shoulder for you to lean on."

"He's out of the question, Mama," I said, my voice sounding weary to my own ears. "You know why."

"Babies ain't the only thing men find attractive in a woman, Katia," she said. "You don't add up the full measure of what you bring to the table."

Mama saw that I wasn't going to debate the issue and sighed. "Okay then. I'm going to go finish watching *Bandstand*. Ain't too much to see. Glen Campbell and some white folks group called The Sunshine Company is on today. I sure wish they had something like *Bandstand* for Negroes, 'cause Dick Clark is mighty slow to bring our musicians onto his show."

I smiled. "Maybe one day, Mama."

She gave me a final hug and went out of the kitchen. I took the phone to the kitchen table and sat down. As I was about to dial Alicia's number, the phone rang. I picked up and it was Jason.

"Sorry to bother you, Miss Katia, but the police called and said they've received word that if Chad's funeral goes on as planned, some of Cobra's associates are planning to retaliate," he said.

"Are they going to provide protection?" I hadn't even considered there being any type of violence at Chad's funeral. I recalled the pregnant girl at the hospital. Was it her people? Cobra's? A combination of the two?

"No, ma'am. From the tone of the policeman, they couldn't

care less what we do. They're staying out of it, until the worst happens, I guess."

"Let me call the funeral home and—"

"I just called," he interrupted. "They suggested we wait a week or two for things to cool down, and instead of having a funeral, they could bury Chad without any fanfare. I'm so sorry."

"A week or two? No funeral?" I couldn't wrap my head around what I was hearing. We were supposed to put that precious baby into the ground like some dead animal we'd found on the street? No prayers over his body? No words of condolences? Just throw him into a hole and forget about him?

"I've got to go, Jason. I'll call you back." I hung up and ran out of the house, slamming the door behind me. I needed to scream and rail against the injustice of it all. I climbed into my truck and closed the door right before the first scream escaped my throat. I wanted to do more—to hit something or someone.

"Why?" I yelled. "Why? Why? Why?" My crying became loud, uncontrollable wails. I didn't know how to contain my rage. My little brother was lost somewhere in the jungles of Vietnam. My poor big little boy was dead and I'd never see his face again. And the job that had defined me half of my adult life had been snatched away from me.

"And I can't have any babies!" I moaned. "I can't have any babies!" I began to hit my steering wheel, my all-consuming grief overpowering me.

Suddenly I heard a knock on the truck door. Though I could barely see through my tears, I recognized that it was Marcus.

"Open the door, Katia!" he yelled.

"I'm fine," I choked out. "I'm fine."

"Open the door."

I unlocked the door, and he ordered me to scoot over. He climbed inside and pulled me close.

"What's wrong?" he demanded. "Why are you out here crying like this? Is it Aaron?" His face hardened but his eyes were panicked.

I shook my head, trying to stop the sobs. "I can't have any babies, and I can't bury Chad. They fired me from my job. And we don't know where Aaron is."

I fell into his arms, trying to stifle my screams, but I couldn't control them. It was as if decades of grief were bubbling to the surface all at once. For the first time ever, Marcus comforted me, giving me the love and attention that I'd always given him.

"It's okay," he said softly. "It's okay. You cry. Nothing wrong with crying sometime."

I was grateful for Marcus's strong arms. He held me as we sat together inside our daddy's pickup truck, underneath the barren pecan trees in our backyard.

25

AFTER MY MELTDOWN, I WAS EMBARRASSED, but Marcus shrugged it off as he linked arms with me as we ventured back to the house.

"How many times have you comforted me throughout the years, sissy?" he asked. "I owe you at least a few brotherly hugs like that. You've always been there for us. It's time we're here for you."

Once inside, I went straight to the phone and called Alicia.

"Hey, girl," she said. "You sound funny. What's going on?" I told her about everything. I was surprised I made it through the telling without breaking down again.

"Lish, I don't know what I'm going to do with myself after Monday," I said.

"Come to Prichard," she said with excitement in her voice. "I know we just saw each other, but why don't you take a few days away from Troy and come down here? Let me spoil my cousin. I'll make gumbo and some beignets."

She knew I couldn't resist her gumbo or beignets. Whenever we visited, I begged her to make them for me.

"Oh, Lish, I can't come down there now. It's almost Christmas, and—"

"Christmas is still on December twenty-fifth. Today is December second. You can stay a week and still get back home before the holidays," she said. "Go finish your last day on Monday, and then head down to Prichard on Tuesday. Say yes. You haven't been down here for the longest time. You ought to invite that handsome handyman of yours to come down with you."

"He's just a friend, and it wouldn't be appropriate," I said, even though there was nothing I'd love better than to have Seth accompany me to visit my family.

"All the more reason to do it," Alicia said with a laugh. "I saw how that man acted around you at Thanksgiving and I saw how you acted around him. You need to talk to him and let him tell you whether your inability to carry a baby matters. There are many different ways to be a parent, Katia, and he didn't come across as the kind of man who'd make a stink over something like that."

"Maybe." I didn't add that I was too scared to have that conversation. It was one thing for me to *think* he'd reject me because of my hysterectomy, but it was another thing entirely for it to actually happen to my face. "Yes—I'll come visit."

"Woo wee!" she exclaimed. "I can't wait! My sister-cousin is coming to town."

I couldn't help but be excited too. Over the last ten years that I'd been executive director at the group home, I hadn't taken many vacations or even days off. The longest time I'd been away was when I'd had the hysterectomy last year, and the second the doctor said I could return to work, I did. I wasn't even sure what it would feel like to be on vacation without worrying about the group home.

After Alicia and I finished talking, I joined Mama, Leon, and Marcus in the living room. I didn't really want to be alone. I told them about Alicia inviting me to come stay in Prichard, and then we watched *The Lawrence Welk Show* until the *NBC Saturday Night at the Movies* came on. Tonight they were showing *Rawhide*, which starred one of Mama's favorite actors, Tyrone Power. The evening was relaxing, and it was sweet watching Mama and Leon try to act like they weren't smitten with each other. I knew they were both nervous about me and my reaction. During a commercial, Mama hopped up to make some popcorn. I followed her to the kitchen.

"Mama, I've told you this before, but it doesn't bother me if you and Leon want to be a couple," I said. "There's a lot going on in my life right now, and I know you're concerned about me, but seeing you and Leon as a couple won't hurt my feelings. I promise."

Mama set down the pan she used for popping popcorn and reached for my hands. "Leon and I have both agreed to put that in God's hands. I'm not in any rush to be in a relationship, in spite of my advanced age, and neither is he. This is an adjustment. The majority of my life I've been either Marcus Harold Daniels II's girlfriend, fiancée, wife, or widow. I don't know how to be anything but that."

I kissed both of Mama's hands. "I love you, Mama."

"And I love you, my sweet girl. I want you to go down to Prichard and enjoy yourself with your cousin. You deserve this time. Marcus and I will be just fine. I'm gone see if I can get him to go back to those meetings. I think it will do him good."

"I'll encourage him to go too," I said.

After the movie ended, I went to bed. In spite of everything that was on my mind, I slept well. Maybe my body's exhaustion finally caught up with me, because I didn't wake up once and I didn't have any bad dreams. Before going to sleep, I'd prepared myself for more nightmares about leeches, but mercifully they didn't make an appearance in my dream world. Instead, I dreamed about Daddy. He was standing on the other side of a huge lake, waving and smiling at me. His wave seemed to say, *Don't worry about me, little girl—I'm doing just fine. Live your life.*

When I woke up, I was smiling—my first genuine smile in the last several days. Oh, I couldn't deny the sadness; it was still there. But seeing Daddy in my dreams was enough to put me on the road toward what I hoped would be healing.

The only thing that would have made that dream better would have been to see Chad standing beside Daddy, also waving and looking happy. I prayed that at some point I'd have that dream as well. I was thankful that my little brother, Aaron, wasn't standing beside Daddy. I tried to tell myself this meant Aaron was still alive and in due time we'd find him, and our little family would be complete again.

I took my time getting up. Sunday school was at nine o'clock, and church didn't start until eleven. Jason was bringing the boys to church so I could have more time with them before we told them the news later today. I dreaded it, but I knew the boys would be in good hands—and maybe this was the radical shift I needed in my life. Years ago, right before I started working at the group home, I'd entertained going back to school to study elementary education. I wasn't sure if that's what I wanted to do, but it was exciting to think about.

I went to the bathroom adjacent to my room and had a nice long, hot shower. By the time I finished, I felt so relaxed. In my bedroom I put on a blue sweater dress with a matching jacket. Then I walked out into the hallway, where Mama and Marcus were waiting. Marcus was wearing his Marine Corps uniform, looking handsome and dapper. Mama was wearing a beautiful winter white dress with matching hat. Mama didn't believe in fashion rules like "don't wear white after Labor Day." Mama's closet was filled with white suits that she wore when the weather got cool.

"Can't nobody but God tell me what to do, and I don't think the Master is concerning Himself with my clothes," she used to say. Daddy used to love it when Mama wore white. He said it reminded him of their wedding day.

"Y'all ready?" I asked. Even though I'd just seen the boys yesterday, I wanted to lay eyes on them again, especially since I only had today and tomorrow.

"Ready," Mama said. We went out and got into my truck. I let Marcus drive and I sat in the middle. He hadn't been behind the wheel of a vehicle in a while, but he drove with steadiness. I was proud of him and how hard he was fighting to go on without

Aaron at his side. Mama looked at me and smiled. I knew she was thinking the same thing.

When we pulled into the church parking lot, the van from the group home was already there. I hopped out of the car and hurried into the church as soon as Marcus parked. The boys were standing with Jason and David. When Pee Wee saw me, he ran and wrapped his arms around my waist.

"Miss K-K-Katia," he exclaimed like it had been weeks since we'd seen each other. I was just as happy to see him. Darren and Charlie stood back, but they smiled and waved. "C-C-Can I sit with y-y-you?"

"You sure can," I said. "Once Sunday school is over with, you can sit right between me and Gran."

"I wouldn't have it any other way," Mama said, walking up to the two of us. Pee Wee moved out of my arms and hugged Mama. I'd miss seeing him, but I prayed that life would be good for him with his grandmother. She seemed like she had a good heart.

A bell rang, which signaled the start of Sunday school. Normally when I brought the boys to church, we only made it in time for the main service, but Pee Wee insisted he remembered where the children's classes were, so we watched as he led Darren and Charlie up the stairs.

"How are you doing, Miss Katia?" Jason asked, coming over to hug me. David followed behind him and hugged me too.

"I'm fine," I said. "Nice of you to come to church with us today, David."

"I wanted to be with the family. One more time," he said with a watery smile.

I touched the side of his face. "You'd better not get teary on me, David Snell. I'm going to have to pull on your strength and Jason's today."

"We are right here," Jason said.

Sister Miller walked up to us. "Y'all come on into the main sanctuary so we can get started." Sister Miller was the adult Sunday school teacher and she ran a tight ship. She and Mama embraced, and then she hugged Jason, David, and Marcus. "You looking mighty handsome in the uniform, son. Thank you for your service."

"Thank you, Sister Miller. It's my honor," he said, sounding confident. I knew he missed serving in the Marine Corps. My prayer was that they wouldn't try to send him back, but we knew that was a possibility. I didn't know if Mama could handle having another son beyond her reach, but I was equally uncertain that Marcus could be comfortable sitting out this war. He'd been reluctant to enter the Corps, only joining because of Aaron. But I knew when we saw him after basic training that this was his calling—fighting for this country that didn't always fight for him.

We went into the sanctuary, and just like when we were children, Mama led us to the front pew. She used to say, *"Nobody ever got saved sitting in the back of the church."* When the twins were younger, they'd pout because she wouldn't let them sit with their friends. And just like then, I reached into my purse, pulled out a piece of Juicy Fruit gum, and passed it to Marcus. He grinned at me. Mama gave us a stern look, but a glint of laughter shone in her eyes.

After an opening hymn and prayer, Sister Miller told us the Scripture for the day: Matthew 5:16: "Let your light so shine before men, that they may see your good works, and glorify your Father which is in heaven."

"So often we strive to do things for our own adoration, but we must be reminded that any good thing we do is for the glorification of God," she said.

When I was younger, this was the time when I'd often escape into my daydreams. I'd think about whatever book I was currently reading, or I'd plan my outfits for the week. I'm grateful that now I truly did try to see how God's Word applied to me and my life. I wanted to believe that my motives were selfless, that I didn't act to receive praise. But Sister Miller's words were definitely thought-provoking. Sunday school continued for another forty-five minutes before we let out in preparation for morning services.

The boys hurried back into the sanctuary, and almost all of the older ladies, with Sister Miller leading the pack, gave Pee Wee a special hug, telling him what a good boy he was. He soaked it in like one might sop up syrup with a biscuit. I prayed his home with his grandmother would give him warm moments like this.

The choir began singing "Nothing but the Blood of Jesus," signaling that it was time for us to be seated. As I'd promised, Pee Wee sat between Mama and me, and when she stood to sing and clap along with the choir, Pee Wee stood and clapped right with her. It was times like this I wanted to remember—to imprint onto my mind so I'd never forget that these boys touched my life in such an incredible way.

Pastor Bennett's sermon was a continuation of Sunday school. When he referenced John 15:8, I couldn't help but grimace when he said, "bear much fruit." He wasn't talking about babies, but that's where my mind went. Across from us, a new mother and father sat with their baby in her lap. I tried not to be envious or begrudging of anyone else's good fortune, but I wished for a life like theirs. If I closed my eyes, I could see myself sitting in the pew, cradling my own baby, sitting next to my husband, who vaguely resembled Seth.

I felt a hand on my arm. I looked at Mama. She mouthed, *Are you okay?* I nodded.

For the rest of the service, I tried my best to remain focused on Pastor Bennett's words. Once the church services ended, I went to talk to Pastor Bennett about what the police had said about the threat of violence if we had Chad's funeral service at the church.

"I just hate to have him put into the ground without even acknowledging his life," I said, feeling tears threatening to spill over again.

Pastor Bennett put his hand on my arm. "Don't worry, Katia. We'll figure something out. I think waiting a couple of weeks for feelings to calm down isn't a bad idea."

I nodded in agreement. "I don't want there to be any more violence or bloodshed. I just want to honor Chad's life."

Then I told Pastor Bennett about losing my job. He was such an easy person to talk to, and since he was a spiritual leader, it seemed natural to talk to him.

He hugged me. "You are a phenomenal young woman, Miss Katia Daniels. Don't allow the actions of those people to make you think otherwise. You've done a good work at that group home. Clearly God has other plans for you. I'll pray for your strength and your discernment in finding out what the next leg of your journey is going to be."

I thanked him and made my way through the crowd of worshipers, people I'd known since I was a child. This church was an extension of home.

I rode home with Mama and Marcus so I could get my truck. I planned to spend the night at the group home, maybe play some board games or watch television with the boys. They loved to watch *Walt Disney's Wonderful World of Color*. I'd do anything to keep things as light as possible.

When I got to the group home, Pee Wee ran to the truck and offered to carry my bag for me.

"I-I-I didn't know y-y-you were staying t-t-tonight," he said.

"I need to talk to you boys about something, and afterward I thought we might play some games or watch television," I said.

"Yeah! I-I-I'm glad you c-c-came to be with u-u-us," he said.

I held back the tears. I didn't want to start blubbering before I even assembled the boys. This wasn't going to be easy, but I had to find the strength to let the boys and the staff know that with or without me, life at the group home would go on.

"Let's go inside," I said and took Pee Wee's free hand in mine.

26

IN ONE DAY, I SOMEHOW MANAGED to pack up my personal belongings in my office. I made certain not to take a single thing that wasn't mine, not even a pencil or a paper clip. Jason helped me load the items onto my truck: My framed degree from Alabama State College. Photographs of me and the various boys who'd come through the group home doors. Knickknacks the boys had made for me during arts and crafts, and stacks upon stacks of letters written by former residents—as well as their parents, grandparents, aunts, and uncles—thanking me for the support I'd given them.

The last twenty-four hours had been difficult. Packing was emotionally draining, but it couldn't even begin to compare to telling the boys the news the night before. When we gathered them in the meeting room and told them I'd be leaving, the tears flowed liberally, but especially from Pee Wee.

"B-b-but why?" he'd cried, running over to the couch where I was sitting and burying his head against my chest. I hated adding to his ever-growing list of losses—his mother, Chad, and now me. I knew that I couldn't come up with a reason for my leaving that he'd understand, so I instead tried to comfort him.

"It's going to be okay," I said, as much to myself as to him. I rubbed his back, but nothing seemed to soothe him. He sobbed like his heart was broken, and I knew it was, because mine was too. I didn't want to leave this place, these boys, and these colleagues. Nothing felt fair about the situation, but one thing I'd learned from working at this job was that fairness wasn't a guarantee in life.

"Can we talk to somebody, Miss Katia?" Darren asked. "Tell them how good you do your job?"

I smiled at him. It amazed me that the sullen young man who'd entered the group home a few days ago now wanted to advocate for me. It was yet another reminder to me that we'd done good work here. Maybe not the way the board wanted us to, but I was certain that I'd played a role in making sure these boys felt safe and loved and seen.

After our conversation, Jason, David, and I had tried to divert their attention to playing games. They usually loved playing Monopoly and Clue, but no one was in the mood. The movie of the week was *A Boy Called Nuthin'*, which starred Ron Howard, a favorite of the boys from *The Andy Griffith Show*. But the boys seemed disinterested, so everyone went to bed early.

The next morning, the tears started fresh with Pee Wee. He didn't want to go to school.

"L-l-let me st-st-stay with you," he cried, clinging to me when Jason told them to go to the van.

"I'll still be here when you get home," I said. "I promise."

"Okay," he said as his sniffling subsided.

I stood on the front porch and waved as Jason drove them away, and at the same moment, Seth and his crew pulled up. I watched as they got out of their trucks and Seth instructed them on the day's duties. After they left to begin their work, he approached me on the porch. Our last conversation had been awkward, and I didn't want that today. Perhaps more than any other day, today I needed peace.

"Good morning, Seth," I said, trying to smile.

"Good morning, Kat," he said, returning my smile. "How are you doing? And if that's a stupid question, just ignore it."

"I'm doing much better than I thought I would be. Probably because I have so much to do before the day ends."

"I won't keep you then," Seth said and turned to leave, but I reached out and stopped him.

"Seth, I want to apologize to you for how I've behaved. You've been nothing but kind to me, and I've been all over the place. There's a lot of things going on with me that I don't feel comfortable discussing right now. Just know that I appreciate your offer of friendship and I hope it's still on the table."

"It will always be on the table, Kat," he said, smiling once more. "You never have to worry about that. And if we can only be friends, then that's what we'll be."

"Thank you." I wanted to tell him the truth about why I hesitated to consider a relationship with him, but I didn't want to see the look I expected to see in his eyes. "Well, I have a lot to do. I'll see you later."

"See you."

I went back inside, my mind processing the day's responsibilities. I was determined to put things into place that would ensure Pee Wee's grandmother could take him home as soon as possible. I called Mrs. Gonzalez and explained the situation. She was extremely excited and thought she might be able to get him to his grandmother by the end of the week if everything checked out. I ended the conversation by telling her this was my last day at the group home.

"I'm so sorry to hear that, Miss Daniels," she said. "You've been a joy to work with and I wish you well on your future endeavors."

I thanked her, and as soon as I hung up I phoned Darren and Charlie's caseworker. She assured me that she was working on a placement for them, possibly with an older cousin who'd expressed interest in taking both boys. Six more boys were scheduled to come to the group home over the next week, so it was nice to have an action plan for the current boys. That way Jason would be able to focus most of his attention on the new residents.

When Jason and I met, I reviewed every detail with him, and I reminded him I'd always be just a phone call away.

"I don't know how you did all of these things, Miss Katia," he said, sitting at the table in my office.

"Time," I said, reaching over and patting his hand. "I didn't come here knowing everything and I'm not leaving knowing everything. You'll learn this job over time, and you'll make the running of this place your own. I have total and complete faith in you."

By the time school was ready to let out, I was almost finished with everything on my to-do list. There was nothing left to do other than eat the final meal Mrs. Kennedy and Miss Grant had prepared. I didn't even know what it was because every time I'd tried to go into the kitchen, they shooed me away. Whatever they were preparing, it made the entire house smell amazing.

I was sitting at my desk, signing some paperwork, when I heard voices—lots of voices. I went to the door and looked out at the desk where Leslie normally sat, but she wasn't there. I couldn't imagine three boys and the staff making that much noise, so I went into the hallway. Jason met me with a huge smile on his face.

"Who's making all of that noise?" I asked, trying to peer around him, but he blocked my view.

"We couldn't let you leave without letting a few people come by and say their goodbyes," he said.

I looked at him suspiciously. "What people?"

"Just follow me," he said and led me to the meeting room. He swung open the door, and the room was filled with people. When I looked closely, I recognized many of the faces. Some of them were young men who'd lived at the group home over the years, and others were former staff members who'd moved on to other careers.

"Oh, Jason," I said as the tears began to flow down my face. I couldn't believe what I was seeing. "How did you do this? Why did you do this?"

He hugged me tightly and whispered in my ear as he pressed a handkerchief into my hands. "I did this because you needed to be reminded of the legacy you've created, Miss Katia. You needed them to come back and have the last word. It doesn't matter what those board members say—it's about what these people say and what we say," he said, pointing toward the crowd of people.

"Oh my," I said, dissolving into a full-blown cry, dabbing at my eyes with the handkerchief. "I don't believe this. There are so many people here. You planned all of this in two days?"

"There would have been more people if I'd had more time," he said. "There are a few more people here who wanted to come and celebrate you too."

I looked over to where he was pointing, and Mrs. Hendricks, Mama, Marcus, and Seth were sitting on the couch, smiling at me. I shook my head. I'd never done this work for any fanfare. It was always about the boys. I felt like I might topple over, so I gripped Jason's arm to steady myself.

"I couldn't track down everybody in such a short period of time, but you also have tons of messages that some of the young men wanted me to pass on to you—I already packed them in your truck," Jason said, squeezing my shoulders. Then he turned to the crowd. "Everyone, line up and come give Miss Katia her flowers."

Every single young man in the room who had been part of the group home, including Pee Wee, Darren, and Charlie, lined up with a single white rose in his hand. One by one the boys hugged me and told me how much my support and love had helped them become the young men they were today.

"I never would have gone to college if it hadn't been for you constantly telling me how smart I was, even though my report cards said something different," Lester Kilpatrick said as he gave me a rose and a big hug. He was one of the first residents who'd come to the group home after I was hired as executive director. Now he was an elementary school science teacher.

Next in line was Tyler Carruthers, a huge success story. He was sixteen when he'd come to the group home five years ago, and he read at a fourth-grade level. After a bit of probing, we discovered that Tyler had a reading disorder but was a wiz at mathematics. I made sure we got him a tutor, and by the time he left the group home, he was reading at an eighth-grade level.

"I have my own lawn care service, Miss Katia, and I employ boys in the foster care system," Tyler said as he kissed my cheek and handed me his rose. "Couldna done it if you hadn't believed in me."

The testimonials went on and on, and I cried like I'd never cried before.

The very last person to bring me a rose was Pee Wee.

"Th-th-thank you for l-l-loving me and t-t-telling me I'm smart e-e-even though I st-st-stutter," he said, hugging me tightly and handing me the last of the roses that made up my bouquet. I handed the bouquet to Jason, then reached down and lifted Pee Wee up so I could look him in the eyes.

"I do love you, Mr. Mason Pee Wee Jones, and you are one of the smartest people I know," I said in his ear. "Don't you ever let anyone tell you anything different."

I eased Pee Wee back down onto the floor, and then I turned to everyone else. "I don't even know what to say. I was dreading today because . . . because . . ." I took a deep breath, and I noticed that all of the young men in the room were taking a deep breath with me. They remembered. That almost sent me over the edge, too, but I held it together. "Thank you for reminding me that good things came out of this group home, and you all are that good thing. I love you."

Mrs. Kennedy came into the room, smiling at everybody. "Food is ready. Y'all come get it. And, Miss Katia, you're first in line."

"No, you all go ahead of me," I insisted. "I want to hug everyone. Just make sure you save me some."

Everybody laughed and formed a line, and I hugged the rest of the special guests. Seeing people I'd relied on to help me run this group home was so beautiful. When I got to Mrs. Hendricks, I was crying all over again, and she was too.

"This place won't be the same without you," she said, hugging me tightly. "Thank you for being such a bright light. If you ever need me, you call."

As she stepped away, Mama and Marcus moved close enough to give me hugs.

I hugged them back tightly. "Y'all knew about this?"

"Jason told us about it yesterday at church," Mama said, wiping away her tears. "This is quite the honor, baby, and you deserve it. You gave this place everything you had, and now you get to see how the seeds you planted grew."

"Proud of you, sissy," Marcus said, kissing my forehead. Once again he was dressed in his Marine uniform. "Aaron would be . . ." His voice faltered as he swiped at a tear. "Aaron would be proud of you too."

"Thank you, Bubby." I hugged him again. "Go eat. You and Mama get in line."

He squeezed my hand and guided Mama to the food line. The last person to come up to me was Seth. He'd changed into dress pants and a nice shirt.

"You knew too," I said accusingly. "And you told me nothing."

"It was a surprise," he said. "Surprise!"

I laughed. "This was wonderful. Thank you for coming back to be part of this amazing evening. I appreciate it."

"Anything for you, Kat," he said and kissed my cheek. "I know nothing will make leaving this group home easy, but I hope knowing how many lives you've touched will help."

"It does."

"Here, get in front of me," he said. "I can't have you at the end of the line at your own party."

I stepped in front of Seth, and as we moved along the food line we chatted about my upcoming trip to Prichard to visit Alicia.

"That will be good for you," he said. "Your cousin seemed like an amazing woman. When you get back, maybe you and I could go out for lunch. As friends—just friends."

"That sounds nice," I said. As long as Seth and I remained friends, I didn't see any harm in going to lunch with him.

When we reached the front of the line, Mrs. Kennedy started preparing plates for me and Seth. Everything I'd enjoyed eating over the years was on the menu: baked ham, fried chicken, collard greens, candied yams, macaroni and cheese, deviled eggs, and peach cobbler. I looked from Mrs. Kennedy to Miss Grant.

"When did you ladies have time to cook all of this food?" I

asked. "There's no way you did all of this today for all of these people."

They laughed, and Mrs. Kennedy answered. "We started working on the food over the weekend at our homes. We finished it here today. Nothing is too good for you, Miss Katia."

"Thank you, ladies," I said. "I'm going to miss you so much."

"You gone miss our good cooking," Miss Grant said with a laugh, coming around the table and hugging me. "We gone miss you too, baby. So much."

The rest of the evening went by fast. Way too fast. I visited with as many people as I could, getting caught up on all of their news. I looked at photos of wives and girlfriends and new babies. I heard about jobs and promotions. After a while, people started filing out, and before I knew it, the only people left were the current staff and residents.

I quietly slipped out of the room and went to my office. I grabbed my bag and coat, looking around the room one last time. Then I walked to the door, turning out the light before exiting Jason's office.

27

"HOW'S THE GUMBO, KATIA?" ALICIA ASKED as she hovered over me at the table, both of her hands resting on her protruding belly. There was no denying that my cousin was "with child."

"Delicious as always," I said, eating another big spoonful of the treat I only got to eat when I visited my family in the Gulf region. I'd been in Prichard four days, and today Alicia felt well enough to make gumbo. I helped as much as I could, cleaning the shrimp and stirring the roux according to her specifications, but making gumbo was not my forte. I was a glorified sous chef and that was fine with me. "Come sit down, Lish. I don't want Curtis mad at me when he gets home from work."

Alicia lowered herself into the chair beside me. "Girl, that man works so hard, I'm in bed when he goes to work in the morning and usually in bed when he comes home in the evening. I wish he'd let go of that second job at the hospital. Garbageman by day and janitor by night. He works way too hard, but he said he doesn't want me or this baby to lack for anything."

I reached out and squeezed her hand. "Curtis is a good man, and I'm thankful he takes care of you the way he does. You deserve it."

"You deserve someone like Curtis too," Alicia said.

I groaned. Any chance Alicia had to bring up my love life, or lack thereof, she did. "Lish, I don't want to talk about that. Can't we get through one day without me being the topic of discussion?"

"Nope," she said and grinned. "It's not often that I have my sister-cousin with me, so I plan on teasing you every chance I get."

"You are too much," I said, but I laughed. It was hard not to laugh around Alicia. She was my favorite cousin for a reason. As serious as I tended to be about everything, she'd always been able to help me see humor in almost any situation.

"Hey, cousin, are you tired?" she asked.

I didn't know what she was up to, but I could tell it was something. "No, not really. Why do you ask?"

"Oh, no reason," she said, glancing at her watch. "I think I'm going to take a nap. If anyone knocks or rings the doorbell, will you answer it?"

"Okay," I said. "I'll clean up here, then go into the living room and read. You rest up. Thank you for dinner."

She stood and kissed my cheek. "Anything for my sister-cousin." She waddled out of the kitchen, and I couldn't believe how pregnant she looked. I was grateful that this pregnancy seemed to be going well.

I started collecting the dishes from the table, taking everything to the kitchen. While the sink filled with dishwater, I turned on the radio. The DJ was on fire, and I sang along with every hit song. I thought about when my brothers were young and I used to teach them all the latest dances, like the jitterbug, the twist, and the stroll. We'd have Mama falling out laughing as they tried to keep up with me and my moves. Aaron was the better dancer of the two. I could almost see him now.

"Please be okay, little brother," I said, wiping away a tear as "I Can't Stop Loving You" by Ray Charles came on. I was drying the last of the dishes when the doorbell rang. I wiped my hands with the dish towel. It was probably some of the relatives, coming over to get Lish's gumbo.

I opened the door, and I was shocked when I saw who was standing there.

"Seth," I said.

"It's me," he said, handing me a bouquet of red roses.

"What are you doing here?" I asked as I accepted the flowers.

"I came to see you. May I come in?"

I wasn't dressed for company, as Mama would have scolded me. My housedress was splotched with dishwater. I didn't even remember picking out my hair today, but he was eyeing me like he didn't see any of those things.

"Yes," I said, moving aside. "Come in. I . . . just . . . Come in. How did . . . How?" I was speaking like a dithering idiot.

"I got your cousin's number from your mother, and then I spoke to Alicia on the phone and she gave me her address," he said.

I should have known Mama and Alicia masterminded this

plot. I was going to get both of them when I got the chance.

I led Seth to the living room and offered him a seat on the couch. I sat in the chair across from him, still holding the bouquet of roses.

"Not to be rude, but why are you here? Why did you want to come see me?"

"I came to see you and take you on a date, Kat." He was definitely dressed to go out, and as always he smelled amazing. I truly felt underdressed and unprepared to have him sitting this close to me, looking this good.

I shook my head. "Seth, no. Nothing has changed. I can't go on a date with you. We said we'd be friends. That's all."

"Maybe you should hear where I'm taking you to first," he said with a smile. "You just might change your mind."

"I won't," I said in a firm voice, gently laying the flowers on the coffee table. "I'm sorry you came all this way. Mama and Alicia shouldn't have helped you with this."

"So you're telling me you won't break your 'no dating' rule to go see *the* Nina Simone in concert?"

"Who did you say?" I must have heard him wrong.

"Nina Simone," he repeated, reaching into his pocket. I shifted the roses to the side and took the tickets from his outstretched hand. Printed right on the tickets it said, "Nina Simone, in concert at the Mobile Municipal Auditorium."

"We're on the front row," he said as I remained speechless. "You'll be so close it will be like she's singing just for you. She is your favorite singer, right? I didn't just imagine you'd told me that, did I?"

"Oh my goodness, Seth," I said, shaking my head with disbelief. "How did you . . . ? When did you . . . ?"

"I figured she'd go on tour after she released those three albums this year, and sure enough, I was looking in the papers right after you left on Tuesday and saw that she'd be performing down here in Mobile," he said, looking extremely pleased with himself. "I got them to hold two tickets for me at the box office, and I picked them up before coming over here. Now you know the whole story."

This sounded like something I'd read in one of my romantic novels. I couldn't believe he'd done all of this for me.

"Seth, I can't go with you," I said, handing the tickets back to him. The sorrow I felt wasn't about missing the concert—it was about the reality that I couldn't lead him on.

"Why not, Kat? You've been skirting around seeing me from the first day I walked into the group home. What is it? Why won't you even consider dating me? Is it my leg? Is it because I have a leg missing?" He looked genuinely hurt. All I wanted to do was kiss away his pain and confusion, but I remained still.

"No. That's not it."

"Then what is it?" he demanded. "Because I can't figure out what it is. Sometimes you act like you're interested in me; then other times you seem as if you wish I'd just disappear. What is it?"

"I can't have children," I blurted out. "Last year I had to have a hysterectomy. It's not fair for me to get involved with someone who hasn't had children of his own. I won't do that to you. I just won't."

I had to look away. I couldn't bear to see pity or disgust on his face, or worse, both.

"Kat," he said softly. "Kat, look at me."

I shook my head as silent tears rolled down my cheeks. I was so focused on not having a breakdown that I didn't notice he'd stood up until he was directly in front of me.

"Get up, please," he said, his hand outstretched. I didn't take his hand at first. "Please, Kat."

I hesitated for a moment, and then I reached out and allowed him to help me up. Once I was standing, he tilted my chin until I was staring into his eyes. His expression was more tender than I'd ever seen on anyone's face. He reached into his pocket, took out a handkerchief, and dabbed around my eyes.

"Miss Katia Daniels, I have been working very hard not to fall in love with you because you didn't seem to want it, but in spite of my efforts, I fell hard."

"But, Seth, I—"

He held up his hand. "Shhh. Let me finish. I love you, and I want to tell you why. You are kind and generous and unselfish and beautiful and sexy and thoughtful and the list goes on and on. I'm so sorry you had to have a hysterectomy. I wish I could have been in your life then to take care of you. If you'll have me, we'll figure out together if we want to be parents. I learned from watching you with those boys at the group home that there are many ways to create a family. But the first person I want to create a family with is you."

I searched his face for some sign that he was lying, but I only saw a man whose eyes were just for me. Only for me. My daddy and brothers were the only men who'd ever looked at me with such unconditional love.

"Seth, you say all of this now, but what if tomorrow you wake up and decide you really do want your own children? I can't fix what's broken inside of me. I can never give you your own babies." I tried to turn away, but he wouldn't let me. Instead, he kissed me. The more I tried to talk, the more he kissed me, until I had no words. I didn't realize how much I'd wanted to share a kiss with this amazing man. We were behaving like teenagers, and I should've been concerned about Alicia walking in on us, but I was lost in his embrace and those incredible, soft lips of his on mine.

After what seemed like hours later but was probably only a minute, he pulled away, his breathing almost as ragged as mine.

"Miss Daniels, will you allow me to escort you to the Nina Simone concert tonight?"

"Yes," I whispered.

He kissed me again but abruptly stopped. "And, Miss Daniels, will you allow me to continue to properly court you and treat you like the queen that you are?"

"Yes," I whispered again.

He groaned and went back to kissing me, and there we stayed until we heard a loud cough. We both turned and saw Alicia with a huge grin on her face.

"About time," she said. "Come on, girl. You can't wear a house-dress to go see Miss Nina Simone. Let's get you all prettified."

Before I could leave, Seth kissed me one more time. Then he bent down and whispered, "If you aren't careful, we might not make it to the concert."

"I heard that," Alicia said with a giggle. "Come on, Katia."

I hurried over to her and we linked arms. She then guided me down the hallway to the guest room.

"You know I should be angry with you," I said as we entered the room and she closed the door behind us.

"But are you?" she asked with a twinkle in her eye.

I shook my head. "No, I'm not—I'm grateful. Thank you."

She hugged me. "You don't ever have to thank me for loving you, Sister-Cousin. Now, go take a quick shower while I figure out what you're going to wear. I have a cute purple cocktail dress I wore to a party a couple of years ago. I think it will look perfect on you."

In less than an hour, I was dressed, fully made up, and beyond shy about returning to the living room. But the way Seth gazed at me melted away all of my shyness.

"My God," he said, walking over to me. "You're breathtaking."

"Thank you."

"Are you ready to go?" he asked.

I nodded, and he offered me his arm. I turned and smiled once more at Alicia, then followed Seth out the door.

The lights dimmed in the auditorium and the announcer's voice came over the speakers: "Ladies and gentlemen, the city of Mobile, Alabama, would like to welcome none other than the High Priestess of Soul herself, Miss Nina Simone."

I almost clapped my hands raw when she sat down at the piano and began to play and sing "I Put a Spell on You." I could have died happy in that moment.

For over two hours, Nina Simone performed her greatest hits as well as new music from her three recently released albums. She ended the night by singing "Do What You Gotta Do," and Seth held me and sang along with her. When the concert ended, he and I stayed in each other's arms. I didn't want the night to end.

"Happy?" he said in my ear.

I nodded. "Very happy. Thank you."

"This is only the beginning," he said, and looking into his eyes, seeing the love shining from them, I knew that what he said was true.

Epilogue

I HEARD A GENTLE KNOCK AT my door. Alicia walked in the room, holding her three-month-old daughter, Gracie. The two of them were wearing yellow taffeta dresses. Alicia was my matron of honor, and Gracie was my honorary flower girl.

"It's about that time," Alicia said with a huge grin on her face.

"Come in," I said. The door opened wider, and my twin brothers, Aaron and Marcus, entered the room, both dressed in their Marine uniforms. Seeing them together caused my tears to fall yet again on this magical day—my wedding day. So many things had made me cry today. Mama loaning me the pearls Daddy gave her on their wedding day, as my something old and borrowed. Pee Wee's grandmother allowing him to be the ring bearer. But most of all, having both of my brothers present to walk me down the aisle. The blessings just kept pouring on me like summer rain.

Five months ago, shortly after Christmas, we'd received the miraculous phone call that Aaron had been located. They said he'd somehow escaped from his captors and was found wandering the jungle. He'd lost a considerable amount of weight, but other than some bruises and a couple of cracked ribs, he was okay. When we met him at the bus station, he was our Aaron, eyes sparkling with a hint of a smile on his face. Before Mama or I could get to him, Marcus wrapped him up in an embrace, crying and laughing, saying over and over, "My brother. My brother. My brother." I didn't think he'd ever let Aaron go.

A few days after we got him home, without my knowledge, Seth asked Mama, Marcus, and Aaron for my hand in marriage. On February 14, he proposed to me in our living room with both of our families present.

"I thought about taking this a bit slower, giving us both more time to make sure we're doing the right thing, but, Katia Daniels, I don't have to wait another second to know that you are my heart—my one and only. Whether we do this a year from now or today, my feelings will be the same. So I ask you, in front of everyone we love on this side of heaven, will you marry me?" Because of his leg, he couldn't get down on one knee, but I didn't care.

"Yes," I cried. "Yes, yes, and yes. I will marry you, Seth Christopher Taylor."

We set a wedding date of July 27, which was special to me because it was Chad's birthday. That morning, I'd taken a boutonniere like the ones the men and boys in the wedding were going to wear and placed it on his grave. I sat down and stroked his headstone. We had buried Chad the day after Seth and I returned from Prichard. There had been no fanfare. Just the group home staff,

Seth, Mama, Marcus, and me gathered together by his graveside. Since then, I have visited his grave a few times, and today was definitely a day I wanted to somehow share with him.

"I sure wish you could be here with us, Chad," I had said, smiling through my tears. This wasn't the first time I'd visited his grave, but it was one of the first times I'd actually smiled there. *"I know that you and all of the other people I love who aren't here on earth will be present at my wedding in spirit. I just wanted to tell you that I'm happy and loved. I pray that you're feeling that same love where you are."*

Now, here I was, about to marry the man of my dreams. A man like none I'd ever read about in any of my romance novels. I glanced at myself in the mirror and positively loved what I saw. From the vintage lace on my dress and veil to Mama's pearls, I'd never felt so gorgeous. I looked behind my brothers, and Mama was standing with Pee Wee, who was handsome in a blue tuxedo. Mama wore a long, pale blue dress and a matching hat.

"Baby girl, you are so beautiful," she said, the tears streaming down her face. She touched the boys' cheeks. "My babies. I've got all of my babies home."

Pee Wee came over to me, carrying the pillow that the rings would eventually be placed on. "I've been pr-pr-practicing how to walk, M-M-Miss Katia. I won't mess up."

Pee Wee's stuttering wasn't nearly as bad as it had been. Having the stability of a home with his grandmother, even though it was filled to the brim with children, made him more relaxed, which made him stutter less. His grandmother and I had gotten close, and whenever she needed a break, I'd pick up Pee Wee and any of the other children who wanted to grab ice cream or see a movie.

I bent down and hugged Pee Wee. "You are very handsome, Pee Wee."

"And you are v-v-very pretty, Miss Katia," he said.

"We all look amazing," Aaron joked. "Sissy, are you about ready to go get hitched?"

"Yes," I said.

The twins escorted Mama to her seat, and then they came back for me. Alicia handed me my bouquet as my brothers stood on either side of me, and I kept careful hold of it as I tucked one hand into the crook of Marcus's arm, and the other hand into the crook of Aaron's arm. When the bridal music started, they escorted me down the aisle to Seth, who also looked sharp in his own Marine Corps uniform. Aaron and Marcus kissed my cheeks, transferred my hands from their arms to Seth's hands, then backed away.

"You are so beautiful," he whispered.

"And you are so handsome," I whispered back.

"Okay, you two," Pastor Bennett teased. "There's a script we must follow. Y'all settle down and let me handle things decently and in order. Amen?"

Everyone laughed, including us, but then, with all seriousness, Pastor Bennett began speaking the oh-so-familiar words of the wedding ceremony.

I looked around the sanctuary and paid close attention to every face in the room. In this room were people I had loved my entire life as well as those I had just recently met. I also felt a warmness enveloping me, like a gentle hug from all of those I loved who had transitioned on. I looked up at Seth and he smiled down at me, brushing away a tear that had slid down my cheek.

I couldn't believe this was my life now, and to think, it was only just beginning.

Author's Note

This book was very different from previous books I have written. Yes, *Untethered* is historical fiction since it was set in 1967-1968, but it wasn't my usual historical novel. This book was far more focused on the human experiences than it was on the timeframe or historical figures of the day, except for the phenomenal and incomparable Nina Simone. Note: I did bend historical details a bit by having Nina Simone appear in concert in Mobile, Alabama. This concert did not happen, but Simone was on tour at that time, and the playlist I used for her was based on her actual concert playlist.

Of course, there were some people that I consulted such as good family friend Dr. Kathy J. Pendleton and former schoolmate Penny Baker. I am also grateful for their invaluable knowledge of the inner workings of the foster care system and group homes. If there were any mistakes or misrepresentations, please chalk that up to me. To orient myself to the child protective services industry, I read *Helping in Child Protective Services: A Competency-Based Casework Handbook* edited by Charmaine R. Brittain, MSW, PhD and Deborah Esquibel Hunt, LCSW, PhD.

I also consulted the following books about the Vietnam War, specifically how it related to African American soldiers: *Fighting on Two Fronts: African Americans and the Vietnam War* by James E. Westheider, *The African American Experience in Vietnam: Brothers in Arms* by James E. Westheider, and *Bloods: Black Veterans of the Vietnam War: An Oral History* by Wallace Terry. And of course I immersed myself in newspapers and memoirs. One memoir in particular was *Ward of the State: A Memoir of Foster Care* by Karlos Dillard. I also appreciated reading Elliott Glover's story in *Those Boys on the Hill.*

Acknowledgments

AS I ALWAYS DO, I DEDICATE this book to my daddy, M.C. Jackson, the man with the tenth-grade education who had the vision to see his daughter becoming an author someday. He did not live to see it happen, but he never lost sight of that dream, encouraging me until the very end. *Thank you, Daddy, for seeing what even I could not see for myself. Every word I write is a love letter to you.*

I am also grateful to my family for always encouraging me. Thank you, Aunt Brenda and Aunt Yuvonne. I see and hear my mother in both of you every time we speak or meet, and it makes her feel close even though at times she seems so far away. Thank you, Aunt Jean and Aunt Lenoria, two amazing women who have celebrated my love of writing from the moment I first knew you. To my sisters (Renee, Joeli, and Eddress) and brothers (Derrick and Terry), I love you and I am honored to be your sister. To Paw Paw Joel, thank you for always loving and encouraging me. Thank you for helping to heal so many wounds. To Mama

Kem, thank you for always supporting my writing by reading my books and encouraging others to do so. To my love, Robert L. Brown, thank you for never giving up on me even when I gave up on myself. You constantly challenge me to grow and soar. To my son, Justin, you mean the world to me. No mother ever had a louder cheering section than you. Even though we are miles apart, you are always close to me. Ashya, my dear daughter, I love you immensely. I never knew how much I needed a daughter until I got you. Thank you to my future son-in-law, David, for being my daughter's touchstone and always being that calming force we all need at times.

Thank you to my friends who are more like sisters: Kiesha, Anita, Elaine, Adrienna, Julia, Libby, Lauren, and Alita. Sometimes we don't talk for long periods of time, but I know that always and forever, you have my back.

To my agent and friend, Alice Speilburg: Thank you. We have been on this journey together for a while and there truly is none like you. Thank you for getting my vision and fighting for me and my work time and time again.

Thank you to the Harper Muse team, especially Kimberly, Becky, Nekasha, Savannah, Margaret, and Taylor. You all are an amazing group of people, and your love for the written word is evident with each project you support.

Finally, to my dear readers: thank you for continuing to rock with me! If my Creator wills it, there will be many more books to come. So, hang on.

Discussion Questions

1. How does Katia's role as a caretaker shape her identity throughout the novel? In what ways do her responsibilities impact her personal desires and dreams?

2. How does the setting of 1967 Troy, Alabama, influence the story and the characters' actions? Discuss the significance of this historical period in shaping the novel's themes.

3. Katia's family history and responsibilities play a significant role in her life. How do her relationships with her mother and brothers affect her decisions and emotional state?

4. Discuss Katia's romantic relationship with Leon and her rekindled friendship with Seth Taylor. How do these relationships reflect her inner conflicts and desires for comfort and connection?

5. How do the losses Katia has experienced (her father's death, her brother missing in Vietnam, her inability to have children) influence her actions and outlook on life? How does she cope with these losses?

6. Katia faces challenges with the board at the group home. How does this power struggle reflect the broader social changes happening in the South during the 1960s? How does Katia navigate these challenges?

7. Throughout the novel, Katia grapples with making choices for herself. How does her journey toward self-discovery unfold, and what are the pivotal moments that lead to her growth?

8. Discuss the symbolism of Katia finding solace in romance novels and Nina Simone's music. How do these elements contribute to the novel's themes and Katia's character development?

About the Author

Ankh Productions LLC—
Photography by Chandra Lynch

ANGELA JACKSON-BROWN IS AN AWARD-WINNING WRITER, poet, and playwright who is an Associate Professor in Creative Writing at Indiana University in Bloomington, Indiana and a member of the graduate faculty of the Naslund-Mann Graduate School of Writing at Spalding University in Louisville, Kentucky.

Angela is a graduate of Troy University, Auburn University, and the Spalding low-residency MFA program in creative writing. She has published her short fiction, creative nonfiction, and poetry in journals like the Louisville *Courier Journal* and *Appalachian Review*. She is the author of *Drinking from a Bitter Cup*, *House Repairs*, *When Stars Rain Down*, *The Light Always Breaks*, and *Homeward*.

angelajacksonbrown.com
Instagram: @angelajacksonbrownauthor
Twitter: @adjackson68

LOOKING FOR MORE
GREAT READS?
LOOK NO FURTHER!

*Illuminating minds
and captivating hearts
through story.*

Visit us online to learn more:
harpermuse.com

Or scan the below code and sign up to receive
email updates on new releases, giveaways,
book deals, and more:

@harpermusebooks

For more from Angela Jackson-Brown, check out *Homeward*

"This is a harrowing novel about the push and pull of fidelity, family, and faith under the crush of history. Angela Jackson-Brown has written a deeply emotional novel that feels timeless while also speaking to the particularly troubled times in which we live."

—Wiley Cash, *New York Times* bestselling author of *When Ghosts Come Home*, for *Homeward*

Available in print, e-book, and downloadable audio